Becoming Bea

Books by Leslie Gould

THE COURTSHIPS OF LANCASTER COUNTY

Courting Cate
Adoring Addie
Minding Molly
Becoming Bea

Becoming Bea

LESLIE GOULD

BETHANYHOUSE

a division of Baker Publishing Group
Minneapolis, Minnesota

© 2014 by Leslie Gould

Published by Bethany House Publishers
11400 Hampshire Avenue South
Bloomington, Minnesota 55438
www.bethanyhouse.com

Bethany House Publishers is a division of
Baker Publishing Group, Grand Rapids, Michigan

Printed in the United States of America

All rights reserved. No part of this publication may be reproduced, stored in a retrieval system, or transmitted in any form or by any means—for example, electronic, photocopy, recording—without the prior written permission of the publisher. The only exception is brief quotations in printed reviews.

Library of Congress Cataloging-in-Publication Data
Gould, Leslie.
    Becoming Bea / Leslie Gould.
        pages cm. — (The courtships of Lancaster County ; 4)
    Summary: "Ben and Bea have always irritated each other. But when their friends push them together, can they cease bickering long enough to fall in love?"— Provided by publisher.
    ISBN 978-0-7642-1034-1 (pbk.)
    1. Interpersonal attraction—Fiction. 2. Amish—Fiction. 3. Lancaster County (Pa.)—Fiction. I. Title.
PS3607.O89B44 2014
813'.6—dc23   2014017689

Scripture quotations are from the King James Version of the Bible.

This is a work of fiction. Names, characters, incidents, and dialogues are products of the author's imagination and are not to be construed as real. Any resemblance to actual events or persons, living or dead, is entirely coincidental.

Cover photography by Mike Habermann Photography, LLC
Cover design by Jennifer Parker

Author represented by MacGregor Literary, Inc.

For Thao,

Youngest daughter of mine,
strong and beautiful,
faithful and fun.

Cause me to know the way wherein I should walk.

Psalm 143:8 KJV

Thou and I are too wise to woo peaceably.

William Shakespeare,
Much Ado About Nothing, V.II.61

CHAPTER
1

I won the third-grade spelling bee with H-A-R-M-O-N-Y. It was a word I loved but was not a feeling I often experienced—except for this moment, sitting on the porch of our farmhouse with my *Mamm*.

It was mid-October. Autumn. Such a beautiful word and my favorite time of the year. The bright blue sky sparkled above us. Sunflowers, the size of platters, lined the field. And woodsmoke from our neighbor's chimney drifted across the road.

I couldn't explain the feeling that swept over me. Harmony, *jah*, but with a hint of A-N-T-I-C-I-P-A-T-I-O-N, the word that had won me the fourth-grade spelling bee. As if something good was about to happen. To me. And soon.

Although I did my best to follow Scriptures, I was known more for my melancholy than my optimism. But for the moment, I relished the hopeful feeling.

My R-E-V-E-R-I-E, the word Ben Rupp had beat me with in our fifth-grade bee, ended just as quickly as it came when I caught sight of my sister Molly trudging up the pathway, an empty flower bucket in each hand.

"I'm not feeling well." She stopped under the oak tree next to the sprawling pile of leaves that I needed to finish raking. Her skin was pale, all the way to her blond hairline. She was nearly as white as her *Kapp*, which was unusual for her, considering she spent every day working outside. She lowered the buckets to the grass and then leaned against the trunk of the tree.

I clutched my journal in one hand and my Bible, which had belonged to my father, in the other.

Mamm started down the steps. "Bea will go down and help."

"I will?"

Molly lurched, probably at the surprise of Mamm's volunteering me to help with the farmers' market in our lower field.

"Jah, you will," Mamm called over her shoulder. "Go put your things away."

I detested the *Youngie* farmers' market and did my best to avoid it, Saturday after Saturday. But I knew to obey my Mamm, even if I'd just turned twenty-one. She wouldn't have assigned me the task if it didn't need to be done.

As Mamm hurried toward Molly, I headed into the house and up the stairs to my room, stashing my Bible, journal, and pencil in my bottom drawer, next to my dictionary and the book of poems I'd checked out from the library. I couldn't afford to buy books of my own.

I closed the drawer. I was always careful not to leave my personal things out for anyone to paw through. Especially not Molly. She'd snooped once, and I hadn't been able to trust her since.

When I stepped back onto the porch, Molly was sitting on the wicker settee beside Mamm. "You'll just need to help load the wagon," she said. "I decided to close early."

That wasn't like her either, but I didn't comment for fear she'd change her mind.

"The sales have been low for everyone. Not many tourists

out today," she explained. "We've sold out of the pumpkins and asters, but that's all."

Even I could have predicted the decrease in traffic. I hurried on down the steps.

"Bea," my sister called out.

I turned toward her.

"*Denki*," she said.

Mamm nodded in agreement.

I waved my hand as if it were nothing, which they both knew wasn't true. I hated crowds. And being around strangers.

"It's good to see her taking steps to stretch herself," Mamm said as I continued on. I knew she didn't intend for me to catch her words—she'd been talking louder than usual lately, perhaps because her hearing had deteriorated during her illness—but it pained me to know my sister and mother talked that way behind my back. Since *Dat* had died it was as if Molly had stepped into the role of parent. Something I was sure *she* relished.

Molly most likely had a touch of the flu that had been going around our district. Even so, we'd been through enough tragedy that I couldn't help but worry about her. Dat had died two years ago and then Mamm had a brain tumor—benign, thankfully—but still she'd gone through an operation and radiation.

I hesitated for a moment on the other side of the oak tree. In the pasture below, the vendors packed their wares: baked goods, fall gourds, lap quilts, woven baskets, fresh herbs, fall flowers, hope chests, and kraut and sausages. An entire cornucopia of offerings. I had often observed the market while I did the wash on Saturday mornings, taking in the sights, sounds, and smells, thankful I didn't have to interact with the people.

I inhaled and kept marching.

Our yellow lab, named Love, escorted me to the trail and

then stopped and looked up at me with her dark brown eyes. I gave her a pat, even though I wasn't much of a dog person, but I didn't bother to tell her to stay. She knew not to follow me.

Not nearly as surefooted as Molly, I confronted the steep slope, doing my best to keep my balance. I didn't possess the level of comfort my sister had with every inch of our land. Although I couldn't say I excelled at it, I spent much more time doing housework than I did outside chores, leaving the flower farming to Molly.

But still I loved our home, land and all, and couldn't imagine ever living anywhere else, although I wouldn't mind if Molly and her husband, Leon, moved away—close enough to do the work but not in the same house as Mamm and me. I was ready for a break from my sister.

It wasn't that I didn't love her. I did, with all my heart. But with Molly, her way was the only way. We were sisters, true, but as different as night and day, starting with my dark hair and brown eyes. Mamm said when I was born she'd expected I'd be just like Molly. But she said it was obvious from day one I wouldn't be the go-getter my sister was.

All my life I'd lived in Molly's shadow.

I stumbled over a rock as I reached the pasture, my arms flailing as I regained my balance.

I swiped at a trickle of sweat by my temple. It had been overcast and drizzly for several days, but the weather had turned warm again. Maybe we would have a streak of Indian summer before winter came.

The savory smell of bratwurst made my mouth water as I approached the market. A few *Englisch* customers bought up the grilled items and pastries, reaping a good sale price.

I kept my head down, hoping none of the vendors expected a conversation from me. My strategy worked—no one even called out a hello—although a stranger, an Amish man I didn't recognize, turned toward me and stared as I passed him. He was tall, broad, and handsome, and wore a thick, short beard. I could feel his eyes still on me as I hurried along.

When I reached our flower booth, my brother-in-law, Leon, nodded a greeting. He and I were both introverts and had much more in common with each other than either of us had with Molly, proving that opposites attract since she was the one he chose. For a short time, a few hours on a camping trip a year ago last June, I wondered what it would be like to court him, but now he was like a brother to me.

I actually did have a brother—Ivan, my half brother, who at nearly fifty had just married Nell Yoder. She'd been delighted to take on the role of big sister to Molly and me, but Ivan remained more like a favorite *Onkel*.

I grabbed the handles of two buckets filled with purple mums and marched to the wagon. I hefted them into the back and scooted them along the boards as far as I could. Our horse, Daisy, nickered, and I stepped forward to pet her, although besides not being much of a dog person, I wasn't a horse person either.

On my way back to the booth I stumbled over my own two feet at the sight of Ben Rupp, who approached Leon.

"Are you going hunting with us?" Ben called out. "The more the merrier."

Leon responded, "It's not hunting season yet."

"It will be—for muzzle-loaders," Ben replied. "It comes right after bow hunting. Before regular hunting."

Leon, his back to me, shook his head and said something, but I couldn't make out his words.

Ben continued, "I have my *Dawdi*'s old gun. And I talked the twins and Phillip into buying their own."

Leon said something else I couldn't hear.

Ben's voice was loud, too loud. "You're going to Montana?"

"Jah. Next week."

No one had said a thing about Leon going to Montana, especially not as soon as next week. I started marching toward them.

A smirk settled on Ben's face as I approached. He took off his straw hat and ran his hand through his hay-colored hair, still streaked by the summer sun. In an indifferent voice, he said, "Bea Zook."

I took a deep breath. "Ben Rupp," I responded, matching his tone. "And it's Beatrice to you."

"Persnickety"—that had been the winning word for our sixth-grade year, spelled by Ben—"as ever," he said.

"How *pretentious* of you," I retorted. I'd won the seventh-grade spelling bee with that word.

Leon stepped between us. "Hey, you two—" But then one of the vendors called out to him with a question.

Ben didn't miss a beat. "Pernicious." It had been on our eighth-grade list. "The definition being, having a harmful effect, in a gradual or subtle way."

As if I wouldn't remember what it meant!

He pulled his hat back on his head. "That's you, Missy D-I-S-D-A-I-N."

That had been his nickname for me growing up, after we'd had the word on our sixth-grade list. The feeling that someone or something is unworthy of one's consideration or respect. That was how he thought I felt about others. He never knew it, but he'd made me cry with that one.

"You're putting yourself in an awfully *precarious* position," I said now as my hands involuntarily formed fists at my side. That had never been on any of our lists.

He had the same impish expression on his face that had annoyed me all through our years as scholars. "I doubt it. You're just being *perfunctory*," he said, his greenish brown eyes flashing, and then added, "performing routinely, in a superficial way."

We'd never had that word either. "I know what it means," I said as my fingernails dug into my palms, even though I actually didn't. I'd ask forgiveness for my pride later.

Leon returned. "Hey, you two," he said. "Knock it off."

I crossed my arms, hiding my fists beneath them.

"I pity you," Ben said to Leon, "having to travel across the country with her." His dimples flashed.

"I'm not going anywhere," I said, but the puzzled look on Leon's face said otherwise.

My voice cracked. "This is the first I've heard . . ."

Leon stuttered. "Mol-ly didn't tell you?"

"She probably didn't say anything because it doesn't have anything to do with me."

"You can't stay home by yourself," Leon replied.

"What about Mamm?"

"She's going," Leon answered.

"Why would she?" She'd already met Leon's parents when they came out for the wedding nearly a year ago. There was no reason for her to travel to Montana.

Leon's face reddened. "You should talk to your Mamm—and sister."

Ben's smirk turned into a full-fledged smile. "Another reason I'll never marry." He pointed at me and then smiled at Leon. "In-laws."

I turned away from the two men and began walking as fast as I could toward the path, hurt by both Ben's rudeness and Leon's secretiveness. One of the adventuresome barn kittens darted toward me, and I scooped her up, cradling her like a baby. The kitten struggled to get down, but after a minute gave in and began to purr. I lifted her to my face, stroking my skin with her soft gray fur. I may not have been a dog or horse person, but I'd always loved cats.

Ben's boots pounded behind me. "Bea!"

I let the kitten go and hurried on, trying to forget the handful of times Ben had come to court me in the weeks after Molly and Leon's wedding. I'd been smitten and thought he had been too. I even forgave him for all the years he tormented me through school. Foolishly, I thought we had a future. But then he'd abruptly stopped coming around—without even a hint of explanation.

I struggled up the dusty trail, stubbing my toe on a root. My foot slipped.

"Wait!" he yelled.

I regained my balance and kept moving forward. Reaching the top, I shoved my hands into my apron pockets and persevered, heading toward the front porch as Love fell in step beside me, her wagging tail bouncing off my leg. Mamm and Molly sat side by side on the settee, framed by our old white house.

Molly pointed at me just as Ben reached my side and touched my arm. I turned toward him and saw a pained expression fall across his face when I jerked away.

Leaving Ben behind, I continued on toward the steps. Determined to keep my voice calm but not caring if Ben heard, I asked, "Why didn't you tell me about going to Montana?"

Mamm and Molly exchanged one of their looks, and then Molly said, "When we were just thinking about it, we didn't want to get you all worked up if it wasn't necessary." She glanced at Mamm, who nodded, and then back at me. "Then once we knew for sure, we were waiting until the right time to tell you."

"But you're leaving next week."

"True," Mamm said.

"*We're* leaving next week," Molly added.

"I'm not going," I answered.

"Bea," Ben said again.

I whirled around to face him.

"Can we talk?" he pleaded.

"No," I snapped, and stormed up the steps, past my mother and my sister and into our house, fleeing up the stairs to my room. It was so like Molly to withhold information from me— and so like her to conspire with Mamm to keep it a secret.

Mamm stood in the doorway of my room. "Come get supper. Then we'll talk."

"I'm not hungry." I flopped over on my bed, tucking my journal beneath me.

"Come on down anyway."

I shook my head. Unlike lots of other Amish families, we rarely traveled. Camping in the Poconos was as far as we'd ever gone—and I was perfectly content with that. "I'm not going to Montana," I said. "I'll stay here and see to the farm."

"That's all taken care of. Edna is going to do the chores the first week, and then Mervin and Martin will take over when they get back from hunting."

I'd never felt so humiliated in my life, at least not since Ben dumped me. Edna was my older half sister, and Mervin and Martin were our neighbors. Did the whole county know before I did about the trip to Montana?

"Come on," Mamm said. "Molly feels horrible."

I didn't believe her.

15

"Bea . . ." Mamm's voice softened. "I made biscuits."

I loved Mamm's baking-powder biscuits.

She added, "And we're having apple butter." We'd put up twenty jars of it last week but hadn't opened one yet.

"Molly wants to apologize," Mamm said.

I inched my way to the edge of the bed. I *was* hungry. And who was I to thwart an apology? The trip wasn't Mamm's idea, I was sure. In fact, it probably hadn't been her idea not to talk with me about it either. It had to have been Molly's. Mamm had been deferring to my sister ever since Dat died. "I'll be down in a minute," I finally said.

Mamm left, pulling the door closed. I clambered off the bed, straightened my apron and Kapp, and put my journal back in the bottom drawer next to the book of poems, wishing I could escape to the Olde Book Shoppe just outside of Paradise, the village closest to us. It was my favorite place in the entire world. Thankfully the owners of the little store welcomed me to come and browse, even though they knew I couldn't buy.

But it was a Saturday evening, and they were already closed. They wouldn't be open tomorrow. Maybe I'd try to go on Monday. Or sometime soon.

I trudged slowly down the stairs to the kitchen, arriving after everyone else was seated. Leon led us in silent prayer as soon as I'd settled on my chair.

Afterward, no one spoke. I stared at my plate while the rest of them dished up the stuffed acorn squash I had prepared earlier that afternoon. Molly passed the platter to me. I took it, staring at the golden flesh filled with ground beef, chopped celery, and baked breadcrumbs. When I placed it in the middle of the table without taking one, no one—not even Molly—commented.

A long moment later, she cleared her throat. "It was my idea to wait to tell you about the trip."

I kept my head down.

"I knew you wouldn't want to go," she said.

"But you didn't ask." I raised my head. She remained as pale and drawn as she had been earlier in the afternoon.

"For good reason," she retorted.

"Girls," Mamm said, pushing her plate aside.

Leon seemed oblivious to us, gobbling his supper as we spoke.

I muttered, "I thought Molly was going to apologize."

"Pardon?" my sister croaked.

"Apologize."

"For what?" Molly asked.

Mamm ducked her head as I said, "For not consulting me . . ." Mamm had said Molly wanted to apologize—but she must have assumed it. Silly me for thinking Molly would.

My sister said, "You've never wanted to be consulted before on anything around here."

I met her eyes. "A trip to Montana is a completely different issue than how many rows of lilies to plant."

"You're right. How's this? I wanted all of us to go together, and I was pretty sure you'd pitch a fit." Molly stared me down. "Bull's-eye." She didn't flinch. "So I figured the longer we waited to bring it up the better."

"What did you plan to do? Pack a bag for me and tell me right before it was time to catch the train?"

"Something like that." She shrugged and spread apple butter on her biscuit.

I reached for the squash, knowing it would do no good to cross Molly now. Mamm must have misunderstood how she felt about the incident. Molly wasn't sorry at all. In fact, she felt absolutely justified in her behavior.

You would think I'd be used to being treated as an accessory to Molly, as if I were equivalent to her apron or her Kapp, but her attitude still caught me off guard. I'd only stood up to her a few times—I would have to find the strength to do it again. Just not tonight.

I finished filling my plate as Molly put down her fork. "I'm tired," she said.

"Go on to bed," Mamm said. "It's been a long day."

Leon put his fork down on his empty plate, a look of concern on his face.

"I'm fine," Molly said. "I think I'm just feeling overwhelmed with the trip." Her eyes met mine. "And everything else."

✤

Once I finished washing the dishes and cleaning the kitchen, I retrieved my books and journal from my room and slipped out the back door.

I shivered as I hurried toward the greenhouse. The welcomed crisp air of the autumn night filled my lungs. The stars shone above me, and Love, roused from beside the barn, yawned and then followed behind. She stopped outside the greenhouse, familiar with my routine. I slipped inside and lit the *Ladann*, placing it on the desk.

I doubted Mamm and Molly would barge into my room at night, but I didn't want to take the chance that they'd see the book I was reading. I put my journal and Bible down and held the book. The brown cover was old and worn, yet soft and comforting.

I'd found a similar volume in the Olde Book Shoppe about a year ago and then started looking for old books of poetry in the bookmobile. I suspected the librarian now added them to the collection just for me. True, I liked the words and the emotions of the poems. But I also treasured the age of the volumes. I'd always liked old things—furniture, dishes, and quilts—but I especially liked old books.

Mamm had been a teacher before she married, and she saw nothing wrong with reading biographies and an occasional novel, but she'd frown on anything that had to do with romance. I doubted she'd approve of the poetry I read.

I opened my journal. It wasn't that I wanted to be a writer. I had no delusions that I was talented enough. My writing was for myself. And honestly, it was mostly what I copied from other books—Scripture, lines from poems, quotes, words from my dictionary. Words, *Vatts* in our language, were what I loved most.

I folded my hands over my stack of books and bowed my head. I recited the Lord's Prayer and asked for forgiveness for my trespasses again, in a routine way, mostly out of habit, I admit. The word *perfunctorily* came to mind.

What were my trespasses? My only conflicts were with Molly and Ben Rupp. If I didn't have any contact with them, I wouldn't have *any* trespasses. That made me smile. I knew that probably wasn't true, but it certainly felt like it. I added my pride from earlier and then moved on and thanked God for his blessings. Mamm's health. The farm. Plenty to eat. The gray kitten who'd brought me joy just that afternoon in a moment of despair.

God was good. That I knew.

I opened my journal. It was time to address the Montana problem. Most people I knew would be excited to go. A long train ride. The Wild West. Leon's family. But not me. I was a homebody. I didn't like to go anywhere. Staying in Lancaster

County with Edna or a neighboring family would be much better than a long, arduous journey.

I couldn't fathom what would make Mamm let me stay—unless I got a job. Molly had suggested the idea several times in the last few months, as Mamm regained her strength. My sister didn't feel there was enough work to warrant my being home all day.

I started jotting down a list of possible jobs I could find.

Schoolteacher. Sure I knew the material, but being in a classroom with thirty students day after day sounded daunting. Plus school had started over a month ago. I was too late for this year, whether I could tolerate the work or not.

Next I wrote down *seamstress.* Mamm and I had made a wedding quilt for Molly, plus I sewed most of our dresses now, but my work was far from spectacular. It was barely passable, in all honesty. My hems were continually ripping and usually had to be repaired by Mamm.

Shop worker. I'd have to talk with people, including Englisch people.

Mother's helper. That was probably my best bet. I could let my sister-in-law, Nell, know I was looking for some sort of position. She was the best source of advertising I knew.

I doodled a shelf on the page and then wrote *bookstore clerk.* That's what I really wanted to do. Work at the bookstore in Paradise. Shelving books would be my preference, but in a pinch I could talk to an Englisch person if it meant working there. But Albert and Willa Schmidt didn't need any help. It only took two people to run the place.

I closed my journal, determined to contact Nell in the morning, and opened the book to the first page, but found myself reading the first line over and over:

"It lies not in our power to love or hate . . ."

The words didn't mean anything to me, and each time I read them my mind wandered. I'd been procrastinating finding a job because I preferred working at home. But now I couldn't help but wish I'd found a job sooner. Molly wouldn't be expecting me to go to Montana if I had.

It was my own fault. It wasn't that I was lazy—but I certainly did lack my sister's drive.

I read the first line of the poem once again, but this time Love's barking interrupted me. I closed the book with a thud.

It was probably Molly coming out to harass me. I gathered up my things, arranging the Bible on the top of the pile, and blew out the lamp. I would read my Scripture passage back in my room. As I opened the door Love's barking grew louder.

"Who's there?" I called out. Too frightened to chastise her, I held my breath as footsteps fell alongside the greenhouse. It wasn't Molly.

A man rounded the corner.

As he pulled off his hat, I realized it was Ben. "Hello," he said.

I barked as loudly as Love. "You frightened me!"

"Sorry." His expression turned sheepish. "I wanted to see how you were doing, after this afternoon."

I took a deep breath, surprised at his consideration.

"Are you going to go to Montana?" he asked.

I shrugged.

"I mean," he said, "it could be a lot of fun, and . . ."

I must have discouraged him with my facial expression, because he stopped talking. In the silence, I noticed his hair had curled along his forehead and the scent of the crisp night air clung to him.

He smiled then, his eyes shining as he did, and he reached toward me, brushing my arm just as Love barked again.

Heavier footsteps fell on the gravel around the side of the building. Love growled.

"Who's there?" I called out.

"Bea?" It was one of the twins. "Have you seen Ben?" As he came around the side of the greenhouse, I could see it was Martin, who was a little heavier than Mervin.

"Fancy meeting you here," he said to Ben and then laughed. "Although it was my first guess."

Ben didn't respond. I stepped back.

"We need to finish going through the hunting gear," Martin said. "You're the one who wanted to get packed a week early."

"Jah," Ben said. "It's better to know what we need now than the night before." Then he turned toward me. "We'll walk you back to your house."

"No," I said. "I'm fine."

Ben shook his head.

"Come on," Martin said, nodding toward Ben. "It means a lot to him." He grinned.

Ben bristled. I hugged my books.

Martin's grin faded. "It's the least we can do after barging over like this."

There was no reason for me to be rude. I started toward the house. Love followed at my heels, and the boys hurried along behind. Ben caught up, bumping against me. I was caught off guard, and the books tumbled from my arms onto the lawn. Ben scooped them up before I could.

"I'll take them," I said, unsettled that my journal was in Ben's hands.

"No, I've got them." He held the books tight.

Love barked again. As we reached the back door Mamm met us, holding a lamp. "What's going on?" she said, her eyes focusing on me.

"Everything's fine," I said, reaching for my books. Ben handed me my Bible. A peaceful expression covered his face. Then, from the bottom of the stack, my journal. Thankfully, he didn't open it. He started to hand me the book of poems, but then he pulled it back. I reached for it. He stepped backward.

"Oh, look," he said, holding it up. "A *Buch* of poetry."

I grimaced as he flipped it open, stopped, and then read, out loud, "'It lies not in our power to love or hate, for will in us is overruled by fate.'"

"Bea," Mamm said, snatching the book quickly, "what sort of foolishness are you reading?"

"Just a book of poems." I stared down Ben as I spoke. I couldn't figure him out. Three hours ago he was insulting me, and then a few minutes ago he seemed concerned about my welfare, only to make an absolute fool out of me now.

Things never went smoothly when he was around.

I stepped around Mamm, clutching my Bible and journal.

"Bea!" Ben said as I hurried on, his voice concerned again. "Wait!"

I kept going, determined to get as far away from Ben Rupp as possible.

CHAPTER

2

I replayed the night before as I readied myself for church, tying my freshly pressed apron around my waist and then twisting my hair into a bun, pinning it tightly. Mamm's concern was unfounded. The book of poems, written hundreds of years ago by Christopher Marlowe, was harmless.

I pinned my Kapp in place over my bun. One of the things I liked about Marlowe's poetry was that he wrote in the same century that the Anabaptist movement began. While my ancestors were being chased around Switzerland, he wrote plays, poetry, and prose in London. Not that he didn't have problems of his own—he was stabbed to death in 1593.

Molly's voice singsonged up the staircase. "Beatrice! We're leaving!"

Leaving? I hadn't even had breakfast. Had I daydreamed half the morning away? "Coming," I called out, slipping my feet into my black Sunday shoes and hurrying down the stairs and out the door.

Leon drove the carriage with Molly up front beside him, while Mamm and I sat in the back. Mamm stared out at the fields as if intent on the corn ready for harvest. Finally she turned toward me and asked, "Is Ben courting you again?" She spoke loudly. Molly shifted in her seat so she could hear us better.

I shook my head.

"Then what was going on last night?" Mamm asked.

"I'm honestly not sure," I answered, pulling my cape tighter against the morning chill. "May I have my poetry book back when we get home? It's not what you think—honestly."

Molly gave Mamm a knowing look, but Mamm simply turned her attention back to the fields without answering me. Obviously she and Molly had talked about the book—and me.

Leon turned the buggy to the right, by the Paradise Stables sign. Church was at the family home of Molly's best friend, Hannah Lapp. The Lapps raised, trained, and boarded horses on their farm.

The poplars along the lane swayed in the breeze. A quarter horse in the pasture raised its head as we passed by. Leon had worked for Owen Lapp, Hannah's Dat, when he first came to Paradise, and I suspected he longed to run a similar business of his own someday. They'd done their best to accommodate horses on our flower farm, but we simply didn't have the acreage to board many of the beasts. When they first courted, Leon considered moving back to Montana, but Molly had been so adamant about staying in Lancaster County that he'd acquiesced.

Leon let us off in front of the Lapps' house and then continued on to park the buggy in the row behind the barn.

The Lapps' house was big, one of the largest in our district. The outbuildings had all been recently updated and newly painted. On a weekly basis Molly commented on how nice things were at Paradise Stables. I wouldn't have noticed if she didn't mention it so often.

The members of our district gathered on the lush lawn,

although attendance was down because of the sickness going around. My brother, Ivan, and sister-in-law, Nell, were nowhere to be seen. Perhaps they'd come down with the flu too. Although it was more likely that they'd gone off on a short trip, taking in the fall colors somewhere nearby. As a childless couple in their late forties with a good income—Ivan worked as an accountant—they traveled more than anyone I knew. I didn't envy them one bit.

I scanned the group for Ben but didn't see him. Nor did I see Mervin and Martin, although their parents, Amos and Eliza Mosier, talked with Cate and Pete and a girl I didn't recognize.

Molly and Mamm headed toward them, and I followed. As we neared, I realized the girl was a young woman—about my age. Hope! She was Nan Miller's niece from New York. I'd met her at Bob and Nan's wedding over a year ago.

She saw me the moment I recognized her and squealed, "Bea!" She dashed toward me, her blue eyes shining. She hugged me and then, with her hands still on my shoulders, jumped up and down. If anyone else had done that to me, I'd be annoyed, but Hope's action made me feel adored, something I didn't often experience.

"I was hoping you'd be here," she said, letting go of me. "I got in last night."

"You're staying at Nan and Bob's?"

"Jah," she said. "I'm helping with the *Bopplis*. I'll be here for a couple of months." She glanced toward Cate. "If not more." Nan had given birth to triplets four weeks ago. Two of them, the boys, had just been released from the hospital.

Molly asked Cate how Nan and the babies were doing. "As well as can be expected," Cate answered, her eyes full of concern. "We're hoping the baby girl will be able to come home next week.

We're trying to get Nan to do nothing but rest so she can nurse the little ones as much as possible and build her strength."

"How's your Dat doing?" Mamm asked.

Cate wrinkled her nose and glanced at Pete. Then she said, "He's worried."

It wasn't like Bob Miller to worry, but then I remembered his first wife had died over two decades ago after giving birth to Betsy, Cate's sister.

"Having Hope here is going to be a big help," Pete said. "It's unbelievable how chaotic everything's become."

Hope smiled. "But I should still have time for fun. Like going to singings and that sort of thing." She purposefully bumped into me. I didn't have the heart to tell her I didn't go to those sorts of gatherings.

"You know, Bea," Cate said. "We're looking for another helper. Would you be interested?"

As Hope clapped her hands together I couldn't help but feel a ray of hope. Imagine that. Maybe I wouldn't need Nell's help to find a job after all. "Jah," I said. "I would, and—"

Molly butted in, saying, "But not until after we get back from Montana."

Cate tilted her head. "Montana?"

"Jah, we're all going to . . ." Molly's voice trailed off as Hannah approached with Mervin, Martin, and Ben behind her.

I shook my head. "Molly, you've been after me to get a job. This is a perfect opportunity."

Molly crossed her arms and pursed her lips into an expression that communicated *We'll talk about this later.*

Cate said, "I see." Then she and Pete exchanged a smile.

I grabbed Hope's hand and pulled her toward the house, determined to get away from Molly, Hannah, and the boys.

"Let's go get a place to sit," I said. Hope came along a little reluctantly, looking over her shoulder. I followed her gaze and at first thought it landed on Ben. But I was wrong. Her attention was directed at Martin, who grinned in return.

Still, I couldn't help but groan. Not surprisingly, Hope didn't notice.

Monday I expected Cate, or maybe Bob or even Nan, to call me. But no call came. Nor on Tuesday. Perhaps they weren't as desperate as Cate made it sound. But I still asked Mamm if I could stay home if I found a job. She said if I did, she'd allow it.

On Wednesday morning Molly came into the house as I swept the kitchen floor. "You have a message on the phone," she said.

I thought she spoke to Mamm, who sat at the table finishing her tea.

"Bea," Molly said, her hand on her hip.

I stopped sweeping. "*I* have a message?" Just when I'd given up hope. . . .

Molly nodded. "From Bob Miller."

I tried not to appear too excited as I asked, "What did he say?"

"Go listen to it," Molly answered.

She left the kitchen as I finished the sweeping. Once done, I headed to the greenhouse. Love darted to my side, leaving Leon, who worked with one of the horses he trained in the corral. Later, he'd help Molly cut the last of the mums from the field to take to the market. Mervin and sometimes Martin used to work for us, but now they worked for Bob in his cabinet shop.

Once Molly and Leon married we didn't need to hire employees. Leon's help plus his work training the horses turned our finances around, mostly. Molly's ingenuity had done the rest. She'd hosted dinners for Englisch people, rented out one of our bedrooms for up to a week at a time, and peddled her herbs to bed-and-breakfasts and restaurants throughout the area. I appreciated the extra income, but did not like having strangers in our home. Thankfully, she held the last Englisch dinner in August—I did the cooking for all the dinners and then disappeared while Molly did the serving—and the last overnight guest stayed the first week of September. Molly had assured me that she was done with all of that, at least for the time being.

When I reached the greenhouse, Love ran back toward Leon, and I stepped inside to find Molly at the desk, with an accounting ledger in front of her.

I stepped to the other side and pushed the Play button on the machine. "This is Bob Miller with a message for Bea. Cate said you might be interested in helping at our house. Could you come by sometime today so we can discuss the possibility? I'll be home—or perhaps in my office."

When the message stopped, Molly put down her pencil. "Maybe they'll still need help in a few weeks. Call him back."

I took a deep breath and headed toward the door.

"Bea," she said. "Where are you going?"

"To hitch up Daisy."

"To go talk to Bob Miller in person?"

"Jah," I said.

"Don't be so stubborn," she said.

"Don't be so bossy," I responded.

"You'll have to tell him you can't start until next month."

"First I'll find out what they need." If they wanted me right away it would be the perfect excuse not to go to Montana. Surely Mamm would agree to let me stay.

I didn't bother to say good-bye to Molly. Instead I firmly

closed the door behind me, went back to the house to tell Mamm I'd be back soon, and then hitched the horse to the buggy and headed down the lane.

Love ran alongside but stopped abruptly and whined as I turned onto the highway. Except for an occasional trip to the bookmobile or bookstore, I rarely left the farm by myself.

I'm not sure why my parents hadn't pushed me to be more independent, but I think they were relieved that I, in comparison to Molly, wasn't such a gadabout. They weren't very social beings either, by far preferring to stay home. Because I took after them, at least in that, they had one less thing to worry about. Until it became obvious I barely went out at all.

I kept as close to the side of the road as I possibly could as a car whizzed by the buggy. Daisy kept steady, plodding along. We passed the willow tree and then the crossroads. In the field to my right, a group of men worked together to harvest the corn, using a thresher pulled by mules. The next farm was a dairy, where the cows grazed peacefully in a pasture. In front of the house, a woman stood in the middle of the garden beside a child, who held a small gourd.

A few miles later, I turned Daisy into the Millers' driveway. To the right was the showroom for their cabinet business and then the shop. To the left was the house and behind it a *Dawdi Haus* that Bob Miller had built for himself before he knew God would bless him with a second marriage and more *Kinner* of his own.

I parked the buggy in the showroom parking lot, tied Daisy to the hitching post, and contemplated whether I should go around the back to Bob's office or enter through the showroom. Finally I decided on the latter, easing open the door, expecting Pete to greet me, but the room was empty.

Not sure what to do, I walked through the room to the door that led to the offices. I opened it, calling out a hello. No one answered.

I stepped into the hall. In the distance, the power tools in the shop hummed. Perhaps Bob was in there. I'd just started toward the double doors at the end of the hall when Mervin came crashing through them, wearing a bandana tied around his head and steel-toed boots.

"Oh, it's you," he said. "I was expecting a customer."

"Bob asked me to come talk to him—about a job."

"In the shop?" Mervin joked.

I simply shook my head.

He exhaled. "That would be good for you to help out with Nan and the babies—then maybe Bob could spend a little time down here. And Pete and Cate too."

"I take it they're in the house now?"

He nodded.

"Denki," I said, determined not to get in any more of a conversation with Mervin.

"Brace yourself," he said as I walked away. "It's as if a tornado touches down every few hours up there."

I didn't respond to his exaggeration. How bad could it be? There were just two babies there right now, until the little girl came home. And five adults, counting Hope. I couldn't imagine why they'd need my help at all. But I was happy to give it, especially if it meant not going to Montana.

⟡

As I neared the house, I debated whether to go to the front door or the back door, but when the back one flew open I hurried toward it. Cate stood in the doorway, a basket of laundry in her hands.

Pete was right behind her. "Give me that," he said.

"I'm fine."

"You're not—" He stopped when he saw me.

As Cate said hello, he grabbed the basket. "You talk with Bea; I'll take care of the wash."

I stared after him. It wasn't that an Amish man would never hang laundry on the line, but it wasn't something I saw very often.

"I can do that," I said to Cate, nodding toward Pete as he rushed across the lawn, easily handling the basket.

"Do you mind? He really should get back to work. We're falling behind."

"I'm happy to do it." I headed toward Pete.

"Come in when you're done," Cate said. "I'll let Dat know you're here."

Pete protested, but when I told him Cate wanted him to get back to work in the shop, he agreed. As a car turned into the parking lot he thanked me and hurried on his way. Diapers—the tiniest I'd ever seen—filled the basket. I picked up the first one, inhaled the bleach used to whiten the cloth, and pinned it to the line, repeating the process over and over, wondering how long it had been since they'd done the wash. The two baby boys hadn't been home long, not even a week.

I kept pinning, wishing Hope would come out to keep me company, wondering what she was doing that kept her in the house. It seemed Cate would have her doing the wash. When they first married, Cate and Pete had done editing for his uncle's publishing business, but I'd heard they were too busy now with Bob's business and the growing household to keep up with that too. Things certainly did seem chaotic at the Millers'.

I inhaled, taking in the scent of roses. To my left was a flower bed. One yellow bloom outshone the dying red ones, which should have been clipped days ago. Clearly the diapers weren't the only things piling up. I shaded my eyes and looked toward the garden. It hadn't been cleaned up either. Weeds and dead vines cluttered the ground, brightened by a crop of pumpkins.

They definitely needed more help.

When I finished pinning the last diaper, I picked up the basket and returned to the house, opening the back door and calling out a hello as I entered. No one responded. The Millers' kitchen was much bigger than ours and much, much nicer. A window over the sink was like a fishbowl—three-sided with views of the lane, the shop, and the backyard and even a corner of the Dawdi Haus.

Beautiful cabinets lined the walls, but the breakfast dishes filled the sink. Their huge oak table sat in the middle of the kitchen—with folded towels stacked on one end and two little tubs on the other. I couldn't help but notice the collection of old kerosene lamps, washboards, and antique crystal vases displayed on top of the cupboards. Obviously someone—Nan, I guessed—liked old things too. Decorations were usually sparse in Amish homes, but the items didn't seem pretentious.

A baby cried. Perhaps everyone was upstairs. But then I realized the sound came from the sun porch Bob had added a few years ago. I put the basket on the table. The cry turned into a frantic wail as I headed down the hall.

The door was partway open, so I pushed on through.

"There, there," Cate chanted to the baby that was screaming. Hope held the other. Both babies were small and red, their faces scrunched and wrinkled with jutty chins and worried foreheads. They looked more like wizened old men than babies. There was nothing plump or soft or round about them.

"Oh," Cate said, "I forgot to tell Dat you're here. Hold on."

She paused for a moment and then extended the baby to me. "Would you take him? I don't want to disturb Nan."

I reached for him. Except for our kittens, I'd never held a living thing so tiny in my entire life. Cate scooted him into my arms and I took him, not sure what to do. Cate was down the hall before I could ask her.

Hope must have noted my dilemma because she said, "Sway— like this." She leaned from side to side with the baby she held. I imitated her, although not nearly as gracefully. It seemed to work though, because the baby calmed down.

"What are their names?" I asked Hope as I sniffed the top of the little one's head, taking in the scent of mild soap.

"This one," she said, dipping her chin down, "is Kurt. The one you're holding is Asher."

"How about the little girl?"

"Leah," Hope answered, and then smiled.

Asher let out a sigh and closed his eyes.

"I'm so glad you're going to help out here," Hope said. "For all sorts of reasons."

"We'll see what Bob says," I replied.

"Oh, he'll hire you." Hope smiled again. "Trust me."

Cate returned. "I thought Dat was upstairs with Nan, but he's not. Head down to the basement—he's working down there."

That seemed odd to me, but maybe he'd set up an office in the house. I slipped Asher back into her arms and made my way back through the kitchen to the basement stairs, my eyes adjusting to the dimmer light as I descended.

"Bob?" I called out as I reached the bottom. In the distance a motor hummed. Maybe he did woodworking in the basement, although it didn't sound like a saw. I walked toward the source of the noise—the laundry room. Puzzled, I opened the door.

Bob stood at the wringer washer, feeding a sheet through the roller.

"We keep getting behind on laundry," Bob said. "My goal is to get caught up today."

"Oh," was all I could manage to say, wondering why women from the district weren't at the house. Then I remembered the flu that had been going through a lot of the children and mothers. The last thing they'd want would be to have Nan and the babies exposed.

"So," Bob said, his eyes on the sheet, "we're barely making it all work, even though we've had help with meals and things like that."

So they had had extra help.

"I think we can make it until next week. However, once Leah comes home from the hospital, we're definitely going to need more assistance. Can you start next Monday?"

"Jah," I said, anticipating how Molly would react when I told her.

"It's a lot of work." Bob dropped the sheet into a basket and pulled another from the tub. "Diapers. Feedings. Walking babies. Cooking. Cleaning. Gardening. Are you up to whatever we need you to do?"

I nodded. "Jah," I said again.

Bob tugged on his beard. "You'll have to be on your toes. This is much harder than just chores. There's plenty of that, but the safety of the babies is the most important thing."

I nodded. They were awfully tiny. I knew I'd have to be really careful. "I'll do my best," I said.

Bob inhaled. Perhaps he was looking for a different answer from me. Finally he said, "Nan thinks it'll be good for Hope to have another Youngie in the house." He chuckled. "Nan also says you remind her of Cate a few years ago." He grew more serious. "But that's not reason enough to hire you. I need to know you're serious about the job."

"Jah," I said. "I am." There was no reason to tell him I was intimidated. Most Amish girls grew up taking care of babies— but not me.

"Come prepared to stay here for a long stretch, but we'll make sure you get some time off too."

"What if I don't want any time off?" I asked. "I mean, what if I don't want to go home at all for a couple of weeks?"

He shot me a questioning look as he eased the rest of the last sheet through the wringer.

"My family is going to Montana. No one will be home—well, except Edna, at first."

"*Ach*, I forgot about that." Bob pulled another sheet from the tub. "And you don't want to go with them?"

I shook my head.

"Under other circumstances, I'd try to talk you into it," Bob said. "But as things are, I'm grateful for your help."

Feeling awkward, I thanked him quickly and headed back up the stairs. I was acquainted with Nan from way back when she used to drive the bookmobile, and we'd gotten to know each other a little better over the last year, since she and Bob married. But there wasn't anything about me to remind her of Cate, I was sure.

And there was nothing about me to make her think I'd be a good caregiver to her babies either. I was pretty sure Bob would agree with me on that.

CHAPTER
3

Mamm stood at the kitchen sink scrubbing potatoes when I returned home. "How did it go?" she asked.

"I start next Monday."

She didn't look happy but said nothing.

"You said if I . . ."

"I know," she answered. "I just didn't expect you to find anything. Molly isn't going to be pleased."

"She should be. It's what she's wanted for the last—"

Mamm's disappointed look stopped me.

"Sorry," I said. "She'll get over it."

That only deepened Mamm's worry wrinkles around her eyes.

Mamm told Molly the new plan as we put dinner on the table.

"Bea," my sister said, "how could you?"

I didn't answer.

"I told her she could stay if she found a job," Mamm said.

It was as if Molly hadn't heard her. "We've never been on a family vacation before, besides camping. This might be our only chance."

Again, I didn't answer. There was no reason to tell her that, though I loved them, I had no desire to go on a trip with my family.

"Mamm," Molly said. "I can't believe you're letting her get away with this."

"She's twenty-one," Mamm said. "She's allowed to make her own decisions."

When Molly started in on me again after the prayer, Leon put his hand on top of hers.

"What?" Molly snapped at him.

He didn't say anything.

She'd been extra wound up lately. Why would I want to spend two days on a train with her? And then another two weeks in Montana dodging her moods? I didn't enjoy traveling—I never had. I said that out loud.

"How would you know?" Molly asked. "You've never been anywhere."

I'd been to the Poconos. That was far enough.

"She'll be a big help to the Millers," Mamm said. "It's important work to help a new mother. Taking care of babies is the most important job in the world."

It wasn't unusual for a family to have twins, but triplets were rare in our community—or any community, for that matter. Nan had been on bed rest for two months before they were born. The babies had come six weeks early, and the little girl's lungs hadn't fully developed. That was why she'd had to stay in the hospital.

Our district and others around had all prayed for Nan and the babies. We'd all felt a part of it.

That afternoon, I headed to the bookmobile with the book Mamm had returned to me. I hoped the librarian had another old volume of poetry waiting.

As Daisy pulled the buggy down the highway, I sat straight, my head high, again anticipating something. Once again, I wasn't sure what it might be, but I felt some adventure was on the horizon. Not a journey to a new place—although I *was* going to the Millers'—but a journey somewhere inside myself.

The bookmobile was parked across from the Englisch school, as always. I returned my book of poetry.

"I don't have any more today," the librarian said. "Sorry. I'll see what I can find next time."

"That's all right," I answered, but I felt disappointed as I left.

When I came to the crossroads, I wasn't ready to go home yet, so I turned left instead of right. I hadn't stopped by the bookstore in a couple of weeks.

I turned down a lane lined with stalks of corn, urging Daisy along. A car passed me, and then a camera popped up in the back window. Most likely tourists. Even though not as many visited our farmers' market as autumn progressed, the season never truly ended in Lancaster County. I kept my face stoic and stared straight ahead.

A half mile later I turned onto the main road, keeping to the side of the road as best I could. Ahead, at the end of a cluster of shops, was the bookstore, with sunflowers growing along the brick building, bidding me inside.

I climbed down from my buggy, hitched Daisy to the post, and hurried inside, my hands in my apron pockets. Inhaling deeply, I took in the musty scent of old books, strong coffee, and shelves made of pine. Albert welcomed me, a sparkle in his eyes and his hair and beard even whiter than the last time I'd seen him. "We haven't seen you for some time," he said.

"Jah," I answered. "I've been busy."

"We've acquired a recent collection," he said. "From an Englisch man. There are several volumes you haven't seen along the back wall."

The shop sold mostly old books, although it also carried

Bibles, copies of the *Martyrs Mirror*, prayer books, and hymnals. Specialty books could be ordered. A few new children's books, coloring books, and workbooks were carried, and they also sold several different kinds of cards, all made by Amish people.

The old books weren't rare books and they certainly weren't in pristine condition, but they were wonderful. Plus, it meant so much that the Schmidts were always so happy to see me. Truth be told, their love for each other reminded me of my parents' relationship, and although it made me miss my Dat, I still relished witnessing it.

I stopped for a moment at a rack of paper dolls and grimaced. They were supposedly Plain, but the designer hadn't researched our Kapps and dresses. Still I understood the store needed to make a profit, and I imagined they were a big draw to the Englisch who made their way through the front door. I continued on toward the back, passing coloring books, picture books, and then Willa Schmidt, her pure white hair and Kapp like a halo resting atop her head. She smiled at me sweetly. I responded in kind and kept on toward the back.

An Amish man, his back to me, stood in front of the shelf of books I aimed for. I stopped in the aisle as a child exclaimed, "Look!"

I couldn't help but turn around. A little Englisch girl had discovered the paper dolls. A woman, who looked to be her grandmother, quickly pulled them from the rack before the girl even requested the set.

I turned back toward the shelf, expecting the man to be gone. He wasn't. He'd knelt down in front of the bottom shelf with a book in his hand, his head down. In the dim light, I peered over the top of him, skimming the title of a very old book above his head. The words *Shakespeare: Sonnets* were imprinted on the spine.

I smiled. *Sonnet* had never been one of our spelling words, but I'd seen the word in some of the poetry books I checked out and looked up the definition in my dictionary: a poem of fourteen lines.

"Pardon me," I said, reaching over the man.

He stood abruptly, bumping my arm. I jerked it away as he faced me.

"Well, well, well." Ben Rupp grinned at me, the book still in his hand. "What are you doing here?" he asked.

I snatched the book I was after and crossed my arms, hiding it. "What do you think?"

"Spying on me?" His dimples flashed.

"Believe me, if I were, I would be standing where you wouldn't be able to assault me."

His smile faded. "Why are you so frosty?" He turned toward the window. "Is there an early snowstorm on the way?"

Before I could come up with a retort, Willa squeezed past me. "Oh, my," she said, "do you two know each other?" Before either one of us could answer, she called to her husband. "Bea and Ben are already acquainted."

My face grew warm, so I turned toward the front of the shop, making accidental eye contact with the Englisch grandmother, who smiled broadly. I spun back around.

Willa caught my arm. "How do you know Ben?"

"We had the misfortune of being in school together."

She grinned at me as if I'd told her we were courting. "Oh, goody," she said. I heard the footsteps of her husband before I saw him, and then he asked his wife if she could help the customer up front as he rounded the corner.

She scurried away, and it seemed Albert wanted to say something but instead he shook his head and asked Ben if he'd found the volume of sonnets.

"No," Ben said.

"It was right there." Albert pointed to the empty spot. He stepped closer. "Where did it go?"

"I have it," I confessed, holding it out, my face growing warm. Ben could probably afford to buy it—while I couldn't. I might as well let him have it, although I couldn't imagine Ben reading poetry.

"Do you want it?" Ben asked me.

I shook my head. Of course I wanted it! My face was now hot and probably beet red. Hot enough to melt snow, if in fact it had been winter.

Ben took it from me, saying he'd have a look. I wandered to the front of the store, hoping Ben would leave. But I had no such luck. I headed to the door.

"Bea." It was Albert, popping out from between two book-cases, his voice a near whisper. "Willa's not herself lately," he said. "She wouldn't have said anything so forward about you and Ben if she . . . " He paused.

"What's going on?" I asked, feeling alarmed, more at Albert's concerns than with what Willa actually said. She wasn't the first person to think Ben and I would make a good match.

He shook his head. "Pray for her, that's all. For us. For our business."

"Jah, of course," I said. I couldn't bear to think of anything happening to Willa, Albert, or the shop.

Molly avoided me until early Friday morning. "Bea," she said as I fried ham for breakfast, "did you plan to do the wash this morning?"

I tilted my head, trying to remember the last time I'd done it, even though it was my responsibility.

"Because," she continued, "I need to finish cutting the mums to get the last load to market. And Mamm, Leon, and I need to pack tonight."

I speared a piece of ham with the fork in my hand and flipped it. I needed clean clothes for my stay at the Millers' next week too. I exhaled and then said, "Jah, I was planning to do the wash. I'll start right after breakfast."

A few minutes later she came through the kitchen with a basket of dirty clothes, followed by Mamm, who carried a smaller basket. They headed down the basement stairs as I continued cooking. It wasn't as if I was the mule of the family. Molly worked far harder than I did—but she had a passion for what she did. I only had a tolerance for my chores.

As I pulled another skillet from the cupboard for the dippy eggs, I reminded myself that I wouldn't want to be taking the mums to market, not for anything. I'd have to talk to people. I'd have to make sure we were paid a fair price. I'd have to ride in the pickup with the driver.

I'd much rather do the laundry.

After breakfast, I soaked Molly and Leon's work clothes in a bucket as I collected my own things to wash. Then I filled the wringer washer tub with hot water and started the whites. After I'd run them through the wringer, I put the regular clothes in the tub and took the basket of whites out to hang to dry. I'd do the work clothes last.

As I headed toward the line, I spotted a buggy turning up our lane in the distance. I squinted. We weren't expecting anyone. I turned toward the loading dock. Leon and the driver lifted the buckets of mums into the back of the truck. Molly was nowhere in sight.

I started pinning aprons on the line, keeping an eye on the buggy as I did until I realized it was Hannah, Molly's best friend.

"She's inside," Leon called out as Hannah jumped down from the buggy.

He said something to the driver I couldn't hear. As Hannah hitched her horse to the post by the barn, the driver jumped into the pickup and then pulled away from the loading dock and headed down the driveway, without Leon or Molly. He had to pull to the side of the driveway to make room for another pickup, this one pulling a horse trailer. Leon greeted that driver and directed him toward the corral. I recognized the man as the owner of the horse Leon had been training. That made sense— why pay someone to see to the horse while Leon was gone?

Hannah waved as she passed me by on her way to the house. I flapped the apron in my hand at her in response and kept on pinning. When I finished, I picked up the basket, choosing to go in the kitchen door instead of the outside basement door, hoping to overhear what Molly and Hannah were talking about.

I'd always been a little flabbergasted by their friendship. They talked more than seemed humanly possible when they were together, going on and on about people they knew, parties they'd been to, and their hopes for the future. I found them both fascinating and repulsive. But I couldn't stop listening.

As I entered the kitchen, they didn't even glance at me.

"No, Mervin's going hunting." Hannah sat across the table from Molly.

"Oh, that's right," my sister said, her hands wrapped around a mug. "Who else?"

"Phillip and his brother."

Molly lifted the mug. "Which one?"

"Don."

Molly's eyes grew wide over the rim of the mug as she took a sip. Then she said, "When did he come home?"

"Two weeks ago. And get this—Phillip and Jessie broke up."

"No!" Molly said, putting the cup on the table with a clatter. Tea sloshed over the side, but she didn't seem to notice.

I put the laundry basket on the counter, started the tap, and pulled a glass from the cupboard, slowly filling it with water.

I couldn't hear what Molly said, but when I turned the faucet off, I heard Hannah saying, " . . . went to a singing in Berk County and met someone—he broke up with Jessie."

"He's a fool," Molly said. "She was perfect for him."

"Jah," Hannah said. "And now the girl from Berk County broke up with Phillip."

"Serves him right." Molly paused and then said, "Bea, how's the wash coming along?"

"*Gut*," I answered, without turning toward her. I put my glass in the sink, picked up the basket, and headed toward the stairs. Everything I knew about men and courtship I'd learned from eavesdropping on Molly and Hannah—except for the painful lesson of rejection Ben Rupp taught me last year. None of it made me want to ever get married.

As I reached the basement stairs, Molly said, "She's not going to Montana with us."

Hannah exclaimed, "Really!"

"Jah, she's going to work for the Millers instead," Molly said. "I wish you could go."

"Jah, but I promised my Aenti Laurel I'd help her. I start on Monday." Knee surgery had sidelined Laurel Cramer, the mother of a household of boys, the youngest less than a year old. My new sister-in-law, Nell, Laurel's sister, used to live with the family and help run the home, but since she married Ivan, Laurel had been on her own. It was kind of Hannah to help, although I figured she had ulterior motives. The Cramers lived just over the creek from the Millers. Working there meant she'd be able to see Mervin every day—except for when he was hunting.

It took me all day to finish doing the laundry, including ironing Mamm's aprons and dresses. Thankfully, Molly pressed her own things and Leon's shirts and trousers, probably because she didn't trust me to do it. I didn't see the point of ironing any of it—the clothes would wrinkle in their suitcases and have to be redone once they reached Montana anyway.

The next morning, I cleaned the kitchen, staying out of Molly's way as best I could as she prepared sandwiches at the table for their trip. After I'd dried the last plate, scrubbed our faded Formica counters, and scoured the sink, I hurried upstairs to check on Mamm, who was finishing up her packing. Her room, like all of ours, was simple with her double bed, a bureau, and a small table by the window. The few dresses she hadn't packed hung from pegs. I'd avoided entering her room since Dat passed away. I felt his absence throughout the house and farm, but especially in their room.

Dat's manly scent left when Molly cleared out his clothes, but the comforting scent of Mamm's lilac talcum remained strong.

She sat on her bed, her back to me, staring out the window.

I cleared my throat. She didn't respond.

"Mamm," I said.

Without turning toward me, she said, "I wish you were going with us."

I walked around the bed and sat down beside her. Not knowing what to say, I said nothing. She clasped my hand. For a moment I wondered if I'd made a mistake.

Until Molly yelled up the stairs. "It's time to go!"

No, I'd made the right decision. I stood and reached for Mamm's bag. "You'll only be gone a couple of weeks."

She nodded and then looked back out the window.

"Dat would be happy you're going, Mamm."

She didn't answer me. The wind played among the walnut tree branches. Love barked at the approaching van.

Finally she said, "It will be good for you to be without us. At least that's what I'm praying."

It was my turn to nod. I'd never been without my family. It was high time I took a step of independence.

Molly shouted up the stairs again.

By then I wondered if agreeing to go as far as the train station with them had been a mistake.

Mamm stood, and I put my arms around her. When I let her go, I retrieved her cane and handed it to her. "Just in case you get overtired," I said.

She patted my arm after she took it and led the way to the landing and down the stairs, with me following, carrying her bag.

By the time I made my way out the back door, Leon had their suitcases outside, along with a small cooler filled with the food. Our usual driver, Doris, stood watching Leon load everything. She was an excellent driver that everyone in our district called first because of her good nature. She pointed to a bag that had fallen sideways in the back and then laughed as Leon hurried to right it. Obviously she was teasing him.

Mamm locked the door and then handed me the key. "Give this to Edna," she said.

I took the key, examining it for a moment. It was spindly and tarnished, as old as the house, it seemed. I slipped it into my apron pocket and crawled into the back seat of the van. Mamm and Molly seated themselves in the middle, and Leon took the front.

As we headed west toward Lancaster, Molly chatted away, talking about the work that would need to be done when they returned. "I hope you don't plan to stay at the Millers' for long. When I wanted you to get a job, I didn't mean one where you wouldn't be available to help at home at all."

I smiled at her, unsure of what to say. I had no idea how long they'd need me.

Molly turned back around, now talking to Mamm. "I'm excited to see Chicago—aren't you?"

Mamm nodded and I turned my attention to the landscape out the window. Corn ready to be harvested. A final cutting of alfalfa. A small dairy herd huddled under an oak tree. A field of pumpkins, bright orange against the dying vines.

Soon the fields gave way to houses and then the freeway. When we exited, Doris turned south toward the train station, and when we were near it, she stopped the van at an unloading area and told us to pile out. "I'll wait here for you, Bea," she said. As Leon grabbed the bags, I took Mamm's arm and we started toward the brick building. I'd only been to Lancaster a few times and never to the train station. It was a beautiful building, two stories high with concrete columns and rounded windows.

Leon and Molly soon caught up with us, pushing a cart with all of the luggage and the cooler, and then led the way into the lobby. Wooden benches lined the area, and the ceiling was high, with a skylight and hanging lamps.

Excitement filled the air as people dashed around us. The

wheels of a passing luggage cart squeaked. A train whistle blew. Molly pointed toward the ticket booth and said, "We need to hurry."

I gave Mamm a quick hug and told Molly good-bye. My sister reached for me then and held me tightly. As she pulled away, a tear spilled from her eye. "We've never been apart," she said, brushing the tear away.

I stepped back. She'd been gone all the time. Overnights at Hannah's. Parties on the river. Hours spent in the greenhouse talking on her phone. Still her emotions caused my voice to falter. "Have a good trip," I managed to say.

She shook her head a little. "You won't miss me, will you?"

I swallowed hard. I hadn't expected to miss her . . . but already I did.

Leon slapped my back and told me to take care. Then he led the way, pushing the cart. Mamm trailed behind, using her cane.

I tried to ignore the emotion that welled inside me as I called out traveling mercies to them. They turned and waved and then proceeded toward the booth. I practically ran back outside.

"Ready?" Doris asked as I reached the van.

I blinked back the tears threatening to fill my eyes and climbed into the passenger side of the van. Doris seemed to sense my emotional state and drove in silence.

By the time we reached Edna's little house in Paradise, I'd composed myself. I hurried toward her front door, but she stepped onto her porch, carrying her bag, before I reached the steps. Seeing her, I felt foolish that I'd been near tears. Her husband had passed away nearly five years before, but she carried on with grace and goodwill to all she knew, never feeling sorry for herself. She'd been a big help to Molly and me, both when Dat passed and when Mamm had been ill.

She dropped her bag onto the chair on her porch and greeted me with a hug, wrapping her arms around me and pulling me close. Her hugs were warm and solid and made me feel cherished and cared for. She had no children of her own, and it was as if I was her baby sister and daughter all in one.

She released me. "So you go to the Millers' place on Monday?"

I nodded, aware for the first time in my life what it meant not to be surrounded by family. I had a new appreciation for Edna's plight. "Will you be all right on the farm by yourself?" I asked.

"Of course," she said. "I'll have Love to keep me company. I'm glad you'll have this experience of living away from home."

I smiled at her. At least one of my sisters was positive about this next step in my life.

CHAPTER

4

That afternoon, while Edna took a nap, I walked down to our pasture and then along the highway toward the creek. The changing leaves of the poplar trees across the field fluttered cheerfully in the breeze, but the gray sky cast a sense of foreboding across the farm, replacing the sense of anticipation I'd felt the week before. All seemed changed without Molly in the flower field, Leon in the corral, and Mamm in the kitchen. Not as bright. And much too quiet.

In the distance, an Amish man hurried along the creek that acted as our property line and then climbed through the fence and cut across to the Mosiers' farm. It wasn't Mervin or Martin, I was sure. They were off hunting, and the man appeared taller. I thought he wore a beard, although it could have been the shadow from his hat. Brush along the fence soon hid him from my view.

As I walked, a few cars slowed, as if looking for the farmers' market, but then sped on by. One driver stopped and asked me directions to the market as Love barked. The driver seemed unduly disappointed when I informed him that the last day for the year had been the previous Saturday.

As I came to the corner of our property, another vehicle slowed. I expected another tourist, but when Love didn't bark,

I turned around. It was Doris's van, with Ben Rupp in the passenger seat. The boys hadn't left yet.

She grinned at me as Ben hopped out. "See you in a minute," she said to him, but she waved at me.

Love wagged her tail at Ben as he stepped toward me.

"I thought you'd already gone hunting."

"We've been delayed," he replied.

My eyebrows shot up.

"Phillip and his brother are going with us. But when Doris and I stopped by their place, Don wasn't there. We waited for a while, but Phillip finally told us to go ahead. There seems to have been a mix-up in our departure time."

I crossed my arms. "So you're going on without them?"

"Phillip said they'll hire their own driver and meet us in the mountains."

"So why did you stop here?" I unfolded my arms and swept them wide.

"Doris's going to pick up Mervin and Martin and then return for me."

I tilted my head. "But why did you get out of the van?"

His face reddened.

"To torment me?"

When he still didn't answer I said, "I guess *torment* is too strong a word considering you're off to kill a deer." It was a stupid thing for an Amish girl to say. Most of our men hunted at least sometime during their lives.

He crossed his arms. "It's the course of nature. Besides, we're using muzzle-loaders. We'll be at a disadvantage." He grinned. "I'll bring you a venison steak."

"I won't eat it," I answered.

"Then I won't waste it on you," he countered, shifting his

gaze toward the flower fields. "So I take it Leon and Molly got off this morning."

"And my Mamm."

"So if they decide to move to Montana, will you go too?" He kicked at a rock.

Molly would never agree to that. I chuckled. "That's not the plan. They're only visiting."

He met my gaze. "Really?"

"You just made that up—didn't you, Ben Rupp? To see if you could get a reaction from me."

"Are you O-V-E-R-W-R-O-U-G-H-T with fear?" he asked and then grinned. That had been on our fourth-grade list of words.

"You have *nary* an inkling of my emotions," I said to Ben. It was an old English word I'd picked up in my reading.

"Ach," he said. "That's a good one. Do you have any more to try on me?"

"N-A-U-G-H-T," I said.

A puzzled expression passed over his face, and then he said, shaking his head, "You always did have to have the last word."

To prove him wrong, I remained silent, meaning that—technically—he'd had the last word. I was tempted to go on home, but what would I be proving then?

He shifted his gaze toward the fence line. At the crest of the hill stood the man I'd seen earlier.

I was thankful for the diversion. "Who is that?" I asked.

Ben shaded his eyes, which was unnecessary considering the day was overcast.

The stranger sauntered toward us.

Ben took a long step toward him. "What are you doing here? Phillip's beside himself."

"I came over to get some things from the market—for our

trip." He took off his hat and jogged down the hill. "I didn't realize it wouldn't be open."

The man—Phillip's brother, I assumed—was the stranger I'd seen at the market the week before. He did have a beard, a sign he was married, which no one had mentioned. He was tall, broad shouldered, and much older than Ben and even Mervin and Martin, who were both Molly's age.

He looked somewhat like his younger brother Phillip but more handsome.

"I told you we'd be by at one to pick you and Phillip up."

The man shook his head. "You said three."

Ben squinted. "I know that's what you said to Phillip, but I told you one."

The man cocked his head. "Believe me, I'd remember. You're the one who has it wrong." He didn't sound angry or even frustrated. Just matter-of-fact.

On the other hand, Ben's frustration was growing. "I wouldn't have told Doris one if I'd told you three."

The man shrugged. "Well, let's get going. Where's the van?"

"Doris will be back in a minute," Ben said, seemingly resigned to the situation. He motioned toward me, saying, "This is Beatrice." Then, glancing at me, he added, "This is Don Eicher."

"You were probably just a youngster when I left Lancaster," Don said, his eyes twinkling.

"Perhaps I was," I answered. "I don't remember you."

I couldn't help but notice the smile spreading across Ben's face. His earlier frustration seemed to have disappeared. "Jah, Don's an old man," he teased.

Don elbowed Ben and said, "Well, I *am* a man."

Ben grinned in a good-natured way and then said, "Beatrice is going to be helping the Millers."

Don's face brightened even more. "I'll see you when I get back from hunting, then. Bob just hired me to work in the shop."

I shaded my eyes. "Is that right?" Phillip worked there now. It only made sense Bob would hire Don too. After all, he was the bishop's son.

Ben cleared his throat. He started to speak, but then the sound of the van coming over the crest of the Mosiers' drive distracted him. He waved and pointed at Don.

As the van came to a stop beside us, Martin, wearing a pair of aviator sunglasses, jumped out of the passenger seat. Love darted around to greet him.

Mervin piled out too, wearing a matching pair of glasses. "There you are," he said to Don. "Now we just need to go get Phillip."

"Jah," Ben said, climbing in after Mervin. "Let's get going." He waved to me as he sat down, and then he called out, "See you soon."

I doubted it.

Don tipped his hat to me and grinned again. "See you at the Millers'."

My hand fluttered. Was he, a married man, flirting with me? Flustered, I called out to the dog, "Come on, Love." My face grew warmer as Don stopped in the middle of the lane and turned toward me.

"What?"

"The dog," I barked. "Her name is Love."

"Oh." He strolled around to the other side of the van, and after he got inside both sliding doors slammed shut at once.

Doris had her window down. She smiled as laughter came from the back of the van. I couldn't see the person it came from, but I knew it was Ben. I used to enjoy the sound of his infectious laugh—not that I would admit it to anyone—but now it riled me.

I had to call Love a second time before she obeyed. She seemed to be drawn to the din. I grabbed her collar and stood holding her as the van pulled away. Doris waved, and I returned the gesture, my face growing warmer by the minute as Ben's laughter welled up again.

The van turned onto the highway, and Love and I resumed our walk. When we returned to the house, Edna sat on the front porch, wrapped in her cape to ward off the chill. She held a mug in her hand. As I walked up the stairs, she asked me if I wanted a cup of tea.

"I'll get it in a minute," I said, sitting down on the chair beside her.

I stared at the highway.

Edna leaned toward me, gripping her cup. "Is something the matter?"

I shook my head. "Not really."

"What is it?" she cooed, as gently as the pigeons in the barn.

"Do you remember Bishop Eicher's son Don?"

Edna sat up straight. "Why do you ask?"

"I just met him."

"Jah, I remember him—I heard he was back. He had a reputation for being wild. I think the bishop was relieved when he left for Ohio."

"How old is he?"

"Oh, twenty-nine. Maybe thirty." She took a sip of tea.

"Oh," I said. "How long has he been married?"

"He's not, at least not that I know of," Edna answered.

"He wears a beard," I said.

She nodded. "His is a sad story."

"Oh?"

"I can't remember the exact details," she said. "But he was married, for a short time."

I leaned forward.

"Maybe just a couple of days—I can't remember for sure."

"What happened?"

"She died. In a buggy accident."

A wave of empathy washed over me. I could be harsh, but I wasn't heartless.

"Jah," Edna said. "That was years ago. He wasn't even twenty, I don't think. It was soon after he moved to Ohio." She paused a moment, most likely remembering her own sad story of losing her husband after a buggy accident.

I wondered why Don's beard was so short. Ten years was a long time. It should have been longer. He must have trimmed it, which certainly wasn't unheard of.

"Poor Don," Edna finally said.

I nodded in agreement, forgetting the beard issue. I hurt for him. For what he'd gone through, he seemed content. But also, with this new information, a bit of a mystery. Why hadn't he married again? And why had he come back to Lancaster County? I wished I'd been kinder to him when we met.

Edna and I spent Sunday in much the same way we did Saturday: quietly. By the time Monday morning rolled around, I missed Mamm, Molly, and even Leon. Edna was wonderful, but there wasn't much conversation and with her there was certainly no drama, which Molly guaranteed me every day of my life.

After breakfast, I finished my packing and then hitched Daisy to the buggy. Edna came out the back door, wearing her cape and black bonnet. I pulled the key from my apron pocket, locked the back door, and handed it to her.

"Denki," she said, slipping it beneath her cape. As we walked toward the barn, I called for the cats, hoping to tell the gray kitten good-bye. Three cats came running, but not the kitten. However, when we reached the buggy, we found her curled up on the seat. I scooped her up, rubbing her soft fur against my face and settling her against my neck. She purred loudly. "Keep an eye on her," I said to Edna.

My sister nodded and took the cat from me, dropping her inside the barn door.

Edna climbed onto the bench and tucked the blanket around her legs, and I urged Daisy forward as Love barked out a fare-well to us. She'd be surprised to have Edna return without me.

With a lurch the horse took off, but soon she was only plod-ding along. Fog hung along the field across from our pasture. But as I waited for a line of cars to go by before I turned left, the low clouds lifted, revealing a pale blue sky.

"Oh, my," Edna said. "Perhaps the weather is changing."

Daisy picked up her pace. A flock of geese flew high above us, in perfect formation. My parents had loved watching birds, a passion I didn't share. But I appreciated the migratory patterns of the geese, the predictability of their lives, and the way they traveled together—so strong and sure.

We passed the willow tree on the left side of the road. Its leaves had turned a gentle yellow but hadn't fallen yet. They fluttered like thin curtains in an open window.

Edna sat straight with her hands in her lap, unusually quiet.

"I hope taking care of the little ones won't be too hard," I said.

She exhaled. "It won't be bad," she predicted. "Many hands make light work."

"Bob said the little girl should be able to come home this week." I turned my head toward Edna as I spoke.

Wistfully, Edna said, "What a blessing."

I'd never thought about her disappointment in not having children. It surely wasn't what she had planned. And then she lost her husband. After the car hit his buggy, he lived for several months. It seemed, by the time he passed away, that Edna was relieved. Not that he'd died but that he was no longer in pain.

But I don't think that relief lasted. She seemed lonelier all the time. I couldn't imagine her ever remarrying—but I couldn't imagine her staying single either. She was one of those people, unlike me, who was meant for marriage.

When Ivan and Nell married six months ago, I noted a pained expression on Edna's face after the service. I know she was thrilled for our brother, but it seemed the pain of her loss was still very real for her.

She clasped her hands tighter. "Those Bopplis are so tiny," she said. "You're taking on a big responsibility."

I nodded as I thought of holding little Asher, who was the biggest of the three but still so small. Daisy had slowed around a curve in the road, and I urged the horse to go faster. "How big was I?"

"Close to eight pounds," Edna answered. "Your Mamm had you at the hospital because she was older." Some women in our community had homebirths, others in the hospital. It all depended on what the woman felt comfortable with and what her healthcare needs were. "We went to see you," Edna added.

I usually didn't mention him, but as I imagined her and Frank in their early twenties, I asked, "How long had you two been married then?"

"Three years . . ." Her voice trailed off. Most Amish couples would have had one baby by then, maybe even two.

"The night you were born, the stars were so bright it seemed I should be able to pluck one from the sky and take it to the hospital, like a flower."

I smiled at the image. I'd been born the first day of autumn.

"And you were such a happy baby—and a happy little girl too."

"Really?" No one had told me that before. I'd suspected I'd always been a little cynical. "What happened to me?" I pondered.

Edna laughed. "Oh, you'll be happy again. You've had a rough couple of years is all. You're just coming into your own. It takes a while. I remember being your age."

I couldn't imagine Edna ever being anything but kind and giving.

We'd reached the Millers' lane, and I pulled the reins to the left. To the right, cows grazed in the field. On the other side of the road, a flock of sheep—probably belonging to Bob's brother-in-law, Cap Cramer—huddled under a shelter.

As we plodded along, I prayed that I'd be up to the tasks ahead of me. It was a stretch for me to leave home and become part of another household. If living with three people drove me crazy at times, what would it be like to live with eight, three of them infants? I prayed I would be able to focus on others first, a concept I'd been taught my entire life but sometimes had difficulty putting into practice.

The sun grew warmer as we approached the Millers' place. First the showroom came into view, with the shop behind it. Then the garden to the side of the house, and finally the three-story home, with the Dawdi Haus behind it.

I pulled Daisy to a stop by the hitching post in front of the showroom. "Want to come in with me?" I met Edna's gaze.

She shook her head. "Not now—I'll wait until Nan has had more time home with her little ones."

I nodded. Edna would stay at our house until next Sunday, when Martin and Mervin would be home and ready to take over the chores. Maybe she would come by after that. Or she might wait longer. She wouldn't want to intrude.

"I'll come back to your house the Saturday your Mamm, Molly, and Leon return," she said. "I'll make supper. Don't you think you could take that evening off and join us?"

"I'll ask Nan." Bob had said I could have some time off—I didn't think it would be a problem. I climbed down from the buggy, retrieved my bag from the back, and headed toward the path that led to the house as Edna pulled the buggy around. I waved to her and hollered, "Denki."

She blew me a kiss and kept on going.

A voice from above called down, "Bea!"

I stopped and shaded my eyes. Hope hung out of a second-story window. "I'll be right down," she called out.

By the time I reached the back door, she'd opened it. "I'm so glad you're here." She gave me a hug, her blue eyes bright, and then ushered me into the kitchen.

Nan sat holding a baby in the rocker next to the wood stove. On the other side was an empty playpen. The house was warmer than it had been the last time I'd stopped by—too warm. This time the dishes were done and the big oak table cleared.

"*Willkumm*," Nan said. She wore a blue scarf on her head

instead of a Kapp. Dark half moons hung under her eyes, and her skin was pale.

I greeted her, but when I realized she was nursing the baby I stopped.

"Hope, show Bea where to put her bag," Nan said, pulling the little one to her shoulder. It looked like Kurt.

As Nan burped him, I followed Hope to the front of the house and up the big open staircase.

"We're sharing a room," Hope said. "The back one. Pete and Cate have the third floor now. The babies are in the nursery—one of the spare rooms, really—or else in with Nan and Bob. She's trying to feed both the boys but is also using some bottles. It will be harder when Leah comes home. We'll have to help in the middle of the night then. I've had to do a few of those feedings already—it's not so bad. Are you a sound sleeper?"

Before I could answer that I was, she said that she had thirty-two nieces and nephews and had helped with babies since she was a little girl. I could see why Nan hired her.

We reached the landing, and I followed her down the hall. A door was wide open, showing a single bed, two bassinets, a dresser, and a changing table. The dresser was covered with diapers, spit rags, and stacks of tiny clothes. "This is the nursery," she said. "The bassinets are on wheels." I could see that. "So we can move them from here into Nan and Bob's room when needed. That's where Asher is right now."

Hope continued on down the hall, stopping at the bathroom. "There's another one downstairs," she said and then grinned. "We only have an outhouse back home. I'm *loving* it here." In a split second she was off again to the next room. Inside were two twin beds, two dressers, and two side tables. Creamy yellow paint covered the walls, and the buffed oak floor shone under the light of the morning sun.

Hope spread her arms wide. "This room was Cate and Betsy's before they both married."

There was a cork bulletin board on the far wall with a calendar on it but no other decorations.

Hope opened a door revealing a wide closet. Dresses filled half of it, but the other side was empty. "I made room for your things," she said.

I'd only brought three dresses. I scanned the room again. There were no pegs—only the closet. We didn't have closets at our house. It was too old.

"You can have that bed," Hope said, pointing to the one on the far side of the room. I placed my bag beside it and stepped toward the wide windows. From the corner of the window I could see the backyard and the Dawdi Haus. Straight on was a view of the showroom and shop.

"Do you see the workers much?"

Hope sat down on her bed. "Some, but most of them are gone this week."

"Jah, hunting," I said.

She nodded. "Which has made Bob nervous. They're behind on a big order."

I'd never known Bob Miller to be unsettled. I sat down on my bed, bouncing on the mattress. It felt like a pillow.

Hope continued, "In fact, Bob and Pete are working in the shop today."

"Why'd he let the boys go hunting?" I asked. They should have stayed and helped.

"He promised them months ago. . . ."

"Where's Cate?"

"Working in the office and seeing to the showroom."

"Have you met a new worker? Someone named Don?"

"Phillip's brother?"

"That's the one."

She shook her head. "I haven't met him yet." She grinned. "But Martin said he was going hunting with the rest." She stood. "I'm so glad you're here."

I couldn't help but smile at her, but before I could say anything, the frantic cry of a newborn startled me.

"That's Asher. His cry is the loudest." She headed toward the door. "He doesn't start out with a whimper—he wakes up screaming at the top of his lungs."

I waited in the hall, feeling awkward, while Hope retrieved the baby. He continued to cry after she picked him up. "Come here," she called out to me. "I'll show you where everything is in this room."

The room was messier than what I'd seen from the hall. The bed wasn't properly made—the covers were pulled up but nothing tucked in. A water glass, prescription bottles, thermometer, bottles of lotion, and a can of powder were strewn on the bedside table.

Not only were more diapers and clothes piled on their dresser too, but so were books and papers. "Don't Bob and Nan mind us being in here?"

"Oh, heavens no," Hope said. She grabbed a diaper and headed toward the changing table along the wall. The baby continued to scream, sounding as desperate as anything I'd ever heard in my entire life. His face turned redder and redder.

I followed Hope to the table. "Is he all right?"

Hope wrinkled her nose as she put him down. "He's fine, believe me." She unwound the thin blanket and took off his sleeper, which was soaking wet, revealing just how small he was. Much smaller than he'd seemed the other day, when he'd been bundled in a heavier blanket.

The enormity of caring for such a tiny being nearly overwhelmed me. "He's so little."

"He's the biggest of the three," Hope reminded me.

She worked quickly, taking off the wet diaper, opening the adjacent pail with her foot, and dropping the used diaper inside.

"I'm surprised they're using cloth diapers," I said over Asher's screaming, thinking of the diapers I'd hung on the line the week before. "Wouldn't disposable be easier?"

Hope chuckled. "Nan's talking about going that route."

After cleaning Asher, Hope pinned the new diaper, slipped on rubber pants, then a new sleeper, and reswaddled the baby. All while he continued screaming. "Take him while I wash my hands."

"Sure," I said, remembering Mamm saying that I'd be doing the most important work in the world. I wrapped my arms around Asher and lifted him to my chest as Hope walked away. I must have startled him, because his crying faded to a whimper for a moment. I cradled him, staring into his murky eyes. He pursed his lips.

I whispered, "Hello, little one."

He scrunched his face.

I braced myself for another round but he hiccupped instead.

That made me smile, which startled him. I bounced him up and down a little. He yawned. The red of his face faded a little. I touched the top of his scalp, rubbing his fine, dark hair. He yawned again.

I stepped into the hallway to wait for Hope.

A minute later, as she came out of the bathroom she said, "Look at you."

At the sound of her voice Asher began screaming again. "I think he wants you."

She put up her hands. "He's all yours."

I pulled him closer. He continued to scream.

"Come on," Hope said. "Let's go see if Nan is ready to feed him."

I took the steps carefully, one at a time, as if I were an old lady. By the time I reached the kitchen, Hope had taken Kurt, who was sound asleep, in her arms and Nan was waiting for Asher. As soon as I handed him to Nan he stopped crying.

She kissed the top of his head and positioned him to nurse.

"I'll take Kurt upstairs," Hope said.

"Denki." Nan leaned back in the chair. "I plan to go to the hospital in an hour."

I stammered, "What if Kurt and Asher need to be fed?"

"Cate is coming to help," Nan replied. "She'll be able to get them to take bottles."

There would be three of us—surely it wouldn't be a problem.

"Bea," Nan said. "Would you like to come with me?"

"To the hospital?"

She nodded. "I thought you might want to see the neonatal unit."

"Would you like to go?" I asked Hope.

She grinned. "Sure."

Nan shook her head. "Hope went last week. I'd like you to go today."

I wanted to say no. I didn't feel comfortable in hospitals. It had been a stretch for me to visit when Mamm was ill, and I'd avoided it as much as possible. I dreaded interacting with the

Englisch nurses and doctors, not to mention having the other patients and visitors stare at me.

Besides, what if Leah got worse while we were there? What if something bad happened? I was awful in a crisis. I'd never had a chance to prove otherwise, because Molly had always been there to deal with every single crisis in our family, but I was sure, if I had the chance to handle one, I'd do badly.

But I had prayed that I'd be up to the tasks Nan asked of me. I didn't want to let Nan down.

"Bea?" Nan said again, as she rocked the baby.

"I'll go," I answered. "If you're certain."

Nan smiled and then said, "I'd like that very much."

We didn't leave until after noon—Nan fed both of the babies while the rest of us ate our dinner. Then she handed off Kurt to Bob and Asher to Hope and said she was ready to go. Bob reminded her she hadn't eaten.

"Oh," she said, a confused expression on her face. "How did I forget? I'm starving."

"I'll dish up for you." Cate grabbed Nan's plate and began filling it.

Bob held Kurt with one hand and put the other on his wife's shoulder. "Are you sure you don't want me to come along?"

"Jah," she answered. "You go back down to the shop." She grabbed his hand and squeezed it. "Beatrice is going with me."

Bob smiled at me but didn't seem relieved by the news. She squeezed his hand again and sat down at the table. I began clearing the food as Cate took Kurt from Bob and settled in the rocker. Bob told Nan good-bye and then followed Pete out the door.

Hope settled Asher down in the playpen and helped me with the food. We'd just started on the dishes when a horn honked.

"Doris is here," Nan said, standing and hurrying to the sink with her plate. She returned to the rocker, bent down to kiss

Kurt, thanked Cate, and then peered down into the playpen at Asher for a long moment.

I dried my hands. The horn honked again.

"Go," Cate said. "So you'll be back as soon as possible."

I grabbed my cape, and Nan grabbed one too.

"That's mine," Cate said.

"Oh." Nan returned it and looked at the others hanging on the pegs for a moment and then grabbed another one. Then she grabbed a Kapp and pulled her scarf from her head.

I led the way out the door, happy to see Doris behind the wheel of her van.

"You sit up front," Nan whispered to me as she positioned her Kapp. "I'm going to try to sleep a little."

The hospital wasn't more than twenty minutes away, but I didn't protest. Coming back from the train station had been the first time I'd sat up front with Doris. As I climbed in, Nan asked me if I had an extra pin.

I took one of mine from my Kapp and passed it back to her.

"How are those boys doing hunting?" Doris asked as I climbed in.

I must have made a funny face because she laughed. "That's right—they don't have cell service up there."

As far as I knew none of them had a phone.

"I wonder if they took warm enough clothes," she said. "I hope they don't freeze to death."

As she drove, she talked about where she'd dropped them off. "At the end of nowhere," she said and then laughed. "They took a mess of cold boxes, thinking they'd each get a deer." She shook her head. "Hunting with muzzle-loaders sounds like a shot in the dark to me." She laughed again.

I knew nothing about muzzle-loaders or hunting.

I glanced back at Nan. She'd tilted her head against the seat, her Kapp a little askew and eyes closed. Her lids looked nearly translucent. Wisps of grayish blond hair fell from beneath her Kapp.

Doris kept talking. "That Ben sure is a sweetie." She gave me a sideways look.

I didn't respond.

"He took a stack of books along to read—but no fuel for his lantern. Said he had a flashlight but I doubt the batteries will last long."

I couldn't help but smile.

"And the other guys were teasing him about keeping a journal." She chuckled. "Especially the one with the beard. What's his name?"

"Don?"

"That's right," she said. "Phillip's brother." She turned onto the highway. "He seems like a nice fellow."

I nodded but then said, "I only met him for the first time Saturday." I didn't want it to seem I was familiar with him.

I glanced back at Nan again. She appeared to be in a deep slumber. The smooth ride had probably lulled her to sleep.

Doris and I continued to chat until we arrived at the hospital, an impressive brick structure, and Doris called out Nan's name.

"Are we here already?" Nan slowly sat up straight. As she opened the sliding door, she said, "We'll only be an hour. I need to get back to the boys."

I climbed out and offered my arm to Nan. She took it and stepped down gingerly.

"I'm going to run an errand," Doris said, "but then I'll wait right here."

I thanked her and slammed the door shut, following Nan

toward the building. A few minutes later we were in the elevator and then at the door to the neonatal ward. Nan checked in and introduced me. As we scrubbed, my hands began to shake, even though the water was hot. It had been a mistake to come—I was sure of it.

I inhaled deeply as we put paper gowns over our clothes and masks over our noses and mouths, willing myself to be brave. The last thing Nan needed to do was take care of me too.

She led the way into a big room and started making her way around little clear plastic baby beds, with two holes on each side. One of them held a tiny, tiny baby, not bigger than a man's hand, hooked up to tubes and wires. Another had a baby with what looked like purple blinders over its eyes.

Nurses and other parents greeted Nan. She introduced me to each one. A hum from the machines filled the room. I jumped at the sound of a high-pitched beep. Nan put her hand on my arm and said, "It's nothing to be alarmed by."

Finally we were at Leah's bedside. Her nurse gave Nan a hug and said, "She's having a really good day."

"Praise God," Nan said, which surprised me. She usually seemed so reserved. Then she introduced me as she placed her hands into the bed, stroking Leah's cheek. The baby had lighter hair than her brothers and she was much smaller. Her arms and legs looked like twigs. Wires and cords crisscrossed her body but no tubes. She wore a disposable diaper and nothing else.

"It's time for her feeding," the nurse said.

"Oh, I hoped it would be," Nan answered.

The nurse left and returned with a bottle and a couple of blankets. Nan lifted the baby, wires and all, and wrapped her quickly in a blanket. Then Nan settled into the rocking chair only a foot away. She cooed to the baby, sounding like a mother dove, as she settled in, pulling the little girl close and then rubbing the nipple of the bottle across the baby's cheek. Leah turned toward her mother and latched onto the bottle.

The nurse stood with her hands clasped together, staring at the two. "I have good news," she said.

Nan's head shot up.

The nurse grinned. "She's almost met her weight requirement. And her body temperature has stabilized. The doctor says you can take her home soon—maybe even tomorrow."

Nan sank against the back of the chair, drawing the baby even closer. "Thank you, Jesus," she whispered, her eyes filling up with tears.

I hadn't cried since my Mamm's medical problems, but my eyes grew teary too. Nan continued to feed Leah while the nurse changed the sheet on the baby's bed. I stood still, feeling out of place, my eyes finally wandering to a young couple standing over a baby nearby. The man had his arm around the woman's shoulder. She wore a pair of jeans under her paper gown. After a few minutes they headed toward us.

Nan stopped rocking. "How is he today?"

"Not good," the man answered.

Nan leaned forward, focusing on the woman. "I'll keep praying," she said.

"Thank you," the young mother said. Then she knelt down beside Nan and peered into Leah's face. "She's looking better."

Nan nodded.

"I'm so glad," the woman said. "And how are your boys?"

Nan simply nodded, appearing too choked up to talk.

The woman stood and patted Nan's shoulder. "See you soon."

Nan nodded again.

After the couple left, Nan began humming "Das Loblied,"

the praise song that we sang at every church service. The baby stopped sucking on the bottle and with her inky dark eyes stared up at her mother. The words played in my head as Nan hummed:

> O Lord Father, we bless thy name,
> Thy love and thy goodness praise;
> That thou, O Lord, so graciously
> Have been to us always. . . .

The baby began to suck again. And I prayed silently, for Leah, for Nan, and for the baby of the young Englisch couple—until a whooshing sound startled me.

"That's just the temperature monitor," Nan said, lifting the blanket a little to show one of the pads with a wire adhered to Leah's chest. "The other three are EKG probes. And the clips on her thumb and toe are to check her oxygen."

"Oh," I answered, trying to comprehend it all.

"We don't have to use any fancy equipment once we take her home," Nan said, her eyes shining.

I nodded.

"But we still have to be vigilant. In fact, we have a stack of books—Cate has them now—about caring for newborns, especially preemies. All sorts of good information, including what to do in an emergency. Instructions on infant CPR. That sort of thing. Ask Cate for the books."

I nodded but couldn't imagine taking charge during an emergency. It's not like Nan or Cate or Bob or even Hope wouldn't be around to help.

"Would you grab me the second blanket?" Nan nodded toward the edge of the bed.

I stepped forward, leaving my spot of safety without glancing down at the floor. My foot wedged against a cord just under the base of the bed. I stumbled forward. The cord gave just as a machine began to beep again, but much louder than before.

I jerked back. "What happened?"

Nan nodded toward the floor. "You unplugged the isolette. That made the alarm go off."

I must have given her a blank stare.

"The bed," she explained, nodding toward the floor again. "It's called an isolette."

I followed her eyes, moving a half step sideways. Under the edge of the bed on the floor was an outlet and beside it was a black cord. I kneeled down and quickly plugged it back in. The beeping stopped.

"I'm sorry," I said as I stood.

"It was an easy mistake," Nan said.

I sucked in my breath as my face grew warm. I didn't belong in a neonatal unit. There was no telling what harm I could do.

"How about handing me the blanket?" Nan smiled.

"Oh," I answered, stepping forward again, this time very carefully, and handing it to her. I retreated back to my spot and stayed there, silently, until the baby was fed and it was time for us to leave.

The next morning as I climbed the basement stairs with a basket full of wet wash to hang on the line, Bob burst through the back door. "Nan!" he called out.

"She's upstairs." I'd reached the kitchen and paused as he hurried through.

"Nan!" he yelled, rushing down the hall and then pounding up the stairs. "We can go get her. As soon as Doris arrives."

Another set of footsteps, not as heavy, came down the steps.

I waited until Hope came down the hall. "I'll help you hang the wash," she said. "Before Nan and Bob leave."

She led the way back to the door. "We'd better hurry. Both babies are sleeping but they won't be for long."

We stepped out into the bright morning. I hoped it was the beginning of a stretch of Indian summer as we began our task.

Hope and I were only halfway through the basket when Bob opened their bedroom window. "Asher is awake."

"I'll go," Hope said.

I continued to hang the sheets and towels until Doris's van eased up the driveway. She stopped it and rolled down her window.

"They'll be right out," I called out.

Doris nodded and then said, "What a happy event, jah?"

I nearly laughed at Doris using one of our expressions but stopped myself. "It is, indeed," I answered.

Bob opened the window again. "We're coming," he said.

A moment later, as I hung the last of the spit rags, Hope opened the window. "Hurry. Kurt's awake too."

I finished as Nan and Bob, who carried a baby car seat, hurried out the door, and then I rushed inside.

Behind me, before I closed the door, Nan called out, "Get Cate if you need help."

I assured her we would. There was no way I planned to be responsible for more than I could handle.

Hope met me in the upstairs hallway with a screaming Asher. "You take him." She passed him to me before I could say I'd get Kurt.

Asher let out another wail but then toned it down to a whimper. I followed Hope into the room, where she scooped up Kurt.

"Are they hungry?" I asked over Kurt's crying.

"Shhhh," she said to me—not the babies. "Don't remind them."

Kurt wailed again, causing Asher to cry too.

Hope wrinkled her nose. "Nan fed them about two hours ago."

Which in Boppli time was forever ago.

"Let's go get the bottles ready." Hope led the way down the stairs to the kitchen. Once there, she said, "I'll take Asher too while you work on the bottles."

I'd seen Nan hold both babies at once but not Hope.

"You should sit." I nodded toward the rocker.

Kurt was screaming now. She sat down, and I slid Asher into her free arm. Hope began rocking back and forth, but Kurt kept crying. Asher began to scream.

I took two bottles from the cupboard and then turned back around. "We should go get Cate."

"No," she said. "She needs to work. We can do this."

Sunshine streamed through the windows of the kitchen, across the countertops and over the floor as I filled and heated the bottles, my nerves growing more and more taut as the crying and screaming continued. I couldn't fathom how Hope stood it.

"I'm so glad you're here," Hope said to me once again above the racket.

At the moment, I couldn't manage to agree. She didn't notice. She continued on. "I'd been praying for a friend."

"Denki," I said. The truth was, I hadn't been praying for a friend. I hadn't even known I needed one. How sweet of God to answer a request I didn't even know to ask.

As I removed the bottles from the pan of boiling water, I prayed that all would go well with the babies, and that I wouldn't do anything stupid that would harm them. Then I said a prayer for the Englisch couple and for their little boy in the neonatal unit. Next I prayed for Mamm and Molly and Leon. Then I felt compelled to pray for the boys on their hunting trip. It'd been a long time since I'd prayed for Ben Rupp and even though I did it with some reluctance, I felt God's nudge. I asked God to bring them home safely so they could finish Bob's order and give the man some peace.

Hope and I finally managed to get the babies fed and back to sleep, and soon after we heard a vehicle in the driveway from the kitchen, where we'd started fixing the noon meal. We hurried out the back door. Cate and Pete must have heard the van too because they stepped out the shop door at the same time.

Doris shifted the van into park as Bob swung the side door open. First he opened the front passenger door and helped Nan down. And then he retrieved the car seat. Tucked inside was little Leah.

Hope and I stayed back as Cate approached her Dat and baby sister, her hands clasped together. "Look at her, all big and pink."

The baby's face was rosy, as if she'd cried herself to sleep. She was far from big, though, but it had probably been a week or more since Cate had seen her.

"We need to get Nan and Leah upstairs," Bob said as Doris drove the van away. "They're both worn out."

Nan took Bob's free arm as he passed the carrier to Pete.

"We just put the boys down in your room," I said to Nan.

"That's okay," she said. "Did they eat?"

"Jah," Hope answered. "They took the bottles just fine."

"Denki." Relief filled her voice.

"We'll bring up a tray of food for you," I said. "We're making chicken potpie."

She nodded, as if too tired to speak, but then she said, "Do you remember the Englisch couple we saw yesterday?"

I nodded, fearing the worst.

"Their little boy is better," she said. "He's going to make it."

"Praise God," I said, surprising myself. I'd never said that out loud before. The intensity of my empathy surprised me.

Nan reached for my hand and squeezed it. Hope and I followed the others into the house, but we stopped in the kitchen as the rest paraded upstairs. Pete came down right away, but we could hear the footsteps of the others overhead, and I imagined Bob helping Nan get situated in bed while Cate held the baby.

Pete poured himself a cup of coffee and asked how long until dinner was ready.

"A half hour," I answered.

"I'll be back by then," he said.

Cate came down a few minutes later and headed out the door to the shop too. I added peas to the chicken potpie.

Once the food was ready, I prepared a tray for Nan and started up the stairs. The bedroom door was wide open, but I knocked.

Bob stood at the bassinets, staring down at his sons.

I knocked again.

Startled, he looked up and then smiled at me. "Come on in," he said quietly.

I did.

"Nan's asleep," he said.

I turned toward the bed. Leah slept in her bassinet, pushed to Nan's side of the bed.

"Put it on the table," Bob said. "She may wake up in a few minutes, hungry."

I did as he instructed.

"Listen closely for the boys," he said. "When they wake up, give them bottles. Then keep them down in the playpen. We need to give Leah and Nan extra time together."

I nodded and headed for the door. Bob followed me. When we reached the living room Cate and Pete stood side by side. "Dat," Cate said, "the three of us need to talk."

I kept going, toward the kitchen.

"About?" Bob asked.

"The business," Cate said. "We need our crew back. If we don't meet this order, we'll be in the red this month. And lose a big account."

I stopped halfway down the hallway.

"They won't be back until Sunday," Bob said.

"We need to send for them," Cate said. "They'll come back if they know how desperate we are."

"I don't think any of them have cell phones. Besides, they wouldn't have service up there anyway."

"Send someone, then," Cate said.

"I have no idea where they are."

"Doris knows," I said. "She drove them up there."

CHAPTER
6

That afternoon, the darkness caught me by surprise. The imminent time change would soon bring it even earlier. I lit the propane lamp and then concentrated on finishing supper.

Cate held a fussy Asher, who began screaming even though he'd just taken a bottle. Kurt, who'd been asleep in the playpen, began crying too. Hope abandoned setting the table and scooped him up. Some households might have believed in letting a baby cry, but not this one. Honestly, most Amish parents I knew wouldn't let a baby cry for long. By the time a child was a toddler, he or she started to learn to sit through services and obey, but caring for a baby meant meeting their needs in a timely manner.

A few minutes later Nan came downstairs, carrying Leah, and settled in the rocking chair. She smiled at me as I dished up the roast and arranged carrots and potatoes around it.

"It smells delicious," Nan said over the racket of Asher's crying. "The cookies too."

"Denki." I'd made a quadruple batch of peanut and raisin oatmeal cookies, thinking the extra protein and calories would be good for Nan. I planned to freeze half of them.

Kurt began to scream again, rivaling his brother's cries. "Can you take him?" Hope asked as I positioned the serving fork on the platter. "I'll set the table."

"Oh, I can do that," I answered. "Why don't you take Kurt down the hall? Away from Asher."

She didn't look happy with the idea but rubbed his back as she walked out of the kitchen.

"Bea," Nan said softly, "why don't you go give Hope a break?"

My face grew warm. Did Nan think I hadn't been pulling my weight? I'd been cooking for hours. But I didn't question her. "All right," I answered, turning to wash my hands.

When I entered the sunroom, Hope seemed surprised to see me. "I'll take a turn," I said. "You set the table."

"Denki," she said, relief flooding her voice. She quickly slid the crying baby into my arms. I held him faceup for a moment, watching him cry. His eyes were crunched closed. His mouth quivered as he worked up to a scream.

I pulled his swaddled body close and lifted him to my shoulder, patting his back as I did. "There, there," I cooed. "You're all right."

Mamm often said how Molly and I had changed her life, how she had no inkling how much she would love being a mother, even though she'd been a teacher for years. I never gave her words much thought until now. But I couldn't relate. Becoming a mother probably was the key to being enthralled with a newborn—because, though I was happy to help, learning to tolerate the babies was the most I could muster.

Kurt shuddered, let out one more cry, and then snuggled against me and ceased his crying.

Maybe someday I'd know what it was like to be consumed by love for a little one . . . What was I thinking? I'd never have any babies of my own. I'd need a husband for that.

When Asher's cries stopped too, I headed back to the kitchen. Cate and Hope put the last of the food on the table, while Nan rocked both Asher and Leah.

Nan shifted her gaze from the two babies in her lap to the third one in my arms. "Ach, Beatrice, you've got a gift with the little ones."

I stopped myself from laughing at the absurdity of such a statement and touched the top of Kurt's head with my chin as Bob and Pete came through the back door.

Cate stopped at the table with the platter of meat and vegetables in her hands. "Did Doris call back?"

"No," Bob said.

"Were you in the shop? Maybe she left a message."

Bob shook his head. "I checked."

"I'll leave a message for Betsy after supper." Cate positioned the platter in the middle of the table. "Maybe Ben told them where they were going."

When it came time to eat, Bob took Asher from Nan, but when he began to scream, Nan said to give him back to her. She rocked him, along with Leah, until he settled back down. I tried to put Kurt down in the playpen, but he began to cry too.

"We'll have to eat in shifts," Nan said.

"I've read that babies have to get used to crying," Cate said. "It's not good for them to be held all the time."

Bob shot Cate a look.

"Jah," Nan said, seemingly oblivious to the interaction between her husband and his daughter. "I've read that too. I'm just not ready to do it—not any more than we have to, at least."

By the time we all took turns juggling the babies, I was the last to finish eating. It was pitch-dark outside but felt cozy in the kitchen. Bob and Nan had taken the babies upstairs, while Cate and Pete had returned to the shop.

As I ran the water for the dishes and Hope cleared the table, a vehicle came up the driveway, its lights shining bright.

"Who could that be?" I said. Surely not a customer this late in the day.

I peered out the window. It was the van. "Doris is here," I announced.

"With the hunters?" Hope put down the bowl of applesauce on the counter and headed toward the door.

"No," I replied to Hope. "She couldn't have gotten Bob's message, gone to the mountains, and been back already."

"Oh." Hope opened the door anyway. "Cate's coming out of the shop to talk to her." Still Hope waited. Finally she said, "I can't hear what they're saying." She shut the door and returned to the counter, picking up the bowl.

I nudged her with my elbow. "Martin will be home soon enough."

She nudged me back. "So will Ben."

I froze. "What?"

She laughed.

I turned toward her. "Who said anything about Ben?"

Hope blushed. "Mervin did. And Hannah. And even Martin . . ."

"They don't know what they're talking about."

She nodded. "Jah, they do."

"Hope," I said, "they're making it up."

She shrugged. "Martin said the two of you courted for—"

"One singing. Okay . . . two," I said.

"What happened?"

I paused and then said, "You'd have to ask Ben."

Cate came in and said Doris would go up in the mountains the next day to bring the boys home. Then she yawned. "Are you two okay cleaning up?"

We nodded in unison.

"Good." She yawned again. "I'm really tired. I'm going to go to bed."

That's when it dawned on me that she'd probably been getting up at night to help with the boys. And now there were three Bopplis to feed.

"Get your rest," I said. "You don't want to get that flu that's been going on. We'll get up with the Bopplis."

She didn't reply directly to me. Instead she said, "Hopefully, they're asleep, and Nan and Dat are going to bed too. Dat's too old to be getting so little sleep—it's taking a toll on our business."

I couldn't imagine Bob lacking energy to do anything. He'd always been a whirlwind of activity with his businesses and caring for people in our district. But I could see the current situation was hard on him.

When Hope and I finished the dishes, I turned the lamp down, leaving just enough light for Pete when he came in from the shop, and then we traipsed upstairs. I slowed at Nan and Bob's door, not wanting to make any noise, but Hope bumped into me and began to giggle. I put my hand over my mouth to encourage her to be quiet, but she giggled even louder so I grabbed her hand and pulled her down the dark hallway to our room.

Her laugh was contagious and by the time we collapsed on our beds I was laughing too, as quietly as I could—until I heard a baby cry. I stopped to listen.

Hope stopped too, a stricken look on her face. The giggles

welled up in me again and I dove under the quilt, pulling my pillow over my head. Maybe if we didn't look at each other we wouldn't laugh.

It wasn't that I thought Bob and Nan would be angry with us, although they'd have every right to be. It was that I truly wanted the babies to sleep so their parents could too. Cate was right. Nan and Bob *were* awfully old to be taking care of three newborns—which was the whole reason for hiring Hope and me, plus the sheer workload of running a home.

I listened as best I could with my head covered but didn't hear any more crying. Finally I poked my head out. Hope sat on the floor with her pillow in her lap. My eyes had adjusted enough to know she was staring at me. When our eyes met, she broke out into a wide grin—but that was all. The giggles seemed to be over. As Hope headed to the bathroom, I took off my Kapp, unpinned my bun, and started brushing my hair. As I did, my thoughts turned to friendship.

Molly and I had had separate rooms our whole lives, except after Dat died I moved into hers for a short while. We'd shared a camaraderie then unlike any other time, but it was short-lived.

Molly had other friends—mainly Hannah, but also many more that she spent time with. She never needed me. Besides, we couldn't have been more different.

The question wasn't why Molly and I weren't closer. It was, why didn't I have friends of my own?

I had acquaintances, sure. Girls from school. Girls who lived in our district that I attended services with. But never a best friend.

Molly said it was because I was distant. And too focused on myself. She said if I didn't spend so much time writing in my journal maybe I'd notice other people.

But now I had Hope.

"A penny for your thoughts," she said, stepping back into the room in her nightgown, her dress in her arms.

I continued brushing. "Oh, goodness," I said. "I was counting my blessings."

She smiled as she hung her dress. "I've been doing the same. My third oldest sister pressured my Dat into sending me down here. I'm so thankful she did. She said I needed to get out of the house more or I'd never marry."

I frowned. "You're only twenty."

"Jah," she said. "And I'm not getting any younger." Hope climbed into bed. "I'm so glad Dat let me come to Lancaster County."

"Because of Martin?"

She blushed and then said, "Don't you want to get married?"

I shook my head.

She laughed. "That's what I like about you. You're not afraid to be different."

I wasn't sure that was a compliment.

She pulled her quilt up to her chin.

I put my brush on my bedside table and divided my hair with my fingers.

"Your hair is so pretty," she said. "So thick and wavy. And the color of chestnuts."

"Oh, goodness," I said. "I'd give anything to have blond hair like yours." Molly's hair was close to the color of Hope's, just a little darker.

She shook her head. "Mine's thin and ordinary. Yours is beautiful."

Before I could think of what to say—she'd embarrassed me—she turned her head back so she looked straight at the ceiling and then said, "Time to say my prayers." She closed her eyes.

"Mind if I leave the lamp on for a few minutes?" I flipped my long braid over my shoulder.

She shook her head but didn't speak.

I kept forgetting to ask Cate for one of the infant care books to read. I'd told Nan I would. I needed to do it, even though I had little time to read at all.

I sighed. Tonight I just wanted a minute or two to myself. I grabbed my journal from under my bed, holding it as I said my prayers silently. I asked forgiveness for my sins, those I was aware of and those I had no idea about. Then I went through my mental list of things I was thankful for. I yawned several times before I finished. Too tired to write much, I simply penned, *I've made a friend. I'm so thankful I didn't go to Montana.*

By the next afternoon, the day was as warm as summer. Hope and I hung more wash—this time baby sleepers and T-shirts, spit rags, diapers, and blankets. The tiny clothes were the cutest things I'd ever seen. I shook each out and admired it before pinning it to the line.

Halfway through the load, Doris's van appeared.

Hope dropped the blanket in her hands. I quickly scooped it up off the grass and shook it out.

"They're back," Hope whispered, grabbing my arm.

I expected a vanload of dirty, mangy guys to descend on us but instead Bob's daughter Betsy climbed out of the passenger seat, tucking a strand of honey-blond hair under her Kapp. She'd been pretty and trim as a teenager. Now she appeared tired and a little plump, but still attractive. But why was she here?

Maybe Doris had picked her up when she dropped Ben off.

When Doris got out of the van my heart began to race. Had something happened? Usually she just dropped people off or picked them up. She was always in a hurry.

"Where are the boys? Are they okay?" Cate stood at the door to the shop.

"Jah," Betsy turned toward her sister as she spoke. "Doris couldn't find them—they were out hunting. Except for Ben. He was at camp."

I rolled my eyes. Leave it to Ben to stay back while the others were doing all the hard work.

"He's going to tell them all to be ready in the morning. Doris will pick them up then." Betsy's back was toward me but she was speaking loudly. "Ben got a deer—"

My face warmed. He hadn't been lazy.

Betsy started walking toward her sister. "He had it all dressed out, cut up, and wrapped, and he sent it back with Doris. Could we put it in the freezer here? We don't have room."

"Sure," Cate said. "I'll get Pete to carry it down."

She stepped back into the shop. Betsy turned toward us and, once she saw us, waved. "Bea," she called out, "I didn't realize you'd started helping out here already."

"On Monday."

Betsy walked toward us, followed by Doris. "Are you surviving?"

"Jah," I said. "The Bopplis are so sweet."

Betsy laughed. "Well, when Nan doesn't need you anymore you can come help me." Betsy'd had three children in three years. I wouldn't be surprised if she had another one on the way. Her oldest, Robbie, was going on four now and was one of the cutest kids I'd ever met. He was smart as a whip and a tease to boot.

88

As much as I liked Robbie, I couldn't imagine being a mother's helper for Betsy. She wasn't much older than I was.

Doris held a brown package in her hand. As she neared us, she extended it to me. "It's from Ben."

I wrinkled my nose but didn't reach for the package.

Hope giggled. "Is it the buck's heart?"

"Eww," I said.

Doris shook her head. "It's the liver." She thrust the package toward me.

I didn't know what else to do but take it. "Why did he send it?"

"He said you'd know." Doris wiped her hand on her jeans even though the package wasn't wet—just cold.

"I have no idea," I said. On the package he'd written, *You said you wouldn't eat a venison steak. So I sent this instead. Make sure and share it.* Usually Ben was at least funny. This was just stupid.

Betsy put her hands on her hips. "That Ben."

"Cook it for Nan," Doris said. "The extra iron will do her good."

"Oh," I said. "Good idea."

Pete approached, going straight to the back of the van, followed by Cate. "Who's watching the kids?" she called out to Betsy.

"Levi's Mamm. Doris is taking me to an appointment, so we need to get going."

I glanced sideways at Betsy, wondering if she was expecting again, even though it was none of my business. Pete came around the side of the van, lugging a big cold box, and headed for the house.

"Go peek at the babies before you leave," Cate said. "They're getting cuter and cuter."

Betsy frowned a little. "I'm happy for Dat and Nan and all, but I can't quite believe, after all these years, we have siblings."

"Isn't it wonderful!"

"Jah . . ." Betsy turned toward Doris. "What time is it?"

"Two ten."

"We'd better get going," Betsy said, giving Cate a quick hug. "I'll come back soon."

Betsy gave a little wave to all of us. Doris said she'd see us the next day. As they climbed back in the van, Cate said, "We're way behind. I need to get back to work."

I nodded—I'd gathered that—and followed Hope toward the house, holding the package out in front of myself. I glanced backward, checking to see if Cate had reached the shop door. She had. And Doris had turned the van around. Pete came out of the house empty-handed. He must have left the cold box in the basement.

After he passed us, I said, "I feel bad for Cate."

"Why?" Hope opened the door, and we slipped inside. The kitchen was empty. I hoped all three babies were still asleep, allowing Nan to nap too.

"Well . . ." I wasn't one to gossip or talk about private things. At least I hadn't been before. "Because it appears Betsy might be having another child soon . . . and Cate hasn't had one yet."

"But she will."

I stopped at the top of the stairs to the basement. "I hope so. . . ."

Hope stared at me with a bewildered look.

"What?" I asked.

"Nothing," she said. "Let's take a break and have a cup of tea."

"You make it." I started down the stairs. "After I put this liver in the freezer, I'll start on supper."

After the noon meal the next day, Cate pushed her chair back and sighed.

"Are you okay?" Bob pushed his empty plate forward.

"Just tired." Cate put the fork down.

"Go take a nap," Pete said.

"I can't." She stood, her untouched plate in her hand. "I'm expecting several orders."

Bob drained his coffee cup. "I'll take them."

"You won't hear the phone in the shop."

"I'm working in my office for a couple of hours," Bob said.

Cate nodded and stood, heading for the stairs. I was surprised she didn't put up a fight. She must have been up with the babies more than once in the night—or maybe she was getting sick.

A few minutes later after Bob and Pete headed down to the shop, Hope and I were left alone in the kitchen. "I wonder if Cate's coming down with that flu that's been going around the district," I said.

"Jah," Hope said. "That's the last thing we need around here." She grabbed a towel to dry the dishes I'd already washed. "But it's probably just her condition."

"Her condition?"

Hope smiled. "You know . . . "

Perplexed, I shook my head.

"Oh," she said and then blushed. "I was thinking maybe you didn't know, after our conversation yesterday." She lowered her voice. "Cate is expecting. She's pretty far along—seven months or so."

91

I couldn't help but grin. I was such a fool, as obtuse as Molly often claimed.

"But they've all been pretty nervous about this pregnancy, because she's lost several—one pretty far along."

My heart sank as I scrubbed a frying pan. "Poor Cate."

"Jah," Hope said.

No wonder Nan had been so gentle with Cate—and no wonder Cate had been so tired. No wonder they'd hired me to help.

Hope quickly changed the subject, asking me what I thought we should fix for supper. "The boys are going to be starving," she added.

"We'll feed them steaks." I placed the pan in the rinse water. "There's a whole shelf of them in the freezer." That was Leon's favorite meal, and I guessed it was true for other young men too.

"Cate said they'll be taking all of their meals with us for the next few days . . ."

"Oh, goodness," I said. It was one thing to come up with one meal to feed everyone, but three meals a day would be a challenge.

"And they'll be sleeping in the Dawdi Haus," Hope added.

"Do we need to get it ready?" I asked.

She shrugged. "Cate said it's fine. The boys won't notice a little dust."

I nodded in agreement. They'd been camping for the last few days—anything had to be better than that.

All through the afternoon, Hope kept looking out the windows—first while we cleaned up in the kitchen, and then while we changed the babies' diapers in Nan and Bob's room. She was clearly impatient for the boys' return.

We scrubbed potatoes back in the kitchen as Nan and the

babies napped. Not for long though. Just as we were finishing the potatoes, we heard Asher screaming.

"That was the shortest nap ever," Hope said as she rinsed off the last potato.

"Poor Nan." I turned the defrosting steak over on the counter and then washed my hands. "Let's go," I said.

All three were crying by the time we reached the bedroom. Nan was holding Leah and Asher. Hope scooped up Kurt and changed his diaper and then handed him to me. Then she changed Asher. Nan had settled back on the bed with Leah.

Nan suggested we take the boys outside. "Some fresh air will do them good," she said. "I'll see if Leah will nurse. Bring the boys up to me in about half an hour. Oh, and bring me a snack too, would you? I'll be starving by then."

It wasn't that long until suppertime, but it seemed as if a nursing mother didn't need to worry about spoiling her appetite.

Hope and I swaddled the boys in blankets and then headed downstairs and out the front door into the sunshine. Both babies closed their eyes against the brightness. Hope started to sit in one of the rocking chairs on the porch, but I suggested we walk up to the garden. We hadn't been getting much fresh air either, except when we did the laundry.

The babies didn't fuss as we strolled along the side of the house. Kurt seemed to be watching the leaves of the oak tree shimmer in the late afternoon sunlight.

Hope sighed as we neared the garden. "I wonder what's taking them so long."

"Maybe they weren't ready when Doris got there." I didn't want to imagine what their camp looked like. "Or maybe one of them got another deer and they had to cut it up." I had no stomach for that sort of thing and didn't want to imagine it either.

The leaves of the squash plants had begun to die back, show-ing even more of the pumpkins and the last of the zucchinis and acorn squash. "We should pick some for supper," I said, starting to hand Kurt to Hope.

"You hold the babies," she said, handing Asher to me instead. "I'll pick." She slid Asher into my arms, his head opposite Kurt's. Alarmed, I shifted the babies until my arms were balanced. Then I stood as still as I could, afraid one of them might slip.

Hope bent down, pulling back the plants, reaching for the smaller zucchini.

Asher kicked against his brother. I tentatively bounced the boys up and down a few times. They seemed to enjoy that. I began to sway.

I heard the vehicle before Hope did and turned toward the driveway. Doris's van was covered in dust.

Phillip sat up front. Doris waved and then honked when she saw me.

Hope sprang to her feet, a grin on her face, appearing much too eager to see them, in my opinion.

Doris pulled up past the showroom and parked between the house and the shop. Cate stepped out, followed by Bob and Pete.

The boys started clamoring out of the van. First Phillip, and then Mervin and Martin. Hope dropped the acorn squash in her hand onto the grass by the zucchini and started hurrying toward them. I followed, walking slowly. As soon as Mervin and Martin saw us, they headed our way—their matching sunglasses directed toward the babies.

Hope skipped ahead of me, distracting Martin, but Mervin kept coming toward me. "Ach, Beatrice," he said. "You have the little ones."

"Two of them," I said. "Leah's in the house with Nan."

Mervin put out his hands—as if I'd turn the little ones over to him.

I turned sideways. "You're filthy. Maybe you can hold one after you shower and change."

He narrowed his eyes at me, looked down at his dirt-caked shirt and trousers, and then burst out laughing. "You're right," he said.

Hope and Martin joined us.

"Aren't they adorable?" Hope cooed.

"Triplets." Martin stepped closer. "I can't imagine. Our Mamm says she can't remember the first year of our lives. I wonder what it will be like for Nan and Bob."

I nodded toward the van. "Speaking of . . ."

Bob and Pete had joined Phillip in unloading the back as Don climbed out of the sliding door, followed by Ben.

"What's he doing here?" I asked.

"Don?" Mervin bumped my elbow as he shifted around, making Asher stir. "He's working—"

I stepped away. "No. Ben. Why didn't Doris drop him off at his place?"

"Bob needs all of us to get the job done."

"But Ben isn't trained . . ."

"No, he is," Martin said. "He's been working here for a few weeks."

"Oh," was all I could manage to utter, a bad taste forming in my mouth. Why hadn't someone told me before I took the job?

Ben began waving his arms at Mervin and Martin. "Hello!" he called out. "Come get your stuff."

"He's such a stickler for fairness," Mervin said. He chuckled and then added, "No wonder he doesn't have a girlfriend."

Ben *was* into fairness. I remembered that. He often feared I cheated during the spelling bees, which of course I never did.

However, I understood his black-and-white thinking and pursuit of fairness because I was that way too. There was no reason for people not to do the right thing.

We all started down toward the van, although I trailed behind, keeping my distance from Ben.

Pete pointed toward the Dawdi Haus. "You'll sleep in there. There are two bathrooms, so go ahead and get cleaned up. Then come over to the big house—we're going to barbecue steaks for supper."

"What a relief," Mervin said. "We're nearly starved from Ben's cooking."

"Jah, I can imagine," I said.

"After supper we'll have you put in four hours of work. And we're looking at twelve tomorrow, at least." Pete turned toward Bob. "Have I forgotten anything?"

Bob held a box in his hands. "Just that we're grateful to each of you for coming back early. We really appreciate it."

"Ach," Martin said, "Ben got the only deer in the whole forest. Another couple of days wouldn't have made a difference."

Ben put his hand up, and Martin slapped it, as if in victory.

"So has Ben found a new best friend in Martin?" I asked Mervin.

He shrugged.

"You know how fickle Ben is," I said. "They'll be friends for a time, and then Ben will move on. He's a bundle of contradictions—expecting people to be fair to him but not treating others the same."

Mervin shook his head. "That's not Ben at all."

That was the way he'd been with me. I sighed, chiding myself. He probably wouldn't treat others as badly as he'd treated me.

"I take it he's not in your good book," Mervin said.

"If he was, I'd burn—" If I hadn't had two babies in my arms, I would have clamped my hands over my mouth. What a horrible thing to say. I'd never burn a book. Mervin laughed.

Bob started toward the Dawdi Haus, stopping for a minute to say hello to his sons. They both turned their heads toward his voice. Then he continued on, followed by Phillip. Don followed his brother, but then veered off toward Hope and Martin. "You must be Bob's niece," he said.

She nodded.

"Don, this is Hope," Martin said. "She's from New York."

"Pleased to meet you," Don said. "I heard about you when I started here." He glanced at Martin. "But didn't have the opportunity to meet you."

Hope nodded as she blushed.

Then Don looked at me. "Beatrice," he said. "So good to see you again."

My face warmed, and before I could think of what to say, Asher began to fuss again, turning his head toward me.

"I hope I'll be seeing more of you," Don said above the baby's cries. I gave a polite nod and Don kept on walking.

"Mervin," Ben called out. "Come get your stuff!" He stood in the middle of a pile of sleeping bags, duffel bags, and boxes. Didn't he know no one was paying attention to him?

I turned toward Hope. "We should go check on Nan."

She ignored me, whispering something to Martin.

"Hope," I said, "go get the squash."

She gave me a hurt look and said, "You sound like Ben."

My heart fell as Mervin and Martin both laughed. "I'll help you," Martin said to Hope, and off they went toward the garden, practically skipping. I headed toward the house, bouncing both babies as I did.

"Ach, hello to you too, Bea," Ben called out.

I couldn't wave because my hands were full. I also didn't bother to tell him to use my full name. That would only get more of a laugh out of the others. I kept on walking.

When Hope finally joined me in the kitchen, I said, "Why didn't you tell me Ben was working here?"

She simply said, "I thought you knew."

⟨ornament⟩

The mouth-watering scent of the steaks barbecuing filled the kitchen. Hope stood idle at the open door, a smile breaking across her face.

"Who's out there?" I teased, approaching with a stack of plates.

She took the plates from me. "Just Martin." She smiled. "Coming this way with Phillip."

Thank goodness Ben wasn't with them.

"Come back in and get the glasses." I headed to the oven and took the potatoes out, placing them on a platter and covering them with a towel.

Cate called from the staircase, "Can you come get Leah?"

I hurried down the hall and up the stairs, passing Cate, who held the boys. "Denki. That will give Nan a few minutes."

The baby was in her bassinet fussing, and Nan was in the bathroom. I picked up the little girl and walked carefully down the stairs with her. By the time I reached the kitchen, Cate had the crew parading through, gathering up all the needed items, and heading back out again. But there was still no Ben. Perhaps he'd gone home. I could dream, at least.

Once all the food had been placed on the table, Bob led us in a silent prayer. He dished up first, heaping food on a plate, and then slipped back into the house with it. I guessed he intended to share the food with Nan.

Still, Ben didn't appear.

I turned toward my friend as she positioned herself behind Martin in line. "Hope, you should let Cate go first."

"I'm fine," Cate said, sitting down in one of the lawn chairs with Asher and Kurt. The babies fussed a little but she jiggled them up and down until they settled.

"Denki," Hope said. "I'll eat quickly."

I sat beside Cate, holding Leah, while the others dished up and then gathered around the picnic table.

I heard Ben before I saw him. "It would have been nice for someone to tell me it was time to eat."

"Everyone else seemed to be able to figure it out," I said.

He stopped in the middle of the yard. "Ach," he said. "It's Missy D-I-S-D-A-I-N."

Mervin chuckled. "Definition, please."

"*Missy*—a disparaging form of address to a female who is not married," Ben replied. "*Disdain*—full of contempt, scorn, derision, and disrespect."

My face grew warm, and I could feel splotches forming on my neck.

"The opposite of courteous," Ben added.

"Believe me," I replied, "I'm plenty courteous with everyone but you."

Ben crossed his arms. "Isn't that a coincidence? All the girls—except for you—respect me. Too bad I'm not looking to court any of them."

I replied, "It's a B-L-E-S-S-I-N-G for them you aren't. *Blessing*—" I couldn't resist. "God's favor and protection."

Don hooted. "She's got the last word on that one."

Ben headed toward the food table, muttering, "I wish my horse moved as fast as her mouth."

"I heard that," I answered. "And you've said that before." Back when we were all camping summer before last, with the Youngie. Not that I was keeping track. "Can't you come up with something original?"

Ben held up his hands. One clasped his empty plate.

That was so like him to back out of an argument.

Hope frowned. A crow cawed from the oak tree. I realized I was patting Leah's back a little too vigorously and stopped. The baby began to fuss. I began again, but gentler.

Ben finished filling his plate and sat down with the others, his back to me.

I bristled. Cate shook her head and leaned toward me. "Try to ignore him," she said. "He's just trying to get your goat."

"He should know by now that I can kick."

"Jah," she said. "I think we all know that."

My face grew warmer.

"I don't mean that in a bad way. It's just that you're usually so sweet and gentle—except around Ben."

"I have my reasons," I said.

"I'm sure you do."

Don elbowed Ben and, looking straight at me, said, "I like her style."

I did my best to ignore them both.

After everyone had eaten except for me, Hope and I took the babies back into the house and up to Nan and Bob. "I'll be back after I eat," I said. "And then I'll put away the food." Hope and I could do the dishes later.

There was no reason for me to eat outside, so I began carrying the food in. The rest of the boys must have gone with Pete to the shop, but Martin and Ben still sat at the table. I couldn't help but overhear snippets of their conversation as I traipsed in and out of the house.

Martin asked, "What do you think of Hope?"

I stopped on the steps to the kitchen, the pasta salad in my hands.

"Hope?" Ben's voice was louder than Martin's. "Is she the same girl you were talking to Sunday before last?"

Martin's voice fell. "Stop teasing me."

"Ach," Ben replied. "Do you want my honest answer? Or do you want me to criticize her, as I seem to do so well these days?"

"Neither," Martin answered. "It doesn't matter what you say. I think she's the most beautiful girl I've ever known."

His voice came closer. "Marry her, then," Ben said, his tone flippant.

I hurried on into the kitchen.

When I came back out, Phillip, Martin, and Ben stood together at the edge of the lawn.

Ben stood with arms crossed and feet spread wide. "You guessed right," he said to Phillip. "Martin has fallen in love."

I beelined for the table, concentrating on listening, sneaking a glance at the group.

Phillip had his arm around Martin, pulling him close and yanking his hat from his head. "How sweet," he said. "Are you ready to talk to Bob?"

Martin pulled away, plucking his hat from Phillip's hand. "Not yet."

"I'll mention it," Phillip said. "Tonight while we're working. And tell you his reaction."

Ben yawned dramatically.

"Just wait," Phillip said, "soon enough it will be your turn."

"That would be as likely as a snowstorm tonight," Ben said, wiping his brow.

Phillip grabbed Ben by both shoulders and began to shake him. "When it happens, we'll all remember the fuss you've made."

I couldn't help but laugh, drawing their attention. I hurried back to the steps, dashing into the house. From the window over the sink, I watched the boys head toward the shop.

"Why the sad face?"

I spun around. Cate stood to the side of me.

"Sad? I'm not sad," I answered. "I was just thinking . . ."

"About?"

I answered, "Martin and Hope."

"Ach," she said. "They seem to be a good match." She continued on to the back door. "But you can be happy for Hope and sad for yourself."

I shook my head. "But I'm not sad for myself. Not at all."

Cate gave me a sympathetic smile. "I'm going out to the office for a bit—less than an hour. Nan's extra tired, so come get me if you need to."

I assured her I would.

CHAPTER
7

As Hope and I washed the bottles before we headed off to bed, Pete stuck his head in the back door, requesting we take a snack out to the boys. "I'm hoping to get another two hours of work out of them," he said. "A plate of cookies and a pitcher of milk might do the trick."

Hope nearly squealed in delight.

I, on the other hand, couldn't help but be aware that we might be up giving babies their bottles in another three hours. "Let's hurry," I said. Fortunately I'd baked the batches of oatmeal cookies the day before. I grabbed the plastic container, the size of a shoebox, from the cupboard because I hadn't gotten them down to the freezer yet. I pulled a stack of paper cups from the pantry shelf as I instructed Hope—who seemed to be becoming more and more oblivious to what needed to be done—to get the milk.

Darkness had chased away the warmth of the day, and it had grown downright chilly, especially without our capes. Woodsmoke mixed with the sweet scent of apples from the trees on the slope above the garden filled the air. Pete had already picked several basketfuls and stored the apples in the cold room in the basement, and I imagined the boys helped themselves straight from the trees on break. Besides picking the rest of the ones on the tree, Hope and I needed to collect the fruit that had fallen to the ground and was about to rot. I added *Make applesauce and apple butter* to my ongoing mental to-do list.

Above, the stars shone bright—thousands and thousands of them. I breathed in deeply again, full of gratefulness for everything. My new friendship with Hope. The opportunity to help Nan and Bob. The beautiful night. The autumn weather.

Everything except for Ben being on the premises.

I sighed, but Hope didn't seem to notice, because the shop door swung open and revealed Martin with some sort of light behind him in the hallway.

She pranced toward him.

"Ach." He started toward her. "Pete said you'd be bringing a snack." He took the milk from Hope, and we followed him into the building. A light bulb shone from the hallway ceiling.

Hope pointed up at it.

"Solar," Martin said to her. "Haven't you noticed the panels on top of the building? It's what runs the power tools. And the fax machine and computer in Cate's office."

I followed Martin and Hope down the hall and into the shop. A fine sawdust filled the air. The men all wore masks, but I tucked my mouth and nose against my shoulder. I wished I could plug my ears against the whine of the machines.

Bob and Phillip talked in the corner, their masks hanging. When Bob saw us, he pointed toward the door. "We'll meet you in the break room," he said.

I didn't know where that was and Martin didn't budge as he continued to stare at Phillip and Bob.

"Come on." I started toward the hallway.

Ben strode toward us, pulling his mask from his face and then taking plugs out of his ears. "I'll show you."

"Take the milk from Martin," I told him. "Before it turns into a sawdust shake."

Ben complied, barely garnering Martin's attention.

I nudged Hope. "Come on."

She followed, reluctantly, and Don and Mervin followed right away. By the time we reached the break room, Martin was behind them. The boys each grabbed several cookies and downed the milk, although Don poured himself a cup of coffee from the machine on the counter. Bob, Pete, and Phillip didn't come get a snack at all. By the time the others were done, Phillip finally stepped into the break room. "Back to work," he said, looking directly at Martin.

It seemed he was some sort of crew boss. Or perhaps he was just the self-appointed leader of the group.

The boys trailed out of the room, and Phillip grabbed two cookies. I poured the rest of the milk into a glass for him and then put the lid on the cookie container, moving it to the middle of the table. Perhaps they'd finish them off later.

Phillip waved toward the outside door. "Hope, could I speak to you for a moment?"

She nodded and followed him. I stacked the used cups and picked up the empty pitcher, trailing the two as far as the picnic table, where they sat down. I hesitated for a moment, not sure if I should stay or keep going.

Light flooded out from the shop behind me, and thinking I'd failed to latch the door, I turned to go back. Martin stood in the doorway, watching Hope, his jaw set and his arms crossed. I continued on to the house and into the kitchen. After I'd washed the pitcher, Hope still hadn't returned so I slipped my cape over my shoulders and grabbed Hope's, taking it out to her.

She and Phillip were deep in conversation. I didn't interrupt as I handed her the cape.

"Denki," she said.

Phillip didn't stop talking—about the camping trip and hunt. Not about Martin at all. Could it be that Phillip was trying to court Hope? Breaking up with Jessie was the stupidest thing he'd ever done, in my humble opinion—until now.

The door to the shop was shut, and Martin was nowhere to be seen. I yawned. Phillip didn't seem to notice.

I yawned again and then said, "Hope needs to get to bed. We have babies to feed soon. And breakfast to prepare in the morning."

"Oh." Phillip looked up at me in surprise.

"And don't you need to be helping the others?"

"I already finished my part," he answered.

The shop door opened again. This time Don stood in the doorway. "Let's go stay at Dat's," he said to Phillip.

Phillip stood. "I'd rather stay here."

"Suit yourself," Don said.

"How are you getting there?" Phillip started toward his brother.

"I'll walk. If I cut through the fields it won't take long." He started toward the Dawdi Haus, most likely to get his bag. "See all of you in the morning," he said.

"Come on." I tugged on Hope's cape. "We should see if Nan needs any help. And then get to sleep."

"Jah," Don said as he breezed by. "The young ladies mustn't miss out on their beauty sleep."

It was a silly thing to say, but I was too tired to be annoyed with Don. Hope had my full attention.

I found her arm and yanked. "Come on."

Hope and I didn't talk that night, because I ended up giving Asher a bottle and she was fast asleep by the time I came to bed. In the morning I woke, wondering if I'd dreamt that I gave Kurt a bottle sometime around three a.m. Probably not.

By the time I reached the kitchen at five twenty, Hope had already started the bacon, and it was sizzling on the stove as she washed her hands, staring out the window a moment longer than necessary, looking for the boys most likely. It was pitch-dark out, but she must have been able to see something—or maybe sense when Martin was near.

Bob padded into the kitchen and poured himself a cup of coffee, yawning as he did.

I pulled out the griddle from the vertical cupboard, one of the fancy features of the Millers' kitchen, and put it on the stove to warm as I mixed the batter. Hope stayed at the window as she dried her hands.

"The bacon . . ." I finally said.

She didn't seem to hear me, but when she smiled, I knew the boys were on their way. Mervin came in first. Then Ben. Thankfully, he didn't say anything. He simply collapsed into a chair. Mervin grabbed two mugs and filled them with coffee. Next Phillip came in.

Hope kept staring out the window.

"The bacon," I said again, this time not as gently.

"Oh." She stepped back to the stove and quickly turned it.

Between flipping hotcakes I pulled down a stack of plates and handed them to Mervin. "Pass these around," I said.

Hope stepped to the kitchen window again. Still no Martin. Or Don. But maybe he planned to eat breakfast at home.

Hope gave me a pleading look that had Martin written all over it.

"Where is he?" I whispered to Mervin.

"Who?" he asked in a normal tone. Everyone looked at me.

"Your brother," I answered. "Remember, that *being* that was born the same day as you."

Mervin shrugged. "He got up before any of us. I don't know where he went."

As Hope and I put the food on the table, Bob asked Phillip if he'd talked to Martin the night before.

"About . . . ?" Phillip asked as he stabbed several hotcakes and slid them onto his plate.

"What we talked through." Bob nodded his head toward Hope.

"Oh, that," Phillip answered, reaching for the butter. "No, I didn't have a chance."

I doubted that. Phillip *was* interested in Hope.

She gave me a pleading look.

"I'll go find Martin," I whispered. "You take care of things in here."

I grabbed my cape and a flashlight by the back door and slipped out into the darkness. Because none of the others had seen him, I didn't go to the Dawdi Haus. Instead I headed behind the barn, dodging a calico cat probably just back from her hunt, and then I headed toward the creek.

I stopped at the edge of the sycamore grove, waving the flashlight around. The limbs of the trees, nearly bare now, cast eerie shadows in the beam of light. Below the grove, I could see the creek, which divided the Millers' property from Cap Cramer's farm. Hannah was staying with them. I was surprised she hadn't been over the evening before, but because Mervin had returned I expected her by noon today, at the latest.

I exhaled slowly, sending a cloud of vapor out from my face. "Martin," I called out.

I turned toward the sound of a twig snapping.

"Everyone's eating breakfast." I shone the light toward the noise, hoping it was Martin. My heart skipped a beat. What if it was someone else?

Another twig snapped, but still no one answered. Below the babble of the creek seemed to grow louder and louder. I turned and hurried away from the grove, keeping the beam on the ground. Still I tripped over a rock but caught myself before I fell. When I reached the fence, I shone the flashlight down the property line. Past the shop was a tree. Perhaps Martin had gone there.

A figure scurried to the other side of the tree. "Martin?"

He popped his head out from behind the trunk.

I exhaled as I shone the flashlight in his face. "What are you doing?"

Instead of responding he turned his head up toward the branches of the tree. For a moment I thought he saw something up there and moved the light skyward, revealing the flaming orange and red leaves of the maple tree. The weeks of rain and warm temperatures had delayed the changing colors, but with the colder nights the leaves had finally turned.

"Come on, Martin." I turned the flashlight off. "All the food will be gone if you don't hurry."

He crossed his arms. "I'm not hungry."

"Is this about Hope?"

Again, he didn't answer but shifted away from me.

"Phillip told Bob he hadn't talked with you."

"He didn't need to," Martin said. "It's pretty clear what's going on."

"What?" I didn't intend for my voice to sound so shrill. I lowered it. "What's going on?"

"Hope is interested in Phillip. They talked forever last night. And seemed quite cozy."

"No." I felt for Martin. "Hope cares about you—only you. She's been looking for you all morning—peering out the kitchen window every few seconds, long after Phillip came into the house. She's not interested in him."

Martin's voice cracked as he said, "But he's interested in her."

"I don't think he is . . ." I stopped, not wanting to lie. I couldn't figure out Phillip's motivation. Was Phillip so distraught over his breakup with Jessie that he would be so foolish as to want to court his friend's girl?

"But why would Hope want to court me if she could court Phillip? He's the bishop's son. He'll be ready to buy a farm soon. He's tall and—"

"Stop it," I said. "You're handsome." Technically he wasn't as good-looking as Phillip, but I found Martin much more attractive. "And a hard worker."

"I'll never have my own farm, not with Mervin needing one too. He'll be first in line for our place."

"Don't say that. You have no idea what God will provide." I grabbed his arm with my free hand. "You have to take it a day at a time." I turned on the flashlight. "A step at a time. Toward the kitchen." I tugged on him. He complied.

We marched along in silence. When we neared the house, Hope was in the window. When she saw Martin she smiled.

"See?" I jabbed him with my elbow.

Still he hung back as I entered the house. "Come on." I tugged on his sleeve. As he entered, Hope actually clapped her hands together. Never would I have done that. I couldn't help but appreciate her honest enthusiasm, though. Nor could I help but steal a glance at Phillip, who had a frown on his face.

Most of the boys had left, presumably for the shop, but Don, who sat beside his brother, looked up at Martin and asked, "What's wrong? Why so sad?"

"I'm not," Martin answered through clenched teeth.

"Sick?"

"No." Martin stared at Phillip now.

"He's neither sad nor sick." I put my hand on my hip and drilled Phillip with my eyes as I answered Don. "He's simply trying to be civil." Then under my breath, I muttered, "Unlike your brother."

"Goodness, little lady. You are spunky." Don leaned toward me.

Was he trying to flirt again? At least now I knew he wasn't married. My face, even though it had been icy cold a minute ago, grew warm. If Bob overheard what was going on, he didn't let on. "Martin!" he said. "There you are. Come sit down." He patted the chair next to him. Then he motioned to Hope to join them.

As Hope dried her hands, Bob turned his attention to Phillip. "Go ahead and get started in the shop. I'll be there in a minute."

I headed back to the mud porch and was hanging up my cape when Phillip bumped into me.

"Excuse you," I said.

"How about you?" he asked. "Are you looking for someone to court too?"

I shook my head as I draped my cape over a peg, wishing away the warmth spreading from my face down my neck.

"Even if she were, she's not your type," Don said, stepping around us, his voice light. "She's too lively for you." As he opened the back door he turned back and winked at me.

I raised an eyebrow and turned around, walking with my head high back into the kitchen. Truth be told, I wasn't sure how to respond to him. Perhaps he flirted with all the girls.

" . . . so Hope's father told me," Bob was saying, "if a young man should want to court her while she stayed with us that he would trust my judgment as to the character of the young man."

I stepped to the sink, my back to the others.

Bob continued, "I have to tell you, Martin. There's not a young man I'd recommend more highly than you."

No one said anything for a long moment. True, this wasn't the way things were usually done in our community, but this was a special case. I listened for a response from Martin. I waited until I felt I might burst and then turned around, slowly. Martin sat staring at Hope as if Bob hadn't spoken at all. He seemed paralyzed—by love or fear, I couldn't be sure.

"Martin, say something," I blurted out.

He cleared his throat. "Jah, I would like to court you, Hope. If that's all right with you."

She beamed, her blue eyes dancing, but didn't answer.

I stepped behind her and whispered, "Hope . . . respond."

She spoke softly, "Jah. I'd like that. Denki, Onkel Bob."

"Whew," I said, settling into the chair beside her. "I'm glad that's finally taken care of."

Bob chuckled as he stood. "So who's next on our matchmaking list?"

I was tempted to say "Phillip"—except I knew it would rile Martin. And besides, I certainly didn't want Hope or Martin saying I needed to be added to the list.

"No one." I stood. "Let's concentrate on the Bopplis. And good health." I knew it sounded as if I was referring to Nan, but I meant Cate too. "And strong families."

"Ach," Hope said, standing. "I know someone who could use a little help."

"Jah." Martin looked directly at me, a smile spreading across his face.

"Oh, no." I stepped toward the sink. "Please. I don't need anyone interfering. I'm not interested in courting—I've got my hands full right now." I turned the water on, drowning out their chatter. I knew their intentions were good, but I didn't want to be matched with anyone.

However, I couldn't help but feel a sense of satisfaction at having intervened on Hope's behalf. No wonder Molly enjoyed her time with her friends. Being involved in people's lives was a blessing, not something to avoid as I'd done, foolishly, for so many years.

The rest of Friday was a blur of washing bottles, mixing formula, filling bottles, feeding babies, and changing diapers. It
helped that Cate left the office early and lent a hand fixing
supper—meatloaf, mashed potatoes, creamed corn, and greens.
I'd meant to make a batch of bread but hadn't found the time,
so I was thankful when a woman from our district dropped by
four loaves. She'd had two sets of twins a half-century ago and
said Nan had been on her mind all week.

I thanked her profusely, hopefully enough that she'd bring
another batch soon.

"My goodness, Bea," she said. "I didn't take you to be so
outgoing."

I must have blushed, because she added, "No need to be
embarrassed. It suits you well."

I couldn't imagine how someone without a community of
support could manage more than one baby at a time, or even
manage one at all, for that matter—not at first anyway. After
the woman left, I offered up a prayer of thanks to God for her,
her bread, and how he was taking care of all of us.

I couldn't explain it, but I felt something shifting inside of me. I was aware of it again when I volunteered to give Asher his bottle after finishing up the dishes.

As I held him, staring into his inky eyes that were glued to mine, an odd feeling welled up inside of me. He was so vulnerable. So dependent on my care. So trusting.

I took a raggedy breath. I cared for him, and for his brother and sister too, in a way I couldn't have imagined possible a week ago. The funny thing was, the more I cared, the more my confidence grew.

That wasn't the only thing growing—the laundry kept piling up, until Saturday morning the two hampers in the upstairs bathroom overflowed.

After breakfast I said I'd start the wash and told Hope to come get me if she needed help. She did, a lot. Asher had spit up all over his bassinet while Nan was nursing Kurt. Leah wouldn't take a bottle. The diaper pail was full.

I tackled the laundry in short spurts, and it wasn't until nearly noon that I got outside to hang the first load on the line. The boys were all outside eating sandwiches they'd made from the meat, cheese, and bread Cate had spread out on the kitchen table.

Sure enough, Hannah sat with them. She called out to me. I waved and then started pinning baby blankets to the line as fast as I could, anticipating a holler for me to help inside at any moment.

I tried to ignore the group at the picnic table, but Hannah spoke so loudly it was impossible. "Now that Martin's been matched, who's next?"

I groaned. What was wrong with people? I listened for an answer, and when it didn't come, I couldn't help but glance—in a natural way, I hoped—over at the group.

All eyes were on Ben. He stood, a sandwich in his hand. "Not me." He took a couple of steps backward. "I'm never getting married."

What a blessing for all women, I thought, as I grabbed another blanket and pinned a corner to the line. Ben would be a pernicious suitor. He'd certainly been so with me.

"Funny," Hannah said. "Beatrice has always said she'll never marry either."

My face grew hot. I turned my back to them, pinning the second corner and then grabbing another blanket.

"Bea, don't pretend you can't hear me," Hannah called out. What all had Molly told her about me? Probably everything—and more.

"I'm not pretending anything," I answered, flipping the edge of another blanket over the line. "I'm choosing not to respond."

Hannah laughed and then said, "I think your not answering must communicate something."

Mervin said, "Ach, Hannah, let her be. She's had some peace with Molly gone."

Someone stirred. I held my breath, hoping Ben wasn't walking toward me—because someone was.

"Where's Hope?" It was Martin.

I faced him. "Helping Nan. As soon as I finish this load, I'll see if she can come out for a bit." If I'd known they were all gathered around outside, I would have sent her out to hang the wash. That way she and Martin could have had a few minutes to chat.

"Thank you," he said, drifting back toward the picnic table.

As I started to hang another blanket, someone else approached. I peeked around the blanket.

Don cleared his throat, his hat in his hand. "Don't let the others get to you," he said. He was uncharacteristically serious.

I dropped the blanket. "Pardon?" I said as I reached down to grab it.

"They're teasing," he said, stroking his beard.

"Don't worry about me," I said. "I'm fine." I pinned the blanket between us. His seriousness concerned me more than his flirting.

He reached out and lifted the blanket so he could see me. "Jah," he said. "I can tell you're able to take care of yourself. I just wanted you to know I'm here if you need anyone to talk to."

I inhaled quickly and grabbed a spit rag. "Denki," I replied, knowing I'd talk with Hope first. Before he could respond, I scooted the basket down the line. A moment later, Don followed Phillip, Ben, and Martin toward the shop. Hannah had moved to the other side of the table and sat on the bench next to Mervin. She couldn't have gotten any closer to him unless she sat on his lap.

The boys would have a break in a couple of hours. Maybe Hope could go out then. I definitely wouldn't—not if I could help it. I'd hang the next loads before they came out again, and then take it all down after their break.

I finished the pinning and hurried up the back steps, surprised to have Hope meet me at the back door. She held it wide open for me. "What did Don say?"

I breezed past her, put the empty basket on the table, and gave her a brief account of the conversation.

"That's nice of him to offer to listen," she said.

I nodded and placed the basket on the table. It was thoughtful of him. "I just wish I knew what his intentions were."

"I think he's sweet on you." Hope smiled.

I shook my head.

"No, he is," she said. "Which one do you prefer? Ben or Don?"

"Hope," I groaned. "Stop. I'm serious—I'm never going to get married."

She grinned. "I'm pretty sure you're wrong. By this time next year, you'll be married. The only thing left is for you to choose which one. If you don't, someone else is bound to choose for you." She giggled.

Her teasing was ridiculous. I picked up the basket and headed downstairs. Ben despised me, and I had nothing in common with Don. But at least he seemed to be a decent human being, which was more than I could say about Ben.

Hope did manage to sneak outside during the next break, while I took a turn with the babies, giving Asher and then Kurt bottles. After I finished, I headed to the kitchen for a glass of water before I put the last load of wash through the wringer. Cate and Hope sat at the table, folding the blankets that the warm autumn sun had already dried.

"Oh, there you are," Hope said, as if surprised to see me.

I grabbed a glass from the cupboard.

When neither of them spoke, a sense of awkwardness spread through me. "Did I interrupt?"

"Oh, no," Cate said. "We were just talking."

Hope nodded her head and then said, slowly, "Jah . . ." She turned toward Cate, her eyes wide.

"Oh," I answered. Hope was a terrible liar. "About anything in particular?"

"Not really," Hope said. "Just that . . ."

"I'd better get back to the office," Cate said, with a hiccup. Or maybe she suppressed a chuckle. "I'm going to finish some paperwork—then I'll be back to help with supper."

"What are we having?" I asked.

Cate froze. "Oh, I hate this part of the day. Do you have any ideas?"

I shook my head. I thought she'd taken something out to thaw. Then I remembered the meatballs in the freezer and mentioned them.

Her face lit up. "Perfect. Aenti Laurel left those before her surgery." She wrinkled her nose. "Except they're frozen."

"They'll probably thaw in time. If not, I'll put the plastic bags in a pan of hot water," I said. "And get the potatoes scrubbed and peeled."

I expected Hope to chime in on what she would do to help, but she stared past Cate instead, toward the back door.

"How about if you hang the last load on the line," I suggested to her. "That will at least give you—"

She was up and headed to the basement door before I finished my sentence.

I called after her, "You'll have to run it through the wringer first."

Cate shook her head and smiled as she left for the office. "She's got it bad."

"Jah," I answered. I pulled the meatballs out of the freezer, and when I returned I checked on Nan and the babies.

She sat on the edge of the bed. "We're almost out of wipes." With so many babies, wipes were much more sanitary—plus they cut down some on the wash. Any little bit helped. Nan continued, "I was sure we had another box. We must be going through them faster than I thought."

"I can go to the store," I said.

"Denki." She looked odd sitting there without a baby in her arms. "And we need milk—buy three gallons, since the boys are eating here. Put it all on our account. And ice cream—so take a cooler."

I grabbed a pad of paper and a pencil and started a list.

"Bob's going to buy disposable diapers, in bulk, on Monday, but you should get a couple of boxes. We can't keep doing cloth diapers. It's too much work."

I jotted down *diapers*, relieved. We'd been doing laundry nearly every day.

"Get a couple of different kinds of ice cream. You could ask the boys what flavor they want."

I wouldn't need to. They'd be happy with whatever I got.

"Denki," she said, a tender look on her face. "I love my babies. I am so grateful to God. I have never felt so blessed. But Beatrice, if you and Hope and Cate weren't here to help, I think I'd be absolutely crazy by now."

"You wouldn't be," I said. "You're doing great."

Her eyes filled with tears.

"Nan." I sat down beside her and put my free hand around her shoulder. "Are you all right?'

She smiled as she swiped at her cheeks. "Just tired. All of it—what the pregnancy did to my body, recovering from surgery, trying to nurse—is so hard."

"I can send one of the boys to the store."

She shook her head. "Bob needs them. I'm going to rest while I can."

It wouldn't be long, I knew.

"I'll hurry," I said. "Hope is finishing up the wash. I'll tell her to check on you when she's done."

"We'll be fine," Nan said. "Take a little extra time if you want to, really. Stop by your place and see how Edna's doing."

"Denki," I said. That was a good idea.

I told Hope Nan had asked me to go to the store, grabbed a stainless-steel cooler from the basement, and then stepped into the shop office to tell Cate. "I'm almost done here," she said. "I'll go help Nan. And get supper started." She leaned over her desk toward me. "Take Thunder. Dat's horses are all so slow."

I'd heard about her horse, so I wasn't so sure that was a good idea. But he was getting older, so maybe he'd mellowed some. "See you soon." It felt good to be getting away from the farm. I'd only been at the Millers' six days, but it had felt like a lifetime. Well, that was a bit of an exaggeration, but not much.

The afternoon sun warmed me as Thunder trotted along the highway. I passed a field of corn, the stalks tall enough to provide shade. Harvesters cut the corn in the next field, sending bits of stalks and dust whirling toward me. I squinted as Thunder, without my urging, trotted faster. I squared my shoulders and clasped the reins.

We reached the store in no time. Being as efficient as I could be, I hurried through, tossing what we needed into the cart. I paused for a moment to select the ice creams, choosing chocolate-peanut butter for Nan and mountain berry and rocky road for the boys, all in the gallon-size tubs.

When I pulled out of the parking lot, I directed Thunder to the right instead of the left, toward the covered bridge and home.

As we passed the bookstore, the door to the shop opened and Albert stepped out. I wished I could stop. I knew Nan wouldn't mind, but I couldn't justify it. Not when there was so much to do—and I had ice cream in the cooler. So I just waved.

Albert stepped to the edge of the porch and, when he recognized me, waved back. As he did, Willa came out the door too.

He put his arm around her, as if to steady her. She didn't seem to recognize me at all.

I waved again anyway, pushing away my sadness at their predicament, and then urged Thunder to go even faster, delighting in the wind against my face. I'd never felt so independent—and so needed—in all my life.

By the time I turned up our driveway, I was sticky with sweat and thirsty. No doubt Thunder could use some water too. A loud bark came from the crest of the hill, but as soon as Love realized it was me, she rushed toward the buggy, her tail wagging. She ran alongside the front wheel until I pulled up by the barn.

"Hi, there, girl." I jumped down and rubbed around her neck with both hands. "Are you glad to see me?"

She turned so her tail thumped against my leg. Her version of a hug. I unhitched Thunder, led him to the trough, and then tied him to the hitching post. The gray kitten poked her head out of the barn, but when I called out, "Here kitty, kitty!" she bolted. Disappointed, I headed toward the back door.

Edna stepped out, drying her hands on her apron, a grin spreading across her face. "I was hoping it would be you," she called out. "Are you going to spend the night?"

I shook my head. "I can only stay for a minute." Love nuzzled my hand as I spoke. "I went to the store for Nan. I have milk and ice cream in the cooler."

Her smile faded, but just for a moment. "I have an apple crisp on the counter." Her eyes twinkled. "Come on in and have some."

No one baked like Edna. My mouth began to water at the thought—not to mention the smell coming through the back door. Then I remembered that Hope and I needed to pick the apples. I'd totally forgotten about it. I couldn't fathom how busy mothers kept up with everything.

A couple of minutes later, I sat at the kitchen table enjoying the dessert along with a cup of tea. Edna had fixed it the same way Mamm did—with milk.

"I have two crisps for you to take back with you," Edna said.

"Denki," I said, relieved because we had nothing for dessert that night. "I should have bought vanilla ice cream," I said.

"There's a tub in the freezer you can take."

I took a sip of the tea, grateful for both the offer of ice cream and the caffeine.

Love whined outside the screen door.

"She's been out of sorts," Edna said. "She misses all of you terribly."

"She's always been more Molly's dog than mine," I said.

"Oh, I don't know about that—not after seeing the way she reacted to you just now."

It was rather sweet.

"How about you?" Edna sat across from me. "Do you miss everyone?"

"Some," I said, "but mostly I've been too busy. I never would have guessed taking care of three babies would be so much work."

Edna smiled. "Has Nan had many visitors?"

I shook my head. "Just a couple of people dropping off food."

"What do they need?" Edna asked.

I chuckled. "Anything. The crisps will be a big help." I told her about Laurel's meatballs and that we were having them for supper. "I'm going to come up with a menu list," I said.

"Good idea." Edna took a sip of tea.

I put my fork down. "I used to tease Molly about her lists—"

Edna looked at me over the brim of her mug. "Tease?"

I rolled my eyes. "Okay, maybe *mock*."

She nodded.

"Anyway," I said, "I'm regretting it. Managing people and chores is a lot harder than I used to think it was."

Edna nodded but didn't say any more.

I told her about Mervin and Martin staying at the Millers' to get the order done.

"That's what their Dat told me," she said. "But he said they'll be home by tomorrow and can do the chores here after that."

I nodded. I knew that's what Bob hoped for.

"I'm worried about Love when I leave though," Edna said.

"Maybe she'd stay over at the Mosiers'."

"Oh, I doubt it," Edna said. "I'm not sure she'd even stay here with everyone gone."

"I'm sure Martin and Mervin will figure something out," I said.

Love began to bark again, but not out of alarm. It was her welcoming tone—the one she used when she recognized the visitor.

"Are you expecting anyone?" I took my last bite of crisp.

Edna shook her head as she stood.

I finished my tea and then took my dishes to the sink, rinsing them.

"Just leave them," Edna said. "I'll wash them after my supper. But don't forget the ice cream." She stepped to the freezer above the fridge and pulled out a small container. It would be gone in no time. Still, I was grateful.

I picked up the two pans of crisps, putting one on top of the other, and followed Edna to the door and then outside.

Our brother, Ivan, waved from his buggy. His wife, Nell, sat beside him.

"Oh, they're back." Edna waved back.

We walked toward them as Ivan tied his horse to the post and then scurried around the buggy to help his wife.

"Oh, Bea," Nell called out, holding onto Ivan's arm as they came around the back of the buggy. "I'm so glad you're here." The two made the cutest couple. Both were a little plump with gray around the edges of their hair. And both were very happy, joking and laughing much of the time.

As we met, Nell reached out and touched my forearm as I held the crisps out in front of me, not wanting to bump against the sticky edges.

"I talked with Laurel this afternoon," Nell said. "She told me you're having a wonderful time at the Millers'."

"Jah," I said, wondering exactly what her sister had said. Anything she knew would have come from Hannah—and who knew how reliable that would be. "Taking care of the babies and helping Nan is a challenge, but I'm enjoying it." In that moment, away from my duties, I realized it was true. In fact, it was the most rewarding work I'd ever done.

Nell's eyes sparkled. "She didn't say anything about your work, but she did mention the Youngie."

"That's true," I said. "I've become friends with Nan's niece Hope."

Nell laughed. "She actually didn't say anything about Hope either. But she did mention that we should expect you to be courting soon."

My face grew warm. "Oh, goodness." I struggled to sound calm. "I don't know about that. But I do know I need to get back and help Nan. It's good to see all of you." I hurried on to the buggy and positioned the crisps in the back, wedging grocery bags around them. Then I took the ice cream from Edna and managed to make room in the cooler for it too.

125

Ivan, Nell, and Edna all gathered around me. After telling them good-bye, I climbed into the buggy and turned it toward the lane. The three waved as I hurried on my way.

I wondered whom Laurel had said I'd soon be courting—Don? My stomach lurched. Or Ben? "Ugh, ugh, ugh," I said out loud.

I'd have to ask Hannah if I wanted to know for sure.

Love looked forlorn as I left, but before I reached the highway, she was tearing through the field, barking at a crow.

C H A P T E R

9

By the time I reached the Millers', the sun had grown heavy against the hill, casting a golden hue through a bank of thin clouds along the horizon.

I stopped Thunder by the house to unload before I went to the barn. The back door opened, and Mervin and Martin hurried out, scurrying around to the back of the buggy, followed by Don and Phillip. By the time I'd jumped down they had everything in their arms and were headed to the house.

"Denki," I called out.

The others kept going, but Don turned around. "I appreciate it," I added.

He smiled. "You're welcome." He started on toward the back door but then turned again. "Go on into the house. I'll unhitch Thunder."

I thanked him again as he went back into the house.

I stopped next to Thunder, and he nuzzled my hand. "You'll have to ask Don for a treat," I said. "Sorry."

As I headed toward the house, Don bounded out, a carrot in his hand. He grinned. I smiled back. Our eyes met for an awkward moment until I glanced away. He wasn't a bad sort, not at all. But that didn't mean I wanted to court him—or anyone else.

127

"See you in a bit," he said.

I nodded. "Denki for thinking of Thunder."

He waved the carrot above his head as he passed by.

I braced myself for chaos as I entered the house. Instead I found the meatballs simmering in a tomato sauce on the stove and the potatoes boiling on the back burner.

"Who made the crisp?" Mervin asked, standing next to the two pans on the table.

"Edna," I said. Then I asked if they'd be able to take care of the chores at our house for the next week.

"Of course," Mervin said. "We'll finish the order up tonight and be back at our place by tomorrow."

A strange sense of sadness overcame me. Cooking for the boys definitely added to the workload, but it hadn't been all bad to have them around. I'd started to enjoy the community that had been a part of Molly's life for years.

I noticed a plate, empty except for a few cookie crumbs, on the table.

Phillip reached for it, but I snatched it up first. "I've got it," I said.

"We were just having a snack," Phillip said.

"Jah," I said. "That's *gut*." They must have found the stash in the cupboard.

"Except for Ben," Mervin added. "And Pete. They're busy in the shop. We need to get back too."

Martin said to send someone down when it was time for supper. I assured him I would. "Maybe Hope," I teased as he hurried out the door.

However, when it was time to call everyone to supper, Hope was upstairs giving Asher his bottle, so I headed down to the shop. Don, Bob, and Pete were on their way up to the house.

Don stopped to talk with me, drawing a concerned expression from Bob. But I smiled kindly at Don, and Bob kept on going.

"Ach, Bea, I—"

"Beatrice," I said.

He shook his head in confusion.

"Only my family calls me Bea," I explained. And close friends, but I didn't add that.

"Oh . . ." He touched the brim of his hat but didn't continue with whatever it was he wanted to tell me.

"What is it?" I was growing impatient. I still had a long evening of work ahead of me.

He took a deep breath and then said, "I just wanted you to know how much it meant to me for you to acknowledge me earlier."

Confused, I asked, "Oh?"

He blushed a little, which surprised me. "When our eyes met, when I was coming out of the house."

I nodded, realizing he was talking about that awkward moment earlier.

"You don't know how much that means to be acknowledged. Especially for someone like me, who's gone through so much."

"Oh," I said again, nodding empathetically. He had been through a lot. "Jah," I said. "I've heard about some of your troubles. I'm truly sorry."

"Denki," he said, stepping toward me.

It was my turn to blush. I had no idea what to say to him. I had no experience with men. My brief courtship with Ben was nothing, really. Awkwardly, I pointed toward the shop. "I need to go tell the others about supper."

He nodded. "Perhaps we'll have a chance to chat sometime." He touched the brim of his hat again. "To get to know each other better. I'd like that."

129

"Sure . . ." I took a step toward the shop, wondering exactly how I'd looked at him earlier—and what it had meant to him. "See you at supper."

"Beatrice . . ."

I hurried on as if I hadn't heard. By the time I reached the door, Martin, Mervin, and Phillip were coming out, giggling. When they saw me they all three stopped and then burst out into laughter.

"What?"

"Oh, nothing." Martin held the door for me.

"Just a private joke, between the three of us," Phillip added.

"Jah." Mervin sputtered. "Although—"

Martin threw an elbow into his twin's side. "What do you need?"

"Nothing," I answered, ready to return to the house, not wanting to deal with men, giddy boys, or the opposite gender at all. Although I didn't feel awkward with the twins and Phillip. Just miffed. "They sent me to call you to supper. But it looks like I don't need to."

But Martin pointed toward the door. "Ben."

"What about him?" I answered.

"He needs to be called to supper."

I rolled my eyes. "One of you"—I pointed at Martin—"is quite capable of calling Ben."

Martin stepped wider. Mervin and Phillip started toward the house, nearly running.

"I'm not sure where he is," Martin said. "But I need to go wash up." He took off running too.

"Oh, bother," I said, stepping into the hallway. "Ben! Supper!" I called out as I headed down the hall. "Ben!"

I pushed through the door of the shop, expecting him to be

using a piece of machinery and unable to hear me. But the shop was dark and silent. Only the scent of sawdust and varnish greeted me.

I heard a rustling in the back of the room. "Ben?"

A head popped up from behind a worktable. Then an entire body. "Bea, is that you?"

I squinted into the dim room. His face had a look of anticipation—and shock. As if he'd just received really good news.

"Supper's ready," I said.

"Denki for going to the trouble to let me know." He smiled.

"It was no trouble," I answered, even though it was.

"So you were happy to do it?" He stepped out from behind the table toward me.

"Happy?" I stepped toward the door. "Indifferent, perhaps." I turned and pushed open the door, calling over my shoulder. "If you don't want to eat, that's fine. If you do, I'll see you at the house."

I marched down the hall. But by the time I reached the exit, Ben was behind me.

He stepped to my side. "Let me open the door for you."

"I'm perfectly capable," I said.

"And I'm perfectly able," he answered, swinging it open.

I marched on with him at my heels and then at my side. I gave him a sideways glance. He smiled at me. What was going on? First Don. And now Ben.

I marched faster, keeping my eyes on the house. For a moment, a crowd of faces filled the kitchen window, but then they all disappeared.

"Denki again for coming to get me," Ben said as we reached the door, hustling ahead of me to open it.

I hurried in, trying to gain distance on him. The only thing worse than a smarty-pants Ben was an attentive one. But why the sudden change? Was he mocking me—again?

An hour later, after everyone was fed, it was time to feed Kurt and Leah. I headed upstairs with the bottles to help Nan while Hope and Cate started on the dishes, but when I arrived, Nan asked me to get a bottle for Asher too. "I nursed him," she said, putting the little one on the bed beside her, "but he's still hungry."

I handed Nan the two bottles and then retrieved the other two babies from their bassinets and handed them to her too.

"I'll be right back." I hurried along the landing and then clomped down the stairs. As I rounded the corner into the kitchen, Hope said, rather loudly, "Jah, Martin says Ben's crazy about her."

I froze. Who was Ben crazy about?

"Pete seems to think the same," Cate said.

I took a step backward, around the refrigerator.

Hope said, "Jah . . ." again, drawing it out.

Flattening up against the wall, I held my breath.

Cate's voice grew louder. "Did they want you to tell Bea?"

Me? My hand flew to my chest. Ben was crazy about me?

There was another pause. Then Hope said, "Jah . . . they wanted me to, but I convinced them it was a bad idea."

"Why?" I whispered and then clamped my hand over my mouth. Had they heard me?

Hope continued, "I don't want Ben to be hurt any worse than he already is. She'll never love anyone—she's said so herself. Least of all Ben Rupp."

My hand fell to my side. *What?* I mouthed.

Hope continued, "It's a pity. She's so critical . . . and overbearing. And he's so sweet. Ben could never please her. I'll tell him not to bother."

My face began to burn. I dreaded Cate's answer.

One of them opened a cupboard door and there was clanking of one dish against another. "Well," Cate finally said, "she could change. Perhaps she hasn't found her true self yet. I know I was far past her age before I learned enough about myself to be able to love Pete."

I took a raggedy breath, grateful for Cate's belief in me.

"Personally," Hope said, "I think Don's a better match for her."

I shook my head.

"Oh, I don't know about that," Cate said. "I think being a childhood friend gives Ben the advantage."

Hope giggled. "Jah, I guess I can see that. He truly knows what he's getting into—and I mean that as a compliment to Bea. I doubt Don could ever appreciate who she truly is."

When neither said anything more, I tiptoed back to the stairs and up a few steps. I didn't blame Hope for her words. She was just being honest.

I bounded back down the last few stairs, trying to be as loud as possible, and then rushed down the hall, saying, "Asher needs a bottle," as I entered the kitchen, proclaiming it as if I'd just arrived, hoping to interrupt them if the conversation had continued.

"Oh." Hope had a look of panic on her face.

Cate pulled a bottle from the pan. "Here you go. It's just been warmed."

I took it from her and said, "Denki," as kindly as I could. "I'll be back down to finish cleaning up as soon as the babies are fed."

"We're fine down here," Cate said. "Take your time."

I wondered if Cate and Hope felt I'd been critical of them too. My face warmed at the thought. I hoped not.

When I reached Nan's room, I found her dozing but still holding the bottles in Leah and Kurt's mouths. Both of them had also fallen asleep. I took the bottles out and put them on the bureau. Then I lifted Asher, who was fussing, from his bassinet and changed his diaper and put a clean sleeper on him. After I washed my hands, I took him to the nursery so he wouldn't wake up his siblings and settled down in the rocking chair. I cooed at him as I did, saying in a singsong voice, "It's all right. Here's your bottle." A week ago I would have been mortified at talking in such a babyish way, but as Asher latched on to the nipple and relaxed against me I realized baby talk served a purpose.

I continued. "Asher, do you find me critical and overbearing?" Cate and Hope hadn't actually said Ben thought that—but I could only surmise he did. And yet he saw through me and thought I had some sort of quality that made him crazy about me.

"No," I said to Asher. "I don't think it's true." Perhaps some-one—named Ben—had a trick up his sleeve, determined to hu-miliate me one more time.

The lamp cast a shadow over Asher's face, but still the baby's inky eyes met mine.

"I don't think he would ever love me," I clarified, rocking harder. "I do think he finds me critical and overbearing." I sighed. "Do you think people can change?" I asked the baby. "Like Cate said?"

He hiccupped but then kept on sucking. A moment later he closed his eyes.

I turned my head to watch the shadow against the wall. The

flame of the lamp sputtered and the shadow leapt. A sense of *Shohm*—shame—overtook me. I hadn't meant to be *that* critical. It started small, over those spelling bees, and grew through the years. I suppose Molly was right. The bickering was annoying.

I didn't truly feel critical of Ben until he jilted me. True, it wasn't as if we'd grown serious even though half the district thought we would eventually marry. But couldn't he have at least communicated something to me?

Oh, God, I prayed. *Was Molly right all along? Am I a horrible person? Was that why Ben had rejected me?* Tears stung my eyes. Asher drained the last of the bottle and pulled his head away, arching his back and then relaxing again. I shifted him to my shoulder to burp him. Here I'd been so proud of what a good girl I was. Not going to parties. Not gossiping. Not ignoring my family to spend time with others.

But I'd been petty and meanspirited. That wasn't how Christ had wanted me to live.

"I'm sorry," I whispered.

Asher stirred and then wiggled closer to me.

I knew that I was sinful. It was part of our theology, taught to us our entire lives. Had I forgotten? Here I'd tried to convince myself that I wasn't prideful, but I had been. I'd been hurt by Ben and I'd lashed out at him. *Hohchmoot*. Pride. It was to be avoided at all cost.

I had failed.

Tears blurred my vision.

"Forgive me," I prayed and then inhaled deeply, holding my breath and then releasing it slowly. Asher stirred again.

A peace settled over me. The baby wasn't mine, but I had come to love him. I was God's, I knew I was, and he loved me even more.

I rocked Asher for a few more minutes until I heard Leah whimpering—funny how I knew each of their cries from the first little sound now. I stood and placed Asher in his bassinet. Then I hurried into Nan's room and scooped Leah up from the bed along with her bottle, putting her in the nursery. I'd finish feeding her in a minute. I returned for Kurt, not wanting him to wake Nan.

But she was awake and rolled toward me. "Where's Bob?"

"Still out in the shop," I said. "Go back to sleep. The babies and I are doing just fine."

It was true. We were. And it wasn't because the Bopplis had changed. It was because I had changed. God was working in me. My eyes misted over. Perhaps he could change me in other ways too.

After I finished, I headed back downstairs. The lamp had been turned down to its low setting, and there was no sign of Cate or Hope.

My guess was Cate had gone to bed and Hope had sneaked outside, hoping to catch a few minutes with Martin. I sighed, deciding to go to bed myself and get a head start on a night's sleep that would soon be interrupted.

I'd started toward the hallway when a bark stopped me. The Millers didn't have a dog. Thinking it was a neighbor's, I kept going. The dog barked again, but in a welcoming tone.

Curious, I headed to the kitchen door, hoping to catch a glimpse of it. It took a moment for my eyes to adjust to the darkness as I stepped down to the walkway. But then the dog barked a third time, over by the picnic table. Ben was there too, stooped over. A yellow tail wagged, hitting Ben's leg.

I made my way toward the pair. "Is that Love?"

It was. At the sound of my voice she turned toward me. "What are you doing here, girl?"

She barked again and waved her tail frantically. Ben let her go, and she bolted toward me.

I bent down and hugged her neck. "Did you come all this way in the dark?" Through the fields and not along the highway, I hoped. "Edna will be worried." I looked up at Ben, trying my best not to be critical of the dog, or him, or anything at all.

He smiled, kindly. "Edna might not realize Love's gone until morning."

That was true.

"Mervin and Martin can take her back tomorrow. You can leave a message for Edna. Cate won't mind if you use the phone."

That was a good idea. "Come on, girl," I said to Love and headed toward the office. Ben started walking too, catching up with me. "I'll keep you company."

He had a funny expression on his face—not his usual sarcastic look. Could what Cate and Hope said possibly be true? Love drifted away from me—and closer to Ben.

I couldn't help but smile. "How's the order going?" I asked.

"We're done with our part. Bob and Pete are finishing up the paperwork."

"Great," I said.

"Jah. We could all go home tonight, but it's a long ways . . ."

It was for Ben. Not so far for Mervin and Martin. And not far at all for Phillip. He could easily walk home—Don did it every day. But they would all leave soon enough.

As we approached the shop building, Pete stepped out. I explained that I wanted to use the phone to let Edna know about Love and then asked if it would be okay if Love stayed until the twins could get her home the next day.

Pete assured me that was fine and said there was a water dish in the barn I could use for her and a bag of food. "It belonged to our last dog," Pete said. "Things have been too chaotic to get a new one just yet." Then Pete asked about Cate.

"She must have gone to bed," I answered.

He tipped his hat at me and hurried toward the house.

Ben held his arm wide for me to go through the door first. Love stayed outside. Down the hall, in Bob's office, a light was on. I stepped into Cate's office, sat in her chair, and quickly dialed while Ben leaned against the edge of the desk, staring at me.

I swiveled away from him a little, my face growing warm. Finally Molly's voice came on the machine, and I left the message for Edna. I doubted she would check, but if she noticed Love was missing, she might phone to see if the dog had turned up at a neighbors' before she started searching.

When I hung up the phone, Ben said he'd walk me to the barn.

"Denki," I said. "That's very kind. But only if you're sure."

"It's no trouble." He grinned. "Honestly."

My heart pounded as we walked along. Afraid if I said anything it might be critical—habits were hard to break—I decided not to say anything at all.

As we neared the barn, there was a rustling from the side— then a giggle. I hoped it wasn't Hope with Martin. Surely she knew better. But who else would it be?

Whoever was there started walking away from us, farther around the barn.

Ben quickened his step, and I followed his lead. When we reached the barn, he opened the door, holding it wide. "You stay here," he said. "I'll find what you need."

Love seemed torn between following Ben and remaining with me, but when Ben told her to stay, she did. I peered into the cavernous barn after Ben entered. It was so dark I didn't see how he could possibly see a thing.

A moment later he yelped, "Ouch!"

"You okay?" I called out.

"Jah—it was only an encounter with a rake."

I heard another rustling and thought it must be whoever had hurried behind the barn. Love stepped closer to me. But then someone, who was whistling, came from the other side of the barn, from the direction of the Dawdi Haus.

"Bea?" It was Don, approaching quickly.

"Beatrice," I corrected.

"Sorry," he sheepishly said. "Whose dog?"

"Mine."

He reached down to pet her, but she darted around me to the other side, pressing herself against my leg. It wasn't like her to be unfriendly.

"Ach," he said, "she's shy."

"Not usually," I answered.

"Would you—and your dog—like to go for a walk?" Don asked.

"Not tonight," I answered.

Before I could give my excuse, Ben yelled again and then added quickly, "I'm fine. I just made contact with an aerator."

Don crossed his arms. "What's he doing in there?"

"Looking for dog stuff—Love is spending the night."

Don shook his head, pulled a flashlight from his pocket, and headed into the barn. "Look on the right side, by the bench," he called out to Ben.

A few minutes later they both reappeared, Ben carrying the bag of dog food and the chain while Don carried two stainless-steel dishes. He reached out for the bag.

Ben didn't give it to him, saying, "Pardon?"

"I'll help Bea—"

"Beatrice," I said.

"—get the dog situated." Don turned away from me toward Ben. "Go along. Do whatever you were doing." Don thrust his shoulders back. "Wait. Isn't it past your bedtime?"

Ben ignored the last comment and said, "What I was doing—am doing—is helping Bea."

"Beatrice," Don corrected.

I shook my head, so only Ben could see. Then I smiled at him, bouncing to the balls of my feet. I wasn't a bouncy person, until tonight.

He grinned and then turned his attention back to Don, squaring his shoulders.

"There's no need for you to help now," Don said. "I'm here."

"Love knows Ben," I said. "We're doing just fine."

Don turned around, waving the flashlight behind me, casting an eerie light, and said quietly, "He's just a boy."

Pretending I didn't hear what he'd said, I blurted out, "Thank you for your help." I reached for the dog dishes, taking one in each hand.

"Suit yourself." He turned away abruptly and headed toward the sycamore grove.

Ben and I stood, frozen, until the beam of the flashlight had totally disappeared. Again there was a rustling along the other side of the barn. Perhaps a cat.

Once Don had completely disappeared, I said, "That was awkward." Don had seemed so pleasant before, but there was something unsettling about him tonight. "I wonder what he's doing, out by himself in the dark."

"He's not so bad." Ben started toward the house. "He means well."

I aimed to be pleasant—not argumentative—with Ben, so I didn't question his statement. Instead, as I walked beside him, I asked, "Do you think that people can change?"

"Jah," he said. "Of course. Isn't that what life is all about?"

I pondered that as we reached the oak tree. We all stopped and Love inched toward me, her tail thumping against my leg again. Ben put down the bag of food and took the bowls from me, putting one on the ground. He headed over to the spigot with the other. I expected Love to go with him but she didn't.

I filled the dish with food and then Ben returned with the other, putting it beside the first.

Love drained the water dish.

I rubbed her head. "You're so thirsty. You shouldn't take off like that."

"She must have really been missing you." Ben reached down to pet the dog, our hands touching as he did. I almost jerked my hand away out of habit but caught myself. We both stopped petting the dog, our hands side by side.

"I feel bad," I said. "There's enough going on around here without adding a dog to the mix."

Ben chuckled and grinned.

My heart melted at his schoolboy look. "What?"

He shook his head. "Why did you ask me if people can change?"

I shrugged. "I've just been thinking about that . . . lately." I looked up at him. Under the dim light from the stars I couldn't make out the expression on his face.

"I'm going home tomorrow," he said.

"After breakfast?"

"Jah." He stepped away from the dog. "I know you're not fond of singings, but I was wondering if you'd like to go with me tomorrow evening. It's at the Funks' farm. They've made a corn maze."

I inhaled deeply, fussing with the ties of my Kapp.

He smiled. "Only if you'd like to. . . ."

I exhaled. "I would. I'd like that a lot."

"*Gut.*" He wrapped the chain around the tree. Once he had it secured, he clipped it to Love's collar. When he stood, he said, "You'd better go on inside."

I nodded.

I expected Love to whine as I walked away, but she hardly noticed because Ben stayed at her side. He was still with her when I glanced out the landing window. When I reached our room, I was surprised to see Hope sitting on her bed in her nightgown, brushing her blond hair.

"I thought you were"—I pointed toward the barn—"out with Martin."

"I was. We were talking. I just came in." She grinned. "I saw you and Ben headed toward the barn."

"With Love," I answered.

Her eyebrows shot up.

"She's my dog," I explained. "Her name is Love."

Hope smiled. "That's so sweet."

"My Dat named her that because he wanted the mockingbirds to repeat her name." It sounded corny.

"Did it work?"

"Jah," I said. "It did. And they still do." I couldn't explain how nice it was to have the mockingbirds calling out "Love!" It was a gift from Dat.

"So . . ." Hope put her brush on the bedside table. "Are you and Ben getting along better?"

I couldn't help but think about what she'd said, that she planned to warn him. Obviously she hadn't yet.

"Maybe," I answered, trying my best to be pleasant.

Hope slipped beneath her quilt.

I quickly changed the subject. "How's Martin?"

"*Gut*," she said dreamily, looking across the room at me with her blue eyes. "I can't wait for the singing tomorrow night. There's going to be a maze."

I nodded. "So I heard."

"And a hayride," she said. "And a couple of uninterrupted hours with Martin."

I pulled my nightgown from the top drawer, glancing back at Hope. She was on her back, one arm above her head. I stepped closer. Her eyes were already closed.

I shook my head. She fell asleep faster and slept more soundly than anyone I'd ever known.

That left me thinking about Ben and all the time I'd known him. During our school years, he was who I looked forward to seeing every day, although I'd never admitted it to him or anyone else. I'd barely admitted it to myself. Every morning, as soon as I arrived, I'd locate him. Usually he was chopping wood or feeding the fire. At recess, he was always the one organizing a game. Everyone wanted to be on his team, including me, although I never made it obvious.

During class, he was the first to raise his hand to answer a question—unless I beat him to it. I pretended he annoyed me—and more often than not, he did—but secretly I loved every minute of it. I didn't have a best friend that was a girl. But it didn't matter. Ben was my best friend.

I was heartbroken when eighth grade ended. I wished so badly our days as scholars could continue. We both loved learning.

We both loved, I was sure, the camaraderie. Even though the other girls flirted with Ben, which I'd never dream of doing, it was my approval he sought. That was obvious, even to an awkward girl like me.

I'd missed Ben over the years and in response had guarded my heart more and more. Then after his brief attempt at courting ended, I'd been hurt. Badly.

Could I let my guard down again? By the way I felt tonight, I thought I could.

As I turned over onto my side, ready to sleep, my mind landed on the memory of Ben choosing me for his kickball team. His quick grin. The flash of his dimple. The momentary feeling of belonging that washed over me.

That was what I longed for again.

CHAPTER
10

That night was our worst yet with the babies. I'd only been asleep an hour when Nan woke me.

"Sorry," she said. "Bob's still working."

I slipped out of bed and into my robe, registering the cacophony of crying babies as I did. Hope didn't stir. I decided not to wake her. If we needed her too, I'd come back.

When I reached the bedroom, Nan already sat in the rocking chair with Leah and Asher. I picked up Kurt from his bassinet, putting him to my shoulder and patting his back. "How long have they been awake?" I asked Nan.

"Asher for a half hour. I fed him, but he won't stop crying." She nodded toward Kurt. "He's probably hungry too."

"I'll go fix a bottle," I said. "Should I make one for Leah too?"

"Jah," Nan said. "I fed her some, but I don't think she got much."

Ten minutes later I was back in Nan's room, ready to wake Hope to help us, when I heard Bob come up the stairs in his stocking feet.

When he entered, he took Asher from Nan and walked the baby back and forth across the landing. For the rest of the night, we took turns with the babies. Halfway through, I recruited

Hope to give me a break for a couple hours, but by early morning we were both back in the nursery. That was when I noticed, as I changed Asher's diaper, that he kept pulling his legs up toward his belly.

"They have colic," Nan said from the rocking chair. She yawned. Bob was asleep in the guest room.

At five thirty, Cate came in, ready to relieve one of us.

"You go back to bed," I said to Hope as I walked Asher around the room. He stayed settled, until I put him down. Hope accepted my offer without any protest.

By six all three babies were asleep.

"Go back to bed," Cate said to me.

I slipped Asher back into the bassinet. "What about breakfast for the boys?"

"They can figure it out," Cate said. "Maybe Pete will make pancakes."

"As long as you don't do it," I said.

"I might help," she said. "But I promise not to overdo it."

When I woke, sunshine filled the room and Hope was gone from her bed. I turned toward the clock on the tabletop. Nine a.m. I bolted out of bed, expecting to hear babies screaming. But all was quiet.

I showered, dressed, and tiptoed down the landing to the stairs.

Bob sat at the kitchen table, both hands wrapped around a coffee mug.

"*Guder Mariye*," I said.

He looked up at me, dazed.

"How are the babies doing?" I asked as I poured myself a cup of coffee.

"All right," he said. "They've been asleep for a long stretch now. Nan's asleep too."

I sat down across from him. "Where is everyone else?"

"Church," he said. "Hope rode with Cate and Pete."

"Oh." I was sorry to have missed Ben. That made me think of Love. I hurried to the window. The chain was still around the tree, but she was gone. Mervin and Martin must have taken her home.

"There are leftover pancakes on the stove," Bob said.

"Denki." I wasn't hungry. My eyes fell to the sink. The breakfast dishes had been done but not the bottles. I filled the stockpot with water to sterilize them and lit the burner.

"Not that I've ever experienced war," Bob said, "but having three babies feels a little like I expect combat would—in a supportive role, not a fighting one, mind you. But still . . ."

I understood what he meant. Mamm had told me taking care of a baby was the most important work one would ever do—I just hadn't expected it to be the hardest.

"Denki," Bob said to me. "For all your help. I don't know what we'd do without it."

"You'd have someone else here," I said, turning to look at him. "But I'm honored to help. Your babies will be special to me my entire life."

I couldn't tell for sure, but I thought Bob's eyes grew a little misty—until we both heard the wail at the same time.

"Asher," we said in unison.

"Ach," he said. "I'd better get up there. Poor Nan. She must feel as if she's been turned inside out by now."

The day progressed pretty much the way the night had—with fussy, fussy babies. Bob, Nan, and I had sandwiches for our noon meal, grateful that Cate, Pete, and Hope would eat after church. Although I'd miss having the boys around all the time, it was a relief not to have to figure out supper for everyone. There was soup in the freezer from earlier in the week. I took it out to thaw.

I was sterilizing bottles in the kitchen again when Hope, Cate, and Pete returned. I thought Pete and Cate had gone on up the stairs, when I whispered to Hope, "Don't get your hopes up about the singing tonight. Things have stayed chaotic around here."

Cate was still in the hall and somehow overheard. She hurried back into the kitchen. "No, you two are definitely going. I'm going to get a nap now. I'll be able to help with the babies." She looked exhausted. And bigger even than she had yesterday.

"Let's wait and see how things are going when it's time to leave," I answered.

Hope pursed her lips together. I nudged her with my elbow. "Jah," she said. "We'll stay if needed."

Cate had already returned to the hallway though, and a moment later we heard her trudge up the stairs.

Hope gave me an exasperated look.

"What?" I stuffed my hands in my apron pockets.

"You don't need to go out of your way to ensure we don't go to the singing," she answered.

"Helping with the babies is our primary responsibility."

"Jah," she answered. "But we should be allowed some time off—a chance to have a little fun."

I returned to the bottles without answering, realizing that Hope and I had switched roles. She'd started out the more experienced one—but I'd ended up taking more responsibility. Perhaps because Hope was so distracted by Martin. Or perhaps I was finding a role I finally excelled at.

When Hope and I went upstairs ten minutes later, Leah and Nan were asleep in the bedroom and Bob held both Asher and Kurt in the nursery, sitting in the rocking chair staring at them. The boys were awake and not crying, both gazing into their Dat's eyes.

"We'll take them outside," I said. "For fresh air. You try to sleep."

"Denki," Bob said. He yawned as he stood and surrendered the babies to us.

We put caps on the babies' heads and swaddled them tightly, but when we stepped outside I realized they'd be more than warm enough. The temperature had to be in the seventies.

"It's going to be such a nice evening." Hope walked beside me on the path, cradling Kurt.

I headed toward the apple trees. "Jah," I said, lifting Asher to my shoulder so he could see better. I wondered if Mamm, Molly, and Leon had as nice of weather in Montana. Or perhaps it was snowing there by now.

We stopped at the edge of the apple trees. "We need to pick the rest of these," I said. "We could do that in the morning. And make applesauce and apple butter."

"Jah," Hope said. "In our spare time."

"Well, let's see what we can do. It would be a shame for the fruit to go to waste." We started walking again, around the barn and toward the sycamore grove. Both babies seemed to enjoy being outside. I knew they couldn't focus on a lot, but the fresh air, sounds, and shapes seemed to distract them from crying.

"I hope we can go tonight," Hope said.

I exhaled. She had a one-track mind.

"I told Martin I'd be there," she added.

"It seems as if things are pretty serious between the two of you," I said.

She blushed, right up to her blond hairline, and her blue eyes grew even brighter.

"So," I said, trying to keep my voice light, "are you sure you two weren't out by the barn last night?"

Her face grew even redder. "I told you we were just talking."

"Oh, come on, Hope, you can tell me. I'm not going to judge you. I know you and Martin are crazy about each other."

She giggled and I let it go.

We skirted around the sycamore grove and then down between the shop and the property line. When we reached the silver maple, we cut back around to the house. The babies were so content that we lapped around two more times and then sat on the porch as the babies dozed. We'd been outside for a good hour before Asher started to fuss.

"He's probably hungry," I said. I rubbed my face against his. "You must be starving," I cooed. It had been at least two hours since he'd eaten, practically a record.

He let out a wail.

As we neared the back door, Hope turned toward the driveway. Even over Asher's cries she'd heard the buggy headed toward us.

Martin, Mervin, and Hannah were inside. I craned my neck, hoping Ben was with them, but he wasn't. Why hadn't I asked him what his plan was for the evening? Better yet, why hadn't he told me? Was he coming to get me—or was I supposed to meet him there?

I insisted to Cate and Nan, who both seemed rested for the first time all week, that I didn't need to go to the singing. Perhaps Ben had changed his mind about me. Perhaps he'd done exactly what he'd done before—led me along only to dump me. Maybe it was all part of a plot to get back at me. To hurt me. Again.

Hope and Cate had it all wrong. Or maybe Mervin and Martin had made it all up as a big joke.

The truth was, I didn't want to go to the singing. I didn't want to set myself up to be hurt and humiliated again, but I could hardly explain all that to Nan and Cate.

Hope assumed I was riding with them. So did Martin, Mervin, and Hannah. Rather than make a fuss, I decided to pretend that was what Ben and I had planned all along.

An hour later we headed to the singing. I did my best to be pleasant, even though I felt like the fifth wheel on a four-wheeled buggy. Ben or no Ben, I didn't want to be the critical young woman that I'd been. I really did, sincerely, want to change.

But as we turned off the highway, my anxiety increased. Ahead, Youngie gathered in front of a grove of pine trees. Off to the right was the Funks' white farmhouse and large barn, with a row of buggies parked to the side closest to the house. On the other side of the barn was the corn maze.

As we passed the grove, Martin spotted Phillip by the barn and called out a hello. I was surprised to see Don with him—he was much too old to come to a singing. Jessie Berg came around the corner of the barn with a group of girls and nearly collided with Phillip. She spoke to him kindly for a moment, not seeming embarrassed at all. I couldn't help but admire her poise, something I'd never possessed.

One of the girls with her grabbed her hand and pulled her along. She waved and smiled at Phillip as she allowed herself to be dragged away. Perhaps she didn't truly love him before. How else could she be so civil to him now?

Mervin parked the buggy at the end of the row. I sighed as I climbed down. "Ach?" Martin extended his hand to me a little too late.

"Ach, nothing," I answered.

"Ach, something," he countered.

"I just don't understand . . ." What? What didn't I understand? "Relationships," I managed to say.

He chuckled. "Welcome to the club," he answered, draping his arm over Hope's shoulder. "Aren't they wonderful?"

I swallowed, trying to get rid of the lump growing in my throat. Ben had asked me to the singing—and now he was nowhere in sight. I couldn't believe I'd fallen for his antics a second time.

"Come on." Hope grabbed my arm, pulling me along. "Let's go in the corn maze." Hannah and Mervin already led the way.

I complied. There was no reason for me to stick around and wait for Ben. Dusk began to fall as we scurried around the barn and entered the maze. I stuck close to Hope, asking, "Does anyone have a flashlight?"

"We'll be fine," Mervin said. "It won't take long to get through it."

"This might be harder than you think," I replied. "Does anyone have a cell phone? In case we don't find our way."

No one did. At least not in our group. I could only hope someone would come along with one if needed.

We strolled over straw spread across the dirt. The corn stalks towered far over our heads and rustled from the breeze—or maybe from small animals scurrying along the ground. The air was dry and growing colder.

Mervin and Hannah raced ahead, followed by Martin and Hope. That left me in the back, by myself. I must have taken a wrong turn. The others were too far ahead for me to see what route they'd chosen. I hit a dead end and headed back the way I'd come. Or so I thought. A minute later I was at another dead end. Panic began to overcome me. I headed to the left. Another dead end.

I took a deep breath and turned to the right. As I rounded the corner, I plowed into someone—a man.

Don, to be exact.

I staggered backward.

"There you are," he said, tugging on his beard.

I straightened my Kapp. "You were looking for me?"

He nodded, the shadow of his hat dark on his face. "Phillip said you came alone."

My face grew warm.

"So it's not like you and Ben are a couple?"

My face was burning now.

He crossed his arms. "Well?"

I shrugged, hoping to indicate I didn't know for sure. "Regardless of Ben," I said, "I'd be willing to walk out of here with you."

He smiled, a little. "Meaning?"

I smiled back, relieved to have a little levity. "Honestly?"

He nodded.

"I'm lost. Not that I couldn't find my way out—I'm sure I eventually would." I didn't want to admit I was beginning to panic.

"Come on," he said. "I figured it out once. I'm sure I can again."

Ahead, Hannah's laughter rang out, followed by Mervin's. Then Hope said, as if just realizing I was gone, "Where's Bea?"

"She was just behind us," Martin said.

A wave of relief washed over me. I wouldn't have to maneuver the maze alone with Don after all, but then he held his finger to his mouth. I shook my head. "I'm fine," I called out. "Wait." I started off in their direction.

Don pointed to the right. "This way."

I shook my head. "Let's go with them."

Reluctantly, Don agreed. When we reached the others, he led the way out of the maze. I trusted the others wouldn't read anything into the two of us arriving together, but both Hope and Martin gave me concerned looks.

Darkness fell completely as we exited the maze. Ahead a group of Youngie milled around. Several lanterns hung on stakes, illuminating the area. To the side was a wagon lined with hay bales, with a lantern hanging next to the driver.

Don grabbed my hand and said, "Let's go."

I pulled my hand away, searching the group, still hoping Ben had shown up. When I didn't see him, I followed Don. But just as Don helped me into the wagon, Ben appeared at the edge of the crowd.

The brim of his hat and the shadows of the lanterns kept me from seeing his face clearly. As I sat down on a bale, I waved to him—I wasn't exactly enthusiastic but, hopefully, I was inviting.

He waved back, but as Don plopped down Ben's face fell. That much I could see. Martin and Hope climbed up into the wagon and sat across from us. I craned my neck. A crowd of Youngie had encircled Ben, just as they used to during our school days. He jumped, making eye contact with me, but then he was back on his feet and the group grew larger, completely blocking my view of Ben.

Don inched toward me. I scooted away, ramming my thigh into a piece of straw that stuck out of the bale.

Hope wrinkled her nose, probably at the expression on my face, as Martin leaned forward and said, "Don, do you plan to stay in the area for a while?"

He inched even closer. "Jah. Of course. I have a good job. I'll soon be able to get a place of my own." He put his hand down on the bale, between us, brushing against my thigh. "And be ready for . . . other possibilities."

I inhaled sharply.

"Do you miss Ohio?" Hope asked.

He shook his head. "Too many bad memories."

Hope's expression turned sympathetic.

The wagon hit a rut, and we all lurched a little. I turned my attention to the driver. Someone's Dat—although I wasn't sure whose. He turned the draft horses onto the highway.

Martin and Hope kept Don talking about himself the entire time. About a half hour later, as the wagon turned back down the lane to the Funks' house, a buggy approached from that direction. I turned my head toward it.

Ben drove it, passing by us, without even a wave. I kept my eyes on the lane, not wanting to face the others. Hope reached across the wagon, put her hand on my leg, and then staggered across and squeezed onto the bale beside me.

"It'll all work out," she whispered. "Besides, if it doesn't, Don's not so bad. He could be your backup plan."

My eyes filled with tears. I hoped Don hadn't overheard her. I blinked, shaking my head, trying to ignore the sensation of my heart breaking inside my chest. It would take me a long time to get over Ben again.

I didn't speak the entire ride home. Martin drove with Hope up front beside him, while Mervin and Hannah sat in the very back. Hannah giggled every once in a while, and the two whispered back and forth, although I couldn't hear their words.

Hope and Martin didn't talk at all, probably in deference to my angst. I felt bad but wasn't sure what to do about it. I didn't want to be unkind, but I had no idea what to say that might make them feel better.

The lantern swung as we traveled, casting long shadows over the fields. October was nearly over. The seemingly endless Indian summer would come to an end. Mamm, Molly, and Leon would return. Eventually I would leave the Millers'.

And then what? I closed my eyes, dreading my future. What sort of life was I destined to? I'd been fooling myself to think I wanted to be single, especially after living with the Millers. The truth was, I wanted to have babies some day—not three at once—but maybe three altogether. More if that's how God blessed me.

Jah, it was difficult to admit, but I wanted a husband. I wanted a relationship like Nan and Bob had. It was obvious they loved each other because they served each other. Considered each other. Put the other first, even in impossible circumstances.

I wanted what Pete and Cate had too. Granted they weren't as stressed as Nan and Bob—weren't in crisis mode, yet. But Pete's concern was more endearing than any love poem, and the way Cate lit up when he walked in the room, even though they worked together, spoke volumes more than any story.

"Really, Bea," Hope said, shifting toward me, as if we were in the middle of a conversation. "Don's not so bad. He—"

Martin interrupted her. "Hope . . ." His voice trailed off.

"But I can tell how much Don cares for her by the way he looks at her," Hope said to Martin, quietly but not low enough so I couldn't hear her.

"Oh, don't worry about me," I said, sitting up straight, doing my best to inject some cheer into my voice. "I've been set on not marrying all my life. There's no reason to change that now."

Martin and Hope turned their heads toward each other. I imagined "a look," although I couldn't see their faces enough to have an idea of what exactly they were communicating. I turned my head toward the dark fields again.

I woke up as we pulled onto the lane to the Millers' house. I kept my eyes closed until we came to a stop and Hope asked, "Whose buggy is that?"

"I'm not sure," Martin replied. He set the brake and jumped down. I opened the door, determined to be in the house before Martin and Hope started their long good-bye, giving the buggy a glance but not a second thought. Perhaps Pete and Cate had gone out.

But then a voice stopped me. "Beatrice."

I turned around slowly, fully aware it was Ben.

"Oh, hello," I said.

"Could we talk?"

I tried to ignore Hope clapping her hands together from the buggy. Instead of acknowledging her, I nodded toward Ben.

He pointed toward the oak tree and then led the way. I followed, my head throbbing. When we reached the tree he stopped and turned toward me. I stepped around him, stumbling over the dog dish that I should have put away, and then grabbed the tree. I leaned against it, acutely aware of my sleep deprivation mixed with the tension of the evening.

"Did you go to the singing with Don?" he asked, looking down at his feet.

"No," I answered.

"But you were there with him."

"I got lost in the maze. He led us out."

"Oh." He looked up at me. "Why didn't you wait for me?"

"I had no idea if you were going to show up." I leaned into the tree even more, pressing my hands against the bark.

"But you knew I would."

157

"I didn't know if you planned to pick me up or meet me there. And then you did neither."

He took his hat off and ran his fingers through his hair, which was in need of a haircut again.

My heart ached as badly as my head. "You don't communicate very well, at least not with me. It's what you did last time."

"What?" He pulled his hat back onto his head. "I don't know what you're talking about."

I shook my head. I'd been so hurt by the way he'd treated me before—and he didn't even remember. Or else pretended not to, so he didn't have to talk about it. Don was right. He was still a boy.

I started toward the house.

He called out after me. "Bea—"

I spun back around. "My name is Beatrice."

He stepped backward.

I kept going.

"I'm sorry," he said.

I turned around again, this time slowly. Had I heard him right? I didn't remember him ever apologizing before.

"I got distracted today, working on a project. I lost track of time," he said. "Maybe we can talk more—not right now but sometime soon."

I nodded, not wanting to make a fool of myself now, in front of the twins and Hannah and Hope, who all still stood beside the buggy.

"See you tomorrow," I said to Ben.

The others drifted out of my path as I headed toward the back door.

I didn't bother to say good-night. My goal was to get in bed and pretend to be asleep before Hope came up. That could only happen, though, if Nan didn't need my help.

I practically ran through the kitchen and up the hall but then started to tiptoe up the stairs. There was no reason to, however. All three babies were screaming.

The nursery door was wide open, and inside Bob held the boys like two logs, one on top of the other, and walked back and forth while Pete held Leah.

"I'll be right back," I said and hurried into the bathroom to wash my hands. When I returned, Bob told me Nan was trying to sleep as I took Asher from him.

"And I sent Cate up to bed," Pete said. "She's exhausted."

"Oh, dear," I said. "Have they been crying all evening?"

"Most of it." Pete spoke over Leah.

"We hoped they wouldn't be colicky—to no avail," Bob said.

"Any ideas of what to do?" I held Asher tightly and began shuffling back and forth.

"Nan did some research, and she's going to try eliminating certain foods. Cabbage, in particular." I'd used that in the soup I'd made, the one Nan had eaten for supper. "And some other things," Bob answered. "She wonders if maybe they have allergies."

I hoped it wasn't the formula.

Bob added, "She's going to try drinking fennel tea, too, and see if that helps. She read that it's a good natural remedy."

We continued walking the babies for the next hour. Leah fell asleep first, and Pete slipped her into the bassinet. Next Asher fell asleep. "Go on," Bob said. "By the time Kurt settles down Leah will be ready to eat. I'll wake Nan then."

"Make sure and have her wake me when she needs me," I said.

Bob raised his eyebrows as he spoke. "Oh, she will."

As I stepped into our room, Hope said, "He really does care about you."

159

I hadn't realized she'd come up. "Don or Ben?" I asked, stalling.

She giggled. "Well, both, I suppose, but I was thinking about Ben."

"Well," I answered, sitting on the edge of my bed, "he has a funny way of showing it."

"Martin says Ben's been crazy about you for years."

I shook my head.

Hope leaned forward. "No, it's true. Ben said you were his best friend all through school. That he would have been bored without you. That you kept him in line."

I smiled, just a little.

"If he did something stupid, you let him know. He said he could always trust you."

I crossed my arms. "What about me being able to trust him?"

"Martin said Ben wants to make that up to you."

I wrinkled my nose.

Hope whispered, "So, will you give him another chance?"

Tears filled my eyes. I was exhausted. And distraught. "I can't talk about it tonight," I said. Again I was afraid of saying something I'd later regret.

CHAPTER

11

The next morning, as Hope washed clothes in the basement and I swept the kitchen floor, someone knocked on the back door. I stopped, pulling the broom close. Could it be Ben? I took a deep breath and walked to the door, swinging it wide.

Don stood on the stoop, holding his left index finger with a paper towel soaked in blood.

"Oh, dear," I said.

"It's not as bad as it looks," he said. "I don't need stitches. Just butterfly bandages. Cate said they're in the downstairs bathroom."

"Come in." I was the last person he wanted to help him with an injury. I started down the hall toward the bathroom, feeling queasy. Don followed, saying, "Cate already scrubbed it out before she realized she was out of that type of bandage."

I wished she'd come up with him.

He waited in the hall while I opened the medicine cabinet. I retrieved the box. "Go on back to the table," I said. I grabbed a clean washcloth, ran hot water over it, then wrung it out, and followed him down the hall.

I sat down next to Don so I could get a good look at his finger. As he unwrapped it, I handed him the washcloth. "What happened?"

"I was using the hand saw, and it slipped." He cleaned the blood off his finger.

"At least it wasn't the electric saw." He could have lost all of his fingers if it had been.

I unwrapped the first bandage. From the looks of the cut, I'd need several. I took a deep breath and secured the first one. "I'm afraid I'm not very good at this sort of thing," I said.

"You're doing great." He glanced up at me.

I quickly looked away and put three more bandages on, focusing on the cut.

"Denki," he said.

"I'll go get a piece of gauze to tape over all of it," I said. "Hold on."

When I returned, Don said he had a good time the evening before.

I concentrated on not wrinkling the gauze into a big mess.

He continued, "You seem more mature than the rest of them. An old soul. Especially more than the boys—because that's really what they are."

I had the gauze ready for his finger, and he lifted it toward me. "Hold it," I said.

He obeyed. "You must get tired of their antics."

"Oh, I don't know about that," I answered, cutting the tape with the scissors I'd found in the cabinet too. Of course I did! But I didn't want to discuss it with him.

"Well," he said, "I'd like to go out again."

I tilted my head. *Oh!* I stood. Did he think we'd gone on a date? "Oh," I stammered, "I don't go out much. I never have."

He smiled.

I shook my head and turned my attention to cleaning up. My face grew warmer and warmer.

Don said, "I'll go ahead and get back to the shop. . . ."

I nodded without looking up.

As the screen door banged, I realized I should have sent the box of butterfly bandages with him. There was a second box in the bathroom. I grabbed it and headed out the door. He was halfway to the shop. "Don!" I called out, waving the box.

He turned, stopped, and then started toward me. I kept moving forward.

Ahead the door to the shop building opened and Ben stepped out just as Don and I met, blocking my view.

"Give this to Cate," I said to Don.

"Denki," he replied, rather loudly.

The door closed. I started back toward the house, glancing over my shoulder as I did. Ben was nowhere in sight. He must have gone back into the shop. My face grew even warmer as I guessed what my encounter with Don must have looked like.

Ben and I weren't meant to be together, not as a couple, I was sure.

The rest of the morning, Hope and I did the wash and cleaned, while the babies slept and slept. I was relieved that she didn't ask me anything more about my feelings for Ben—or Don.

After dinner, we helped Nan feed the triplets their bottles, and then they immediately settled down again. Nan was going to take a nap too, saying she was afraid the babies were getting their days and nights turned around.

As we pinned the last load of laundry on the line, I suggested to Hope that we gather up the apples. The morning had been chilly but sunny, and the afternoon was beautiful and warm.

We left the laundry basket under the line and headed toward

the orchard. "Let's check the barn for baskets," I said, veering to the left. "We won't be able to carry much in our aprons."

I pushed open the door of the barn, and a swallow flew out, startling both of us. Hope screamed and my hand flew to my chest. Then we both laughed. A calico cat bounded down from the stack of hay, but when she realized we weren't there to feed her, she disappeared again. Once our eyes adjusted we spotted a stack of baskets along the far wall on a shelf, probably near where Ben and Don had found the dog food and dishes.

Breathing in the scent of hay and leather from the stables at the end of the barn, I grabbed four baskets and met Hope back at the door. We started at the end of the orchard closest to the barn. It was a small orchard, with only six trees—but that was still a lot of apples.

We'd make what we could into applesauce and apple butter and then store the rest in the basement, along with the apples Pete had already picked and the potatoes, onions, and turnips he'd harvested. I had quite a few recipes I could make using apples too. Crisps, of course. Pies if I had the time. I had a pork loin recipe that called for apples, along with one with sausage. I'd peruse Nan's recipe books and see if I could find more too.

As Hope began gathering up the good apples on the ground, I said, "We're going to need a ladder." I hadn't really thought things through. "I'll go get it," I said. I hadn't seen any in the barn, but I'd probably just overlooked them.

Sure enough, they were on the far side, hanging just above the floor, behind the buggy. It took me a minute to wiggle the medium-size one off its hooks, but I managed to get it out from behind the buggy without hitting it and out the barn door. I staggered a little, trying to balance it. Molly carried ladders all the time—and then climbed them to prune branches off trees. I squared my shoulders. I certainly could manage this on my own.

I did, staggering again as I walked, but still making my way. When I approached the trees, Hope began laughing. "You should have asked one of the boys to help."

I shook my head. "I'm fine."

I put the ladder down in front of the first tree, spreading it wide and securing it, and then climbed with the basket in one hand, reaching as best I could with the other. Hope continued to collect apples off the ground and from the lower branches.

We'd worked that way for about an hour, from tree to tree, when a wasp began buzzing around my head. I ducked, making the ladder quiver. The wasp buzzed me again. I swatted at it. Growing up on a flower farm, I appreciated bees. However, wasps were an entirely different matter. I'd been stung as a child when I'd been helping Molly pot mums outside the greenhouse.

The memory of that sting came back clear as day when a second wasp joined the first. I climbed down the ladder as calmly as I could. "Hope, I think there's a nest up there. Come on." I grabbed her arm and started marching away.

A chuckle from the end of the shop caught my attention. Ben stood clutching the handles of a wheelbarrow full of sawdust.

I stopped and turned back toward the trees. I considered that I might have overreacted . . . until I felt a tickle on my neck. I swiped at it, turning toward Hope.

"It's a wasp," she squealed.

I swiped again, but my hand came away empty. "Can you get it?"

Hope hit at my neck. "Oops," she said. "It crawled under your Kapp!"

I screamed as I yanked my Kapp off, pins and all, and then

grabbed at my bun, twisting it undone, flinging my head down, swatting at my hair as I did. My wavy, chestnut hair reached the ground, swinging this way and that, brushing over the dirt.

The wasp fell, and Hope stomped on it, stepped backward, tripped over a rock, and landed on the ground, giving out a yell. I fell to my knees beside her, laughing. She grabbed my hair to keep it out of the dirt, twisting it on top of my head. "Ach, Bea, it's so beautiful."

Embarrassed, I took it from her and scooted it down, re-working my bun in the proper place. Then I remembered Ben. I couldn't help but look at him.

He stood staring at me, his eyes wide.

Hope nudged me. I diverted my eyes. It wasn't proper for him to see my hair down. I began searching the ground for my bobby pins but couldn't find them. I must have flung them far and wide. My Kapp was off to the side, between Ben and me. I started to stand, but before I could, he started toward us. I froze.

He retrieved my Kapp and handed it to me, our hands touching. An electric current surged through me—as real as a wasp sting but not as painful. Not painful at all, actually.

"Denki," I finally said, taking the Kapp from him.

Hope quickly pulled a couple of bobby pins from her bun and handed them to me. Then she hurried back toward the trees, picking up the basket she'd abandoned. I did the best I could, tucking my hair under my Kapp.

"Beatrice," he said. "I—"

"Bea," I corrected.

"Bea," he said and then grinned.

I smiled in return, fastening my Kapp with a pin that had clung to the fabric.

Ben whispered, "Could we talk tonight?"

My first instinct was to correct him, to say, *May* . . . But the truth was I had no idea if *may* was the right word or not. *Could*, actually, was probably the better choice. "We could try," I said. "Depending on the babies."

"Ah, the *Tropplis*," he said.

"The what?" But then I registered the word play, his combination of *Bopplis* and *triplets*, and smiled.

He grinned and started to walk away.

"Ben," I said.

He stopped and turned back toward me.

I placed my hand on the top of my Kapp. "I hope the Tropplis will cooperate."

His eyes sparkled. "Me too."

I inhaled deeply as I walked back toward the trees. I couldn't deny it. I wanted a relationship with Ben. I really did.

Ben ended up working well past seven, finishing a special-order hutch, so Bob told him to spend the night in the Dawdi Haus. "There's no use you going back and forth."

We'd already eaten supper, but he came into the house and I fixed him a plate. Before he was done, there was a racket upstairs with more than one baby crying.

"It's their fussy time," I said. "I might be a while."

"That's all right," he said. "I'll wait by the oak tree. Come out when you can."

Two hours later, I managed to sneak away. "For just a few minutes," I told Hope, after I'd taken a second cup of fennel tea to Nan.

When I reached the back door, I flung my cape over my shoulders and hurried out. The night sky was bright with a million stars, every one of them twinkling, as if sending down more blessings than I could ever count. I hurried down the walkway toward the tree, feeling optimistic.

There was Ben, sprawled out on the lawn, a backpack to the side of him. He had his coat on and his hat off and his head resting on . . . something. At first I thought he'd brought a pillow out—a big one—but then I realized it was Love.

"Oh, goodness," I said, approaching the two. Love stirred but Ben was fast asleep.

I touched his arm. He rolled toward me. "Ben," I whispered.

He opened his eyes slowly and then raised himself to his elbow. "Bea," he said, wiping his mouth as if maybe he'd drooled, which he hadn't.

I leaned toward him, but Love scampered to her feet and pressed up against me, nuzzling my face. "Why did you come back?" I cooed.

"She couldn't stay away," Ben whispered, petting the dog. She wedged herself between us.

I glanced toward the house.

"I don't see any faces in the windows," he teased.

"You never know," I said.

He reached up and slipped a strand of my hair behind my ear, his hand coming to a rest on my neck.

My stomach fluttered. He'd made the same gesture back when we were courting, ever so briefly. I grabbed his hand and pulled it away. I needed answers. "What happened a year ago? After we'd gone out a couple—"

"Ach, Bea," he said. "Do we have to rehash the past?"

"I need to know," I said.

He sighed. "What are you asking, exactly?"

Before I could respond, the back door screen banged and a

light cast across the yard. Hope called out, "Bea! Are you out here?"

"Over here," I said, scrambling to my feet.

"Can you come take a turn with Asher? It seems you're the only one who can calm him down." Then she looked past me to Ben, a smile spreading across her face. "Sorry!" She held the lamp high as she spun around. If both her hands had been free I'm sure she would have been clapping.

I sighed.

Love rolled away from us.

"What should I do about her?" I asked.

"She can stay. Bob won't care." He bent down and hooked the chain to her collar, saying, "Just in case," as he did.

"Denki," I answered.

"Bea, hurry!" Hope called out. "Asher is going to wake up Cate." As if Hope hadn't already.

"Sweet dreams," I said to Ben and then hurried toward the house. When I reached the door, I turned. In the starlight, I could see Ben sitting beside Love on the grass, his back against the tree but his eyes on me.

I waved.

He returned the gesture and called out, "Good night, sweet Bea."

I stumbled going up the stairs. No one, in all my life, had ever referred to me as sweet. And what a great play on words. Sweet pea. Sweet dreams. Sweet Bea. I was definitely letting Ben Rupp have the last word tonight.

CHAPTER

12

Bob was fine with Love staying. I thought perhaps he'd changed his mind when she barked at the mailman, but a few minutes later he came through the kitchen door with a postcard for me.

It was a photo of the Kootenay River, a wide blue ribbon bordered by evergreen trees and hills on both sides. At the bend of the river was a fisherman. On the back, Molly had written, *Missing you SO much. Wish you were HERE. See you SOON! Your sister, Molly*

I assumed they were having a good time, although she hadn't said so. I slipped the postcard into my pocket and thanked Bob for bringing it to me.

He nodded and headed back toward the shop.

I finished making bottles for the babies and returned upstairs. By midmorning the babies settled down again, exhausted from their late night of screaming, and Nan said she thought she'd take a nap too. "Don't wake me when it's time to eat," she said. "I'd rather sleep."

We assured her we'd check on the babies in half an hour. "We'll pick more apples first," I said, as Hope and I hurried out the nursery door, shutting it quietly behind us.

As we tiptoed down the stairs I whispered to Hope that it was break time for the boys.

"Jah," she answered. "My thoughts exactly."

They were all sitting around the picnic table, along with Hannah, when we headed out with our baskets. Ben, with Love beside him, met my eyes and smiled. I nodded toward the orchard, but before Ben could move, Don sprang to his feet. "Good morning, girls," he said, tipping his hat.

Hope giggled. I smiled. We stopped at the end of the table.

"How is everyone today?" Hope asked, looking straight at Martin.

He grinned.

For the first time in my life I felt as if I truly belonged to a group of Youngie. I could see why Molly liked these people.

But Hope and I couldn't linger. I figured the babies would sleep for at least a half hour, but after that it was anyone's guess. Plus, we still had dinner to fix. I nudged Hope.

She nodded her head and started around the picnic table, stopping at Martin and whispering something in his ear.

"Sure," he said, scooting off the bench.

I smiled at Ben again as Don, who stood behind me now, asked if I needed help.

I shook my head, turning toward him. "You should relax," I said. "It's your break."

Martin and Hope started toward the orchard, but I hesitated, wondering if Ben would decode my smile. He didn't—or else the fact Don started following me convinced Ben to stay put.

"Well," Hannah said, rather loudly. "Bea, do you still plan to stay single?"

I pretended I didn't hear her.

"How about you, Ben?" she asked.

Mervin said, "Hannah."

I hurried on toward the orchard. We'd left the ladder out because there was no chance of rain. Once I reached it, I realized Don had followed me—or had at least started to. He'd stopped halfway between the picnic table and me, a troubled look on his face. He turned back slowly.

Hannah giggled.

I scampered up the ladder and set the basket on the platform. Then with a branch in front of my face, snuck a peek at the others. Don had started walking toward me again. Ben stood, his arms crossed, looking my way.

Hannah was standing now too. "I need to go," she said. "I'm supposed to be out running errands for Aenti Laurel."

"Jah," Mervin said. "Break's over." As he swung his leg over the bench, he called out, "Come on, Martin."

Hope told Martin good-bye, and as he headed toward the shop, she started collecting apples along the ground again. I reached for an apple in the tree, just above my head, and then another one.

I picked a third apple and then, as I put it in the basket, watched Ben head to the shop too. Below me, Don had reached the ladder. He put his hand on a middle rung and tugged. "Come on down a second," he said.

I shook my head. "We only have a short time to work—until the babies wake up. And we plan to make applesauce this afternoon."

"I'll only be a minute," he said.

"Don't you need to get back to work?" I grabbed a branch.

"Come on, Bea. Please."

I'd prefer he called me Beatrice, but I didn't want to point it out—again.

"Come down." His voice sounded so serious, I decided to comply.

As I stepped to the ground, I asked, "What is it?"

He squinted, even with his hat on. "What's going on? With Ben."

"We've been friends for a long time."

"You could have fooled me," he said. "You acted like you despised him."

I wasn't sure how to respond. He was right. I had acted that way. But once I knew Ben cared about me, I realized I'd suppressed my feelings for him. At least I thought Ben cared for me. He'd hinted that but hadn't actually said it. The truth was, I wasn't exactly sure what Ben's feelings were—but I guessed they were positive.

I wasn't sure enough though to tell Don I was interested in Ben. I'd been burned once by Ben—I needed to protect myself this time.

Don crossed his arms.

"We're just friends," I said.

"What did Hannah mean then? Just now."

I shrugged. "She's my sister's best friend. She's been teasing me for years."

Don inhaled slowly and then blew his breath out in a rush. "So what about us?"

I leaned back against the ladder, panic filling my chest. "Us?"

"Jah," he responded. "Where do we stand?"

"You and me?"

He nodded.

"We're friends too," I managed to say.

I expected him to be annoyed, but instead he smiled. "So I'm still in the running?" Before I could think of what to say, he stepped away and turned toward the shop. "Just you wait, Bea. I'll win you over. I'm sure of it." Then he took off at a march.

I grabbed the side of the ladder as Hope scampered over to my tree. "What was that all about?"

"He wanted to know what was going on between Ben and me."

"What did you tell him?" Hope braced herself against the tree.

"Nothing."

"Bea. That's not entirely true."

"But I don't know what's going on with Ben." I felt *something* was, but he hadn't communicated anything clearly. It seemed prideful for me to imply something was going on, especially if it wasn't true. Even if Ben and I were courting again, I'd feel awkward discussing it with Don. It was hard enough talking about it with Hope.

"Martin says Ben's crazy about you." She crossed her arms.

I sat down on the bottom rung of the ladder.

"Don't lead Don on," she said.

I shook my head. "I'm not—honestly."

"I thought he'd be a good match if Ben didn't work out," she said. "But Ben really cares for you."

I groaned. "Well, he should make it clear, then," I said. "And soon."

❧

The next time the boys were outside was for their noon meal. I couldn't bear to go out, but Hope did. I watched from the kitchen window as everyone laughed and chatted. Both Ben and Don appeared fine. It seemed I was the only one in a dither.

Hope and I had managed to get the babies fed and back to sleep, giving Nan the longest nap she'd had since they were born. But they'd probably be awake again soon, so we started the process to make applesauce as soon as we got back downstairs, first retrieving the canning supplies from the basement and setting up a production line on the table.

I started water to boil on the stove, dunking the jars and lids, while Hope peeled the apples and began slicing them. Once the jars were sterilized, I got the apple wedges cooking, and then helped Hope cut the rest, adding them to the pot along with the spices and sugar. After it had all cooked we ran it through the food mill and then put it into the jars, placing them back into the canner.

I stepped toward the hall. "Is that Asher crying?"

"I don't hear him," Hope said.

I sighed. "I do. We'll have to make the apple butter tomorrow." I headed to the sink to wash my hands.

"I'll clean up," Hope said.

When I returned with Asher in my arms, the kitchen was only partially done and Hope was outside at the picnic table with Martin and Hannah and Mervin. They appeared to be deep in conversation. I stepped to the center of the window, where I had a view of the shop. Don and Ben walked toward it.

I placed Asher in the playpen and talked to him as I worked, first clearing the table and then washing up the remaining items. I put the uncanned applesauce in the refrigerator. We'd turn it into apple butter the next day. Then I took the chicken out of the refrigerator and put it in the roaster pan, drizzling oil over the top and then sprinkling it with salt and pepper. I grabbed three apples from the basket beside the table and sliced them over the chicken and then sliced up an onion too, dabbing at my crying eyes as I did, and spread it over the bird and apples. Next I chopped several sprigs of rosemary that I'd stashed in the refrigerator from the garden the day before and sprinkled that on top of everything.

After I popped the chicken into the oven, I glanced out the kitchen window. The twins had returned to work but Hannah and Hope continued talking. I headed downstairs with a bowl to retrieve potatoes from the basement. When I returned, I glanced out the window again. Hannah had left and Hope was working in the garden.

Bob must have asked her to do that. If we needed help with the babies, I'd simply go get her. I busied myself peeling potatoes.

As I made a salad, Hope and Cate came through the back door. Hope scrubbed her hands in the mudroom sink, and Cate scooped up Asher, who had started to fuss, and headed down the hall.

"Tell Nan it's almost time to eat," I said, grabbing the pot-holders. When Hope came into the kitchen, I kept my voice low as I asked her how Ben was.

A puzzled expression settled on her face.

"You know—did he say anything about Don talking with me?" I asked as I lifted the roasting pan out of the oven.

Hope's face brightened. "He didn't say anything at all. In fact, I wouldn't worry about any of that. Martin said everyone's fine."

I nearly lost my grip but managed to get the pan to the stovetop. Maybe neither one of them was all that interested in me.

The next few days were mostly worry free—except for my dilemma over Ben. He and I managed to say hello to each other and exchange a smile or two, but we didn't have time to really talk. I bit my tongue, deciding not to be pushy, and prayed for patience.

A few times he helped me pin laundry on the line if I was out during one of his breaks or over the dinner hour, but there were always other Youngie within earshot, so we didn't say much to each other, except to chat about the weather and the work we were doing.

Don was friendly enough and didn't put me on the spot.

Hannah came over nearly every day to see Mervin. One noon hour the two sat off by themselves, intent on their conversation, as Ben helped me hang towels on the line.

"They're getting pretty serious," Ben said.

"Haven't they been? For several years now?" True it had been on and off, but it was past time for them to either get hitched or call it off for good.

Ben stepped closer to me. "They're thinking about marriage—and soon."

I leaned toward him as I placed a wooden pin. "How soon?"

"Maybe within a month or so."

That meant Hannah's family would already be busy with the planning, although quietly. It was a good thing that Molly would be home in a few days. She'd want to help. But then again Molly probably knew before she left for Montana what Hannah's plans were. She just hadn't told me.

The back screen banged, and Hope stepped out, looking around—for Martin, I knew. He hurried toward her from the picnic table.

"They'll be married soon too," Ben whispered, stealing a pin out of my hand.

I swatted at him, playfully, surprised at my ability to flirt. "How soon?"

"Probably not too long after Hannah and Mervin." Ben grinned.

"No," I said, my voice a whisper too. "They hardly know each other."

"But, regardless, don't you think they know they're meant to be together?"

"Jah," I answered. "But Hope hasn't said a word about marriage."

"Neither has Martin," Ben replied. "I'm just guessing—"

I swatted at him again but this time he grabbed my hand. I twisted my arm, playfully trying to get away.

"I have something I want to show you," Ben said. "Do you have time?"

"It depends what it is," I teased.

"It's a book." His voice was serious. "In my buggy."

He didn't have to twist my arm to get me to go with him. I walked with him willingly toward the far side of the barn, where the workers parked.

It wasn't like we were going off alone or anything—at least not far—but still I felt self-conscious. When we reached the buggy, he grabbed his backpack out of the front and led me around to the back.

As he opened his pack and pulled out a book another fell to the ground, sending up a cloud of dust as it landed. "Oops," Ben said, picking it up and brushing off the book, and cramming it back into the bag in a quick motion.

"What's that book?" I asked, leaning against the back of the buggy.

"This?" He held up the first one, still in his other hand.

"No, the one you don't want me to see."

"Who said I don't want you to see it?" He scooted closer to me.

"You did—by stuffing it away so quickly."

He grinned at me, his brown eyes dancing. "This is the one I want you to see." He held it up again.

I wrinkled my nose. "Okay, you win. You can show me the other one next."

"We'll see," he said as he focused on the book in his hand. He opened it, going by a slip of paper that served as a bookmark. "It's the book of sonnets, written by Shakespeare. It was still at the Olde Book Shoppe the last time I went in. Albert had set it aside for me."

I couldn't help but feel a little jealous. I took it from him and flipped to the front cover. Sure enough, there was an illustration of the author on the cover, under the words *Shakespeare's Sonnets*. He had bushy hair, a mustache, a pointy beard, and steely eyes. I opened the book again to the marker and handed it back to Ben.

Ben put his hand on the page nearest him and then pointed to the other one, pressing against the book. "This is my favorite of all the poems," he said. "Number 116. It uses nautical symbols—which I had to ask Albert about. But once I understood all of it, I really liked it." He picked up the book and held it closer to his face. As he did, his shoulder brushed against mine. A shiver shot down my spine.

Then he began to read,

> "Let me not to the marriage of true minds
> Admit impediments. Love is not love
> Which alters when it alteration finds."

I thought about that as he continued to read. It seemed the author was saying that love must remain constant.

I focused again on what Ben read.

> " . . . it is an ever-fixed mark
> That looks on tempests and is never shaken."

He stopped reading and said, "A tempest is a storm."

I smiled. I knew that. A rustling along the barn caught my attention. I expected a cat—or maybe Love—but it was Don, coming our way.

"Back to work," he said and kept on walking.

Ben blushed.

My face grew warm too as Don disappeared.

Ben flipped to the back of the book, took out a piece of paper, and handed it to me. "I copied the sonnet for you."

"Denki," I said, slipping the page into my pocket. I'd read the rest of it as soon as I could.

"You've been kind to Don," Ben said as he slipped the book back into his backpack.

My face and neck started to grow even warmer. "I've been trying to be kinder—to everyone."

"Well, it's working," Ben said.

I wasn't sure if he meant it was a good thing. My face grew as hot as the fire I'd made in the wood stove that morning to ward off the chill. "Denki," I said, "for showing me the sonnet."

He smiled a little.

"I'll read the rest of this one—and I'd like to read the others too. Later, of course."

He nodded and then jerked his head toward the shop. "See you soon."

He put his pack in the buggy and headed back to work, and I started toward the house. Was Ben jealous of the attention Don paid to me? If he was, that might not be a bad thing. I'd decided not to force Ben to reveal how he felt about me. That would come better from him, in his own time.

When I reached the clothesline, I stepped behind a towel

and pulled the paper from my pocket, starting to read where Ben left off.

> It is the star to every wandering bark,
> Whose worth's unknown, although his height be
>   taken.
> Love's not Time's fool, though rosy lips and cheeks
> Within his bending sickle's compass come:
> Love alters not with his brief hours and weeks,
> But bears it out even to the edge of doom.

That sounded a little ominous.

> If this be error and upon me proved,
> I never writ, nor no man ever loved.

I folded the paper and slipped it back into my pocket, shivering even though I wasn't cold. I couldn't figure Ben Rupp out. "'But bears it out even to the edge of doom,'" I whispered out loud. He certainly hadn't done that when we courted briefly last year. He'd simply disappeared.

One minute I thought he was interested in me again, and the next I had no idea. Ben Rupp was an E-N-I-G-M-A, a person or thing that is mysterious, puzzling, or difficult to understand. It had been a sixth-grade spelling word. That was Ben, for sure.

⁓

That afternoon I found Nan crying in the nursery again. She wasn't making any noise, but tears streamed down her face. She held Asher on her shoulder, patting his back as he screamed.

I froze in the doorway.

"Don't mind me," she said, "I'm just feeling a little weepy."

How could I not mind her? She was a sight.

"Hormones," she said, her hand dashing from Asher's back to her cheek and then to his back in one smooth motion. "Or sleep deprivation. Or happiness."

"Ach, probably all three." I stepped into the room. "Do you want me to take Asher?"

"Denki," she said. "I need to take a shower. I can't remember the last time I had one. Betsy and her kids will be here soon."

Involuntarily my eyebrows raised.

"Oh," she said. "Didn't I say anything about them coming?"

"Not to me," I answered, as I stepped toward her.

"Ach. Maybe I told Hope." Nan handed Asher to me. He gulped a breath of air and then continued screaming.

"Will they stay for supper?" I asked, rubbing Asher's back, holding him firmly against my shoulder.

"I'm not sure. . . ." Nan stood, holding on to the arm of the rocking chair for an extra-long moment. "But probably. Is that all right?"

"Of course," I answered. We were having a roast, but it was enough for company."

"I need to get some fresh air today." She started toward the hallway. "After my shower, maybe we can take the babies out on the porch." Once she reached the door, she turned back around. "If you weren't here to help, I don't know what I'd do." She'd said that before—she didn't need to say it again.

"Ach, you'd be fine," I said.

"Well, I'm glad you think so. But I wouldn't be. Neither would Bob." She sighed. "I can't imagine having more children. Of course if that's what God has for us . . ." She smiled, wearily. "Although at this point it's not like Bob and I even have time to hug each other, let alone . . . " She laughed. "I'm sorry. I'm babbling. And saying stupid things. I feel like I've lost my brain."

I couldn't help but smile. I really liked Nan.

She patted the wet spot on her dress where the spit-up had soaked through. "Lovely, isn't it?" Tears welled in her eyes again. "I mean it is—it's all so lovely. And exhausting."

I nodded. "Go get your shower," I said. "And take your time."

"The other two are in my room." She shuffled into the hall.

I sat in the rocking chair and continued to pat Asher's back. He wiggled a little and then stopped screaming. Soon he stopped crying. A few minutes later, he'd fallen asleep and I slipped him into his bassinet.

Next I picked up the overflowing laundry basket to take to the basement. Even though I'd told Nan she and Bob would be fine on their own, I couldn't imagine what they would do without Hope and me either. Bob rounded the corner from the hall as I came down the stairs.

"There you are," he said, extending an envelope to me. "Here's your pay."

I said, "Denki," as I took the envelope and slipped it into my pocket. I'd never had any money of my own before.

"We appreciate you," Bob said. "You've exceeded my expectations as far as your work, and you've become a leader with Hope. Plus you have a positive attitude that has, frankly, surprised me—it's had a ripple effect on all of us."

My face grew warm at his comments. I wasn't used to being complimented. It wasn't the norm for our community—we feared it would lead to pride. But I could see why the boys all valued Bob as a boss. He inspired them to do their best. I certainly felt that way now.

"Anyway," he said, "God has blessed my family through you."

"Denki," I said again and then held up the basket. "I'm headed to the basement."

He smiled. "And I'm headed upstairs."

"The babies are all asleep," I said.

"*Gut*," he replied as he reached the stairs. "I'll just take a peek and then get back to work."

When I reached the basement, I put the basket on the laundry table and then took the envelope out of my pocket. As I counted the money, a sense of satisfaction unlike I'd ever known overcame me. The thing was, I would have taken care of the babies for free. Not at the beginning, of course—but now I would have.

But now I could buy some books. I tucked the money back into the envelope. Maybe Ben would go with me to the Olde Book Shoppe.

An hour later, Nan, Hope, and I had the babies out on the porch. As the boys trickled out of the shop for their break, they headed our way. All of them were crazy about the babies. And none of them had seen much of Nan lately. It was clear they were all crazy about her too. Except Don. He stayed back at the bottom of the steps by himself.

As Ben held Asher, I couldn't help but admire him. He'd had a lot of experience with babies because Betsy and her brood lived with him and his parents. Until the last week, he'd had a lot more experience than I had.

"Hey, little guy," he cooed to Asher. The baby's gaze fixed on Ben for a moment, but then he began to fuss. "Ach, none of that," Ben chided. "Or I'll have to hand you back to Bea."

The baby began to cry.

"Ach." Ben lifted his head, a helpless expression on his face. Asher began to scream.

"He wants you." Ben's eyes met mine. In the old days, he

184

would have followed the comment with a jab, but now, he grinned at me. "Can't blame him," he whispered, leaning toward me.

My heart skipped a beat as I took the baby. Our hands tangled for just a moment, the little one wedged between us. I quickly pulled mine, now holding Asher, away. I wanted Ben to communicate how he felt about me—but in private. Not on the porch in front of everyone.

"Hey, Ben, what's the matter?" Don called out as I drew Asher close to me. "Can't you handle a baby?"

"Jah, that's right. I can't," Ben answered, looking over his shoulder as I lifted Asher to mine. "But thank goodness Bea can."

Don smirked a little.

His response surprised me. He hadn't been harsh before, but perhaps his wife had been pregnant when she died. Bob said he appreciated my positive attitude—a first for me—I wasn't going to fall back to being critical.

I smiled at Don.

Ben turned back toward me.

"Ignore him," I whispered.

"Jah," he answered quietly. "I will."

Nan, sitting near us in one of the many rocking chairs on the porch, asked Ben if he planned to stay for supper. "Betsy and Levi and the kids are coming," she explained.

He laughed. "It's going to be absolute chaos here, then," he said. "Are you sure you're up to an invasion?"

Nan nodded, halfheartedly.

"I wish I could," Ben said. "But I told Albert I'd stop by on the way home. He has a broken bookcase he needs help with."

Then Nan told me that I'd have the next afternoon off. "Bob and I are taking the triplets to the pediatrician." She turned her attention to Ben. "And he's giving all of you the afternoon off too. Because you worked so hard getting that last order filled."

Ben raised his eyebrows as he glanced at me. "Perfect," he said, stepping closer, touching my shoulder with his arm as he did.

Over Asher's head, I asked, "Would you want to go back to the bookstore with me tomorrow afternoon?"

"Are you asking me on a date?" His eyes twinkled.

I wrinkled my nose, embarrassed.

"Jah," he said, this time quietly, "I'd like that."

CHAPTER

13

After Ben left and before Betsy and her family arrived, Don approached as I took a load of towels off the line, folding them as I did and dropping them in the basket, enjoying the warm autumn afternoon.

He came toward me from between the barn and the Dawdi Haus, carrying a book in one hand. I folded the last of the towels as he neared.

"What do you have there?" I asked. I couldn't pass someone who was reading without trying to see the title of the book. My curiosity got the best of me every time.

"Oh, this?" He held the book up a bit.

I nodded.

"It's a history book—about Colonial America."

"Oh," I said. It wasn't a topic I was particularly interested in.

"Want to borrow it when I'm done?" he asked.

I shook my head. "I don't have much time to read lately." I patted the sonnet in my pocket. I hadn't had a chance to read it again. Nor one of Cate's books on caring for babies.

"Too bad," he said. "I have a stack of other books back at my folks' place. Maybe one of those would catch your fancy."

I shaded my eyes against the sun. I doubted it.

"Well, see you tomorrow," Don said.

I waved and picked up the basket, wishing I hadn't asked him about the book, afraid he'd read too much into my interest.

When I reached the kitchen, Hope and Cate were frantically trying to get supper finished. "Help," Hope said. "The gravy isn't thickening."

I stashed the basket of towels in the sunroom and took over at the stove.

Ben was on target when he said having Betsy, Levi, and the kids for supper would be chaotic. It wasn't that they weren't *gut*—they were. It was just that his nephew and nieces were kids. And really close together in age. Robbie was three, going on four, and the baby was one, with their sweet sister Tamara in between the two.

I couldn't help but dote on them though. I didn't want to assume they might someday be my nieces and nephew too, but I hoped it might be true. I walked to the garden with the older two, Robbie leading the way. It was the last day of October, and soon the garden would need to be completely cleared, but there was still a crop of squash to use.

"Dawdi and I planted these pumpkins last spring," Robbie said, skipping along. It wasn't unusual for families in our community to overlap, for grandfathers to also be fathers of young children, still busy parenting their own offspring; for children to have aunts and uncles close to their ages. But right now to have three little preemies be uncles and an aunt to Robbie was a little hard for me to comprehend. I wondered if he'd call them Onkel Asher, Onkel Kurt, and Aenti Leah.

When we reached the garden, Robbie waded into it, jumping

over a few boat-size zucchinis that clung to the vines. Robbie maneuvered around the bean poles, toward the back. "Look at that one!" He pointed to a pumpkin that must have been sixty pounds or so. He tried to lift it and then yelled, "Dawdi!"

I turned back toward the house. Bob held Betsy's baby in one arm and Asher in the other. The size difference between the two was almost comical.

"He looks a little busy," I said to Robbie.

The little boy frowned. It must have been hard for him to go from having the sole attention of so many adults to having to share it with five other children, soon six. The Millers had certainly been blessed.

Robbie moved to a smaller pumpkin and wrapped his arms around it, pulling hard. As he lifted, it tore from the vine. Tamara attempted to do the same but couldn't budge her chosen pumpkin. I directed her to a smaller one and then helped her.

The children started back to their grandfather, walking off-kilter. I kept behind them a few feet.

When he saw them coming, Bob called out, "Look at you big kids! Take those home with you—get your Mamm to make you some pumpkin bread."

Betsy, who had been sitting on the porch, leaned over the railing so she could see what was going on. "Oh, goodness."

Levi grinned at his children. "I'll clean those out and cut them up when we get home. Then your Mamm can make something yummy."

Betsy shook her head. "Baking is the last thing I want to do."

Robbie's face fell.

Levi tousled his curly hair. "We'll figure something out," he said quietly. "Your Mamm's tired—that's all."

With their straw-colored hair and wide smiles, Levi and Ben

looked like brothers. Both were kind, although Ben had a much smarter mouth than his older brother. And though not necessarily more intelligent, he was quicker. Levi seemed fine following someone else's lead—mainly Betsy's.

By the time Betsy and her family left, both Nan and Cate were exhausted. I sent Hope to help with the babies, while I finished cleaning up the dessert dishes.

"Ach," Bob said as he held Leah, ready to follow Nan up the stairs. "You really earned your wages this evening."

"They're fun," I said.

He raised his eyebrows. "Betsy's so used to coming over here and having Nan and Cate wait on her that she takes it for granted she won't need to help when she's here."

That was the closest I'd ever heard Bob Miller come to criticizing anyone.

"She'll figure it out," I said.

Bob headed on down the hall. Before I would have been critical of Betsy, but I could see she was learning, just like all of us. She probably never dreamed she'd have her little ones so close together, and now she had to figure out how to make it all work.

That night was another blur of fussy babies. It was becoming so routine, I could practically feed them, change them, and walk them in my sleep. The next morning it seemed as if maybe I'd dreamt it—except for how tired I felt.

This time Cate stayed in bed without coming down to breakfast. Pete seemed worried and took a tray up to her. When he came back down he consulted with Bob over their coffee as I washed dishes. I couldn't hear what Pete said, but Bob replied, rather loudly, "By all means, call the doctor. The sooner the better."

Pete hurried out the door. Bob drained his coffee and then

followed his son-in-law. I said a silent prayer for Cate and her baby as I continued to scrub the dishes. After I finished, I joined Hope in the basement to help with the laundry. Back home, we only did the wash on Mondays, but at the Millers', even with using disposable diapers, it was still nearly a daily chore. Spit rags. Blankets. Sleepers. Sheets. Towels. It never ended.

Hope had one load through the wringer and in a basket. As I picked it up, she said, "Do you think it's possible to know you want to marry someone after having spent just a few weeks together?"

I put the basket back on the table, remembering what Ben had said. I grinned at her. "Why do you ask?"

She smiled. "Why do you think?"

I placed both my hands on the edges of the basket and leaned toward her. "Tell me," I said.

She twisted the hot-water handle. The hose lurched a little as the water poured into the tub. "We've talked about it some. In a kind of roundabout way. And actually, we've known each other for over a year, fifteen months to be exact, since Nan and Bob's wedding."

"But you didn't see each other for fourteen of those months."

"True," she said. "But we wrote to each other."

"Really?"

She nodded and then chuckled. "Mostly I wrote. Martin isn't good at corresponding—but he'd send short letters in response to mine. But he was thinking about me all that time." She added the detergent to the tub and turned on the agitator. "You and Ben are so lucky."

"How's that?"

She began dropping the dirty spit rags into the tub. "You grew up together. You've known each other all these years."

191

"Oh, that just made it worse." I chuckled. "We tormented each other all that time. And we still can't seem to figure things out."

"You will," she said, dropping more spit rags into the tub. Funny how she was doing them one by one instead of a handful at a time. "And the thing is, you truly know each other."

That was true. Warts and all.

"Are you worried you don't know Martin?"

"That's the odd thing," she said. "I feel as if I know him better than anyone I've ever met. I feel like I could marry him tomorrow. I'm sure he's the right one for me."

"The two of you really do make a great pair," I said. "I can see you getting married—give it some time, though."

"But I don't want to go back to New York," she said.

"Nan is going to need help for quite a while. I don't think they'll be sending you home anytime soon."

"Jah," she said. "But my Dat said a month to start with. That will be up soon."

"Have Nan or Bob leave a voicemail for him."

"They'd have to write a letter."

"They'd do it." I picked up the basket of laundry again, sure each load grew heavier, to carry up the stairs.

She dropped the last spit rag into the tub. "What are you going to do this afternoon?"

I looked over my shoulder as I crossed over the cement. "Go to the bookstore."

"With?" she asked, a teasing look on her face.

"Guess!" I reached the bottom step and turned around. "What are you going to do?"

She blushed. "Go to the Mosiers' farm."

"With?"

She grinned. "Guess," she retorted. Then she added, "We're going to visit with his parents." I knew she'd met Amos and Eliza Mosier at church but that was all.

"That sounds pretty serious," I said.

"Jah," she answered. "It is. That's why I don't want to go back to New York. Not ever."

"You'd rather get married here?"

She nodded.

"Why?"

She shrugged. "I like it here. Everyone is more relaxed."

I wanted to laugh but didn't. Relaxed, with three babies in the house and a high-risk pregnancy?

She continued, "Plus, I feel part of the group here. I never felt that way back home."

I nodded. "I understand what you're saying," I said. "I'm feeling that too—for the first time, even though I grew up here." The basket of laundry was about to break my back. "See you in a few minutes," I said as I started up the stairs.

I only got as far as the kitchen when I heard babies crying upstairs. I held the basket for a moment, torn between dashing out the door and hanging the wash as quickly as possible or running up the stairs. Going upstairs won. So I put the basket on the floor and hurried to help Nan.

By late morning, Doris arrived to take Cate and Pete to the doctor. And then after dinner, Doris returned for Nan, Bob, and the babies. Hope and I helped carry the babies, in their car seats, out to the van. Bob asked if Doris had any word on Cate.

"They were going to do some tests," Doris said. "They told me to check after I drop you off."

As excited as I was to go off with Ben for the afternoon, Doris's report gave me pause.

"They're still at the doctor's office," she said. "If things were bad, they would have sent them to the hospital."

Bob exhaled. "That's a good insight," he said.

Hope and I stood to the side, watching as Bob and Nan fastened the car seats to the bench seats. Then Nan crawled into the back of the van and Bob sat up front with Doris.

As soon as the van pulled away, the boys poured out of the shop, while Hope and I ran into the house and up the stairs. Hope giggled as I sped past her on the landing.

I envied her. She knew exactly where Martin stood. I wasn't sure with Ben, but I'd been trying to be pleasant and not put him on the spot. I wasn't sure how much longer I could manage not to be blunt.

Kurt had spit up on my shoulder and Hope had spilled rhubarb juice on her apron. We changed as fast as we could, then took turns in front of the mirror, re-pinning our buns and adjusting our Kapps. After we grabbed our shawls, we hurried back down the stairs. When we reached the yard, Martin and Ben had their buggies lined up, waiting for us.

Ben helped me into his, and then we followed Martin and Hope down the long drive to the highway. When we reached the stop sign, they turned right and we turned left. My unsettled feeling continued to grow. I needed to know what Ben's intentions were but still didn't feel comfortable asking.

"When does your Mamm come home?" he asked.

"Tomorrow," I answered.

Ben pulled the buggy as far onto the shoulder as he could to let a car pass. "But you'll stay at the Millers'?"

"Jah, as long as they want me."

"*Gut*," he said, "and they will, for a long time." He took the reins with one hand and reached over and patted my knee with the other, his hand lingering for a moment—long enough to make me shiver. We continued on in silence.

I focused on the beautiful day. Tonight it would be downright cold, but the bright sunshine still warmed the world. The blue of the sky over the trees—gold and red deciduous mixed in with the evergreens—brought tears to my eyes.

Ben glanced my way as I swiped at my cheek. "Are you okay?"

"Jah," I answered. "Just a bit of dust, I think."

"It certainly is a beautiful day," he said.

I swallowed hard, wishing he'd bring up the topic of "us."

"The weather is supposed to hold through the weekend. After that they're predicting rain," he said.

It was early November. The Indian summer couldn't stick around forever.

Ben turned onto a back road, on a lane I'd never traveled before. Ahead was a forest of trees, their leaves fiery red and orange. "Oh, my!" I said.

Ben grinned at me. "Isn't it amazing?"

"It's like a tunnel," I said, as we rolled under the canopy of leaves. "I've never seen anything like it." The sun burst through at the end of the trees, casting beams of light across the pavement, which was littered with dry leaves.

A few moments later, the buggy popped out of the trees, only to roll onto a covered bridge. I gasped as the wheels thumped over the wooden planks. When we reached the other side, I looked behind us at the bridge framed against the fiery forest. "That was amazing," I said.

Ben stopped the buggy. "Want to get out?"

A minute later we stood gazing at the bridge, the glorious

trees all around it. I couldn't help bouncing up on the balls of my feet, feeling as if I might be able to walk on air. Ben's hand brushed against mine, but he didn't take it. "We should be on our way," he finally said.

Once we were back in the buggy, the image of the bridge and changing leaves stayed in my mind as Ben turned onto the highway and then a few minutes later into the Olde Book Shoppe parking lot. He pulled up to the hitching post and tied his horse to it.

I jumped down. The sunflowers alongside the brick wall of the building tilted to the west, toward the afternoon sun. Purple mums filled the flower beds in front of the store. Had they been there a couple of weeks ago? I couldn't remember. Probably so. Everything seemed so cheery. It was as if the entire world had come into focus for me, complete with brighter colors and textures. Unless I'd misread Ben's intentions. . . .

I couldn't stand it anymore. I stopped in front of the flowers and stared down at them.

Ben stepped to my side. "What's wrong?"

I couldn't keep silent any longer. "I need to know what you're thinking."

"About?"

"Us," I managed to squeak.

He placed his hand on my elbow, barely touching it, and then stepped closer to me, his body against mine. He paused a moment and then sighed. "Ach, Bea. Let's go inside. I promise we'll talk—soon."

I stood firm and shook my head.

"I promise," he said. "Before we get back to the Millers' today, we'll talk things through."

He held the door open for me. After a long pause, I finally stepped inside.

Albert and Willa were both at the register, and they greeted me warmly, but when Ben came through the door their faces nearly exploded into smiles. At first I thought it was at seeing him, but then I felt his hand on my elbow. Was the couple responding to seeing us together?

"What brings you in?" Albert asked.

"We both have the afternoon off," Ben answered.

"And you chose to come here?" Willa clapped her hands together, the way Hope often did.

"Of course." Ben stopped at the counter, and so did I, grateful that he was able to be friendly. I found myself feeling shy.

"We're going to browse." Ben pointed toward the back of the store and then led the way. I smiled at the couple and followed him.

"Oh, good," Ben said. "They have some new—I mean, old—books in." The shelves were packed with small volumes of hardbacks, most without their jackets.

"Where do they get the books from?" I asked, sinking to my knees.

Ben kneeled beside me. "Estate sales, garage sales, flea markets—and some people bring them directly here."

"Do Albert and Willa go to the sales?"

"Some," Ben said. "I've gone to a few for them. Also to some thrift shops. It's amazing what families give away."

I couldn't imagine.

We browsed for quite a while, pulling out books and flipping through them. Novels. Guidebooks. Devotionals. Biographies. And a couple of poetry books.

I found one book I wanted to buy and kept it in my hand, excited to make my first purchase.

"Who's the author?" Ben nodded toward the volume.

"William Butler Yeats," I said. "The poems are easier than Shakespeare's."

"But are they as good?" Ben countered.

"We'll have to read them and find out," I teased.

On the way to the cash register, he took the book in my hands from me. "I'd like to buy it for you," he said.

"I finally have my own money. I was going to get it," I said.

"I know. But let me." His eyes met mine. "Please?"

I let him take the book.

After Ben paid, as we walked to the door, he asked if I'd like to get a cup of coffee at the shop a couple of doors down.

"Sure," I answered, anticipating we'd finally have our talk.

The coffee shop was busy, without any open tables, when we arrived, but by the time we had our coffee and the blueberry muffin Ben had ordered, a table in the back had opened up.

After we sat, Ben divided the muffin between us and then asked if he could look at my book. I pushed it across. He leafed through it, reading bits here and there as I sipped my coffee. Music with no words played in the background.

"I'm ready to talk," he said.

I sighed.

"First, let me explain what happened last year."

I braced myself. "When you dumped me?"

He grimaced. "I didn't dump you."

I slumped against my chair. "What would you call it then?"

"We weren't ready," he said. "Your Mamm was ill. We were young." He blushed. "I'd been watching Levi and Betsy for the last two years and knew getting married before you were set could be a challenge. The doctor and hospital bills for the babies. The medicine and formula. Plus, I couldn't figure out where we'd live. My folks' house was too crowded. I couldn't imagine us living at your Mamm's place, not with Molly and Leon there."

It was my turn to blush. He had a point.

He shrugged. "I'm used to chaos, but I figured you'd need a little more peace and quiet."

He was right about that too.

"Why didn't you tell me all of this? Instead of disappearing like you did."

He blushed even more and then spoke in a hushed voice, "Well, wouldn't it have seemed a little presumptuous, on my part?"

He had a point about that too.

He shrugged a second time. "You're right. I'm not very good at communicating."

I crossed my arms. I could only imagine the scowl spreading across my face.

He leaned forward across the table. "Bea, I'm sorry. Will you forgive me?"

His words caught me off guard.

"I'm going to try to communicate better, starting right now."

I sat up straight.

"This is very important," he said, his voice serious without a hint of teasing.

I leaned toward him, my arms crossed on the table.

"I want to court you," he said. "I've known for years that I cared about you, since we were scholars together. There's no one else I'd rather spend time with than you. I figure I can make enough money to support us. We'll never be rich . . ."

I put my hand on his arm. "Wait."

"But I'll do my best—"

I squeezed his arm. "Stop."

He froze, his eyes on mine.

"Go back," I said.

He closed one eye, as if it might help him remember what he'd said.

I smiled just a bit. "To the part about courting . . ."

He nodded. "Isn't that what we're doing? The singing. The talks."

"This is the real thing?"

He nodded.

I exhaled. "You're positive? You won't change your mind in a day or two?"

He grabbed my hand.

Part of me wanted to pull away—I didn't feel comfortable being seen in public holding hands—but as my heart began to race, and this time not out of fear, I held on to him.

"I've never been more certain of anything in all my life," he said. "I C-H-E-R-I-S-H you, Bea Zook."

The background music grew louder.

My entire world shifted. Ben wanted to court me. He was serious.

H-A-R-M-O-N-Y. I'd never felt it so intensely, not in all my life. In those few moments, my fear vanished. He cherished me.

Our eyes locked.

Neither of us moved. Over the hum of the shop, Ben said, "It's true that I've cared for you since we were kids. You were so smart." He smiled. "And sassy, but in a quiet way."

I shook my head, wanting more than anything to be honest with him. "I was awful."

"No, you were great. You were the best part about school."

"I was critical and judgmental."

He shook his head. "You were honest—and still are. I've

always appreciated that about you. And you were so pretty." His eyes lit up. "But you're not anymore."

I swallowed hard.

He grinned. "You're beautiful. The most beautiful girl I know."

My face warmed. "I have my own confession to make," I said. "I've been prideful—first I was competitive and then I was prideful."

Ben's eyes shone. "I think we were even on the competitiveness," he said. "But you didn't seem prideful to me, just honest, like I said. And very Bea-ish."

I laughed. "Well, who else would I be?"

"You'd be surprised," he answered. "How about if we forgive each other?"

I nodded in agreement.

"And ourselves?"

I took a deep breath. That meant not bringing it up again—especially to myself. If Ben could forgive me, I could too. "Done," I said. I let go of his hand and pulled away until just our fingertips still touched. Tears stung my eyes.

"What's wrong?" he asked.

I laughed through my tears. "It's just that I feel so—" I needed a word that expressed more than *harmony*. "So jubilant!"

He grinned. "As in *great happiness*?"

I nodded. It had been on our fourth-grade spelling list.

"As in exultant, exuberant, and elated." He leaned forward over the tabletop, his face inches from mine now.

I shivered. "Exactly," I whispered. The background music swelled.

"Ach, Bea," Ben whispered, clasping my hand—just as Albert came through the door, looking a little frantic.

"There you are," he said, stepping around the other customers to our table.

Ben let go of my hand.

"Bob Miller just called the store." Albert looked straight at me. "He asked if I'd send you on your way to their place as soon as possible. They need your help."

We stood to our feet and hurried to the door, leaving our coffee and muffin behind.

I felt sick to my stomach the entire ride home, afraid of what might have happened. Had Cate lost her baby? Had something happened to one of the triplets? I tried to pray silently but worry kept interrupting me.

Finally, as we neared the lane to the Millers' farm, Ben said, "It's probably not as bad as Albert made it sound. He was in a hurry to get back to the bookstore. And Bob probably didn't tell him much."

I nodded. But I didn't think Bob would call the bookstore if he wasn't desperate. Perhaps Cate was in the hospital and Bob needed to go be with her and Pete. It would be hard for Nan, not to be available for Cate. . . .

"Let's talk about something else," I said to Ben. "How long do you think you'll work for Bob?"

"That depends," he said.

"On?"

He turned his head toward me. "Well, lots of things. What Levi and Betsy decide to do for one. If Levi moves on to something other than farming with my Dat, then that would open up a place for me—although I doubt that would happen. Levi doesn't like change much." He shrugged. "So I'll stay at Bob's until something else turns up."

"Do you enjoy it?" I asked.

"Jah, very much. But someday I'd like to have my own business."

"Farming?"

He shrugged again.

"Cabinetmaking?"

He shook his head.

"What?"

"Oh," he said. "I've had this *Drohm* of owning some sort of a shop—a bookstore, for example. . . . "

I sat up straighter. I'd had that dream too.

He turned his head toward me. "Silly, huh?"

"Not at all," I answered. "Well, practically speaking, maybe so, but as far as Drohms, it's brilliant."

He smiled at me and then turned the buggy onto the lane. We were silent the rest of the way. When we arrived, I told him a quick good-bye as Love barked out a welcome to us.

"I'll wait," he said. "To see how things are."

"Denki. Come on in, then."

He continued on to the hitching post. We both jumped down, and Ben tied his horse and followed me through the back door.

No one was in the kitchen, and the house was quiet. We headed down the hall. "Wait in the living room," I said. "I'll go check upstairs."

The nursery was empty, and so was Nan and Bob's room. I headed up the flight of stairs to the attic, where Pete and Cate had their quarters. I'd never been up there and knocked tentatively on the door. No one answered.

Mystified, I hurried back down to Ben, who stood at the window. "No one's here," I said.

"They just pulled up in the van."

Realizing it didn't look good for us to be alone in the Millers' house, I hurried down the hall to the kitchen, with Ben trailing behind.

But when we met them at the van, Ben and I seemed the last thing on Bob's mind.

"Denki," Bob said, "for coming right back."

"What happened?" I asked.

"The doctor admitted Cate to the hospital. We hope she'll be able to come home tomorrow—on bed rest. We'll need to get the sunroom set up for her."

"Goodness," I said.

Ben stepped forward. "Do you need help moving anything? I have some time."

"That would be *gut*." Bob undid Leah's baby carrier, handed the car seat to me, and then grabbed Asher's carrier, handing it to Ben. Next he grabbed Kurt's. The baby began to scrunch his face up, getting ready to scream.

Nan crawled out next, looking completely exhausted. She wrapped her hand around Bob's free arm.

"Let's get Nan and the babies upstairs," he said. "Then Ben and I will haul Cate and Pete's bed down to the sunroom."

I led the way, with Ben right behind me. Asher started to holler. Then Kurt began to cry. "Hey, hey, hey," Ben said.

Leah began to fuss too.

I opened the back door and started to hold it, but Ben took it from me. "Go ahead," he said. Nan and Bob followed me. I headed straight for the stairs, doing my best not to bump the baby seat against the wall.

By the time we reached the nursery, all three Bopplis were screaming. I took Leah from her car seat and began changing her while Bob and Ben worked on releasing the boys. When I was done with Leah, I took Asher from Ben.

"Give me Leah," Nan said. "I'll feed her in our room."

"I'll make bottles for the other two, once I finish changing them," I said.

"Make three," she said. "Just in case. I'm feeling wrung out."

Ach, that's what we didn't want to happen, for Nan to get so tired she couldn't nurse the babies. When I finished changing Asher, I handed him back to Ben, and then I took Kurt from Bob. The little one sneezed, and his breathing seemed a little rattled. "Is he coming down with something?" I asked Bob.

"The doctor said he's picked up a virus. Hopefully, the others won't." By *others*, I knew he included Nan and Cate with the babies. "Make sure you wash your hands," Bob said.

I nodded. I was certainly doing that. All the time.

Ben made faces at Asher, and the baby tried to focus but then turned away and began screaming again.

When I finished changing Kurt, I said to Ben, "Take Asher downstairs. I'll be right there."

After I'd finished sterilizing the diaper pad and washing my hands, I found Ben at the living-room window again, talking to Asher. I felt as if one of Mamm's favored hummingbirds had been let loose inside my chest. Ben grew more attractive with each passing minute. "Come on into the kitchen," I said.

Ben held Asher with ease.

"I can tell you have experience," I said.

"A little." He grinned. "Onkel Ben has been well trained."

I put Kurt in the playpen, turned on the burner to warm the water, and poured formula from the pitcher in the fridge into three bottles. Then I placed them in the water. "They just need to heat up," I said.

Ben nodded. He knew the drill.

Once the bottles were done, I ran one bottle up to Nan while Ben fed Asher. Bob said he'd be ready to move the bed in a little bit. "If Ben can stay that long," he added.

"I think he can," I answered, grabbing a clean spit rag from the stack on the dresser.

When I reached the kitchen, I handed Ben the spit rag. "Look at you." I'd never seen such a handsome man in all my life.

I picked up Kurt and sat down on one of the straight-back chairs to give him his bottle, but he fussed and turned his head back and forth, spitting out the nipple. I wondered if it was hard for him to suck because he was having a hard time breathing. I knew nothing about babies and colds or any other kind of illness either.

I put the bottle on the table, put Kurt to my shoulder, and patted his back.

"You need one of those bulbs," Ben said.

I had no idea what he was talking about.

"You put it in the baby's nose and squeeze it—to clear out the nose."

"Oh," I said.

"I bet Nan has one. Upstairs."

Kurt had settled down, but his breathing remained raspy. I'd ask Nan about the bulb when I took a supper tray up to her.

While Bob and Ben moved the bed, I put some leftover ham-and-potato soup on the stove to heat, and I put apples in the oven to bake for dessert, after sprinkling them with sugar, cinnamon, raisins, and pecans. Then I quickly made biscuits and popped them in the oven alongside the apples. When everything was done, I put together the tray for Nan and Bob, placing one cup of fennel tea on it.

That left Ben and me to eat alone, at the big table in the kitchen, with the baby boys asleep in the playpen.

As he led us in a silent prayer, I felt as if my heart might fly right out of my chest. When he said *amen* our eyes met.

"Who would've thought?" he said.

"My family will never believe it." Molly would have a cow. I was sure none of them ever expected that Ben and I would court again. But the animosity that was once between us now seemed a distant memory.

"When will Hope be back?" Ben asked.

"I think she planned to have supper with the Mosiers and then come back—so soon."

Ben helped me clean up after our meal. I figured Bob would bring the tray down when they were done.

After Ben dried the last plate, he said he should be getting home and then added, "Denki, for everything."

"You're the one who helped so much." I dried my hands on the dish towel that he still held. "I really appreciate it."

He brushed his hair out of his eyes. "Going to the bookstore and out for coffee was fun—but I enjoyed taking care of the Tropplis the most." He grinned, most likely at using the word he'd made up.

He handed me the towel. "Now I know how hard your work is," he said. "Not that I didn't have an idea, from watching Betsy with her kids. But I'll think of you in here when I'm out in the shop, concentrating on one thing at a time."

I liked this new Ben. A lot.

As I walked him out to the buggy, I remembered I'd forgotten my book. I stepped up to retrieve it as Ben untied his horse. "Any chance I can see you tomorrow?" he asked.

"My family's coming home," I answered. The plan was for me to spend Saturday night back at our farm, but with Cate on bed rest I wasn't sure how that would work.

"That's right." His face fell a little, but then he said, "The singing on Sunday is at the Cramers' farm." The districts had recently been redrawn when new ones were formed to accommodate our growing numbers, and the Cramers had been added to our district. "Do you think you'll be able to go?" Ben asked.

"I'll have to see how things are here."

"It's so close," he said. "Maybe you can come for a little while at least."

"Will you be there at the beginning?" I teased, thinking of the corn maze. "Or arriving late?"

"Definitely at the beginning." He stepped closer to me. "I hope I'll see you then."

"I hope so too." I looked up into his eyes just as a buggy came up the driveway.

Martin and Hope waved as they approached, big smiles on their faces.

Ben seemed a little put out to be interrupted. I patted his arm. Hope jumped down as Ben climbed into his buggy.

"See you Sunday," I said as he pulled away.

"You two looked pretty intent," Hope said. "Are things going well?"

"Well enough," I answered and then smiled. "How about you two?"

"Great. We stopped by the bishop's on the way home."

I could feel my eyes grow large. "Why?"

"Why do you think?"

"You talked to him about getting married?" I swallowed hard. "Already?"

"Jah," she answered. "He's going to contact my bishop. We could be published—in no time."

I couldn't quite fathom what she was saying. Sure, I'd expected they'd marry, but this all seemed so soon to already be announcing their upcoming wedding to the district during a Sunday service. And then to be getting married after barely courting. "So you and Martin might marry before Mervin and Hannah?"

Her eyes twinkled. "We'll see."

"Hope," I said, "what's going on?"

"It's not for me to say." She gave me a knowing smile.

For once I wanted the latest gossip. No matter. Molly would be home soon enough.

I couldn't imagine how Hope's family would react to all of this. I swallowed hard again. "What about your Dat?"

Her smile turned into a frown. "That's a problem. I need to write him tonight—before he finds out from our bishop."

I changed the subject, telling her about Cate and then adding, "And it seems Kurt is coming down with a cold. Hopefully, no one else will get sick."

Kurt was worse at bedtime, but Nan took over while I changed Asher and fed him a bottle. When I put him in his bassinet in the nursery, Nan came in with Kurt, who was still fussy. Holding him with one hand, she began to wheel his bed out of the room. "I don't want him to expose Asher and Leah, if we can help it," she said.

I doubted we could—especially since I'd had both boys in the playpen earlier that evening. I tried to shake off my sinking feeling, but it stayed with me. What if Leah caught it too?

Later that night, after Hope wrote her letter and then fell asleep, but before I extinguished the lamp, I pulled the copy of the sonnet Ben had given me out of my journal, unfolded it, and wrote in pencil at the top: *I've never felt such harmony. Such jubilation. Such anticipation . . . Bea+Ben=Love.*

It was a schoolgirlish thing to write, but I didn't care. My heart contracted as I refolded the paper and then slipped it back inside my journal.

Then I opened the book by William Butler Yeats and flipped through it, reading poems along the way. I read one in particular, "When You Are Old," several times, my heart sinking a little more each time I read it.

It was beautiful, but haunting.

> When you are old and grey and full of sleep,
> And nodding by the fire, take down this book,
> And slowly read, and dream of the soft look . . .
>
> But one man loved the pilgrim Soul in you,
> And loved the sorrows of your changing face;
>
> And bending down beside the glowing bars,
> Murmur, a little sadly, how Love fled.
> And paced upon the mountains overhead
> And hid his face amid a crowd of stars.

"That's so sad," I whispered out loud the final time I skimmed it. I couldn't imagine love fleeing like that. I couldn't imagine that ever happening to Ben and me, not now, not after we'd finally worked things out.

The poem left me feeling unsettled. I'd just had the best day of my entire life, and I was worried over a poem, a baby . . . and something else. What else was nagging at me?

Jah . . . Don. I needed to be clear with him—and soon—that Ben and I were courting. I turned out the lamp and pulled the quilt to my chin, knowing it wouldn't be long until one of the babies awoke.

The next morning I left a message on our machine at home that I wouldn't be over that evening, explaining that Cate was in the hospital, adding that Love was at the Millers' with me and I'd take her home soon.

I decided to cook the deer liver from Ben for the noon meal that day. I sliced it thin, coated it with flour, salt, and pepper, and fried it with onions and bacon. The iron would be good for both Nan and Cate. Just before it was time to eat, as I took the apple dumplings from the oven, Doris dropped Cate and Pete off at the house. They entered the kitchen, slowly.

"Your bed is all ready in the sunroom," I said. I'd changed the sheets that morning and fluffed the pillows.

"Denki." Cate sat down at the table, and Pete headed up the stairs. "He's getting my nightgown," Cate explained.

I hadn't thought about that.

She scooted her chair out and then put her feet up on the next one. In that position, her pregnancy was much more noticeable.

"Do you need anything else?" I asked her.

She sighed. "For this baby to stay put for a couple of more weeks." Her blue eyes swam a little with tears, but then she blinked and they were gone.

"Jah," I said. "That's what we're all praying for."

She nodded and then said, "Your dumplings smell delicious. There's nothing like the scent of apples and cinnamon. They truly smell like home."

"Not to mention the butter and sugar," I joked.

She laughed. "Well, I'm not worried about calories—at least not right now."

I promised I'd bring a dinner tray to her, with an extra serving of dessert, as Pete returned with her nightgown and an armload of other garments. Cate followed him down the hall to the sunroom.

No one commented about the liver, but they all ate it. After dinner Nan asked when I'd be heading home.

"I'm not going," I said. "I already left a message."

"Why?"

I explained that I wanted to stick around to help.

"Nonsense. You need to see your family," she said. "Hope can take more of a turn tonight. Go leave another message. Spend the night—come back in the afternoon." She took Kurt from me and headed to the rocking chair.

A few minutes later I was back in Cate's office, following Nan's instructions but not feeling very good about it. It would be nice to see my family, though, and hear about the trip. Hope could handle things for an evening and a night. Kurt didn't seem any worse, and the other two babies had been calmer today. Maybe they were about ready to turn a corner with the colic.

As I dialed the number, I began to feel excited about going home—but just for the night. I couldn't imagine going back for good, not now. I'd found meaningful work at the Millers, not to mention a community, and most importantly I'd found Ben. For the first time in my life, I saw a husband in my future.

I left my message, retracting the previous one and saying I'd be at our place by five. If their train was on time, they were scheduled to arrive around three. Edna planned to be at the farm and would cook supper. All I had to do was show up.

Bob offered me the use of their buggy, and Cate insisted I take Thunder again. It was another bright day but nippy, so I wore my cape and gloves. I called Love to the buggy as I climbed in. She jumped up and stood beside me. The breeze blew leaves down from the trees as Thunder clopped along. The boughs of the willow trees blew back and forth, the tiny yellow leaves falling like rain. Red and yellow maple leaves floated up and then swirled back down. Every once in a while, a seedpod flew against the buggy, hitting it with a *ping*.

Love barked a couple of times at the wind but then settled down by my feet. Perhaps she was content to go home.

When I turned up our drive, Love stood and began wagging her tail. When I reached the barn, she jumped down and ran toward the house, barking loudly. By the time I had Thunder unhitched, Molly hurried toward me, her arms outstretched and Love beside her.

"Bea!" she called out. "You're here!" She was typically tanned from all the time she spent outside, but now she practically glowed. She wrapped me in her arms, hugging me tightly until I pulled away a little, willing her to let me go.

"I missed you so much," she said. "Every day I wished you had come with us."

Finally she let go.

"Did you miss me?" she asked.

"Jah . . ." I answered. "But I've been really busy, so I didn't have much time to think about it."

"You would have loved Montana," she said. "We went hiking and fishing. Horseback riding."

I didn't enjoy any of those things.

She continued. "Leon's family is wonderful. They all wished you'd come too."

"That's nice," I said as Mamm hurried toward me.

"Bea!" she said. Leon was right behind her. He stepped around

214

Mamm and toward the horse, saying a quick hello to me. Then he took over caring for Thunder.

Mamm hugged me, holding on to me. I didn't push away from her though—I just hugged her back as hard as I could.

When we pulled away, we both had tears in our eyes. "I'm so glad you're home," I said. And I meant it. I'd missed her more than I realized. Love stepped next to us, first thumping Mamm with her tail and then me.

Mamm laughed. "Love is happy to have us all home too."

My mother stepped backward, her hands on my shoulders. "You look well," she said. "I think working for the Millers has suited you."

"Jah," I said. "It's been a good experience. I'm needed there." Not wanting to sound prideful, I hurried on. "I mean, I know they could have hired anyone, but I'm privileged to help them. You were right. Taking care of a Boppli . . . well, Bopplis"—in my head I thought, *Tropplis*—"is the most important work in the world."

"Oh, *gut*," Mamm said. "I'm thankful it's been the right thing." She put her arm around my waist as we walked toward the house. "But I hope you know how much we need you here too. You've contributed so much to running our home all these years."

Did she expect me to come home soon—after Molly had wanted me to get a job so badly and I'd finally complied? Before I could answer her, Molly was on the other side of me. "We have some news to share," she said. "But I'll wait until supper. We haven't told Edna either."

Molly shot a knowing look over my head to Mamm, but our mother didn't respond. Instead a serious expression settled over her face as she looked straight ahead.

After Leon led the blessing, we all dug into Edna's roasted chicken, cooked in a broth flavored with balsamic vinegar, honey, and rosemary. She explained it was a new recipe she'd come across, in a fancy cookbook. It was delicious, but I enjoyed it mostly because I hadn't cooked it. I appreciated the break.

"Do you want help returning the horse and buggy tonight?" Molly asked me.

Puzzled, I said, "Oh, I don't need to take it back tonight. I'll take it tomorrow morning, when I return."

"Return?"

"Jah," I said. "They'll need me until Cate's baby comes and gets settled, I'm guessing. Maybe longer."

"They'll have to find someone else," Molly said.

I shook my head. "No. I like it there."

Molly scooped a spoonful of mashed potatoes onto her plate and then looked up at me with a huge smile spreading across her face. "It might work for another week or so, but wait until you hear our news."

"What news?" Edna asked.

Molly passed the potatoes to Leon. "Actually, we have two

things we want to share. The first is that I'm going to have a Boppli."

A wave of joy swept over me. We were going to have a little one in the family! I was going to be an Aenti! Molly was going to be a mother! I'd never felt so happy for her in my entire life.

"That's wonderful!" Before I realized it, I was on my feet making my way around the table, hugging her. Edna followed me, hugging first Leon and then Molly. I simply slapped Leon on the back.

It took a couple of minutes for us all to settle back down. When we did, Edna said, "What's the second thing you wanted to tell us?"

I'd forgotten there were two things. One was quite enough.

"Well . . . " Molly glanced at Leon. "We're going to be moving. To Montana."

"What?" I wailed. "You can't leave when you're going to have a baby. How could you do that to us?"

She grinned. "Don't be silly. We wouldn't do that."

"Wait," I said, my heart stopping. "Who's moving to Montana?"

"All of us." Molly looked at Edna. "Well, not you, Edna, unless you want to."

"Mamm," I gasped. "Are you moving to Montana?"

"Jah," she said. "And so are you."

I inhaled sharply.

A pained expression passed across Mamm's face as she looked at me. "This probably wasn't the best way to tell you, was it?"

"She'll be fine," Molly said.

I couldn't go to Montana. But where would I live here? I couldn't live by myself on our farm. I'd need a place until Ben and I married. My face grew warm at the thought—but I might as well be honest with myself. That was the trajectory we were on. Maybe the Millers would let me stay there, whether they needed me or not.

"I can't move," I managed to say.

Molly bristled. "Why not? It's not like you have a life here."

I couldn't tell her all of that had changed—not now, not this way. "That doesn't mean I want to move to Montana."

"You'll love it," Molly said. "It's so beautiful. Much better than I thought it would be."

"What about our farm?" I asked.

Neither Mamm nor Molly answered for a moment. Finally Mamm said, "We'll have to sell it."

Edna gasped. But then, she said, "I'm sorry. It's not my business."

"No," Mamm said. "It is your business. It's a family farm, after all."

Molly speared a piece of chicken and passed the platter on to Leon.

He took it, concentrating on getting a slice of chicken onto his plate, his head hanging low.

Molly frowned as she ladled gravy over her potatoes. Obviously the conversation wasn't going as she'd planned.

We ate in silence for a long stretch.

Then Molly spoke, as if the conversation had continued along, saying, "It's just that I want all of us to be together. You too, Edna, if you'd want to move. I can't imagine us being separated."

I wanted to shout that I couldn't imagine living in Montana, but the new and improved Bea didn't respond at all. I'd wait until I calmed down.

Finally, at the end of the meal, after Leon had led us in a final prayer and Molly and Edna began clearing the table, I whispered to Mamm, "Can we talk? Just you and me?"

She nodded and then said, "Bea and I are going out to the porch for a chat."

Molly gave Mamm a sympathetic look as we stood. I took a deep breath. The old me would have been sure Molly felt sorry for Mamm for having to deal with grouchy old me. But I wasn't going to jump to that conclusion, not now.

Mamm and I put on our capes, she grabbed her quilt from the back of the couch, and we settled on the settee. Mamm spread the quilt over both of our laps. Nightfall had given way to the stars, shining so bright it seemed as if I should be able to pluck them from the sky.

Mamm put her arm around me and pulled me close. "Child," she said, "I missed you so much."

Tears flooded my eyes. I'd missed her too, but we needed to talk. "I don't understand what's going on," I said. "I thought Molly and Leon were going to stay in Lancaster. Why did you agree to sell the farm and go with them?"

My mother sighed but said nothing. Finally she started to speak, then stopped.

"Mamm?"

"Montana was lovely. Leon's parents are very nice people. They've found a horse ranch for Leon and Molly to buy. Because of Leon's experience, there seems to be a market for his work. When they decided to relocate and I found out Molly was pregnant, it seemed like the right thing to do."

I doubted Molly purposefully used her baby to manipulate Mamm, but I could see how it would have an influence.

"They didn't ask me to, but I know the sale of our farm would help them buy the place." She paused for a moment. "Of course

I wouldn't give them all the money. You and I would need some of it too, for our home."

"And where did you plan for us to live?"

"We'd build a small cabin on Molly and Leon's ranch."

"And what did Molly plan for me to do?"

"What you've done here. The cooking. The cleaning."

"But there aren't very many Youngie in Montana—right?"

"Some, but Molly pointed out that you've never wanted to marry or have a family of your own. She felt you would be perfectly content to move to Montana."

I sank against the back of the settee.

Mamm pulled her arm away from me and asked, "What is it, Beatrice? What's changed?"

"Everything," I answered, shifting away from her.

I explained how much I loved caring for the babies. Although taking care of three tripled the work, it also tripled the joy.

Even in the darkness I could see her face brighten. "That's wonderful," she said. "And you'll have that opportunity with Molly's baby."

"I want that opportunity with my own babies," I said.

Mamm chuckled a little. "Well, you'd have to want a husband, then."

"I do," I said.

"Sweetheart," she said, leaning toward me. She'd never called me that before, and her voice had a hope in it I hadn't heard her use with me. "That's wonderful. God could very likely have that future husband for you in Montana."

I frowned.

"What?" Mamm inched closer to me.

"At the Millers' place, the boys working in the shop and Hope and me, and even Hannah, who's been staying at the Cramers' farm, have been having a great time. For the first time in my life, I feel part of a community."

Mamm didn't respond. I think she was beginning to see the picture.

"In fact," I said, "Ben and I have . . . patched our differences."

"Ben Rupp?"

"Jah," I said.

She chuckled. "I thought you . . . despised him."

My face grew warm. "I acted like I did, but I didn't. Not really."

"Bea," she said, putting her arm around my shoulders again. "What are you telling me?"

"We've been spending time together. Yesterday we went to the bookstore, just the two of us."

"Oh," she said, as if she grasped the significance of the two of us going to my favorite place.

"It's his favorite place too," I explained. "And then when we got back to the Millers' home he helped me with the babies and then supper. He's a *gut* man."

"I suspected that all along," Mamm said.

I shivered. "I can talk to him in a way I haven't been able to with anyone I've ever known."

Mamm's voice was low. "Oh, goodness. So you love him, then?"

My face fell to my hands and I began to cry. "Jah, I think I do."

"Goodness," Mamm said. "I didn't see this coming. I mean it's *gut*, right? What a blessing." Her voice fell to nearly a whisper. "And yet, what a problem too."

We'd gained an hour with the time change, meaning it was light by six thirty. I didn't mean to sleep in, but I did, awakened by the first rays of sunshine through my window. After dressing, I stood at my bedroom window, wrapped in a shawl, looking over our flower farm. The changing shrubs and bushes were a hundred different shades of green, gold, red, and orange. The ornamental plum trees had completely lost their leaves weeks ago. The field of mums needed to be cleared and tilled, ready for annuals to be planted in the spring.

I stepped closer to the window. The gray kitten, who had grown lanky and fast, darted out of the barn and out into the flower field. Molly was out by the nursery trees, talking to someone. He wasn't tall enough to be Leon. Another man headed toward them, from the Mosiers' property. Mervin. That meant she was talking to Martin. Both of the twins wore their aviator glasses.

My room was cold. The temperature had definitely dropped.

Martin headed back toward their place, but Mervin stopped and talked with Molly. A moment later Leon joined them. Love bounded toward them, barked, and then took off after the gray kitten, who paid her no mind. Love chased a crow instead, but once it landed in the walnut tree, the dog headed back toward the house, where I couldn't see her.

The smell of bacon frying drew me away from the window and coaxed me down the stairs. When I reached the kitchen, Edna asked if I wanted a cup of tea.

"That's exactly what I want," I answered, grabbing a mug from the cupboard. "Where's Mamm?"

"Sleeping in, I hope," Edna said. "I think that trip wore her out."

I could've kicked myself. I hadn't noticed. I'd been so absorbed in my own problems. After I poured my tea, I asked Edna if Mamm was all right.

"I think so, just overtired," she answered as she flipped the bacon.

Edna's eyes appeared red around the rims. "How about you?" I asked, pouring milk from the little pitcher on the counter into my tea.

"Ach, I'm all right," she said. "Although still in shock from Molly's announcement—not about the Boppli. I'm overjoyed about that. But the thought of any of you, but especially you and your Mamm moving to Montana . . ." She took a deep breath, put the fork on the stove, and waved her hand in front of her face. "Well, I didn't see that coming at all."

"I didn't either," I said. "I'd rather Molly didn't move out there—our family is so small it only seems right we should stay in the same place. But if she's set on going, then so be it. But I don't think I could bear to have Mamm go."

Edna nodded in agreement. "Did you tell her about what's been going on between you and—" Edna's hands flew over her mouth.

"What?"

She shook her head. "I shouldn't even know this," she said, speaking through her splayed fingers.

I put my tea on the counter and pulled her hands down.

Edna practically whispered, "Nell told me."

"Oh," I said. "About Ben?" I wasn't surprised. Nell had been looking for it to happen when I'd seen her last. Now that it had, of course she knew. Hope would have told Martin, who told Mervin, who told Hannah, who told Nell.

Edna nodded.

"It's okay." I leaned against the counter. "Everyone is bound to know sooner or later. I told Mamm last night."

"And?"

I shrugged. "She said we had a problem."

Voices outside distracted us. The back door opened and Molly and Leon, followed by Mervin, tumbled into the kitchen. "Where's Mamm?" Molly asked, slipping out of her cape.

"She's not up yet," Edna answered. "Why?"

"Because . . ." Molly gestured toward Mervin. "We've found a buyer for the farm."

Edna's hands flew to her mouth once again, while I froze, as if stuck to the counter.

"Well, I don't know if I can buy it for sure," Mervin said. "I'll need help. But I think I have a great uncle who can assist me. I'll need to talk to him first."

"Isn't that wonderful?" It was as if Molly hadn't heard Mervin. She looked from Edna to me. "My plan is moving forward even faster than I thought it would. We'll be on our way to Montana in no time."

Leon cleared his throat.

"What?" Molly turned toward him.

"Look at your sisters." His voice was quiet and even. "They're having a hard time with this."

She looked from Edna to me and then said, "Oh." She stepped toward me and gave me a hug. I attempted to hug her back, but it was half an effort. Then she hugged Edna, who did better than I had. But after Edna pulled away she began to cry.

"Oh, goodness," Molly said, tears filling her own eyes. "I had no idea this would be so hard. Please come with us, Edna. You'll always have a home with us."

My oldest sister shook her head. "I'm too old for a move like that. . . ."

"But if Mamm can adjust, surely you can too."

Edna didn't reply with words but simply shook her head.

"Give it some time," Molly said. "This will all work out. We'll soon know what's best."

Mervin cleared his throat and then said, "I should get going. I don't want to miss breakfast."

As Molly and Leon walked him outside, I asked Edna what I could do to help.

"Don't move," she said. "If your Mamm decides to go, you could stay with me. You know, until . . ."

I nodded. "I'm not going to leave Lancaster. There's no way Ben would move to Montana. I'm not going to give up my one chance at happiness."

Edna put her arm around me. "That's my girl."

"Now, what can I do to help with breakfast?"

She chuckled. "I forgot what I was doing." She turned back toward the stove and jumped a little, as if surprised by the crisp bacon. She quickly turned off the burner. "Mix up some pancake batter," she said. "I'll get the griddle out."

By the time we had breakfast fixed, Mamm came down the stairs and stepped into the kitchen. "How are you doing?" I asked as I turned toward her.

"Fine," she answered, but she wasn't. Her eyes were as red rimmed as Edna's.

After breakfast, Molly and Leon headed back outside, while Mamm, Edna, and I washed and dried the dishes.

"It really did seem like a good idea when we were in Montana," Mamm said, as she scrubbed a plate. "I felt the most important thing was for us to be together. I had this fantasy that you would come too, Edna. Ivan and Nell seem so happy here—I didn't think they'd miss us much." Her eyes filled with tears again.

"Now, now," Edna said, putting one hand around Mamm as the other held a glass.

Mamm continued. "I never dreamt that you, Bea, would be courting someone here. You always said you never planned to marry."

I had said that—many times. I didn't need to be reminded, again and again. But why had she believed me? Wasn't it obvious that I was wounded? And immature? "I was pretty convincing, wasn't I?"

Mamm frowned. "You certainly were."

"What are we going to do?" I asked.

"Pray," Mamm said. "And wait. There's no reason to rush into leaving or staying. Let's see how God leads us."

Mamm was right. The old Bea would have marched outside and told Molly off. The new Bea wasn't going to do that.

I enjoyed being with Mamm and Edna, but by the time the dishes were all put away, I began to miss being at the Millers'. I wondered how Hope had done with the babies during the night, how Cate was feeling, and who fixed breakfast. Since it was Sunday, the men wouldn't be working in the shop, but I was certain they would still be thankful for my return.

I began to think that if I went back sooner, rather than later, I might have a better chance of going to the singing. I could get caught up on the bottle washing and formula making. I could get dinner on the table and then put together a simple supper before the singing. There really wasn't any reason for me to wait until afternoon to return.

Mamm had retreated to the front porch to enjoy the last day of predicted sunshine for a stretch. I sought her out, sat beside her, and shared my idea of returning early.

She said, "You want to leave already?"

"I think I should, is all," I said.

"All right." She put her arm around me and drew me close. "When will I see you again?"

"Soon," I said. I imagined Ben dropping me off after work and then picking me up on his way back the next morning in a week or two. Of course it would make more sense for me to get a ride with Mervin and Martin, but why would I want to do that?

"I'll see you then," Mamm said.

I told Edna good-bye in the kitchen and then found Molly and Leon in the greenhouse. Molly seemed distracted but managed to give me a hug and said she would see me in a day or two. "I plan to go see Hannah this week. I'll stop by the Millers' place to see Cate—and you."

Leon told me good-bye and then gave me another sympathetic look.

As I turned Thunder onto the highway, a wave of uncertainty swept over me. I'd had one good day with Ben—and then Molly had to go and complicate everything.

I took a deep breath. Life wasn't meant to be easy, I knew that. Jesus had said we would have tribulation. He'd never promised us a worry-free life. And I'd known worse trials than this. Dat dying. Mamm being diagnosed with a tumor.

I exhaled. I could deal with this latest crisis. I sat up straight, concentrating on the crispness of the day and the dazzling blue sky. My spirits lifted as high as they could go with the threat of our family being divided hanging over me. The puffy clouds—as white as freshly laundered sheets—gathering on the horizon and the hint of woodsmoke in the air reminded me that the good weather wouldn't last forever.

I just hoped it would last through tonight's singing.

The dark soil of a freshly plowed field to my right contrasted with the golden stalks of corn littering the edges of the road. Harvest was nearly done. Winter was on its way.

When I turned off the highway, Thunder raced down the lane and straight to the barn. Pete met me there and said he'd take care of the horse. "I'm just finishing up the chores anyway," he added.

"Isn't it a little late for that?" I asked as I jumped down.

Pete just smiled and said, "Go on into the house. Bob will be happy to see you."

I found Bob in the kitchen, his sleeves rolled up, his arms submerged in a sink full of soapy water. He was stooped over, scrubbing a pot. The dish rack was full of plates and glasses. Frying pans covered the stovetop. A platter with two slices of ham on it, a bowl with some potato wedges, and another platter with a bit of runny yolk on it were still on the table.

"Guder Mariye," Bob said, turning his head toward me. He looked as if he hadn't slept a wink. "Or is it past noon?"

"It's still morning," I answered. "Barely."

He turned his attention back to the pot. "We had brunch today—at least that's what we're calling it."

I hung up my cape. "I can help with the cleanup."

"Denki," he said. "But go check with Nan first. She might need some bottles for the babies."

When I reached the nursery, I found Nan asleep on the single bed. Kurt was on a blanket on the floor, on his back, awake, and Leah and Asher were asleep in their bassinets. Kurt began to fuss when I entered the room, but Nan didn't wake up. I picked him up quickly. His congestion seemed to be gone. I headed down the hall to look for Hope. She was asleep on her bed, in her dress, with her quilt pulled halfway over her.

She stirred and then opened her eyes, rolling toward me.

"Thank goodness you're back. I was up half the night. Pete ended up helping too." She sat up, yawning as she did. "What time is it?"

"Around eleven thirty," I said.

"Do you need me?" she asked.

I shook my head.

She collapsed back on the bed. "Then I'm going to try to sleep a little longer if you don't mind." She closed her eyes as she spoke.

"Sure," I said, backing toward the door.

When I reached the kitchen, Bob was drying a plate, probably to make room in the rack for the pots and pans. I put Kurt in the playpen and began clearing the rest of the table.

Bob shook his head. "How'd I overlook those things?"

I smiled. "You were focused on the dishes. These were out of sight, out of mind."

"Jah," he said. "I feel like a lot of things are out of mind right now." He put the plate in the cupboard and grabbed another one. "How's Nan?"

"Asleep. So are Leah and Asher."

"*Gut*," he said. "They gave us a run for our money last night. We thought their colic was getting better, but the boys had a flare-up last night, and Asher seems to have caught Kurt's cold."

"Oh, mercy," I said, thinking about how I'd put them in the playpen together. But at least it didn't seem to be a bad cold or to hang on too long.

But I decided not to get my hopes up about going to the singing. That way I wouldn't be disappointed. Instead I busied myself making apple butter from the leftover applesauce that we hadn't canned.

CHAPTER

16

Hope must have said something to Nan about the singing, because the next time I went upstairs she was awake and said she wanted both of us to go. "You'll be back to help with the babies by the time they're the fussiest," she said. "Bob and I can handle it while you're gone." She yawned. "Pete too if we need him. In fact we'll all sit in the sunroom with Cate, so she doesn't feel left out."

"I'll have supper ready early," I said, not convinced she didn't need us to stay but willing to give it a try. "If you need us, send Bob or Pete over. We'll just be at the Cramers'."

She yawned again and then said, "We'll be fine."

I spent the rest of the afternoon bathing babies, carrying dirty laundry down to the basement to be ready to be washed the next day, fixing bottles, and rocking babies. Midafternoon I woke Hope and told her I was going to start supper and for her to take over in the nursery. As I worked in the kitchen, more clouds rolled in, dark and heavy, turning the sky from blue to gray. By the time dusk fell at five, I was certain the rain wasn't far behind.

Cate and Pete ate in the sunroom, but the rest of us ate at the table—beef-and-barley soup, biscuits with warm apple butter, green beans, and apple cobbler for dessert.

"It's amazing how quickly you can pull together a meal," Nan said to me.

"Jah," Hope added. "We really missed you while you were gone."

I nodded graciously but inside I beamed. "I hope you're not all getting tired of apples," I said.

"Of course not," Nan replied. "I'm just relieved not to have to worry about planning or fixing meals. At least not for all of you." A wry smile crossed her face, and we all laughed.

Hope and I rushed through the dishes, finishing just as Martin and Ben arrived in the Mosiers' buggy. "Go," Nan said, coming up the hall from the sunroom with Leah in her arms when she heard the boys in the kitchen. "We'll be fine."

"We won't be late," I promised.

"We'll just be over at the Cramers' shed," Ben added.

Hope said she was too tired to walk and especially too tired to walk home in the rain, so we took Martin's buggy, lighting the lantern against the dark night. Ben and I sat in the back seat, side by side. He took my hand with his, tucking both between us, covered by my cape. My heart fluttered.

Martin drove the buggy up the driveway, while Hope described the wild night with the triplets. "We really missed Bea," she said. "She definitely has a way with the Bopplis. And with the cooking." She glanced back at me and smiled, then added, "And everything else."

Ben squeezed my hand, causing my heart to race, and then he whispered, "I missed you too."

I squeezed his hand back. Just seeing him had made my thoughts fall back to the whole Montana debacle. My mood fell. It was hard to keep trusting God about it, especially when

Molly had her mind made up. I needed to speak with Ben about it before he heard I was moving to Montana soon.

"You okay?" Ben asked. "You seem really quiet."

I nodded. "Just tired." That wasn't exactly true, although I was tired of Molly trying to run my life. But I didn't have time to explain things to Ben, and I didn't want to try with Hope and Martin along. I hadn't said anything to Hope yet. "I need to talk with you," I whispered. "In private."

"Everything all right?" He sounded alarmed.

"It will be," I said, my heart sinking again.

Ben gave me a worried look. Not wanting to respond, I turned my face away. Why had Molly gotten a bee in her bonnet about moving to Montana?

Martin turned right onto the lane, and headed farther down, over the bridge that spanned the creek. We arrived at the Cramers' farm and followed their drive straight back to the shed, parking past it in the field where the other buggies were. Already quite a group had gathered.

As Ben helped me down from the buggy, Don called out to me and then said, "Just who I was looking for. Got a minute?"

I glanced at Ben.

"Go ahead," he said, a puzzled look on his face.

Don grinned at him. "Be back in a second." He grabbed my hand and pulled me along.

I yanked my arm back. "This is fine," I said, stopping by the side of the barn, confused that my arriving with Ben hadn't made it obvious to Don that the two of us were courting.

"Ah, that sassy spirit." He grinned again. "I have something I want to show you, later."

"Ben and I are courting," I blurted out.

"Jah," he said. "So I've heard. This doesn't have anything

to do with you though. It has to do with me. My girlfriend is arriving this evening."

"Girlfriend?"

He nodded.

I put my hand to my forehead in relief. To think I thought he was interested in me when he had a girlfriend all along.

"I was hoping you could meet her," he said.

"Tonight?" I asked.

"Jah. She had to work around her driver. She's meeting me over at the Millers' shop around nine."

"Where's she staying?"

"Friends of hers. Phillip brought the buggy. I'll have him swing by the Millers' on the way home from the singing. Then we'll drop her off at her friends' house on our way home."

I'd need to be home by nine anyway—the babies were sure to be fussy by then.

"She and I had some problems, but we've worked things out, and everything is fine." He dug his boot into the dirt, his head down. "You've been kind to me . . ."

"So you're not upset?"

He shook his head but didn't look me in the eye. Perhaps he was embarrassed. "I have something for you though. I picked it up a few days ago." He pulled a small book from his pocket and handed it to me. I couldn't read the title in the dark.

"It's a children's book of verses."

"Denki," I said, "but wouldn't you rather give it to your girlfriend?"

His eyes met mine. He shook his head. "It's for you."

I slipped the book under my cape, into my apron pocket, deciding I might as well get meeting his girlfriend over with. I wasn't sure why it meant so much to Don—maybe just to prove to me that she existed and that I didn't matter to him after all. "All right," I said. "I'll tell Ben. When he takes me back to the Millers', we will stop at the shop."

"Oh, he doesn't have to leave early. I can walk you over."

It would be dark, pitch-black, in fact. I shook my head. "I'll ride in the buggy."

When I returned to Ben, a crowd had gathered around him, but when he saw me he slipped away. "What was that all about?" he asked, his eyes on Don.

I shook my head. "He wants me to meet someone." I didn't want to go into detail.

Ben squinted. "So when can you and I talk?" he asked. "It seems something is upsetting you."

"Jah," I said. "We do need to talk. I have something to tell you."

Hope called out my name and pointed toward the shed. Everyone was filing inside.

Ben took off his hat and ran his hand through his hair, exhaling as he did.

"Come on," I said. "We'll talk later." When we entered the shed, I drifted toward the girls' side with Hope while Ben followed Martin to sit with the other boys.

I couldn't help but yawn as the singing started. It wasn't that I was tired. I was the one who'd gotten a good night's sleep. It was more that I anticipated soon being tired.

Part of me wished I hadn't come to the singing at all. I patted the book in my apron pocket. But after tonight I wouldn't have to interact with Don anymore. That was a good thing. Then I just needed to tell Ben about the Montana problem and deal with Molly.

᠈᠍᠋

After the singing, Cap and Laurel Cramer served apple cider, popcorn, cheese slices, and crackers. Their daughter Addie held her baby brother, and the next two youngest—Billy and Joe-Joe, who were still in school—chased each other around the shed. Addie's husband, Jonathan, helped serve the snacks.

Not saying I needed to meet Don's girlfriend first, I told Hope we needed to get back over to help Nan. She agreed, but then she and Martin disappeared. I looked for Mervin or Hannah outside the shed, but I couldn't find them either. Don had been talking to Hannah right after the singing, but I hadn't seen Mervin.

"You stay here," Ben told me. "I'll find Martin. Or Mervin. He'll know where his brother is." He hurried off toward the barn.

Just then Don approached me. "It's getting late."

I answered, "I need to wait for Ben." He'd already disappeared into the darkness. At least the rain had held off.

Before I finished, Don took off. "I'll tell him you're coming with me."

"No," I called out, squinting after him. "Tell him to come back."

A few minutes later, Don returned alone. "He's still looking for Martin. He said, if you don't mind, that you should just go with me. He'll find Martin and tell him to come around in the buggy. Ben will find us, by way of the creek."

"It's awfully dark to go that way," I said.

Don pulled a flashlight from his pocket. "I have this. And it is much quicker, but I understand if you're not comfortable. You can wait. Maybe my girlfriend can stop by tomorrow."

I took a deep breath, exhaling slowly. "No, I'd like to meet her tonight." The sooner I got it over with the better. Then maybe Ben wouldn't be so uptight about Don. On second thought, maybe he wasn't as uptight as I thought since he was fine with me starting back to the Millers' without him.

Don started off across the yard toward the trail down to the creek, waving the flashlight back and forth. I stayed a few steps behind, glancing over my shoulder for Ben every few minutes. I couldn't see a thing except for an occasional beam darting around in the darkness. Probably the light on someone's cell phone.

When he reached the willow tree, Don waited for me. "He'll catch up," he said as I approached. He glanced up at the sky and then sniffed the air. "But I'm sure the rain is going to start any second—we should get going."

He sidestepped down the trail with me right behind him. When we reached the bank he reached for my hand and I gave it to him for my own safety, but he quickly dropped it when we reached the shore of the creek. He flashed the light across the stepping-stones. It was obvious he'd been this way before. He took my hand again, and I followed in his footsteps, managing not to get my shoes wet. When we reached the opposite bank, he dropped my hand. So far so good—except when I looked back over the creek there was still no sign of Ben.

"Come on," Don said, starting up toward the grove of trees.

I heard voices ahead and then the giggle of a girl. I stopped.

"It's nothing," Don said. "Just a couple of kids having fun."

My face grew warm, and for once I was thankful for the darkness so he couldn't see me blush.

As we hurried along the border of the trees, the girl giggled again. I quickened my step. In no time we'd reached the far edge of the trees. Don shone his flashlight toward the gate that separated the Cramers' property from the Millers'. When we reached it, he unlatched the gate and held it open for me. Again, I glanced over my shoulder looking for Ben. Don turned back toward the trees and shone the flashlight back and forth over the path. No one was there.

"I wonder what's taking him so long," I said.

"He probably ran into someone he hasn't seen for a while," Don answered as he yanked the gate closed and then latched it. "He'll be along soon enough."

We stayed to the fence line, on the far side of the shop and showroom. "She's going to meet us in the parking lot," Don said, his voice gravelly. "I told her to have her driver drop her off there."

We stood in the middle of the pavement until the rain started. It'd been so long that I turned my face up to it, holding my mouth open to the heavy drops, but when I realized Don was staring at me, I stopped.

He pointed at me. "Look. She's here."

I glanced toward the lane. "Where?"

He kept his finger directed at me and laughed.

The rain began to pour.

"Let's go under that tree," he said, starting toward the silver maple with the towering evergreens just behind.

Confused at the odd way he was acting, I stayed put.

"Come on," he bellowed.

Frightened, I followed.

Enough of a canopy from the maple remained, combined with the wind block behind it, that we had some cover. I leaned against the tree, wishing Don's girlfriend would show up soon.

He stepped closer to me. "Are you cold?"

I shook my head.

He yawned and stretched his arms. I flinched as his right arm came down around my shoulders. I ducked out from under him. "Don't," I said, quietly but firmly.

He laughed. "You know, Bea, I—"

"Beatrice."

This time he chuckled. "We really could have something special if you'd just relax a little." He inched closer to me again.

I stepped away. "I need to go to the house," I said, walking away from him, into the pouring rain. "I told Nan I'd be back right after the singing to help with the babies."

I thought I was going to make a clean escape but he hurried after me and grabbed my arm under my cape.

"What about your girlfriend?" I yanked away.

He held on tightly, spinning me around toward him and then backing both of us under the tree.

"Let go of me," I said. But he didn't. I jerked my arm away again, but he didn't release me. "I don't want to be with you like this."

He pushed me up against the tree trunk until I could feel the bark through my dress.

"Why did you lead me on?" he asked.

I gasped. "I didn't. Not at all. I—"

"You did," he said.

"No."

"What about on the hayride? And that night outside the shop? And when you bandaged my finger."

I shook my head. "I didn't, honestly."

"Oh. So that's the way it is. You treat every man—or boy, in Ben's case—as if you're interested in him?"

"No." I winced, aware that Hope had told me to consider him "a backup plan." Had I implied I was interested in him?

He waited for a long awkward moment, and finally said, "I'm the better match for you. I'm much more the husband type than Ben."

I shook my head and tried to wrench away, but he tightened his grip and stepped closer until his body was against mine. I flattened myself against the tree trunk and sputtered, "Stop it."

He didn't. He pressed against me, his breath heavy on my neck. I pushed, managing to get my one arm between us.

"That's one of the things I like about you," he said, taking a half step back, "you're a fighter."

Fear gripped me as he reached up, still holding the flashlight, and stroked the point of my chin with his little finger.

I'd never been kissed. But at the moment, from the look on his face, that was the least of my worries. I tried to yell, but it was as if my voice had frozen. With my free hand I managed to knock the flashlight, sending the light helter-skelter as it illuminated the rain for just a moment, before it fell to the ground.

He cursed, pulling me along as he stepped to retrieve it. As he did, he yanked me down hard toward the ground. I stumbled and fell to my bony knees as the sound of a buggy started up the drive.

Relief rushed through me. "Ben!" I called out.

Don shoved the flashlight into his pocket and then clamped his hand over my mouth. I tried to bite it, but he shoved his hand against me harder and then yanked me up. I began to shake as he pulled me back under the silver maple.

The buggy stopped in the parking lot. "Don?" It was Phillip. "Come on," he yelled. "Don't make me have to get out and find you in this downpour."

Don hesitated for a moment and then muttered, "He's early." Then, his eyes beady, he said to me, "Guess my girlfriend got delayed." He dropped his hand from my mouth, let go of my arm, and pushed me.

I stumbled backward against the tree, grabbing it to keep from falling.

Without looking back he started toward the buggy. "See you tomorrow," he said.

"Not likely." I choked on the words as a sob welled inside of me. As I let go of the tree, my hand fell against the book in my pocket. "Wait!"

Don turned as I dug the book of verses out from under my wet cape and then hurled it through the darkness. It missed his head by a couple of inches and fell with a thud to the ground a few feet beyond him. He hesitated for a moment, an angry look fixed on his face.

"Come on!" Phillip yelled.

Don picked up the book and then jogged toward his brother, the beam of the flashlight bouncing up and down, illuminating circles of rain.

After he climbed into the buggy, and as Phillip turned it around, the beam found me for a long moment and then flickered off as they started up the drive.

I touched my Kapp. It was soaked. I was tempted to head back through the sycamore grove and over the creek to the Cramers' to find Ben and tell him what happened. But what would I tell him?

And what had happened? A sob, full of pain, lodged in my throat. And then another. I'd never, in all my life, been treated so badly. I'd never felt such Shohm.

He'd acted as if I'd deserved it—for leading him on. Had I? My vision blurred.

The wind began to blow, and a branch overhead creaked. A wet leaf plastered against my cheek. I peeled it away and clasped it in one hand, wiping my wet face where it had landed with the other. Tears, mixed with rain, flowed down my face.

I took a deep breath, wiped my eyes with the edge of my cape, and started toward the house, making my way in the pitch-black as best I could.

5🐋

Although I couldn't see it until I'd nearly reached the back door, someone had left the lamp in the kitchen on low. I hung my cape and turned the lamp to high, feeling comforted by the light. I examined my arm, expecting a bruise. It was only red and fading quickly. I took the lamp down the hall with me to the bathroom, tiptoeing so as not to wake Cate and Pete, and looked in the mirror. My mouth was a little red but not bruised. Perhaps Don hadn't gripped me as tightly as I'd thought.

My eyes were red rimmed and a wet rope of hair had come loose from my bun. I took off my Kapp and released the rest of my hair, running my fingers through it.

I left the bathroom, still shaking as I did.

What had been Don's intent? Surely more than for me to meet his girlfriend, if in fact, there was a girlfriend. Perhaps he'd made all that up. I slumped down into a chair at the table, remembering he'd pointed his finger at me and said, "*Look. She's here.*"

He'd tricked me.

I buried my head in my hands. Did he think treating me that way would make me change my mind about him? I shuddered.

I placed my hand on the oak table, leaning against it, replaying Don grabbing me and then pressing himself against me. I couldn't think about what might have happened if Phillip hadn't arrived.

Maybe Don didn't have any idea how badly he'd scared me.

I lifted my head. I was trying to fool myself. How could he not know?

I stepped to the sink and poured myself a glass of water, remaining there as I drank it, watching the rain splatter against the window. That was as far into the night as I could see. And all I could hear was the rain coming sideways against the glass and house.

My stomach roiled. Had I led him on?

I heard the faint sound of wheels over the rain and rushed to the back door, finding Hope hurrying toward the house as Martin's buggy turned down the drive. "Oh, there you are." She brushed past me, leaving her cape on.

I followed her into the kitchen.

"I didn't think you'd be here already," she said as she headed straight for the hall.

"Why ever not?" I asked.

I put my glass in the sink, turned off the lamp, and followed her up the stairs. When she reached the landing, she headed straight to our room. I stopped at the closed nursery door to listen but couldn't hear anything. Nan and Bob's door was shut too.

When I reached our room, Hope breezed back past me with her nightgown in her hands, on her way to the bathroom, I guessed.

I got ready for bed in the dark, not wanting to bother with lighting the lamp, and when Hope returned I headed to the bathroom. When I was done, I assumed Hope was in bed.

"What's going on?" I asked, as I crawled under my quilt.

She didn't answer.

"Hope. What happened?"

It sounded as if she flopped toward the wall. "All I know," she said, "is that Ben is really upset."

"Why?" I asked. I was the one whom he'd abandoned to Don. What right did Ben have to be upset?

"He wouldn't say, exactly." Hope's voice was muffled. "I had to guess."

I sat up in bed. "What are you saying?" Had something happened at the singing after I left?

"Ask him yourself," she said and then flopped again, probably onto her stomach, her face in her pillow. "But keep in mind the way you looked when I came in. Hair down. Lips red. Soaking wet. . . ."

"What are you saying?"

"Nothing." She sighed.

How could I sleep after that? The rain seemed to be a lullaby to everyone in the house, including the triplets, except for me. It drummed against the windowpanes of the bedroom, matching the turmoil inside my head.

CHAPTER

17

I did get up twice during the night with the babies. Kurt had totally recovered from his cold, but Asher was worse. In the morning I awoke to the steady beat of raindrops. I wished the incident with Don had been a dream—but it hadn't been. An unsettled feeling in the pit of my stomach weighed me down as I crawled out of bed.

I'd only been in the kitchen a few minutes when Mervin and Martin's buggy drove up the drive toward the barn. A few minutes later, I watched them hurry down the path to the shop. When Phillip and Don came around the corner of the building toward the door, I stepped away from the window.

Ben was usually first to arrive, but not today. I was adding oats to the boiling water when another buggy came up the drive. I stepped to the window. Sure enough it was Ben. For a second I considered running out to him, but the water began to boil and rise to the top of the pot. I turned off the burner, but not before it boiled over. I grabbed the potholders and yanked the pan to the back burner. I'd wait a minute and catch Ben on his way to the shop.

But then Pete came into the kitchen and said he needed to make a cup of peppermint tea for Cate. "She has indigestion," he said.

"I'll make it." I didn't want him to have to work around the mess on the stove. I grabbed a mug and then a tea bag, pouring the water and handing it to Pete.

"Denki," he said, as Hope came into the room. "Nan's nursing Asher, but I need bottles for the other two."

"Guder Mariye," I said, smiling at her.

"Jah, right," she responded, taking the pitcher of formula out of the fridge.

My stomach lurched. I needed to talk with Hope, but how could I possibly tell her what had happened? It was too embarrassing. And what if she didn't believe me?

By the time I cleaned up the oatmeal and glanced out the window again, Ben was at the entrance to the shop building, opening the door. I considered asking Pete to tell Ben I needed to talk with him, but that felt awkward. I'd have to do my best to catch Ben during his break. After breakfast, I scrubbed potatoes for dinner and prepared the round steak I'd put in the refrigerator to thaw the day before, following the menu list I'd made. After I put everything in the oven, I headed upstairs to help with the babies.

Cate had asked if I'd join her in the sunroom, which I was happy to do, because Hope was only speaking to me in monosyllables. I didn't want to expose Cate to Kurt or Asher's germs, so I took Leah down. But after she cried for a half hour straight, Cate asked me to leave. "I'll read," she said.

For the first time since I started working for the Millers I wished I could spend the morning reading too, not that I envied Cate her reason for the opportunity.

Back upstairs I went. At break time I looked out the nursery window, but rain was coming down in torrents. The boys had stayed in their break room. If the rain continued, they'd eat their noon meal there as well.

We finally got the babies settled down for their morning nap, just in time to get dinner on the table. Pete and Bob dashed through the kitchen door, nearly soaked to the bone. Jah, the boys would be eating in the break room for sure.

It continued to rain buckets. Not even Hannah braved the weather to see Mervin that day, but Hope did take a platter of cookies down at the afternoon break time, hunched under an umbrella. She was gone for nearly half an hour. I imagined her and Martin going over the evening before, talking about me no doubt.

When she returned I asked if she'd seen Ben.

"He didn't take a break," she answered. "He worked straight through."

At quitting time, as I washed bottles at the sink, I heard footsteps on the stoop. I expected Bob or Pete but instead someone knocked. Hope, who was just coming down the hall with two empty bottles, hurried to the door. "Come on in," she said, her voice serious.

I dried my hands on a towel as I turned toward the mud porch. Martin, followed by Ben, came through the door into the kitchen.

"Ben needs to talk to Beatrice," Martin said, as if I weren't there. "Does she have a minute?"

"Jah," I said, facing Ben. "I've wanted to talk with you all day too."

He exhaled, slowly, his face pale and his eyes narrow. I'd never seen him appear so—pinched.

"Do you want coffee?" I asked, motioning toward the table. He shook his head.

Hope stepped to Martin's side.

Ben took a deep breath and then said, "I saw you last night. With Don."

I shivered at the thought of what he might have seen.

"I was hoping you'd catch up with us," I said.

He shook his head.

"I thought you were right behind us."

Ben stepped backward, into the frame of the door. "Are you sorry for it?"

For Don forcing himself on me? Jah, I was sorry for all of it. But I had no idea what he meant. "Sorry for what?"

"For cheating on me!"

It was my turn to step backward. "Cheating on you? That's not what—" What had he seen? Don's arm around me under the tree? Don pressing up against me? Or Don pulling me to the ground? My face warmed and then grew hot in a split second. "I don't know what you're talking about."

"It's apparent you do." Ben exhaled again, shaking as he did.

"It's all a misunderstanding." My voice cracked as I spoke. "He . . . I . . . " The harmony I'd felt in the coffee shop with Ben shattered like a crystal vase thrown against a brick wall.

Ben started toward the back door.

"Wait!" I called out.

He kept going, slamming the door behind him.

"Martin," I said. "Stop him."

"There's nothing to stop." He started toward the back door too. "You simply confirmed what Don already told him."

I followed. "What did Don say?"

Martin kept on going. "You already know what Don said."

"He's lying," I called out to Martin as the back door slammed shut again.

❧

That night I did my best to reach our bedroom ahead of Hope, determined to explain things to her, but I ended up walking a fussy Asher back and forth in the nursery while Nan fed Leah and then Kurt.

By the time I reached our room, the lamp was off and Hope was in bed, but by the way she breathed I could tell she wasn't asleep.

"Hope," I said after I'd changed into my nightgown.

She didn't answer.

"I know you're awake. I have some things to say—whether you want to listen or not." I sat down on my bed. The rain had stopped but the wind blew, scraping a branch against the corner of the house. I took a deep breath. "I did not cheat on Ben." Just the thought of it made me nauseous. I swallowed, hard. "I would never do that."

I went on to explain that Don had wanted me to meet his girlfriend. "He told Ben to follow us," I said. "I wanted to wait for Ben but Don insisted we go on ahead. He said it was fine with Ben. I just wanted to meet Don's girlfriend and get it over with."

She rolled toward me. "So you claim Don has a girlfriend?"

"Jah," I said. "At least that's what he told me. She was supposedly coming for a visit." I wasn't sure if I wanted to voice my doubts that she existed or not. I'd have to tell Hope the whole story. . . . Instead, I described what I believed at the time. "I was so relieved that he had a girlfriend, thinking he'd stop acting strangely with me, that I agreed to meet her." My face warmed, and I paused for a moment, thinking that my story sounded both arrogant and fishy at the same time.

"But why would his girlfriend be coming here?"

"Well, to visit him . . . and see Lancaster County."

"In November? There's not much to see," Hope said. "A bunch of cornstalks is about it. Oh, and rain."

That was true. "So on our way back from the Cramers', all

along I expected Ben to be right behind us, because Don told me he would be. We waited in the parking lot for the girlfriend's driver to drop her off, but then it started raining." I debated whether to tell her about Don being physical with me—and then rough—and decided not to. I wasn't sure I could tell her without crying. And I was afraid she might think I led him on too, that I was somehow responsible. "So we moved under the trees. Then Phillip came in his buggy and Don left with him. I came into the house—and then you arrived. That's all that happened."

She lifted her head to her elbow. "But no girlfriend showed up?"

"That's right," I said.

"And nothing happened between you and Don."

My voice shook. "No."

"Then why were you all out of sorts when I came into the kitchen? All jumpy. And your face was all red . . . And your hair down."

"I'd been out in the rain," I said. "My Kapp and hair were soaked."

She exhaled. "I know you, Bea. It was more than that. Something happened between you and Don."

I closed my eyes and fell back on the bed. What could I say? She was both right . . . and wrong.

"And what about Don's girlfriend?" Hope asked. "If she's in Lancaster, don't you think she would have come by today?" When I didn't answer, Hope continued, "Like I said, Martin's never mentioned her. Nor has Phillip, as far as I know." Her head fell back to her pillow. "Martin believes Ben, beyond a shadow of a doubt."

My voice wavered. "And you believe Martin?"

"Jah, we're going to get married. Remember?"

"That doesn't mean you have to believe everything he believes." I shivered. "Hope, I promise you, I haven't done anything wrong." My voice shook again. "My reputation is at stake, and even worse"—I took a raggedy breath—"Ben's love for me."

"Actually, that's not at stake anymore," she said. "He's crushed. Didn't you figure that out this afternoon?"

I wanted to wail that he hadn't heard my side yet, that surely he'd come to understand what really happened, but instead I crawled into my bed, pulling the quilt up to my eyes. Had Don lied to Ben? Or was Ben using all of this as an excuse? Perhaps he'd decided he didn't want to court me after all and this was his way of breaking up without it appearing to be his fault.

Maybe I'd been "had" again. Tears filled my eyes. The A-N-T-I-C-I-P-A-T-I-O-N that I'd felt, that something good was going to happen, completely left me. Why had God allowed me to love and be loved to only have it end so badly? Even worse than before?

Hope's breathing shifted. She'd fallen asleep—just like that. I thought I'd finally found a friend—a best friend—only to have her betray me.

I wasn't going to take my troubles to Nan. She had enough to deal with, and besides, she was old enough that I doubted she'd understand what was going on.

If Cate weren't on bed rest, I would talk with her about all of it, but I couldn't burden her now. There was no way I was going to risk adding to her stress.

I was almost relieved a minute later to hear a baby cry. I scrambled out of bed and grabbed my robe from the end of the bed. I was awake anyway. Hopefully, Nan could sleep a little longer.

The next morning was windy and drizzly, but by ten the rain had stopped. It wasn't exactly sunshine and roses. More like fog and dead leaves as I looked out the living room window, holding Leah in my arms. During the night, she'd come down with whatever Kurt and Asher had. Nan had hardly gotten any sleep, so I was walking Leah around the house now, hoping to give Nan a chance to rest, while Hope tackled the laundry in the basement.

Nan did have one of those bulbs Ben had mentioned. She'd used it on Leah earlier that morning. I hoped I wouldn't need to use it. Leah had screamed and thrashed around until I had to hold her arms and legs. Poor baby. I had nearly cried along with her.

I stood at the window, my stomach still roiling from my encounter with Don, and from Ben's reaction. I'd thought I'd feel better by today, but the truth was, I felt worse. I held Leah up against my shoulder to help her breathe better. When I held her on her back she'd coughed and her breathing grew raspier. I'd need to go get the bulb and use it myself if Nan didn't wake up soon.

Leah began to cough and sputter. I pulled her down so I could see her face. She began to cry along with coughing, causing her face to turn even redder. Her tiny hands curled up alongside her face, and she twisted in my arms.

"I'm so sorry you're sick," I said, holding her up a little and swaying with her, back and forth. She continued to cry. "I wish I could tell you that once you're not a baby anymore life will be easier, but I can't. You might end up going to school with a boy like Ben. I'm truly sorry if that happens to you."

She stopped crying and coughed again.

"If that does happen, don't believe the boy if he ever tells you he cares about you. If he ever acts, even for a day, as if he might love you, run the other way."

Leah stopped coughing and crying.

I stopped talking, surprised by the silence.

Was she breathing?

"Leah!" I lifted her higher. She seemed to be gagging. I put her to my shoulder and patted her back, but then quickly pulled her back down.

Was she breathing?

I could have rushed up the stairs to Nan, but instead I ran to the kitchen and then down the hall. "Cate!" I yelled as I neared the sunroom.

As I pushed open the door, Cate dropped her book, and it clattered to the floor as she reached out for her sister, who was still silent, her mouth open and her inky blue eyes wide.

Cate swung her legs out of the bed, held the baby face down, supporting Leah's body with her arm and face with her hand. With the heel of her other hand she hit the back of Leah's back, alarmingly hard, I thought, for such a tiny thing. After the third hit, Leah began to cry.

Cate turned her around and held her tightly. "There, there," she said to her little sister. Then to me she said, as calm as could be, "Could you get me a tissue?"

I hurried to her bedside table, just out of her reach, and held the box close to her. She grabbed a tissue and then wadded it up in her hand. "She choked on her own congestion," she said.

The baby, still in Cate's arms, was screaming now.

"Go get Nan."

I nodded and hurried from the room.

After Nan determined Leah was all right, she thanked me. I shook my head, tears stinging my eyes. "I didn't know what to do. But Cate did." I turned toward her. "How did you know?"

She nodded to a stack of books on the windowsill. My heart

sank. I was supposed to read those. "Which one would you recommend first?"

"The top one," Cate answered. "It has the most important information—it's not just about babies but about all sorts of medical emergencies."

"Take Leah in the bathroom and start the shower. She needs the steam," Cate said. "And tell Hope to go tell Dat what happened so he can call the doctor."

Nan took Leah up to the bathroom, after I kissed the baby on the head. I'd fallen hard for her and her brothers. I couldn't bear the thought of anything happening to any of them.

After I asked Hope to go tell Bob, I collapsed on a kitchen chair, my head falling to my arms on the table, on top of the book I should have read two weeks before. I couldn't stop the tears. What if I'd been alone with Leah when she began to choke? What if she'd died?

A sob shook me. Then another.

"Bea?" It was Cate, calling from the sunroom, her voice full of concern.

"I'm all right," I called back, ashamed that I'd been so thoughtless to worry her. "I'm going to make some bottles for the boys." I busied myself mixing the formula, fighting shame and despair. I'd been treated badly by Don. I'd ruined things with Ben. And then, by not reading the books Nan had recommended, I'd been negligent with Leah.

Hope came back and said the doctor advised setting up a humidifier in the nursery. Bob was going out to buy one, and then he'd connect it to a battery. She hurried on up the stairs to tell Nan.

As I filled the pan with water to heat the bottles, Hannah arrived on her horse. A minute later a buggy pulled up the drive.

As it passed by, I saw it was our horse, Daisy, pulling our buggy with Molly driving it. No Leon. She and Hannah had probably schemed to meet here.

Ten minutes later there was a knock on the door. I opened it, knowing it would be my sister and her best friend. I invited them in.

Molly hugged me. "We just wanted to say hello to Cate," she said. "And maybe sneak a peek at the babies."

I told her the babies were sick, although I didn't have the fortitude to tell her what had just happened. "Cate's in the sunroom."

Hannah gave me a curt nod, confirming that the gossip mill was up and running. My stomach lurched. At least she hadn't said anything to Molly yet—I could tell by how happy my sister was to see me.

I sent them down the hall. Laughter drifted back toward me. How I wished I had my sister's charm.

As I set the table, Nan came down with Kurt in her arms. "Who's here?" she asked.

When I told her Hannah and Molly, she headed down the hall with the baby, acting as if nothing had happened a half hour earlier. A few minutes later, Molly came back up the hall, holding Kurt.

"Oh, goodness," Molly said to me. "I can see why you like your job so much."

I nearly laughed, first because Molly really didn't like babies, although I was sure she'd adore her own, and next because Kurt wasn't crying. It was the middle of the day, and Molly had only been holding him for thirty seconds. And he wasn't choking.

Nan joined us in the kitchen and said, "Come on upstairs

and see Asher. He's much better. But Leah's sick. Hope is in the bathroom with her."

They left, parading on down the hall. I couldn't fathom how relaxed Nan seemed. I was still shaking inside.

Ten minutes later, they all returned, and Hannah explained they were going to eat with the crew. "We brought our lunches," Hannah said.

"Oh, I see," Nan teased. "You'd rather eat with the crew than with us." Then she turned toward me. "Beatrice, you and Hope should join them. Cate can give the boys their bottles. It would do you good to get out of the house."

She couldn't see the look on Hannah's face—but I could. Clearly she didn't think it was a good idea. But because Hannah hadn't had a chance to share the latest gossip with Molly, my sister said, "That's a great idea. I've really been missing Bea."

"Perfect," Nan said. "I'll go tell Hope." She turned toward me. "Just fix plates for the two of you and you can take it on out. We can serve ourselves."

Before I could respond, she headed toward the stairs.

"We'll go on out," Hannah said, pulling on Molly's arm. By the time I joined them, I was pretty sure Molly would know what was going on. I sighed. I probably should have tried to tell her first. But then again it didn't matter. She was bound to believe Hannah over me anyway.

Hope seemed conflicted about going out to eat with the boys—happy to see Martin but not so sure about arriving with me. She rushed ahead. I didn't try to keep pace with her. Obviously she didn't want to be associated with me.

Ben wasn't at the picnic table, but Don sat at the far end, and the seat across from him was open. He motioned for me to sit there.

I didn't. Instead I stood behind Phillip and asked him to move down, saying I'd like to sit beside my sister.

For some reason he did. I put my plate on the table and squeezed in. Molly gave me one of her looks. Jah, I was right on target. Hannah had told her what was going on.

But Molly wasn't deterred for long. "Anyway," she said to everyone, "about Montana . . ."

"Will your whole family move?" Phillip asked.

Molly glanced at me. "I'm not sure . . ."

Don harrumphed from down at the end of the table. "I can't imagine moving to Montana."

My face grew warm. What was he insinuating? Did he think that because he'd ruined things between Ben and me, I'd court him? My throat tightened.

Molly pursed her lips together and shot me a look. I stared straight ahead. The door to the shop area opened. I expected Ben, but Pete walked out. Before the door shut all the way though, it flew open again, and Ben appeared. He still had that sorry pinched expression on his usually handsome face. He started toward the table but froze when he saw me.

I dropped my head, thinking of the poem about the two people who had loved each other but then love fled and "paced upon the mountains overhead." Tears welled in my eyes as I pretended to concentrate on my meal, carving a trench in my potatoes with my fork for the gravy to pool in, but I couldn't help but notice that Martin got up from the table even though Hope had just sat down.

Molly reached over and plucked one of my green beans from my plate and then another as she began to describe the river they'd fished in Montana. She'd never liked fishing before. I scooted the plate her way.

"I just ate a sandwich," she answered.

"You'll be able to eat this too," I said. She always had a good appetite. I couldn't imagine what it was like now that she was pregnant. "Besides," I said, "I'm not hungry."

She took the plate and started in on the roasted pork. "Yummy," she said. "It's your recipe, right? The one with the apples?"

I nodded. Lasting love might be in short supply, but we certainly had plenty of apples.

I glanced up. Martin and Ben were several yards away from the table, conversing. Hope looked over her shoulder at them and then at me. I smiled. She shrugged.

Molly took a bite of the homemade bread, with the apple butter spread across it. I could smell the mix of cloves and cinnamon. "*Wunderbar*," she said. "Did you make this too?"

"Jah," I said.

"You're amazing," Molly said.

Any other time, her praise would have sent me over the moon but not today.

Martin nudged Ben toward the table. Ben balked. Martin said something I couldn't understand, but then Ben started toward the table. He stopped across from me.

"Beatrice," he said.

I couldn't help but notice he'd used my full name, not Bea. I swallowed hard, twice. I so wanted him to apologize for the way he'd acted, but it didn't seem to be his intention.

Ben took his hat off and ran his hand through his hair as everyone waited. He placed his hat back in place and then placed his foot up on the bench and leaned forward. His voice was quiet, but still, everyone heard him say, "If you ask my forgiveness, I'll give it to you. This one time."

I gasped. I struggled to my feet, got tangled on the bench, managed to get my legs straight, and stood. "Ben Rupp," I said, my hands flying to my hips, "I have nothing to ask your forgiveness for. You're the one that's been treating me like . . . " My eyes fell to a planter filled with rainwater with a murky film on the top. "Like scum."

Hannah giggled. Don chuckled. Obviously I hadn't chosen a strong enough put-down. And Hope glanced toward Martin, who stood behind Ben, giving him a nudge.

Ben placed his foot back on the ground and stood tall. "You can't do what you did and not hurt me. It's not like I am required to give you a second chance . . . but I want to."

I didn't take the time to even take a breath. Instead I hissed, "You're nothing but an I-G-N-O-R-A-M-U-S." I'd wanted to call someone that my entire life—at least since the fifth grade—but not even Ben Rupp had deserved the term. Until now. I turned on my heel and began marching back toward the house.

"Bea!" It was Molly, coming after me.

I increased my speed, my fists clenched together at the injustice of it all. I didn't blame Ben for being hurt by what he thought he saw. I did blame him for not trusting me and, even worse, for not listening to me. My Shohm had turned to *Zann*—anger.

"Wait!" Molly yelled.

Once I reached the stoop, I did. I was crying too hard to go into the house. When Molly reached me, she wrapped her arms around me, pulling me close. "Oh, sweetie," she said, "what's going on?"

I laid my head on her shoulder, my tears soaking her dress, and let out sob after sob. Don had attacked me. Leah had almost choked to death. Ben didn't love me.

"What happened?" she whispered.

I raised my head enough to see the others, still at the table, all of them staring at us except for Ben. He was nowhere in sight. "Hannah told you about Ben—right?" I managed to ask.

"Jah," Molly said, "but I don't think she has the story straight. You're the most chaste person I know. You'd never do that. Tell me what happened."

I let out another sob. I'd never loved my sister more.

Molly led me through the kitchen, past the table where Nan and Pete sat, each holding a baby, my head still plastered to her shoulder. "She's not feeling well," Molly said. "I'm taking her up to bed. I can stay and help with the Bopplis though."

"Oh, dear . . ." Nan said. Although it sounded as if she was alarmed about Molly helping, I knew she said it out of concern for me.

When we got to the top of the stairs, I pulled away from Molly and led the way to my room. I kicked off my shoes and crawled into my bed. She scooted in beside me, and I thought of how, after Dat had died, I'd slept in her room with her. That made me cry all the more. Perhaps if I had a father to watch over me, all of this wouldn't have happened. Maybe both Don and Ben would have been more respectful.

"Tell me everything," Molly said.

I did, starting with what happened with Leah.

"But she's fine, right?"

I nodded.

"And Nan doesn't seem upset. Read the book." She paused a moment, her lips tight, before saying, "And then loan it to me."

I nodded.

"Now, tell me what happened with Don."

I began with the ride over to the Cramers' with Hope and Martin, saying I wanted to tell Ben about the Montana problem but didn't have enough time to give it justice. "I might have seemed a little standoffish," I said.

I could feel Molly's head nod against the back of mine, probably agreeing I could seem that way at times. Probably a lot. "Go on," she said.

I did, giving a detailed account of the entire evening, explaining about Don asking me to go with him, and me saying no. Don going off to talk to Ben and then telling me he would catch up, how at first Don acted gentlemanly, deferring to me, making sure I felt comfortable walking with him back to the Millers'. I gave a play-by-play account, but this time I didn't leave out Don pressing up against me, grabbing my arm, and yanking me to the ground and clamping his hand over my mouth.

"How dare he!" Molly snarled.

I turned toward her.

Her face and neck were red and blotchy. "How could he do that? What a sociopath." I was surprised Molly knew the word.

"Don't tell Bob and Nan," I said.

"Of course I'm going to tell them." She swung her feet onto the floor.

I took a raggedy breath. "But I'm not done with my story."

Molly stopped, turned back toward me, and looked into my eyes. "Okay," she said, wiping her hand across my brow. "Finish telling me what happened."

I did, explaining that Phillip came and Don left with him and I made my way to the house, and then that Hope told me later I'd looked and acted suspicious when she came into the house.

"Did you tell her what Don did?"

I shook my head.

"Why not?"

"I was embarrassed. I was afraid maybe I *had* led him on."

"Did you?"

I shrugged. "I didn't mean to, but looking back I should have discouraged him more. I was just trying to be nice." I wrapped my arms around myself.

Molly groaned. "That's no excuse, whatsoever, for him to act the way he did."

I lowered my head back down to the pillow.

Molly stood and pulled the quilt up around me, tucking it under my chin, and then leaned down and kissed my forehead. "I can wait and talk to Bob with you, once he's back with the humidifier."

I shook my head, unpinning my Kapp and putting it on the table beside me. Then I shook my hair loose. "I just want to sleep. I'm exhausted."

"Okay, I'm going to talk with him when he gets back. You sleep for a while, and I'll come in before I leave."

I did want to sleep but really didn't think I could. But unburdening myself to Molly must have done the trick. Or maybe it was knowing she, with her take-charge personality, was on my side. Whatever it was I think I drifted off before she reached the hall.

I woke with a start, wondering where I was. The room was dim, as if dusk was falling. A baby cried, and I remembered I was at the Millers'. Down the hall, a door opened and then closed.

I couldn't possibly have slept all afternoon. Perhaps the rain had started again, darkening the day. I crawled from my bed and stepped to the window. Dusk *had* fallen. I redid my bun and then took my Kapp from the bedside table and repinned it.

A knock fell on my door, and then it opened. Molly stood with a lit lamp in her hand. "Bea?"

"I'm awake," I said. "Why did you let me sleep so long?"

"Because you needed to." She held something else in her other hand. As she came closer, I saw it was a mug. She handed it to me. "Bob's been waiting all afternoon to talk with you. He keeps going back between here and the shop."

"Oh, dear," I said, sniffing the liquid in the mug. It was tea. With milk. The way we fixed it at home.

I sat back down on the bed and drank it.

"The boys have all gone home," Molly said. "Bob wants us to go down to his office and talk with him there."

"I'd rather not."

"You have to, Bea. He's waiting to talk with Don until after he talks with you."

"Doesn't he believe what you told him?"

"Of course he does." Molly stepped toward me. "But he wants to hear it from you." I sank back down on the bed.

I wrapped my hands around the mug that had lost all of its warmth. "But it's still Don's word against mine?"

Molly put her hands on her hips. "Not necessarily."

"But there's no way to prove what really happened," I whispered.

"Let's go talk to Bob." Molly reached for me, taking my forearm, pulling me up from the bed.

On the way down the hall, I stopped at the nursery door and nudged it open. By the dim light of the lamp in the room, I could see Hope standing at the changing table, Leah in her

263

arms, and Nan in the rocking chair, feeding Kurt. In the corner, the humidifier spouted a mist into the room.

Nan's voice was full of concern. "Are you doing all right?" she asked.

I nodded. "I'll be back in a little bit."

"Take your time," she chirped. Hope didn't say a thing. She just held Leah and stared at me.

Molly pulled me to the landing and then on down the stairs. A pot of something simmered on the stove. I'd taken stew meat out to thaw that morning but hadn't done anything with it. "Who cooked?" I asked.

"I did." Molly smiled. "Cate told me where to find everything. I was hoping you'd make the biscuits in a little bit though."

"Sure," I said as we grabbed our capes on the way through the mudroom. "Did you take care of the babies too?"

"Jah," she said. "I did. I walked Asher up and down the sunroom while I talked with Cate."

I smiled.

A light drizzle fell as we hurried across the yard toward the shop. As we neared the outside door, Pete came out. "Bob's in his office," he said. I felt certain he knew what was going on too. He held the door for us, and I followed Molly inside and down the hall.

Bob must have heard us, because he met us at his door. "Let's go down to the break room," he said, "where we can sit at the table."

It hadn't been that long ago that Hope and I had served the boys cookies and milk in the room. So much had happened in the last couple of weeks.

Bob stood to the side and let us enter first. Even though there was solar electricity in the building, the light in the room was a propane lamp. He lit it quickly, directing us to the chairs. Molly and I sat on either side of the head of the table, leaving that place for Bob, but he told me to sit at the head. "Next to your sister," he said.

Once we were all in our places, Bob said Molly had told him what happened but he wanted to hear it from me. I went through the whole thing again, my voice growing tight as I struggled through the story.

"Do you think Don has a girlfriend?" Bob asked. "Or do you think he was using her as an excuse to win your trust?"

I shook my head. "I didn't know this at the time, but it doesn't sound like he mentioned her to anyone but me." I hesitated and then said, "And as we stood in the parking lot, he implied that I was the 'girlfriend'—that he hoped I'd come around and choose him."

Bob shook his head. "He had a sick way of attempting to win you over."

I didn't answer.

"But he used the idea of a girlfriend to convince you to go with him, to imply he was safe." Bob patted the tabletop with the tips of his fingers. "Don seemed jealous of the Youngie here. I tried to talk with him about it once, but he became defensive."

I hadn't thought about Don being jealous. That was preached against, of course, but it was also human nature.

"I talked with him once about my first wife dying. And about how I had to choose to trust God and live the life he'd given me." Bob sighed. "But Don said my story didn't count. I was happily married again and blessed with a second family."

He certainly had been, but with a time lapse of over twenty years. Bob had waited a long time.

"I'll talk with Don in the morning," Bob said. "And then I'll deal with Ben."

"It really is their word against mine," I answered, repeating what I'd said to Molly before.

"Jah, I realize that." Bob leaned forward, his voice sympathetic. "But I believe you, Bea Zook. You've never given me a reason not to. I can't tolerate anyone working for me mistreating a woman. We'll take this a step at a time. But you have my full support."

My eyes welled with tears as he stood, and we followed him down the hall, me blinking until my eyes no longer blurred.

"A letter came for Hope," he said and then stepped into his office to retrieve it. "I think it's from her bishop." Again his tone was sympathetic. "Would you give it to her?"

I took the letter from him, wondering why he didn't deliver it himself. But maybe it was his way of keeping me in the loop. Hope might not share anything about the letter with me. It would be easier, in light of the fact that I wouldn't be getting married at all, to know if she would be soon.

I started to follow Molly down the hall—until she stopped abruptly. She turned back around and, looking past me, said, "Bob?"

He stepped back out of his office.

She stepped in front of me and asked, "Do we know for sure Don *was* married before?"

I gasped. Bob raised his eyebrows.

"Think about it," Molly said. "If he lied about having a girlfriend, maybe he lied about being married."

"I don't know about that," Bob said. "I guess I assumed his family would have gone to the wedding. And he does have a beard." He looked from Molly to me. We both shrugged. I'd never heard about the Eichers going to Ohio for anything. Then again, I would have been too young to notice, and even if I hadn't been, I didn't keep track of those things. But Molly did.

ॐ

The next morning, as I cleaned up the breakfast dishes, my hands submerged in the soapy water, I couldn't help but glance out the kitchen window, over and over. I knew Bob would talk to Don first thing. I also knew there was no way I would know what Don's response was, unless Bob told me. Or so I thought.

As I dipped a plate into the burning-hot rinse water, my head up and looking out the window, Don came storming out the shop door. I expected Bob—or someone—to come after him, but no one did. He headed around the outside of the shop to the display room, stopping in line with the house and turning toward the window. I ducked my head down, concentrating on the dishes again.

"Please don't let him come to the house," I prayed.

"What did you say?" It was Hope. I thought she was upstairs helping with the babies. I hadn't even realized I'd said it out loud. I kept my eyes downcast.

She stepped toward the sink, placing three bottles on the counter, and then looked out the window.

"What's Don doing?" she asked.

"I have no idea." I dipped another plate in the rinse water and then put it on the rack.

"He's staring this way. I think he sees me," she said.

"Don't make eye contact with him." I scrubbed another plate, still stooped over.

"Why?" She leaned forward and then quickly stepped back. "Oh, dear," she said. "Now he's coming this way."

I wanted to flee upstairs but I didn't think that would be fair to leave Hope to deal with Don alone. I pulled my hands out of the dishwater and grabbed a dish towel. "Let's both go upstairs," I said, dropping the towel on the counter.

"Wait," she said. "Bob's coming out of the shop."

I groaned. "Come on." I grabbed her hand. "Believe me, we don't want to stick around for what's next."

"What's going on?" She pulled away from me and stepped back to the sink.

"Bob talked with Don this morning, and it looks like Don is upset."

"Uh oh," Hope said, still staring out the window.

I couldn't help myself. I stepped to her side.

Bob and Don stood face-to-face. Bob pointed to the lane and said something to Don, who turned toward the window and yelled, "Bea, come out here!"

Bob stepped between Don and the window, blocking his view of us. I held my breath. Finally Don turned and headed toward the lane. He was out of our sight in a few steps, but Bob didn't budge. I assumed he was watching Don until he knew for sure he'd left.

"Here he comes," Hope said.

At first I thought she meant Don. I bristled, but then I realized Bob was marching toward the house. We scurried away from the window.

"Bea," he called as he came through the door.

"Right here," I answered, moving toward the table.

"I tried to talk with Don," he said, his hat in his hand, "but he—" He stopped when he saw Hope. "I'm sorry," he said, turning toward me. "I thought you were alone."

"It's all right." I glanced toward Hope and then back to Bob. "Go on."

Bob seemed to understand that I didn't mind if Hope heard and said, "Don got defensive and then quit, just like that. After he stormed out I was afraid he might come over to confront you, which it appears he planned to do."

"Denki," I said.

"I'm glad you came forward with this. Obviously Don has something to hide, or he wouldn't have reacted the way he did." Bob put his hat back on his head. "I'll be back at dinnertime. If you need me sooner, send Hope out to the shop." He smiled then, kindly, and left.

"Bea," Hope said, "what was that all about?"

"Come dry the dishes." I headed back to the sink. "I should have told you that night, but I was afraid to."

When I finished my story, she said, "I'm so sorry. Please forgive me."

"I do," I said, as sincere as I'd ever been. "So you believe me?"

She nodded.

"Do you think the others will?"

Her face fell.

"Jah," I said. "I don't think so either."

After we'd finished up the kitchen and were ready to go upstairs, Hope pulled the envelope from her pocket that I'd given her the night before.

"It's from my bishop," she said.

I nodded. I'd gathered that.

"He's already sent a letter to the bishop here. He approves of the marriage."

I hugged her, feeling genuine happiness for both Hope and Martin. "What about your Dat?" I asked. "Have you heard from him?"

She shook her head, looking downcast.

"Maybe his letter will come today," I said, giving her a hug, thankful that the rift between us had been mended.

Later, as I fixed the noon meal, peeling potatoes at the sink, I sensed someone watching me. I looked toward the shop, wondering if perhaps Ben might be staring at the house. Perhaps he was working up the nerve to come apologize.

I sighed. I was thinking too highly of myself. Then I had the horrible thought that perhaps Don had gone up on the hill, where he could see the house.

I doubted he could see through the kitchen window though.

I just wouldn't go outside. That would save me the embarrassment of seeing Ben or Don.

That afternoon Nan asked Hope to sort the laundry in the basement so we'd have a start on it the next morning. Then she asked me to help her bathe the babies. In a normal household, with one baby, I guessed the chore was done in the morning or before bed. In the Miller household it was done whenever we could fit it in.

I stoked the fire in the wood stove and then set up the row of tubs on the kitchen table, filling two of them at the kitchen sink, as Nan brought the babies down the stairs one at a time, leaving each in the playpen as she returned upstairs for the next one. Leah's congestion was much better. The humidifier had done the trick.

When all three were down, I spread towels on the table. Nan picked up Leah and I picked up Asher, because Kurt was the one fussing the least, and we began undressing them.

"I'm going to say this quickly, before Hope comes back up." Nan's voice was low. "If you want to go home, I completely understand. I don't want to make an awkward situation worse for you."

My stomach sank. "Oh, no," I said. "That's the last thing I want to do."

"Are you sure?" Nan lifted Leah into the tub.

I swallowed hard and nodded.

"All right," Nan said. "Just let me know if you change your mind." Nan smiled down at Leah, tickling her under the chin, saying as she did, "Bob is going to leave a message for your Mamm this morning and invite her to come over for supper."

"Oh," was all I could say to that. No doubt Molly had already told Mamm everything anyway, but I hated to think of her worrying about me.

Hope's footsteps fell on the stairs. "Laundry's sorted," she said as she pushed the basement door open.

Nan smiled at her. "Go ahead and fill the third tub and then bathe Kurt."

Hope complied. As we worked, I heard Cate in the hall. I surmised she was on her way to the bathroom. It was the only time she was allowed out of bed. But she kept coming to the kitchen, wearing her bathrobe and slippers.

"Are you all right?" Nan asked.

"No," Cate said, sitting down at the end of the table. "I'm on my way to going crazy."

Nan smiled at her stepdaughter and then nodded at the chair next to the one she sat on. "If you plan on taking a little detour," Nan said, "at least put your feet up."

I didn't think she should. I thought she should go back to bed immediately, but if Nan didn't seem too alarmed, I didn't feel it was my place to say anything.

Cate did prop up her feet. Her belly looked even bigger, but maybe it was the angle and the fact her robe was tied above her waist. She reached out and touched Kurt's hand as Hope undressed him.

"You'll have one of these soon," Nan said.

Cate's eyes teared up, and then she said, "Don't mind me. I'm just feeling emotional. A few years ago I would have thought a couple of weeks in bed with nothing to do but read would be a Drohm." She swiped at her eyes. "But not anymore."

"Sit with us while we bathe the babies," Nan said. "It will do you good."

Once we were done, Cate returned to her room and we took the babies upstairs. All three were relaxed and ready to nap.

Nan said she was going to nap too and asked Hope to work on cleaning out the garden while I fixed supper.

It was about time for the boys' break, and it wasn't raining, so it was perfect timing for Hope to be outside. Once we were down in the kitchen, Hope went to the mudroom and pulled on boots. I stood in the doorway. "Don't say anything about me to any of them," I said.

"Even if they ask?"

I nodded.

"I won't," she said, swinging her cape over her shoulders.

I tried to stay away from the window as I scrubbed carrots and then turnips, but I couldn't help but glance up now and then. At first the boys gathered around the picnic table, but then Martin drifted over to the garden. Soon Mervin and Ben joined Martin in helping Hope, while Phillip stayed put. Either Mervin or Martin said something funny, because they all laughed, except for Ben. He stood with his arms crossed, and then headed back toward the shop.

Mervin threw his head back in laughter as Ben walked away. A moment later, Mervin and Martin headed back to the shop too, followed by Phillip. As Hope loaded the rest of the vines from the squash plants into the wheelbarrow, it began to rain. She kept working until the wheelbarrow was full and then pushed it toward the compost pile, moving out of sight.

A few minutes later she came through the back door, pausing to take off her boots and cape. When she entered the kitchen she said, "I'll go back out after the rain stops."

She stopped by the wood stove and warmed her hands while I stumbled over my thoughts. I wanted to ask how everyone was doing. And what the joke had been about. And if anyone asked about me.

But how could I inquire about that when I'd asked her not to talk about me?

She lifted her head. "Don't you want to know what we talked about?"

I grimaced.

"I can tell you do," she said. "Martin asked where you were, because none of them have seen you since yesterday noon."

I nodded.

"They think you've gone somewhere. Back to your Mamm's farm. Or maybe even to Montana already."

I shook my head. That was like all of them to jump to conclusions like that.

"And then Mervin said he bet you'd run off with Don—or that you were planning to."

"Was he serious?"

Hope nodded. "He seemed to be. I mean, he was all jokey, but at the same time he wasn't. Do you know what I mean?"

I nodded. I knew exactly what she meant.

My head began to hurt. "Did you say anything to him?"

She blushed. "I know you didn't want me to, but I told them they were all ignoramuses."

I burst out laughing.

"Is that correct? As far as making it plural?"

I nodded, still laughing. But if she'd called them all *ignorami*, that would have been funny too.

Before I could say more, Cate called my name from down the hall.

"I'll be right back," I said. I hadn't checked on Cate for an hour or so. I thought she was sleeping. But maybe she needed some fresh water or another book to read. I could loan her the book of poems Ben had given me. Better yet, I could give it to her. "What do you need?" I asked as I entered the sunroom.

"To talk with you," she said, pointing to the couch. "Sit down."

I did, not sure what to expect. Had I done something else wrong?

"What's going on?" she asked.

I shook my head. I didn't want to burden her.

"Pete told me some of it. I'm so sad—false accusations are horrible. I can't believe Ben . . ." She sighed. "You two seemed so right for each other."

"It's okay," I lied. "I was mistaken about him. That's all." I stood. "Are you out of books to read? Because I have one for you."

I left the room before she answered and returned with the book of poems, handing it to her quickly and then leaving again to check on the meal.

Later, as I mashed the potatoes, Cate called out my name again. I headed back down the hall, stopping in the doorway. She held the open book toward me, showing me that she was reading the "When You Are Old" poem.

"You know," she said, "whether a story has a happy ending or not all depends on when the author ends the story. If he would have waited a day or two, love might have come back down from the mountaintop and sat beside the fire again. Relationships are like that. You have to work through things. You can't let love flee."

"I didn't let love flee," I said. "Ben chased it away."

"Jah," she said, "I understand that. And it's important that you're loyal to yourself. But even more so, you should be loyal to the truth because it's a big part of love, a love that's healthy anyway."

"I am loyal to the truth," I said. "I'm not going to sprinkle sugar over what Ben has done." I couldn't trust him after this. There was no hope for our relationship.

"I mean loyal to finding out the truth, Bea." She sat up a little straighter. "Until you can get to the bottom of this, to why Ben is so sure you cheated on him, you won't really know what happened."

What happened was that Ben was an idiot. I'd known that in the past. I'd been a fool to think he'd changed. "I'll bring you a tray in a few minutes," I said to Cate.

"Denki." She extended the book to me.

"Oh, you can keep it," I said.

She shook her head. "I don't want to." She took a deep breath as I took it and then said, "I hope Pete will be in soon."

"He will be," I said. And my Mamm would be arriving too. The last thing I wanted was to rehash everything with her around. And it wasn't as if there was anything she could do anyway.

⁂

I shouldn't have been surprised that Molly arrived with Mamm, who brought three casseroles. After I took the pans down to the basement and put them in the freezer, I quickly set another place at the table as she explained that Leon decided to stay home and sort through his tackle in the barn. "He'll take some to Montana and sell the rest."

Pete ate with Cate in the sunroom. A soon as Bob entered the kitchen, carrying Leah, Mamm swooped the baby out of his arms and settled in the rocking chair, cooing at her. Nan entered next with Kurt and put him down in the playpen, followed by Hope with Asher.

As I put the food on the table, Molly knelt down by the play-pen and looked at Kurt. "Pick him up," Mamm said. "Babies need to be held."

Molly did, although a little awkwardly, which made me smile. She was better than me at everything in life—except for babies. Well, she wasn't much interested in words either.

Nan sat on her chair as I put the potatoes on the table. "Time to eat," she said. Poor Nan was always hungry.

Hope put Asher in the playpen and Molly put Kurt beside him, but when Mamm tried to put Leah down, she began to fuss. "I'll rock her," Mamm said. "While all of you eat."

After Bob led us in prayer, taking advantage of my mother's hearing loss, I asked Molly, quietly, what she'd told Mamm.

"Just that there had been a misunderstanding as far as Ben. I didn't give her all the details."

"Denki," I said.

Bob passed the roast to Nan. "I talked with Ben today. He says he definitely saw you, Bea, with a man. He's sure it was Don—"

I started to speak but realized I was interrupting.

Bob continued. "I don't think he's lying—I think he truly thinks he did see you. He's hurt to the core by it."

Molly passed the potatoes to Bob. "Did you ask Ben exactly what he saw?"

Bob actually blushed. "Jah . . ."

"For example, did you ask what she was wearing?"

I shook my head. "Molly, I was wearing my cape and Kapp. Like every other girl at the singing."

"True . . ." Molly said. "How about exactly where she was?"

"Under a tree," Bob answered, glancing up at me.

"That's true," I said, "but Don and I were arguing—and then

he was being . . . rough with me. We weren't doing anything Ben could misconstrue . . . the way he has." Unless he only saw us for a split second.

"I'm going to talk with him," Molly said. "And try to figure this out. I'll come over tomorrow." I was tempted to roll my eyes. Molly thought she could come to the rescue, positive she could do something not even Bob could accomplish. In the background, Mamm hummed to Leah and Asher began to fuss.

"As far as Don's wife," Bob said, "I asked Phillip about it. He said Don was married, but they didn't learn of it until after the wedding. And he said that his wife did die in a buggy accident—at least that's what Don said."

It had to be true. Who would lie about such a horrible thing?

"Well, I'm still really curious about Don's girlfriend story," Molly said. "I think I'll call one of my friends in Ohio and see what I can find out."

I didn't feel like rolling my eyes anymore. The truth was, if anyone could figure this mess out, it was Molly.

Asher's fussing grew louder. "I'll get him," Bob said.

"No, you eat. I'll do it." I stuffed another bite into my mouth and pushed back my chair. As I lifted Asher he let out a wail, his face all red and scrunched. "You're all right," I cooed, swaying back and forth with him. He wailed again but then shifted down to a whimper. I stepped closer to Mamm so I could hear her peaceful humming to Leah, thankful that my mother hadn't heard our earlier conversation.

She held Leah over her shoulder, patting the little one's back. Without missing a beat she reached over and patted my arm, smiling up at me as she did. She said, quietly, "I'm so happy you like taking care of the babies."

"Me too," I answered.

She continued speaking softly. "Molly said you've had a difficult couple of days. I know Nan and Bob would be fine with you coming home if you need to."

I nodded. "I'm fine, Mamm."

She started humming again as the others chatted around the table. I kept swaying. Mamm kept rocking. I could see why she wanted to move to Montana. I didn't want her to miss out on Molly's baby—not for me.

I winced. It wouldn't matter now if I did go to Montana. I'd be the *Maidel* Aenti. And Molly's helper. Still, as much as I'd love my niece or nephew, I couldn't imagine moving to Montana. Ben or not, I didn't want to leave Lancaster County.

Mamm stopped humming. "Is there anything you need?" she asked.

I stepped in front of her, facing her. "Would you consider letting Love come back over here?" Love didn't like Don. If he came around, she'd warn me.

"Molly can bring her by tomorrow," Mamm said. "When she talks to Ben."

I grimaced. So much for her not hearing our conversation. Her hearing was better than she let on. She smiled and started up with the humming again. But then a minute later she leaned close to me again and whispered, "Just don't let the *biddah* bug bite." It was something she used to tell me when I was little—and, honestly, it was timely advice for this particular time too. The last thing I wanted was to be a bitter old Maidel.

Mervin knocked on the back door the next morning, Love at his side. "So you really are still here." Mervin took off his sunglasses, which he didn't need on a foggy morning. "But Don's gone?"

Love pressed my leg with her nose. "I have no idea where Don is," I answered, as I reached down to stroke my dog's head.

"That's the same thing Phillip said."

I doubted Don had left Lancaster, but I decided the best thing to do was change the subject. "Where's Molly?" I asked. "She said *she'd* bring Love."

"She said to tell you she couldn't make it, that she has some things to deal with concerning their move."

I thanked him for bringing Love and then asked if he'd fill her water dish and food. I nodded toward the bag on the mud porch. The last thing I wanted to do was venture far from the house and risk seeing Ben.

Throughout the day, I called Love to the mud porch to pet her. Happy to serve me, she'd come quickly, her tail wagging, knocking against the coats hanging on the pegs and the line of boots on the floor. It was a comfort to have her nearby. I'd changed. I was still a cat person, but Love had won my heart.

By late afternoon, I asked Hope to move Love's dishes under the eaves of the house, next to the back door. She hadn't been chained all day. She wasn't going anywhere.

Friday morning Molly sent a note with Mervin that explained she'd had some more unexpected things come up concerning the logistics of her plans, but she'd be by soon. I hoped they were details that would prohibit them from moving at all.

She added a P.S. at the end of the note, asking me to come to the house Sunday evening to talk things through. *Mervin is serious about buying the farm*, she wrote. *And now Mamm is feeling conflicted about all of it. I need you to talk with her.*

I refolded the note and slipped it into my pocket. Molly was probably too caught up in all of her own problems to remember she said she'd speak to Ben and call friends in Ohio to find out more about Don. It appeared there were some things not even Molly could fix. I'd have to figure it out on my own. I'd been too complacent the last few days, relying on others to help me instead of helping myself.

Minutes before the noon hour, Hannah arrived to wait for Mervin. I hurried outside, wanting to speak with her before the boys came out of the shop.

"I need your help," I said to her quickly. "I'm wondering who Ben might have seen that night, thinking it was me."

"Goodness, Beatrice," she said. "Don't you think he can recognize you?"

"It wasn't me," I answered.

"I don't care who you make out with." She crossed her arms. "But why did you lead Ben on and then betray him?"

Voices came from down by the shop.

"Here they come," she said. "You'd better go."

Dumbfounded, I headed back to the house. With each step, the bitter bug bit at my soul.

A little after noon, Bob came into the house with a letter for Hope. "I know you've been waiting for this," he said as he handed her the envelope.

She sat down at the table, pulled out the letter, and read it silently, a smile spreading across her face. When she finished it, she folded the paper and looked up at me and then turned her attention to Bob. "Dat said if you approve he approves. He trusts your judgment. He's given us his blessing. He even said he wouldn't mind if we married in Lancaster." She stood quickly. "May I go tell Martin?"

"Jah," Bob said, his eyes smiling.

Hope slipped the envelope into her pocket and practically skipped toward the mudroom. As she flung her cape over her shoulders, Bob gave me a sympathetic look.

I glanced away, afraid I might tear up. I was happy for Hope. I truly was. And her marrying Martin meant she'd stay in Lancaster County. Still, I couldn't stop the ache inside me.

It rained all of that day, through the night, and during the next day too. The soggy red and yellow leaves of the maple and the brown leaves of the oak covered the lawn. At dinner Hope said the ground was so waterlogged that it felt as if it were a sponge when she walked across it.

Bob added that the creek between the properties was near flood level, something that seldom happened in November. It was usually only that high after the snowmelt.

I was glad we'd already moved Love under the eaves. She kept dry there and seemed content to see me on the mud porch several times a day.

That afternoon at quitting time Molly finally showed up, coming to the back door to tell me hello. The rain had slowed to a drizzle and the temperature had dropped more. Darkness had completely fallen, bringing a quietness to the house. Perhaps the lull before the storm. The babies had been colicky again, and I guessed it would be another wild night.

"I came to talk with Ben." Molly stood at the back door with Love at her side. "I need to get right back, so I won't have time to stay and talk for long. But you're coming over on Sunday, right?"

I nodded.

"*Gut*. We have lots to discuss. We'll have a better idea of the timing of everything."

I frowned.

"Now that you and Ben have broken up, there's no reason for you not to come to Montana with us."

"Molly . . ."

"Think about it," she said. "It would make everything much easier on Mamm."

"I have been thinking about it," I said.

"*Gut.*" She turned to go. "I'll stop by before I go, just to tell you what Ben says."

She was back in less than ten minutes.

"Come on in," I said.

She shook her head. "I don't have anything to tell you."

"He wouldn't talk to you?"

"No, he did. But I didn't get any new information from him. Just that he saw you and Don. And he's one hundred percent sure it was you, although only seventy-five percent sure it was Don from what he actually saw."

"One hundred percent, huh?"

She nodded. Something else was going on. She didn't seem as sympathetic toward me as she had before.

I narrowed my eyes. "What else did he say?"

She shrugged. "That was it, really."

I wrinkled my nose. "Did you get ahold of any of your friends in Ohio? To ask about Don?"

"Oh, sorry," she said. "I keep meaning to. I need to find my list of phone numbers I wrote down after I got rid of my cell. I think it's in the desk out in the greenhouse." She grimaced. "I've been so busy . . ."

"I'd really appreciate it," I said. "Or give me the number and I'll call."

"Really?" she said. "You hate using the phone."

I shrugged. "I hate being falsely accused too."

"I'll call," she said, wrinkling her nose. "See you tomorrow. Probably at church, jah? And then for supper."

"Jah," I said. "Depending on how the babies are doing. But I'll come by the house for sure."

I hoped Molly would help me. If not, I'd have to figure out how to clear my name on my own.

That evening Bishop Eicher, Mervin, and Hannah all congregated at the Millers' dining room table, along with Hope and Martin. The twins' parents had encouraged a double wedding. I guessed to save money, which I knew would appeal to Hope and her family. Apparently Hannah and her parents, who would be footing the bill for the event, had agreed to the idea too.

As soon as everyone arrived, I headed upstairs to help Nan care for the babies. An hour later, she'd retreated to her room with Leah while I rocked both Asher and Kurt.

When the nursery door opened I expected Hope, but it was Hannah. "Ach, there you are," she said to me. "With the babies." She acted as if nothing had happened between us the other day.

"It's all set," she said. "The marriages will be published tomorrow and held a week from this coming Thursday." She giggled. "Church is at the Mosiers' farm, but Mervin will be with me and I guess Martin will come over here." Our district held to the old tradition of the bride- and groom-to-be not attending the service when their marriage was published. Instead the bride prepared a meal for the groom during that time.

"Goodness," I said. "Your family's been working on the wedding for a while, then."

"Of course," she answered. "I just couldn't imagine getting married without Molly here. So when I found out they were thinking about moving to Montana, I started the planning."

"Wait, when did you start the planning?"

"When they first started talking about the property in Montana."

"But you wouldn't have known until they returned . . ."

She shook her head. "They knew a couple of months ago they were interested in the ranch."

I took a deep breath, until I felt as if I might explode.

She rushed on. "That's not what I came up to talk about, actually. I wanted to apologize for the other day. What you choose to do really isn't my business."

Flabbergasted, I asked, "What do you mean?"

"Whom you . . . spend your time with. What you do."

"But it is your business," I said. "We're part of the same community."

"Jah, I get that," she said. "But I was thinking maybe Ben mixed things up."

I nodded.

"Jah, that's what I thought. So you weren't committed to him like he thought?"

I started shaking my head. "No, I was. Absolutely."

"Then why did you—"

"I'm telling you, I didn't!" My voice may have been a little loud by then.

Hannah stepped back. "Goodness, what a mess. I can't figure any of this out, not for the life of me."

I wanted to say, *Welcome to my world*—I'd heard that from

Molly, probably a phrase she'd picked up at some party—but didn't.

She glanced toward the door. "I should get back downstairs. I've said too much. Don't be mad at Molly about the whole Montana thing. Or at Ben. He's really hurt."

I didn't answer as she turned and fled.

Had Mamm known from the beginning about Molly and Leon's plan to move to Montana? They'd all deceived me.

And why was everyone so sympathetic toward Ben? Didn't they know my heart was broken too?

I didn't go to church the next day either. Bob had to go to announce Hope's wedding so I encouraged Pete to go with him. I didn't want to face Molly and Mamm in a crowd of people. After Bob and Pete left, I took the babies into Cate's room to keep her company, lining them up on her bed, while Nan went back to sleep. Hope started preparing her meal for Martin, who would arrive in about an hour.

Rain pelted the windows of the sunroom. The gray day matched my mood, but spending time with Cate and the babies began lifting it. I handed Leah to Cate, along with a bottle.

"Is it weird to think of these little ones as your siblings?" I asked as I settled a sleeping Kurt into the playpen I'd dragged down the hall and into the room.

Cate shook her head. "No. I'm just so grateful God blessed Nan and Dat. And that all the babies are healthy. What an unimaginable gift. There's nothing like family."

Her words stung as I thought of my own. I considered not seeing them at all that evening. Molly would end up getting her way, no matter what I said. Mamm would sell the farm. They'd all move to Montana. And I'd end up going because I didn't have anything else to do with my life.

I could try to stay with Edna, but I'd need a job, probably more of one than working for the Millers.

"What's wrong?" Cate asked as she shifted Leah to the other side of her big belly.

I shook my head. "Nothing."

"Everything?" Cate asked.

I shook my head again.

Hope came in to chat while the pasta cooked, sitting on the end of Cate's bed while I walked Asher. She asked how many guests were usually invited to weddings in Lancaster County. "I mean, I was at Bob and Nan's and it was huge. Are most that big?"

"It depends," Cate said. "My wedding was pretty small. Around two hundred people. Because you're sharing the day with Hannah and Mervin, it will probably be pretty big. I'd say four hundred or so."

That sounded right to me too. That was about what we had at Molly's.

Hope kept asking questions, but I zoned out, staring at Asher, who for the moment was both awake and calm, while I thought about Ben. I'd been right about him all along. He only thought of himself. E-G-O-C-E-N-T-R-I-C. It had been one of our fifth-grade spelling words.

"Oh, I didn't think I'd ever marry," Cate said, drawing my attention back to the conversation.

"Didn't you court?"

Cate chuckled. "Funny thing . . . I actually went out with Martin and Mervin's older brother a few times. But that was all. I was awfully prickly back then. I still was even after I met and then married Pete."

"What happened?" Hope asked.

"God tamed me," Cate said. "I finally learned to trust him—instead of expecting so much from myself and others. I really had behaved badly up to that point."

"Oh," Hope said.

Hope was so sweet, she'd never have to worry about behaving badly. But I could sympathize with Cate. Hope jumped to her feet. "Oh, no," she said, rushing from the room. "The pasta!"

Soon all three babies were asleep and I put them down in the playpen, where they wiggled close to each other until they were touching, giving Cate a chance to rest.

Bob and Pete would eat after the church service with everyone else in our district. I planned to heat up leftover soup for Nan, Cate, and me—after Hope and Martin finished eating.

He'd arrived by the time I entered the kitchen. "I'm going upstairs," I said to Hope. "Come get me when the Bopplis wake up."

As others in our district worshipped together at the Mosiers' house, I tried to read Scripture, opening my Bible to the Psalms, but I couldn't concentrate. I opened my journal instead. I'd hardly written in it since I'd come to the Millers'. I hadn't had time. Now I didn't know where to start. With Ben wanting to court me? With Molly's return from Montana? With Don treating me so badly and Ben dumping me? I closed my journal, tears filling my eyes.

"Oh, God," I whispered out loud. I'd worked at being so good, done all the right things, and still nothing had worked out. Why had he given me the desire to be married when I'd suppressed it for so long? And the wish to be a mother? Only to take away all of my chances? How absurd life could be. There was a time I might have laughed at all of it. But now I cared.

Maybe because my pride—*mei Hochmoot*—was hurt. That

wouldn't be surprising. It seemed my pride had been part of my problem all along. When it came to my competition with Ben. To my reluctance to spend time with the other Youngie. To my hurt from when Ben stopped courting me the first time.

However, my hurt now wasn't related to my pride. Only to Don's meanness and Ben's stubbornness.

I shut my journal and opened my Bible again, to Psalms, skipping ahead of my reading, looking for something my Dat had marked. I stopped at Psalm 143:8, which was underlined with the faint marks of a pencil. I read it silently and then out loud, "'Cause me to hear thy lovingkindness in the morning; for in thee do I trust: cause me to know the way wherein I should walk; for I lift up my soul unto thee.'"

Pride was the opposite of trusting God. I could trust myself, to no avail, or in humbleness trust him.

I closed my Bible, tiptoed down the stairs, and hurried past Hope and Martin, who sat eating at the table as I listened for the babies. All was silent. Then I hurried out the door and to the shop.

I knew no one would mind if I used the phone. I dialed our number and left a message for Molly. "Please call your friend in Ohio as soon as possible," I said. "I really need to get to the bottom of this."

Afterward, back on my bed, I picked up the book about caring for infants that Cate had loaned me.

ॸॖॖ

By the time the men returned from church, Hope and Martin had gone for a walk. As Pete headed straight down the hall to Cate, Bob said to me, "Your Mamm and Molly both asked about you. They're looking forward to seeing you this evening."

The singing that night was at the Mosiers' farm too. The plan was that I would give Hope a ride there and then spend that time with my family. Martin would soon be returning home to help get ready for the singing.

Bob assured me he could handle supper. "I think I'll make pancakes," he said, a twinkle in his eye. "Pete can fry the bacon."

I took Love with us, in case she wanted to stay home. I was pretty sure Don was long gone. By the time we reached the lane to the Mosiers' place it was pitch-dark, except for the lantern and the running lights on the buggy. I stopped Thunder by the mailbox, tempted to ask Hope to walk up the lane so I didn't have to show my face at the singing. But I realized that was a little over the top and slightly dangerous, considering how dark it was.

When I reached the Mosiers' shed, Hope jumped down, practically into Martin's arms, and told me she'd get him to walk her over to my family's place when the singing was over. "There's no reason for you to come back here," she said.

"Denki," I answered and then turned Thunder around, scoping out who was there. I didn't see Ben. But Phillip stood near the doorway with Jessie. She waved at me, but I pretended I didn't see her, not wanting to draw Phillip's attention.

I had a new empathy for her. How had she stayed so centered after Phillip dumped her? Everyone knew. And yet she didn't seem out of sorts at all—she'd stayed serene, at least by all appearances.

As Thunder pulled the buggy back onto the highway, I whispered a prayer, "Please, God, help me to trust you. To stay centered on you, not myself."

In my mind, I'd called Ben egocentric, but so was I. And I'd continue to be, unless I allowed God to intervene.

Out loud I'd called Ben an ignoramus. And then I'd been so pleased that Hope had lumped all the boys into that category, to their faces. I flinched. I was one too.

But I still wanted the truth and there was nothing wrong with that. "Please, God," I prayed again. I knew he wanted truth and justice, but sometimes God didn't bring those two about until heaven. "I'll trust your timing," I whispered as I turned Thunder up the lane toward home.

Love jumped down from the buggy and ran toward the house, barking. Molly opened the back door and stepped onto the stoop, waving at me. Once Love reached her, she bent down to pet her.

After I unhitched Thunder and put him in the pasture, I stepped into the barn and called the gray kitty. She came running and rubbed my ankle as I petted her. But then she darted off just as quickly, ready to be on her own.

By the time I reached the house, Love had settled into her usual spot under the eaves near the back door, and Molly had returned to the kitchen. When I entered, she and Mamm were dishing up supper while Leon sat at the table.

But he wasn't alone. Hannah and Mervin sat with him.

For a moment I was tempted to hightail it back to the Millers'.

But then Mamm rushed toward me, wrapping her arms around me. "I'm so glad you're here."

I wished I could say the same. Still, leaving wouldn't be fair to Mamm. As I washed my hands at the sink, Molly whispered, "I didn't invite them. Honest. They just came by, said they didn't want to go to the singing."

I simply nodded my head.

After we all sat down and Leon led us in prayer, Molly began the conversation by saying, "I got your voicemail. I kept forgetting, but I finally called my friend in Ohio this afternoon. She gave me the name and cell phone number of a girl from Don's old district who's left the church."

I shook my head, wanting her to stop.

"No, she really did," Molly said, as if I were contradicting her.

I gave her a wide-eyed look, hoping she'd get my hint. I didn't want to talk about it in front of Hannah and Mervin.

"What's wrong with you?" Molly asked, but before I could answer she said, "Don's girlfriend broke up with him and that's why he moved to Lancaster. The girl I talked to said she doubted his ex-girlfriend would come see him here—because she's getting married next week."

"Goodness," Hannah said.

Mervin passed the pork chops to Mamm. "Don never said anything about a girlfriend."

"Not to you or anyone else," I said. "But he did to me."

"He said something about a wife." Mervin looked at me. "She died, right?"

"That's what he said." I put the cooked carrots down in the middle of the table.

"Well," Molly said, "I asked about that too. This girl said he was never married."

I gasped.

Molly nodded.

"That's not right," Mervin said. "He has a beard. And Phillip said he was married."

Molly shook her head. "But none of the family actually went to the wedding. They simply believed Don, and why wouldn't they? The girl I talked to said he wanted to be married, but the girl he asked refused him. And then she was killed in a buggy accident a few months later."

"No," Mervin said, putting down his fork. "The girl you talked to has to be mistaken."

"I don't think so," Molly said.

"How odd," Hannah said, making eye contact with Mervin.

He shook his head as if Molly were crazy and then said, "It doesn't make sense. Don was way too convincing when he talked about his dead wife. He teared up and everything while we were hunting."

"Maybe it was the smoke from the campfire," I said.

Mervin made a face. "But what about his beard?"

"It's not that long," Molly answered.

"Jah," Mervin agreed. "But he probably trimmed it."

"Or started growing it before he moved here, since his family would have all expected him to have one," Molly countered.

"Doesn't it seem odd he could have fooled his family about being married? Doesn't it seem as if some acquaintance in Ohio would have discussed it with them? Or they would have looked for the obituary in the *Budget*?" I asked. I know I would have looked for an article in our newspaper.

Mervin shrugged. "Phillip did say that Don hadn't told them he'd married until months after his wife died. And then years went by without them hearing from him."

"Weird," I said.

"Creepy," Hannah added, a sympathetic look on her face.

"The girl I talked to said Don had this deceptive way about him. He'd stir up trouble with half-truths. Pit people against each other by claiming they'd told him one thing when they'd said another. And talking about people behind their backs."

"I can see that," Mervin said.

I could too.

"Anyway," Molly said. "It seems he's brought trouble to more people than just my little sister." She looked straight at me, her eyes full of compassion.

Everyone was mostly quiet for the rest of the meal. If Don would lie about having a wife, surely he would lie to me and about me too. I couldn't help but think it was obvious.

After the closing prayer, to my relief Leon asked Mervin to go out to the barn with him. As soon as they left, Hannah said, "All the boys believed Don."

"Jah," I said. "I know." I hurt so badly.

"I'm sorry," Hannah said.

"Denki," I answered.

"We all just assumed Don was telling the truth. . . ."

I turned toward Mamm as my eyes filled with tears. I didn't want to make a scene in front of Hannah.

"Come into the sewing room," she whispered to me. "I have something for you." I followed her, half listening to Molly and Hannah speed ahead to a new topic.

"So how are things going between you and Mervin?" Molly asked.

Hannah giggled. I stopped in the hallway.

"What?" Molly asked. She must have turned the water faucet on because the sound of running water drowned out their voices.

"Bea?" Mamm waited for me at the doorway to the sewing room. I followed her on in.

She had stacks of fabric she wanted to show me. "You can take a third of it," she said. "I want to divide it evenly between you, Edna, and Molly."

"Denki," I said, "but let Molly choose first."

She frowned. "I wanted you to have the first choice."

I picked through the fabric, pulling remnants from the stacks for a pile for me. "Are you set on going to Montana, then?" I asked.

"It depends on what you decide to do," she answered.

"What are my choices?" I turned toward her, sorry that my voice sounded so hurt.

"Well," Mamm said. "I've talked this over with Edna and Ivan. They're in agreement with me. I plan to split the profits from the sale of the farm three ways—between you, Molly, and me."

"Mamm," I said. "Will you have enough?"

She nodded. "Because I'll live with one of you." She smiled. "But the idea is, if you decide to stay in Lancaster, you can buy a house. Or a business. In case—"

"I never marry?"

"Something like that," she said.

I felt my old defensiveness building, until I thought of the bookstore. It was both a house and a business. But I doubted I could afford it. Still . . .

Laughter came from the kitchen, and then just Hannah giggling. I could hear them clearly through the sewing room doorway.

"I really let my hair down that night," Hannah said.

"What night?" Molly asked.

I stepped through the doorway.

"The night of the singing," Hannah answered.

Molly's voice rose. "Last Sunday night? When Ben accused Bea of stepping out on him?"

I couldn't hear Hannah's response.

Molly asked, "Where were you and Mervin?"

"In the sycamore grove. Under a tree."

Molly's voice was raw. "And your hair was literally down?"

I'd already started to the kitchen before Molly yelled, "Bea! Come here!"

When I reached them, Molly told me to undo my Kapp. I understood exactly what she was after and had my hair unpinned and loose immediately.

Hannah stood. "What's going on?"

"Let your hair down," Molly said to her friend.

"Why?" Hannah's hand flew to the top of her Kapp.

"Please," Molly pled.

Hannah did, although with a bewildered look on her face. When she shook her hair out, Molly directed us to stand shoulder to shoulder while she stepped behind us.

"Your hair is the same length," she said. "Bea's is wavier but not much. Hannah's is darker, but who could tell at night? And you're within a half inch of each other in height." I was thinner, but I doubted Ben would have noticed that—or cared.

I turned toward my sister. She crossed her arms. "How about Don and Mervin? Are they about the same build?"

"Don's bigger," I said. Hannah turned around.

By the surprised look on her face it looked as if she'd just realized what Molly was getting at.

"You shouldn't have been so mean to Ben about all those spelling bees," Hannah said. "Maybe he wouldn't have been so suspicious."

"That's ridiculous." I froze. The word *bee* made me remember . . . "A wasp got in my Kapp when Hope and I were picking apples. And I yanked it off. Ben saw my hair down." I shivered. "He liked seeing it. I could tell by the look on his face."

Molly gasped and then said, "I'd laugh if this wasn't all so pathetic."

Hannah shook her head.

"Ben saw you and Mervin under the sycamore tree," Molly said. "Not my little sister and Don."

"I already figured out what you were getting at." Hannah twisted her hair back into a bun, turning toward me. "Now I really am sorry."

Molly was to the door before I realized it. "Where are you going?" I called out.

"Ben's over at the singing," Molly yelled. "I want him here—now!"

CHAPTER
21

Ben sank down to the floor, his back against the cupboard, his head in his hands when Molly finished telling him what had happened. Leon and Mervin stood on either side of him.

"Did you see the couple in the sycamore grove?" Molly, followed by Hannah, stepped to my side.

He nodded.

"Not under the trees by the shop?"

He lifted his head, his hands still over his face. "Jah. The couple was under the biggest sycamore in the grove."

Hannah put her arm around me. "Don told me to meet Mervin in the sycamore grove that night. He said Mervin had asked him to give me the message."

Mervin cleared his throat and then said, "Don told me the same." His face reddened. "I mean, that you, Hannah, had asked him to tell me to meet you there."

Molly turned toward me. "Hannah and Mervin have already confirmed they were in the sycamore grove. Who can confirm you were by the shop?"

"Phillip," I answered. "He can at least confirm we were near the shop."

Ben's hands fell from his face and his eyes met mine. "I believe you. There's no need to drag Phillip into this." He struggled to his feet. "Don told me to meet the two of you in the sycamore grove. That you would wait for me there, if I hadn't caught up to you by then." He groaned. "I can see it doesn't even make sense now—why would he wait if he was in a hurry to get over to the Millers' place?" His eyes met mine. "Please forgive me. Can we start over? And court peaceably this time?"

I crossed my arms. I couldn't start over with someone who'd thought so poorly of me. I was devastated that he wasn't the man I thought he was. He was the one who'd betrayed me.

"Bea . . ." Ben said.

"Beatrice to you," I snapped.

"Bea . . ." Molly nudged me.

"I'll do anything," Ben said. "Anything to make this up to you."

"Anything?" I asked.

He nodded.

"I forgive you," I said. "Now leave."

"Leave?" He glanced toward the kitchen door.

"No," I answered. "Leave Lancaster."

Molly and Hannah both gasped, and a look of horror spread over Ben's face as he stuttered, "You're kid-ding—right?"

I shook my head.

"But my home is here. My family." His brown eyes grew wide. "And you."

"That's just it," I said. "I don't want to be reminded, for the rest of my life, that you"—I choked—"didn't trust me enough to let me explain." Every time I saw him, I would recall what might have been. I had loved him. I still loved him. Yet I despised him. The best thing would be to have him gone.

He continued to stare at me without speaking.

Molly grabbed my arm. "Bea, you just said that you forgave him."

"I did," I answered. "I do. But that doesn't mean I want to reconcile with him." That would never happen.

Ben looked as if he might cry.

Tears, quite involuntarily, filled my eyes. I turned and walked away, through the living room and up the stairs. When I reached the landing, Mamm called out to me from her bedroom where she'd retreated earlier—to get away from the drama, I was sure.

I stopped in her doorway. "I'm just getting my lap quilt," I said. "For the ride back to the Millers'." Mamm had made it out of Dat's old shirts. She had a matching one, and Molly had a bed-sized one, her wedding gift from Mamm and me.

"Are you leaving soon?" Mamm asked.

I nodded.

"And what are you thinking about the future?"

I shrugged. "That I should find a business here in Lancaster County to buy," I answered. In a rush, all the tears I'd been holding back escaped, flooding down my face. "Or maybe I *should* just go to Montana." There was no way Ben would honor my request that he leave Lancaster. Sure I asked him to, but I had no control over what he'd do.

"There, there," Mamm said, extending her arms.

I fell into them, burying my head against her shoulder as one sob after another tore through me.

She patted my back and began to hum, the same tune as when she'd rocked Leah. After a while, Molly came up the stairs and said that Ben was waiting for me.

"She's distraught," Mamm said. "Tell him to talk with her tomorrow at the Millers'."

"No," I said, my voice muffled. "Tell him to leave. I don't want to see him again—ever."

Molly stepped into the room and then sat down on the end

of Mamm's bed. "Bea, that's not true. You wouldn't be crying like you are if it were. We can hear you all the way downstairs. Ben's sitting on the bottom step crying too."

My heart contracted, but not enough to sway me.

"I know this has been hard," Molly said. "But love is like that. Believe me."

I shook my head against Mamm's shoulder and took a deep breath, trying to form my words, but another round of sobs overtook me.

"Go," Mamm said to Molly. "Let her be."

It took a moment of stony silence, but finally Molly obeyed. A few minutes later we heard the back door open and close and then Love's happy bark, no doubt for Ben. Mamm pulled me down beside her on the bed, and I dozed until Molly woke me to say that Hope had arrived.

"Are you taking Love with you?" Molly asked as I headed out the back door.

"Jah," I said, deciding I needed her more than any of them did. Love greeted me, wagging her tail, and followed Hope and me toward the barn. The night had grown colder. It wouldn't be long until the first snow fell. Maybe tonight. Maybe tomorrow. When we got ready to go, Love jumped up into the buggy and off we went.

This time I didn't feel excited returning to the Millers' place. Only weary. Molly must have told Hope what happened, because she didn't ask. But she acted in a sympathetic way, mostly by giving me the space I needed.

The temperature fell even more by morning. Bob had a roaring fire going in the wood stove by the time I reached the kitchen and one going in the fireplace in the living room too. "A storm's predicted by early evening," Bob said. "Pete and I have a delivery to make this morning, over in Berks County. We'll be back sometime in the afternoon."

They'd hired a van to transport a set of cabinets for installation. The boys had work to keep them busy until noon, and then they were to go home.

"Are you okay taking charge of the house?" Bob asked.

"Sure," I said.

"Cate says she's feeling fine. Pete kept the fire going all night, and the door to the sunroom is open. I told Nan to keep the babies down here today."

I nodded. "I'll move one of the bassinets down, next to the playpen."

"I wish we didn't have to go," he said. "But this is an important job. I'm hoping for more work from this contractor. He has a bid in on a subdivision."

I knew with three preemie babies that Bob had financial concerns unlike any he'd had before.

I made oatmeal for Bob and Pete and then packed sandwiches for them to eat for their noon meal, adding cookies and apples to the lunch box. Then I filled a thermos with coffee, knowing they'd need something hot.

The panel van arrived on time, and the boys helped them load the cabinets. A couple of times, as they did, Ben glanced toward the window. I ducked each time.

The morning progressed quickly. Hope and I fed the babies and took turns in the rocking chair while Nan took a shower. She came down shivering and stood in front of the wood stove, her long blond hair wet and loose. She ran her fingers through it, trying to dry it.

I checked on Cate several times. Regardless of her door being open, the room was chilly. When I took her dinner tray to her, she said she wasn't feeling very well. "Kind of shaky," she said. "Maybe I just need to eat." She sat up straight, pulling the bed table across her lap. I placed the tray of food on top of it. As she reached for the fork, she grimaced and her hand went to the side of her belly.

"Was that a kick?" I asked.

She shook her head.

"What can I do?" I asked.

She looked at the clock and then said, "I think I'm having contractions. About five minutes apart."

"I'll go get Nan," I said.

"Denki."

The two conversed for a short time, and then Nan came back down the hall. "Bea," she called out, "go call Doris and see if she can come get Cate. I don't want to take any chances."

I hurried to the mud porch and swung my cape over my shoulders, practically flying out the door.

The doctor wanted Cate's pregnancy to last another two weeks. The last thing they needed was another premature baby in the house. Maybe her doctor could do something to stop the contractions.

Storm clouds darkened the day, and the cold air bit at my face and hands as I ran across the lawn. The snow began to fall—not big, fluffy flakes, but small, determined ones. Love followed me, although a little slowly for her. She didn't run circles around me—she simply stayed at my side. The snow fell harder and harder, coming down in a fury. When I reached the door to the shop, Love whined to come in with me.

"Stay," I said.

Thankful that the boys had left for the day, so I didn't have to worry about seeing any of them—especially Ben—I made the call and reached Doris on her cell phone. She thought it would be forty-five minutes before she could get to the Millers' place but said she'd do her best to arrive sooner. I ran back to the house with Love matching my stride.

I left my cape on when I reached the mud porch, hoping to ward off the chill of being outside. Hope was walking a screaming Asher, while Kurt cried in the playpen and Leah fussed in the bassinet. I picked up Kurt and headed back down to the sunroom, where Nan packed a bag for Cate.

"She'll be here as soon as she can," I said. "But it might be forty-five minutes or so."

"Oh, dear," Nan said, looking at Cate. "The contractions are four minutes apart now. We'd better call one of the neighbors." Nan started for the hall. "I'll do it."

I followed her.

"The Cramers are closest, but Mrs. Barnes has a car, although she doesn't drive anymore. Maybe she'd let me borrow it. I don't have a license anymore, but I think, under the circumstances . . ."

"By the time you walk over there, Doris will be here," I said.

Nan stopped at the kitchen table and leaned against it. "I wonder if those new neighbors would be home? The ones out on the highway, to the right. We could take the buggy there."

"You're not going anywhere," I said. "I'm going to call 9-1-1. That's what I should have done in the first place, instead of calling Doris."

"Of course," Nan said. "I'm not thinking straight. Neither is Cate. Denki." She stood up straight, her hand going to her forehead. "Oh, wait."

"What is it?"

She shook her head. "Bob gave me instructions in case there was an emergency, but . . . never mind," she said. "Yours is the best plan anyway."

I headed back to Cate's office a little baffled, but by the time I reached the phone, I didn't give Nan's odd behavior another thought. She was overwhelmed—that was all.

Five minutes later, I was back on the mud porch, kicking the snow from my boots. Cate sat at the kitchen table, her bag by her side. "It'll save time if they don't have to come in," she said, looking up at me. "Will you come along? Nan will send Pete as soon as he gets here. But I need someone with me."

"Of course," I said. A month ago I would have hesitated. Even a week ago. But not now.

Hope looked a little wide-eyed with both Asher and Kurt in her arms, while Nan sat in the rocker nursing Leah.

"Keep the fires going," I said to Hope. "I'll go get one of my Mamm's casseroles out of the freezer for supper."

I heard the wail of the ambulance as I came back up the stairs. Relieved, I wondered again why I hadn't called 9-1-1 in the first place.

Cate was already at the door, ready to go.

"Wait," I called out, running to take her arm. We tottered out into the storm as the ambulance pulled up. An EMT jumped out of the passenger seat, the snow pelting his jacket.

"I'm in labor," Cate called out. "Contractions are four minutes apart. Our driver couldn't get here for another half hour."

The EMT scrunched up his nose. "Chances are you won't deliver for hours."

"I'm early—thirty-four weeks," Cate said. "I'm hoping they can stop it."

"Oh," the man said, hurrying to the back of the ambulance and opening the doors.

Soon we were on our way, me sitting in the back with Cate, the EMT taking her blood pressure as I took in everything around me. There was a monitor above the bed-like gurney that Cate was on, several machines made blipping noises, and shelves of supplies lined the back of the ambulance.

The ride was bumpy down the lane. The vehicle lurched a little to the right and then slid when it turned onto the highway. I put my hand up to steady Cate, afraid she might fall, even though she was strapped down.

"Whoa," the EMT said, as if talking to a horse, as the ambulance straightened out and then picked up speed.

The view out the back window grew whiter and whiter. I wasn't sure how the ambulance driver could see at all. I breathed a prayer of thanks that I'd called the ambulance and that Doris hadn't had to brave . . . My face grew warm. *Oh, no!* I hadn't called her to tell her not to come.

I inhaled deeply, but it just drew my feeling of horror deeper.

The ambulance driver must have slammed on the brakes, because it lurched, and then began to slide again. I grabbed Cate's leg. It was all so disorienting inside the vehicle. Did it slide to the right? Spin around? I wasn't sure. All I knew was nothing was right in the big box we were riding along in. An abrupt bump jolted me upward. I raised my hands to keep my head from hitting the ceiling, but in a split second I was free-falling back to my seat. Another bump, bump followed. With a last jolt, the ambulance came to a stop.

"Oh, my," Cate said, holding her belly.

An odd crackling sound startled me, followed by someone saying, "Is everyone all right?"

I must have jumped, because the EMT beside Cate, his face gray and his hand on the ceiling, said, "That's the driver, checking in on us. It's a speaker. Are you two okay?"

I nodded, and so did Cate, her eyes wide.

"Roger," the EMT answered. "Everyone's fine."

A few minutes later the back opened and the driver peered in. "A cow was in the road. I hardly saw it before having to swerve." As the driver talked, a van pulled up behind him. "I already called for a backup ambulance and a tow," he added.

"*Gut*," Cate said.

A door slammed.

"That was fast," the driver joked, turning around.

A voice asked, "Do you have Cate Treger in there?"

"Doris," I called out, straining my head to see her.

"Oh, Bea." Doris leaned inside, dressed as if she were headed to the North Pole. "Are you two all right?"

"Jah," I answered. "Except Cate's in labor."

"I have chains on," Doris said to the driver. "I can take them. I know these girls well."

The EMTs looked at each other and then at Cate. "It's up to you. It could be another half hour before the next ambulance shows up."

"Unstrap me," she said. "We're going with Doris."

The ride was slow and tense. Cate didn't complain, but it was obvious her contractions were getting closer and closer together. It was becoming less likely, I knew, that the doctors would be able to stop them.

"The most important thing," Doris said, several times, "is that we get her there unharmed." She gripped the steering wheel and plowed along, the snow coming down so fast that nearly all that was visible was white.

Most likely in an attempt to keep Cate's mind off her contractions, Doris asked what names she and Pete had picked out.

"We don't have a girl's name yet, although we're considering Esther, after Pete's Mamm," she said. "But for a boy we've decided on Walter, for sure. After Pete's Dat."

"Nice," Doris said.

Molly had told me there was a time Cate didn't get along very well with her in-laws, but obviously she had worked through it. I admired her for that, along with so many other things.

By the time we reached the hospital, I felt as if we'd been through the ordeal of a lifetime. I couldn't imagine how Cate felt. Doris pulled under the overhang over the ER door, behind several other cars, and I ran in to get some help.

As an aide helped Cate into a wheelchair, Doris apologized to me that she couldn't stay. "I need to get home before the roads become impassable," she said. "Stay with Cate. When she delivers, go in with her. She'll need the support."

I nodded, hoping it wouldn't come to that. It was one thing for me to figure out I truly loved babies and quite another to think of being in the room to support a woman having one.

It did come to that. The doctor said it was too late to stop the contractions. "You're seven centimeters dilated," he said, and then asked, "How many weeks are you?"

"Thirty-four," Cate answered.

"We'll hope for the best," he said. "Things should be fine."

Cate grabbed my hand and said, "Pray."

I did.

Within an hour Cate was pushing. After three hours of that, the doctor said he was going to call the surgical team in to do a

C-section. Just then Pete rushed in, his face and hands red from the cold, wiggling out of his coat, which I grabbed from him.

"You're here," Cate said, tears flooding her face. Another contraction overtook her.

When it stopped, she turned to the doctor and said, "Wait. Let me keep trying, for a few more minutes at least."

"All right," the doctor said. "A few more minutes."

When Cate pushed again, I started to leave.

"Bea, would you stay?" Cate asked through gritted teeth.

I did.

Ten minutes later, little Walter came into the world, screaming his head off as the doctor proclaimed, "It's a boy!"

The doctor let out a sigh of relief, and both Cate and Pete cried. I did too.

Feeling as if it was all too intimate for me to be there, I stepped outside the door, bumping into Bob.

"You're here," I said.

"Jah," he said. "Listening in. The baby sounds good."

I agreed. "Did you hear the doctor?"

Bob smiled. "A boy. Walter—right?"

I nodded.

"You have a visitor," Bob said to me.

"I do?"

"Jah. He caught a ride with us. One of the Cramer boys saw the ambulance in the ditch and came back to our place to tell Ben."

"Ben was at your place?"

Bob nodded. "In the Dawdi Haus. I asked him to stay, just in case. Nan knew. She was supposed to send him for help, if needed, but she forgot until you were ready to call the ambulance." He shook his head.

"Poor Nan," I said, feeling a little odd that they were hiding Ben from me.

"Jah, sleep deprivation is taking its toll on all of us." He yawned. "You did the right thing, Bea. I'm glad Nan forgot about Ben. It probably would have delayed getting Cate to the hospital in the end."

Bob yawned again. "Anyway, Ben's in the waiting room."

I was tempted to head the opposite direction, but out of respect for Bob I walked down the hall, stopping at the entrance to the nearly empty room. Ben stood at the far window, watching the snow fall.

He turned, as if sensing me. "Are you all okay?"

I nodded and then blurted out, "Cate had her baby. A boy."

An expression of pure relief settled on Ben's face. "Are they all right? Both of them?"

"I think so," I said. "The baby was screaming when I left. The doctor was taking care of Cate."

Ben's face reddened a little, and then he said, "Are you hungry? I could buy you a snack. Or some supper."

Truth be told, I was starving and I'd forgotten to bring any money with me. It couldn't hurt to spend a little time with Ben. "Sure," I answered.

I went back and told Bob we'd be in the cafeteria if he needed us.

He smiled. "I won't need you anytime soon—not until I can find a ride home for you and Ben and me."

I imagined he was anxious to get home to Nan and the babies.

Ben led the way to the elevator, down to the cafeteria, and then through the line. I chose a bowl of vegetable soup and a turkey sandwich. He ordered a hamburger from the grill. After he paid for our food, he led the way to a table by the window, where we could watch the snow coming down.

"It's so beautiful," I said.

"Jah," he agreed. "Listen . . . " I expected him to say my name, but he didn't. Probably because he didn't want to get scolded again. "I really am sorry. You put your trust in me, and I hurt you badly—not just once but twice."

More than twice, I thought as I put my hand up. "Don't," I said. "I'm not up to rehashing everything."

He swallowed hard and then said, "Fair enough."

Nothing was fair. I knew that. "Let's just enjoy our meal," I said.

When we returned to the waiting room, Bob was at the nurses' desk, using the phone. He placed his hand over the mouthpiece and said, "Cate wants you two to see the baby. They just got moved down the hall, third room on the left."

"Is Walter with them?"

Bob nodded. "He's a little guy, but bigger than they anticipated—just over five pounds." He chuckled. "So about the same size as his aunt and uncles."

"How are his lungs?" I asked, knowing that was the big concern.

"They're fine. He gets to stay with Cate. No need for the NICU."

Relieved, I led the way down the hall, knocking on the door when we reached it.

"Come in," Pete said.

I pushed the door open. Cate sat up in bed, her face as pale as porcelain. But the brightness of her blue eyes and the grin on her face made her look as beautiful as I'd ever seen her. "Come look," she said, motioning toward me with her free hand.

Little Walter was swaddled tightly in a blanket, his face red under a little cap. His eyes were closed.

I washed my hands and then touched the top of his head.

"Do you want to hold him?" Cate asked.

"Of course." I leaned forward and reached for the baby. Cate slipped him into my arms, and I stood up straight with him, my eyes on his sweet face. Ben stepped to my side. The baby stirred a little, and his eyelids fluttered open for just a minute, but then he settled back down. Ben reached out and stroked his cheek.

"You must be tired," I whispered to Walter. "You had quite the adventure—and gave us all quite the scare."

"Jah," Cate said, "But Aenti Bea came to the rescue. What would I have done without you?"

I turned toward her. "You would have done just fine. I didn't do anything."

"No, you did," Pete said.

Ben was nodding his head. "You're awfully competent, Bea."

"Stop," I said, embarrassed to the core.

Bob came into the room and said he'd found us a ride, and the driver was only ten minutes away. "We need to get downstairs," he said. Then he turned to Pete. "I'll check the messages tonight and first thing in the morning. Let me know if you need anything. And when you can come home."

I passed the baby back to Cate, and Bob bent down and kissed them both. "Get some rest," he said. "And congratulations."

As Ben followed me out of the room and stepped beside me, a wave of sadness passed over me. Just over a week ago, I'd thought a family with Ben was in my future. Now it wasn't. I swiped at a tear, and Ben gave me a concerned look.

I swallowed hard. "I'm happy for them is all," I said. That was true. I was. But it wasn't why I was crying.

CHAPTER
22

Bob had hired a driver with a humongous four-wheel drive truck with an extended cab. The snow had stopped, and Ben and I sat in the back with a huge space between us. When the driver drove up the lane, I was surprised to see Leon riding his horse down it. He gave us a big wave and a grin and kept on going. When the driver stopped in front of the house, Ben got out first and then offered me his hand. I took it because the ground appeared icy. It was. I nearly skated into the splits. Love bounded to my side and then to Ben's as he steadied me, helped me to the door, and then said good-night. As Bob paid the driver, I watched Ben head toward the Dawdi Haus, Love at his side.

I heard a voice I didn't expect when I entered the kitchen. My Mamm's. She sat in the rocker, cradling Asher, talking with Hope.

"Here they are!" Hope exclaimed, coming toward me with Leah.

My Mamm asked, "How is Cate? And the baby?"

I let Bob answer. It was his place to. "*Gut,*" he said. "Walter is tiny but healthy. Cate's tired but grateful. And Pete's as proud as any papa I've ever seen." He glanced toward the hallway. "Where's Nan?"

"In the living room," Hope said. "Napping in front of the fire."

As he hurried down the hall, I asked Mamm why she was here. "Molly got a call from Hannah that you'd gone with Cate. I figured Hope and Nan would need help, so Leon brought me over on his horse, and then he stayed for supper. It was Molly's idea."

"Oh, goodness," I said. "That must have been quite a ride for you."

Her eyes lit up. "It was lovely. Moonlight on snow is one of the most beautiful things in the world."

She was right. "How long will you stay?" I asked.

"Until tomorrow. Whenever Leon can make it back for me."

She slept on the couch. Nan and Bob slept in Cate and Pete's bed in the sunroom, to make it easier for Bob to keep the fires stoked and the babies warm. For once I didn't get up during the night to help.

The next morning, I found out that Mamm had. "Goodness," she said. "I couldn't do that night after night, but it was a joy this once."

Again I understood why she wanted to go to Montana with Molly. And I thought she absolutely should. Grandchildren were a blessing. There was no reason she should experience it at a distance.

As I was preparing breakfast, Ben appeared at the door, surprising me, but I let him in. It wasn't my house or up to me to say whether or not he could eat with us.

Mamm rocked Leah and told the rest of us to eat. Once the baby was asleep, she asked Ben—of all people—if he'd take the baby girl from her and put her in the playpen. "It hurts my back," she said, "to bend over like that." Ben obliged, handling the little one with the expertise I'd seen from him before.

About midmorning, Leon showed up to take Mamm home. I don't think she was ready to go, but she didn't want to ask Leon to come back later. She gave me a hug. "We still need to talk," she said. "I'm going to go ahead with the sale of the farm to Mervin. We'll figure out what to do with the money in time—and what you want to do."

I nodded, hugging her back.

Cate, Pete, and the baby didn't come home that day. The doctor wanted to keep Walter for an extra couple of days, until he began gaining his weight back and maintaining his heat. And there was no reason for Cate to have to find a ride back and forth, so she stayed too, with Pete at her side. I thought that was a good idea. We were having a hard time keeping three preemies warm, let alone four.

Ben stayed at the Dawdi Haus all week, helping Bob with the chores and working in the shop, even though the rest of the crew didn't come in on Tuesday or Wednesday. Bob didn't speak with me about Ben, but he must have decided we'd come to some sort of peace, because he invited Ben to eat with us every meal. I was fine with that—as long as Ben didn't try to talk with me.

He didn't.

Still it hurt to have him around.

On Wednesday evening, Ben stayed in the kitchen after supper. Hope, Nan, and Bob moved into the living room with the babies, probably thinking they were doing me a favor. Ben picked up the platter of chicken.

"I can do that," I said.

"I'd like to help," he responded.

316

I started the dishwater, putting the glasses in the sink and then adding the soap, as he cleared the food from the table.

"Mervin came by this afternoon—he'd been over at the Cramers' house, to visit Hannah."

"Oh," I said.

Ben put the empty mashed-potato bowl on the counter. "He says you plan to move to Montana."

I turned the water off. "Who told him that?"

"Molly." He walked back to the table.

"Oh," I said again. Molly probably assumed I wanted to get as far away from Lancaster County as possible.

He returned and placed the basket of rolls on the counter. "So you were just kidding about me leaving—right?"

"Unless *you* want to move to Montana," I replied.

"Pardon?"

"Montana," I said louder. "Would you like to move there?"

"Jah, I would," he answered. "As long as you're going too."

"Ben—" My voice caught in my throat as my heart lurched. I chided myself. It was no good to be around him, not at all. "I can finish up," I said, turning away from him.

He stepped closer to me, the bowl of apple butter in one hand and the salt and pepper shakers in the other. "I want to help." I could feel his breath on my neck.

I turned to face him, shaking my head. "Go read. Or write in your journal. I'll see you at breakfast."

For some reason, he obeyed me.

❦

The next morning, Thursday, Ben didn't show up for breakfast. Bob said he was already in the shop. "He said he brought some food and fed himself."

I didn't respond. It wasn't like I missed him. Or cared, really, whether he ate or not. I just wanted to make sure I was doing my job.

By then all of the roads were plowed, including the lane, and the shop was back on a normal schedule—except for Pete, who was still at the hospital with Cate. During dinner, Bob said Doris was on her way to pick up the new family and bring them home. "Betsy's going to come over this afternoon to see them," Bob added. "She wasn't able to make it to the hospital."

Hope and I changed the sheets on the downstairs bed. Bob and Nan would be back upstairs with their babies, leaving the sunroom for Cate again until she regained her strength.

A different driver brought Betsy, who came alone, just before supper. "Levi said he'd stay with the kids," she said. "We'll bring them after Cate has more time to rest. I remember how exhausting it is to have too many people around."

We expected Cate and Pete any time, but I went ahead and put supper on the table, with Betsy's help. Just as we were sitting down to eat, the new family arrived. Betsy rushed outside to help them in. Betsy was much more helpful when her own children weren't around.

Cate looked exhausted as they entered, leaning against Betsy as Pete carried the car seat. I imagined being on bed rest for so long had zapped her strength. Nan scrambled to her feet to hug Cate and get a look at the baby. Then Cate said she was going to go to bed.

"I'll bring a tray," I said. "For you too, Pete."

"Denki," he responded.

But a few minutes later, when I entered the sunroom with two plates, Betsy, who was holding the baby, said she'd stay with Cate. "Go to the table," she said to Pete. "Give us some sister time."

Pete obeyed. As I placed the plates on the bed table, I heard someone at the back door.

"It's Ben," Betsy said. "He's getting a ride home with me tonight. But he needs to box up his venison in the freezer first. I made room for it back home today."

I didn't respond.

Betsy leaned back against the chair, the baby secure in her arms. "I hope you know you've broken his heart."

I stood up straight. "Are you talking to me?"

"I'm certainly not talking to Cate."

"Betsy," Cate chided.

"Who told you I broke his heart?" I asked.

"He did."

"Well, I doubt he told you the whole story."

"I'm guessing he did," Betsy replied. "He said it was all his fault."

"You two looked so sweet together the night Wally was born," Cate said, lifting a spoonful of applesauce. "Are you sure you're not getting back together?"

"Positive," I answered. "I'll check back with you in a little bit." I fled but stopped halfway down the hall. Ben stood in the kitchen, a bag in one hand and his journal in the other.

"The cold box you borrowed is still down by the freezer," Bob said. "Use it. You can bring it back whenever you get a chance."

I couldn't help but wonder why Bob said "whenever you get a chance" and not just "tomorrow."

"Denki," Ben said, placing his bag beside the wall and then slipping his journal into the side pocket. I was absolutely opposed to snooping. Molly had done that to me once and it took me years to recover. But I had a sudden urge to read Ben's journal. I couldn't help but wonder if he'd written about me.

Not that it mattered one way or the other. I stayed frozen in the hall, listening as closely as I could.

"Denki," Ben said again. Apparently he wasn't done being grateful. "For everything. You've been so good to me—as a boss and as a friend. I appreciate the advice, honestly."

A chair scraped against the floor. I guessed Bob must have gotten up, because in no time there was the sound of someone being patted on the back—and it wasn't someone burping a baby. These were manly pats. It seemed over the top, considering Ben would be back tomorrow.

A moment later the chair scraped again.

I waited until I heard Ben's footsteps on the stairs before continuing on to the kitchen.

That night, Hope and I dropped into bed exhausted, but for once she wanted to talk—all about her wedding. "It's just a week away," she said.

"Jah," I answered, thinking the Millers were crazy to agree to her getting married so soon when they had so much going on. I doubted Cate would be able to go to the wedding. Nan might be able to, but I didn't see how. She wouldn't want to take the triplets out in public and risk exposing them to so many germs.

"I thought I'd start making wedding nothings," Hope said. "And try to freeze them."

My mouth watered at the thought of the fried pastries sprinkled with powdered sugar, but I didn't think they'd freeze very well. "I can help you the day before the wedding," I said.

Hope continued talking. She'd started a dress that day, a blue one. Her Dat would bring a new black head covering and apron that her oldest sister was making for Hope to wear.

"You'll be my *Newehocker*, won't you?" she asked.

"Of course," I said. I'd never been anyone's sidesitter before.

"Even though Ben is going to be Martin's?"

I pursed my lips together.

"Bea . . ."

"Sure," I said. "But only for you."

She smiled at that. "At least he won't be around anymore during the day."

I shook my head a little. "Why not?"

"He's going to work for the Schmidts, in their bookstore." My chest tightened. "No," I whispered.

Hope leaned her elbow against the bed, her head in her hand. "He told Martin that you're moving to Montana. So it shouldn't matter to you. He said he'd rather work there, away from you, until you leave, than be reminded . . . You know."

I pulled the pillow over my head.

"Bea?" Hope sounded a million miles away. "You can't have it both ways. Don't get me wrong. I don't want you to move to Montana. You're the best friend I've ever had. I want you to stay. I thought you'd marry Ben and we'd all spend our lives together. We'd live in the same district. We'd have babies at the same time. And they'd grow up to be friends, and—"

"Ben was supposed to move away from Lancaster," I muttered, acknowledging my fantasy, if only to myself, that Mamm and I would buy the Schmidts' business and she and I could run it together. She could go to Montana every fall, after the tourist season slowed in Lancaster, to visit Molly.

That was what I'd hoped for. I'd hoped for so much more than that only a couple weeks ago—but now my dream of the bookstore was all I had left.

"Bea, talk to me," Hope said. "What's wrong?"

"Nothing." *Everything.*

A few minutes later, in true Hope fashion, she was snoring gently. I took my journal from where I'd tucked it under the bed and headed downstairs with it. I added a log to the fire in the fireplace and pulled up a chair. In the dim light I poured out my heart, recording the events of the last month. I didn't stop until I heard a baby cry.

23

I didn't see Ben once during the next week. All of my spare time was spent helping Hope with her wedding plans, hemming her dress, writing place cards, and then making the wedding nothings. The snow melted, and we had another spell of bright blue sky with the temperatures just above freezing. Cate grew stronger, first walking around the house and then taking little trips outside. Pete would accompany her, carrying Wally as they walked.

On Tuesday, two days before the big wedding, Hope whispered that she had some news for me after she'd been outside to see Martin on his break. "Come down to the basement when you can," she said. We were trying to catch up on the laundry before her Dat arrived.

A few minutes later, after I'd finished the dishes, I hurried downstairs.

Hope fed towels through the wringer. When she saw me, she said, without fanfare, "Don's back."

"What?"

She nodded. "He came by the shop this morning, asking Bob for his job back. He thought he was a shoo-in, since Ben quit."

"Oh, no," I said.

"Don't worry, Bob didn't hire him."

I blinked back tears of relief.

"In fact, Martin said things got a little heated. Bob said Don owed you an apology and the sooner he dealt with it the better."

I gasped. The last thing I wanted was for Don to seek me out to apologize.

That evening Hope's Dat arrived. He'd taken the bus to Lancaster, and then Bob had sent a driver to bring him the rest of the way. As Hope rushed into his arms, he dropped his bag on the kitchen linoleum and hugged her hard, picking her up and spinning her around.

I felt a pang of sorrow for the loss of my Dat again—but then I breathed a prayer of thanks for my Mamm. We could have lost her too.

Hope introduced her Dat to me. "William Troyer," she said to me. "Dat, this is Bea Zook—the one I wrote so much about."

"Nice to meet you," he said, a kind expression on his face. He looked to be sixty-five or so, around my Mamm's age. His boots were worn and his hat a little shabby, but he made up for it with his warm personality.

"I'll go show you your room," Hope said, picking up his bag. "Plus Nan and Bob are upstairs. They said to let them know as soon as you arrived."

"After you," he said, wrestling the bag from her.

I returned to the sink, to dry the last of the plates, when Love began to bark frantically. I was about to go tell her to stop it when a knock on the back door startled me. I flipped the dish towel over my shoulder, hurried through the mud porch, and opened the door.

There stood Bishop Eicher, filling the doorframe, with Don and Phillip behind him. The bishop was as big as a giant. His sons, who were both good size, looked tiny next to him.

I wanted to slam the door and run, but Love pushed her nose between Don and the bishop and then squeezed through to get to me. I, as graciously as I was capable of, invited them in, shooing Love out and closing the door. She stayed on the other side and whined.

"I'll go get Bob," I said, even though I wanted to run the opposite direction, down the hall to the sunroom, and hide.

I hated tearing Bob away from Hope and her Dat, but as soon as I said who had arrived, he excused himself and followed me.

When we reached the kitchen, Bishop Eicher, who stood with his hat in one hand and the other braced against a chair said, looking straight at me, "We need to talk."

"Let me take your things," Bob said. "And then let's all sit down." He took each of their coats and hats, and then as he headed to the mud porch said, "Bea, is there coffee?"

"Jah," I answered. "And apple cake." I'd made it that afternoon.

"Wunderbar," he said.

I said a prayer at the thought of serving Don anything, and God must have answered, because I managed to keep my composure.

As I dished up the cake and then poured the coffee, the men talked about the weather and how the early snowfall had delayed Bishop Eicher's plowing. "I'll be back on track as soon as the ground soaks up more of the moisture."

Once I'd served dessert, Bob told me to take a seat beside him.

The bishop cleared his throat and said, "I think I'm probably the last one to piece all this together, but between what Phillip told me, the rumors that have been flying around, and what Don has confirmed, I finally realized that something must be done." He shifted his gaze to Don. "What do you say, son?"

I expected an apology, but instead Don said, "You were the girlfriend I wanted that night under the tree."

I nodded. "I gathered that."

He raised his eyebrows and leaned backward.

"Jah," I said, "I figured out there wasn't a girlfriend from Ohio. You were hoping I'd change my mind, but attacking me was an odd way to try to influence me."

He squared his shoulders. "I set it all up."

I didn't respond. He'd thought I was a fool—for sure.

He continued, "I told Mervin that Hannah wanted to meet him. And told Hannah that Mervin wanted to meet her. I told Ben to meet us in the sycamore grove." He picked up his coffee mug. "But I didn't plan to treat you the way I did—I expected that you would be more cooperative. I truly did want to court you."

"No," I said. "You wanted to hurt me. And you did."

The other men grew restless but none of them contradicted me. Don lowered his head and stared at the tabletop. Finally Bob said, "Bea's right."

And the bishop said, "Son, say what you came here to say."

Don kept his eyes on the table. "Will you forgive me?"

"For . . . ?" I asked.

"Lying. Mistreating you . . . All of it."

I supposed that was as sincere as I was going to get from Don.

I stared at him, wondering why he wouldn't look at me. A shiver passed through me. "Were you lurking around that night Love showed up?"

He shrugged, his eyes still downcast.

"Were you spying on the couple on the other side of the barn?"

He shrugged again.

"Who was it?"

"Hannah and Mervin," he muttered.

I'd thought it was Hope and Martin, but it made more sense that it was Hannah and Mervin. "Did that give you the idea to use them to set me up?"

He shrugged a third time, his head still down.

"And then after Bob fired you, were you sneaking around then too?"

He didn't respond, but his mouth turned down.

Bishop Eicher cleared his throat and then said, "It seems Don's had a problem with boundaries, both physical and emotional."

I nodded and then shivered again at the creepiness of what he'd done.

He'd been the pernicious one—the one who'd harmed so many of us. The bad apple in the bottom of the barrel.

Bob said, "Bea, do you feel you can forgive Don? That might free him to do the right thing in the future, to move forward in his own life—because he's a child of God too, just as much as all of us are."

"Jah," I said, "I forgive you." Instead of anger, all I felt for him was pity. But it wasn't up to me to figure out how he was going to experience God's healing. That was up to him. And God. "I appreciate the apology," I added. "It helps."

"Denki," Don said as he continued to stare at the table.

"But," I said, "I want you to be accountable to someone—to a man who can make sure you're respecting others and their boundaries." That would please me the most.

Don nodded.

I knew I'd never know for sure if he was or not, but still I had to state my wishes.

"What are your plans now?" Bob asked Don.

He kept his eyes on the table. "I'm going back to Ohio in the morning. I have some unfinished business I need to take care of there too. I talked to my bishop this morning." He raised his head. "He told me I need to be accountable to him if I come back . . ."

Both Bishop Eicher and Bob seemed relieved. Bob said, "I'll contact the leaders in your district there and let them know exactly what happened."

Don seemed to accept that. I liked the idea. If Bob talked to the bishop and an elder or two, it would make it harder for Don to sneak anything over on them.

The conversation turned to the wedding in two days. Don concentrated on eating his dessert and didn't say anything more. He didn't look exactly cheerful, but he didn't appear as brooding as before either.

Thankfully, they didn't stay much longer. When they left, Phillip said he'd see me at the wedding, "Jah," I said, without much enthusiasm, I'm afraid. "I'll be there." It wasn't that I wasn't excited for the happy couples. It was spending time with Ben that I dreaded, even more after Don's confession.

But at least Don's actions had revealed Ben's true character. It was better that I knew now rather than after I'd married him.

৸৶

I finished cleaning up the dessert dishes and then took a piece of cake down the hall to Cate. Pete had gone out to finish up some work in the shop before bed, so she was alone with the baby.

"Denki," she said, scooting into a sitting position. The little one was tucked in the crook of her left arm. She took the plate with her right hand and then balanced it on her lap. "I'm starving. But I could have come and gotten it."

"I know," I said. One of the lessons I'd learned by working for the Millers was what a pleasure it was to serve others. It was something I longed to do with a better attitude for my own family, including Molly.

"What did Bishop Eicher want?" she asked between her first and second bite.

I explained what happened.

"There's no reason you and Ben can't work things out now," she said.

I shook my head.

"Why not?" She took another bite.

"I can't trust him," I answered.

"Ben made a mistake, one that's devastated him. He still loves you." She tilted her head as she spoke, the fork in midair. "You should give him another chance."

I pursed my lips.

"You still love him. Maybe you thought this would be easy, but I can tell it's not." The fork reached her mouth.

As Cate continued eating, I thought of Bob saying that Don was God's child as much as any of us. It dawned on me that Ben was God's child too, just as much as I was. God favored all of us—not just me. As Cate took her last bite, I said, "But what does it matter if I love him or not? How could I bear to be with him after being so angry? I've never been so mad at anyone in all my life—not even Molly."

Cate laughed. "That's just it. We get the angriest with the ones we love the most."

I shook my head, taking the empty plate from her.

She kissed the top of Wally's head. "Except for babies. But someday Walter will exercise his free will and make me angry too. But I'll love him just the same. That's what true love is—we keep loving, keep working things out. We don't give up."

I'd have to think about that. As I headed to the door, I realized that my anger with Ben wasn't the whole problem. Part of it was how much I'd loved him, how I felt that day in the coffee shop and then later taking care of the babies together. How I felt sitting with him under the oak tree. I loved him with my very being. And he'd rejected me, rejected my love.

How could I go from love to anger and back to love? How could I *feel* that love without becoming angry again?

I retreated to my room after I washed Cate's plate. Hope and her Dat were in the nursery with Nan and Bob, so I had some rare time to myself. I pulled my journal and pencil out from under my bed again, determined to get more of my feelings down on paper. Out fell the piece of paper folded in fourths with the Shakespeare sonnet Ben had written down for me. I ignored what I'd written at the top and skimmed the sonnet, reading parts of it out loud:

> " . . . Love is not love
> Which alters when it alteration finds.
> . . . it is an ever-fixed mark,
>   That looks on tempests and is never shaken. . . .
>   Love alters not with his brief hours and weeks,
>   But bears it out even to the edge of doom."

I sank down onto my bed. Shakespeare knew love was hard work. So did Cate. And Bob and Nan. And my Mamm. Ben expected it would be. Even Molly knew.

Why had I been so naïve? My idealism had gotten the best of

me. I took my pencil from my journal and wrote, *Still, love fled,* at the end of the sonnet, knowing I was mixing poets.

As an afterthought, I wrote, *If only. . . .* What? If only Ben hadn't been unreasonable? If only I could trust him? If only we could have another chance?

I refolded the paper and put it on my bedside table as the tears started to pool in my eyes. I swiped at them, but they kept on coming. I tried to write in my journal, to pour out my soul again, but the tears kept me from seeing my words.

Nothing came, except for a particular memory—and I certainly didn't want to write about it. But I couldn't help thinking about it.

Cally Wetzel had been the teacher of our one-room schoolhouse all through our school years. When we started school, she was in her midtwenties, never married and didn't seem to want to be. She loved words, both in the Pennsylvania Dutch language and in English. And she loved me. And Ben.

When I started school and began studying English, it was as if my world doubled. I had an entire new vocabulary to learn and love. English enchanted me. Soon we studied German too, but although I enjoyed it, it didn't hold the same power over me that English did.

Cally started the spelling bees hoping to encourage her students to study our accumulative list of words all school-year long. Every year, either Ben or I won our grade's contest. Our last year—the spring of eighth grade—he was ahead by one win. Cally didn't keep track of our standings from the previous years, but we did. I could either tie him or he'd win it all.

On the night of the end-of-the-year program, the two top spellers from each grade had their runoffs. For some grades, it merely took two words. For Ben and me it took forty-three.

There we stood, in front of the blackboard, going back and forth while the younger children squirmed and the parents yawned.

Finally Cally said she was going to add new words, off the top of her head. "Except, I'll give you the *definition* and you give me the word and the spelling," she said. She was tired too. She looked at Ben and then at me and said, slowly, "A lover of words."

I felt giddy with excitement. I knew the word and how to spell it, thanks to my Dat. He had told me a few months before that he was an ornithophile, a lover of birds. Together we figured out what a lover of words—*logos*—would be and then I confirmed it by looking the word up in my new and very large dictionary that I'd just received for Christmas.

But it was Ben's turn. He grinned. My heart sank. He knew it too.

Quickly he said, "Dictophile. D-I-C-T-O-P-H-I-L-E."

I grinned. He'd taunted me with that word about a year ago, calling me one. But it was the wrong answer for this question.

Her voice matter-of-fact, Teacher Cally said, "Incorrect. Beatrice?"

"Logophile," I answered.

Ben groaned.

I continued. "L-O-G-O-P-H-I-L-E."

"You've got to be kidding," Ben said, as his head fell into his hands. I knew he was embarrassed that he'd assumed he knew the word—instead of figuring it out.

I stood there and beamed until I saw my father with his eyes cast down in Shohm. He loved me unconditionally. I always felt special to him, validated by him, but that last spelling bee was the one time I felt I'd disappointed him.

It turned out to be the last spelling bee the board allowed at our school. Obviously Ben and I were both too competitive and too prideful. No one cared if we loved words and dictionaries.

No, the school board members were much more concerned with our souls, as they should have been, than who won the eighth-grade spelling bee.

Ben reminded me the next day that overall we'd actually tied.

"Jah," I answered and then said, "But I got the last word."

Tears filled my eyes as I closed my journal. I'd gotten the last word in the eighth grade and now too. But it wasn't what I'd wanted—not at all.

The next day Hope went with Martin and her Dat to Hannah's house to get ready for the wedding, while I managed things on the home front. None of the boys had come to work because they, too, were helping over at the Lapps' horse farm. The plan was to use the barn, one of the biggest in the county, for the service and the meals. That would take a lot of sweeping, dusting, and mopping of the cement floor to get it ready. I was thankful to be taking care of babies and not mucking out stalls.

When Hope and her Dat arrived home, way past dark, she said Molly had been there too. "I told her I didn't think Nan would be able to make it tomorrow. For sure Cate won't."

I nodded.

"But it would be nice if Nan could be there," Hope said.

I thought so too. After all, Nan was Hope's aunt.

"Anyway," Hope added, "Molly said she had an idea."

I smiled. That was my sister. She always had an "idea." I was certain it had turned into a "plan" by now.

We went to bed as soon as we could, because we needed to be up by four to get over to the Lapps' farm so we could help with all the final details. I didn't sleep well that night, but Hope did—and that's what mattered.

When we rose, we dressed in our work clothes and packed our wedding clothes. As I retrieved my brush from my bedside table, I slipped the poem from Ben inside the pocket of my work apron. I didn't want anyone snooping while we were gone—not that anyone would. Still, it made me feel better to have it with me.

I patted my pocket as I turned to grab the garment bag. Hope was watching me.

My face warmed, even in the icy chill of the unheated room. "We'd better hurry," I said. We'd eat breakfast at the Lapps' house with all the others who would gather to see to the last-minute details. All I needed to do was hitch Thunder to the buggy and we'd be on our way, along with Hope's Dat. Bob would come later.

When we reached the kitchen, the lamp was already lit and Mamm and Edna, along with Nell and Ivan, sat at the table, their hands wrapped around mugs of coffee. Hope's Dat and Bob sat with them.

"Mamm!" I rushed toward her, giving her a hug. "What are you doing here?"

"We're going to watch the babies," she said, "so Nan can go to the wedding."

"Ach," I said. "Molly did come through with a plan."

Mamm and Edna nodded in unison.

"What about you?" I said to Nell. "You're going, right?" After all, she was Hannah's Aenti.

"Of course," she said. "I wouldn't miss it for the world. We just dropped Edna and your Mamm off." She stood, followed by Ivan. "Don't you just love a wedding?" she asked him, rhetorically, of course.

He nodded. Ivan used to be talkative before he married Nell. Not anymore—but it seemed to suit him just fine.

"I want everyone to be as happy as we are," Nell said to him, a twinkle in her eye.

He smiled. "So do I, dear." Then he told Hope and me that we could ride along with them.

"Do you have room for my Dat?" Hope asked.

"Of course," Ivan answered.

Hope had suggested long ago that maybe her Dat and my Mamm would fall for each other once they met. That was the last thing I wanted. Mamm still loved Dat. She always would.

So I couldn't help but smile when William said to Edna, "It's been a pleasure to meet you."

Edna blushed and then managed to say, "I feel the same way."

"I'll see you after the wedding," he said to her, pushing his chair away from the table.

"We'll be here," she replied, a smile spreading across her face.

The wee hours of the morning whizzed by as we ate breakfast and then helped with the finishing touches for the wedding. As we worked, the stars shone brightly in the cold early-morning darkness, and when the sun began to rise, it was evident the day would be sunny. Thanksgiving was only a week away, but it seemed the day would get fairly warm, much like those endless Indian summer days of October.

An hour before it was time for the service to start, Hope and I headed up to Hannah's room, where our garment bag hung, to get dressed. Hannah and Molly were in the room too, laughing and joking and taking their time. Molly, because she was married, wouldn't be one of Hannah's sidesitters—her sisters would—but she was still the one that Hannah wanted with her before the service.

I, on the other hand, dressed quickly. After I tied my fresh apron, I took the sonnet from my work apron and slipped it into my pocket. Once again, when I turned, I caught Hope watching me. She smiled a little and turned away. Had she opened up the scrap of paper earlier in our room? I wasn't about to ask her now.

The barn was the perfect place for the service. It easily seated five hundred people, and the Lapps had rented heaters to keep it cozy. The barn was so big that they'd been able to set up the tables at the far end.

We waited in the tack room until it was time to march in. Through the single window, I caught sight of Mervin and Martin under the trees, both wearing their aviator glasses and looking rather handsome in their new suits. Ben stood with them, a shock of his hay-colored hair sticking out from under his new black hat. They laughed about something, but then Ben's smile faded as he looked my way. Had he seen me?

I stepped away from the window.

When we met the boys at the back of the barn before walking down to be seated on the benches at the front, the twins had their glasses off and looked very serious, as they should have.

The service was like any other Amish wedding—first the hymn singing, starting with "Das Loblied."

> "O Lord Father, we bless thy name,
> Thy love and thy goodness praise. . . . "

Next was the Scripture reading and then a long sermon given by Bishop Eicher. Finally, the two couples stepped forward and the bishop married them, followed by prayers by the father of the grooms and fathers of the brides.

Afterward the bridal couples and sidesitters sat at the *Eck* tables, two corner tables, and were served, along with the first seating of guests. Nan and Bob ate with the first group, sitting with Hope's Dat. Nan seemed a little lost without her babies and as soon as she finished, she hugged Hannah and Mervin, then Hope and Martin. For once she was done eating before Bob and went back to tug on his sleeve.

He stopped by the Eck table and said he'd take her home and then, if things were going well, come back to help with the cleanup.

After we'd finished eating, the couples mingled with the guests, thanking everyone for coming. I wandered outside to get some fresh air and then on toward the house. Some of the Youngie had started a game of volleyball on Hannah's parents' lawn. I wore my cape over my dress, but the sun had warmed the day enough that I barely needed it, and after a while I took it off, spread it on the ground, and sat on it. A few minutes later, Molly joined me.

"How are you feeling?" I asked.

"Great," she said. "I was tired those first few months, but now I'm feeling fine." Molly turned toward me. "Have you decided about Montana?"

I shook my head.

"But you don't really want to go, do you."

I exhaled.

"It's okay. I shouldn't have tried to force you. Mamm's right. You need to make your own decision." She patted my hand.

"Denki," I said.

"So what will you do?" She leaned back, her hands behind her. "Since things didn't work out with Ben."

"I don't know," I said. "Keep working for the Millers." I took a deep breath and exhaled loudly. "Maybe move to Montana after that." There really wasn't any reason not to.

She smiled.

It wasn't like I could buy the bookstore, not with Ben working there. Of course, I could fire him. But I suspected the Schmidts were thinking of selling it soon and moving in with one of their children, and I imagined they'd offer it to Ben first.

"If you don't come, I'll miss you terribly," Molly said. "More than anyone."

That was hard for me to believe. "Not more than Hannah," I couldn't help but say.

"Ach, of course more than Hannah. You're my sister. We've been through so much together. No one else understands me the way you do."

A pang overtook me. I leaned against her shoulder.

She patted my head. "It's true," Molly said. "And I'm guessing I'm starting to understand you better too."

Before I could answer, she nodded toward the pathway. Ben came toward us, holding something in his hand. "For example . . ."

My face grew warm. Maybe Molly did understand me more than I knew. She knew I pined after Ben—but she hadn't tried to force me to sacrifice my principles.

I leaned toward her. "I'll miss you," I said. "Much more, I'm sure, than I can imagine right now."

A commotion on the path caught my attention. Martin and Mervin had rushed to Ben's side and grabbed for whatever it was in his hands. Hope and Hannah stopped behind them. In a burst of action, the boys spilled out onto the lawn and rolled right in front of us. I stood quickly, to protect Molly.

"Got it!" Mervin said, popping up from the ground with Ben's journal.

338

Mervin opened it and, as Ben sprawled out on the grass as if defeated, began reading,

"It lies not in our power to love or hate—"

I rushed at Mervin. He turned his back to me, twirling around as he did to keep away from me, and kept on reading:

"For will in us is overruled by fate.
When two are stripped, long ere the course begin,
We wish that one should lose, the other win . . ."

I managed to pretend to go one way and then cut back, snatching the book from him. Not much was sacred in this life, but one's journal should be. Ben was on his feet now, and I handed it back to him.

Mervin stood empty-handed. "Did you write that, Ben?"

"Of course not. Christopher Marlowe did." Ben winked at me, causing a fluttering in my chest. It was the poem he'd read from my book that night over a month ago, after he'd walked me to the back door from the greenhouse.

Ben handed the book back to me. "Read what I wrote after the poem."

Curiosity got the best of me, and I opened the journal.

"Last page," he said.

I flipped to the back.

After the poem, he'd written: *I want Bea to win. I'd do anything for her. Even move to Montana—without her—if that's what she truly wants.*

The hummingbird in my heart returned, flapping against the walls of my chest. I looked up and shook my head at Ben.

"Keep going," he said.

Silently, I read, *I think winning means loving, and I know I love her more now than I ever have. God showed me what a fool I can be, so quick to judge. I know what I've gone through makes me appreciate myself less—and her more.*

I glanced up at him again. For the first time in my life I was speechless. But it didn't matter because Hope was at my side, digging in my apron pocket. Before I could react, she had the sonnet in her hand.

Ben grinned. "I recognize that," he said.

"I'll read it," Hope said, scanning the poem, her mouth turning downward. Finally she said, "Well, how about if I just read the last of it.

> "Love alters not with his brief hours and weeks,
>   But bears it out even to the edge of doom.
>   If this be error and upon me proved,
>   I never writ, nor no man ever loved."

Hope made a face. "Whatever that means."

They all laughed as Hope handed the paper to Ben. Then she clapped her hands together as she looked at me. "You two really are a match."

Ben read the paper and then stepped closer to me. "Is this true?" he asked as the others lost interest in us and wandered away. Molly followed, most likely to give us privacy.

"Is what true?" I asked, even though I knew exactly what he was referring to.

He held the paper up and pointed to the top, reading, "'I've never felt such harmony. Such jubilation. Such anticipation . . .'" He blushed as he read, his tongue tripping over, "'Bea plus Ben equals Love.'"

I inhaled, sharply, thankful the others had drifted away.

"When did you write that?" he asked.

"After our trip to the bookstore and coffee shop. The night you helped with the Tropplis." I winced. I'd meant to say *Bopplis*.

"Oh," he said, reading more. He pointed to the bottom of the page. "And when did you write this?"

"Night before last."

He read it out loud, "'If only. . . .'" Then he looked at me again. "Do you mean it?"

"Theoretically, I meant it when I wrote it."

"Oh," he said, refolding the paper and handing it to me.

My heart skipped a beat. Who was I trying to fool? He loved me—more now than he ever had. And I still loved him.

"But now I mean it sincerely." I met his gaze. I wanted to be with him. I wanted to trust God with Ben Rupp.

He wrapped his hands around mine, the paper wedged between, and then pulled me close. For a moment we embraced, but then, as if we both remembered at once where we were, we stepped away, inhaling in unison.

My eyes filled with tears, and a wave of emotion came over me, as if I'd just had a good cry—one that had lasted two weeks.

"Ach, Bea," he said.

For a moment everything stopped as we stared at each other. Then as I dried my eyes, he said, "Would you come around to my buggy with me?"

I nodded, yanking up my cape and following him.

When we reached the buggy, he pulled me around to the side facing the woods, away from the barn, and he took me in his arms. He kissed me on the forehead first and then, finally, my mouth. The wings—*Flikkels*—of my heart beat frantically, and then it was as if they took off in flight.

When the kiss ended I met his eyes. "That was my first kiss," I said.

"Mine too," he whispered.

The hug that came next was far more intimate than the kiss. Finally I stepped back and smiled up at him.

"What?" he asked.

I shook my head. "It's nothing."

He hugged me again.

I nestled into his arms. "It's just that I'd thought love had fled."

"No," Ben answered. "It was only waiting."

"Cate told me that a happy ending depends on where the author decides to end the story."

"Ach," Ben said. "I'm so thankful God gave us another chapter, because"—his eyes met mine—"I love nothing in the world, except God, as much as you."

Later, after supper, as Ben and I drove away, he called out to Phillip. "Get yourself a wife!"

Phillip stood at the entrance to the barn. Down the path was Jessie in the midst of a group of girls. Phillip shifted his gaze to her.

Ben nodded. "Exactly."

As Phillip headed toward her, Jessie smiled. Ben took my hand, squeezing it gently as he drove me on home to the Millers'.

CHAPTER

24

Mamm and Mervin finalized the sale of the farm a month later. She sent Molly and Leon off to Montana with a check as a down payment on the ranch they intended to buy. Then she stayed with Edna until March, while Love stayed with me at the Millers'.

Phillip and Jessie published their wedding in the middle of December and were married in early February. Martin began working full-time with his Dat, and the twins made plans to expand our flower farm over to the Mosiers' property. Phillip kept working for Bob, and along with Pete, trained a whole new crew.

I didn't hear anything, good or bad, about Don. He never returned to Lancaster. I hoped for the best for him, and that he'd made peace with those in Ohio that he'd hurt too.

I worked for the Millers for the next six months, until Nan and Cate were strong enough to take over the care of the babies with help from Hope. Martin's Mamm was still plenty capable of running their house, so Hope continued to help the Millers three days a week.

My friendship with Hope grew over the months, and with Molly gone Hannah and I grew closer too. She invited me to our old farm often, saying she always wanted me to feel welcome. And I did.

Hope's Dat and Edna corresponded for a couple of months and then, to the surprise of no one, married in March, before Mamm went to Montana. Edna gladly moved to New York, promising to visit when she could. Although she'd never have children of her own, she now had thirty-two grandchildren—and counting. Hope and Martin were expecting by the end of summer.

Ben and I married in May. It was a small celebration, by our Plain standards, with just family and our closest friends, including Albert and Willa. We didn't have a big place to host it, just the bookstore that Mamm had gifted us a down payment toward. We scooted all the bookcases along the walls and held the service in the open space and then the dinner too.

Mamm returned from Montana to help us celebrate, along with Molly and Leon and their two-month-old baby, Anna Bea.

I was a little miffed that Molly used Mamm's name, which meant I wouldn't be able to, but once I saw the little one, I was so smitten I thought the name perfect for her. And I couldn't help but be honored they'd used mine too.

I couldn't wait until I had a baby of my own. Ben and I planned a trip to Montana the next fall. Hannah said she'd watch the Olde Book Shoppe for us and, jah, we'd take the train. I was up for an adventure—as long as Ben was at my side.

Mamm announced on our wedding day that she would return to Montana with Molly and her little family, but she'd be back by winter. We had a room for her in our upstairs living quarters.

Besides Anna Bea, little Wally—still a babe-in-arms himself—and the triplets, who were the same size as their nephew, all attended our celebration, which soon spilled out onto the lawn in the warm spring weather. I counted my blessings, over and over, as Ben and I thanked our guests.

That night, after we sent everyone home, saying we'd finish the rest of the cleaning ourselves, the scent from the spring honeysuckle outside the open window filled the room. As I swept, Ben stepped beside me, as if dancing. I put the broom aside and fitted into his arms.

"Ach," he said, drawing me close. "I'm so glad you're Bea."

"Jah, that's me," I answered. "At least who I'm becoming." I wanted to be the strong woman God had created me to be. Not the critical girl I'd been. And not the nice girl I'd tried to be.

And here I was, in my favorite place, in the arms of my favorite person—the man I loved with all my heart, so much so that I had absolutely nothing to protest. "H-A-R-M-O-N-Y," I spelled.

He grinned. "L-O-V-E," he replied.

Pulling him toward the stairs, I spelled, "A-N-T-I-C-I-P-A-T-I-O-N."

We both laughed, and then he said, "Ach, imagine that. I let you have the last word—once again."

Acknowledgments

I'm humbled by all the people it takes to make a book success-ful—early readers, resources, agents, editors, publishers, mar-keters, printers, salespeople, distributors, booksellers, readers, bloggers, and reviewers. I am grateful to each person who has had a part in this process.

As always, I am especially grateful to my family. My husband, Peter, and children, Kaleb, Taylor, Hana, and Thao, keep me writing—both through their physical and emotional support and through the many ideas they toss my way. Thank you!

Early readers for this story included my critique group—Melanie Dobson, Nicole Miller, Kelly Chang, Dawn Hill Ship-man, and Kimberly Felton. Laurie Snyder read the manuscript multiple times and Libby Salter also read for me. I'm grateful for all of you!

Another special thank-you goes to Marietta Couch, who read for me and also answered my many questions about Plain liv-ing. I'm so grateful God connected us at a book signing—and for the friendship that's resulted. (Any mistakes are mine, and mine alone.)

Kerri Brown Scott also deserves a mention for giving me a great idea, during my visit to her book group, as far as wrapping up one of the details of the COURTSHIPS OF LANCASTER COUNTY series. Thank you, Kerri for suggesting another baby for Laurel. I truly treasure feedback from all my readers.

The entire team at Bethany House Publishers has my thanks for all they've done for my books. Dave Long, Karen Schurrer, Jenny Parker, Steve Oates, Noelle Buss, and Amy Green are just a few of the many people I am grateful for.

I'm also very appreciative of my agent, Chip MacGregor, who has guided me through over a decade of writing. From the beginning he supported my crazy idea of retelling Shakespeare plays in Plain settings. I'm very thankful for his ongoing support.

Leslie Gould is the coauthor, with Mindy Starns Clark, of the #1 CBA bestseller *The Amish Midwife*, a 2012 Christy Award winner; and the author of CBA bestseller *Courting Cate*, first in the Courtships of Lancaster County series, and *Beyond the Blue*, winner of the Romantic Times Reviewers' Choice for Best Inspirational Novel, 2006. She holds an MFA in creative writing from Portland State University and has taught fiction writing at Multnomah University as an adjunct professor. She and her husband and four children live in Portland, Oregon.

Learn more about Leslie at www.lesliegould.com.